THE HARROWS

THE HARROWS

A Novel Of The American Century

Matt Pavelich

Bar R Books

THE HARROWS
A Novel Of The American Century

By Matt Pavelich

Published by Bar R Books,
Helena, Montana
© 2025 by Matt Pavelich

Bar R Books celebrate the art and literature of Montana and the
West. The press's name derives from the brand owned by Louis
Kaufman and Louis Stadler, Helena, Montana, butchers who
became prominent cattlemen during the open-range days of the
Montana frontier. Louis Kaufman was the rancher to whom Charlie
Russell sent his famed watercolor, *Waiting for a Chinook,* during the
disastrous winter of 1886–87.

Helena, MT & San Francisco

Also by Matt Pavelich

Beasts of the Forrest, Beasts of the Field

Our Savage

The Other Shoe

Survivors Said

Himself, Adrift

But Tell it Slant

A portion of *The Harrows* originally appeared in
The Montana Quarterly.

FOR

Marnie, Nick, and Riley,
and for the Elizabeths, all of them

With *The Harrows,* Matt Pavelich offers us a third splendid novel—this one a true family saga of the American West.

The novel begins at the start of the 20th century with Charlie Harrow, erstwhile freighter, and his beloved Dove, schoolmarm and homesteader in her own right, establishing the family farm on Montana's fabled Square Butte Bench, a "place of haunting, receding horizons." The novel ends on the same place with the return of a great-great-granddaughter intent, unaccountably, on continuing the family operation.

While one member of each generation stays on to make the home place thrive, others travel far afield, to the killing fields of World War Two, to drug-running adventures off the coast of Morocco, to the jazz clubs of Great Falls and Los Angeles, to military drudgery and tragedy on Okinawa during the Vietnam Conflict, to the quiet, bookish neighborhoods of Portland.

The intertwining stories of these remarkable Harrows—Charlie and Dove, George and Verity, Tel and Jeet, Carrie and Elizabeth—tell us of a beautiful, often unforgiving place and of what it means to be family, in all our imperfections, our sorrows, and our joys.

The Harrows is a gorgeous piece of work. It seems destined to become an American classic.

Rick Newby, author of *A Regionalism that Travels: Writings on (Mostly) Montana Arts, 1975-2022*

CONTENTS

Charlie   1
Dove   11
Charlie   37
Dove   47
Verity   49
Charlie   55
Dove   57
George   75
Dove   103
Verity   105
Charlie   113
Ulyssess Purefoy   119
Verity   137
Jeet   197
Tel   233
Ulysses Purefoy   265
G. C.   271
Carrie   323
Elizabeth   349
Verity   359
Carrie   369
Jeet   371
Elizabeth   377
Tel   389
Acknowledgments   398

THE HARROWS

Charles Harrow m. Dove (Appleby) Harrow
Hope
Honor
Faith
George Harrow m. Mary Lou (McQuiston) Harrow—Unknown Father
George Charles Lloyd Harrow (Jeet) (G.C.)
Verity Harrow Ulysses Purefoy
Tel Harrow m. Donna Emmert
Carrie Harrow Brett Manfredi
Elizabeth Harrow

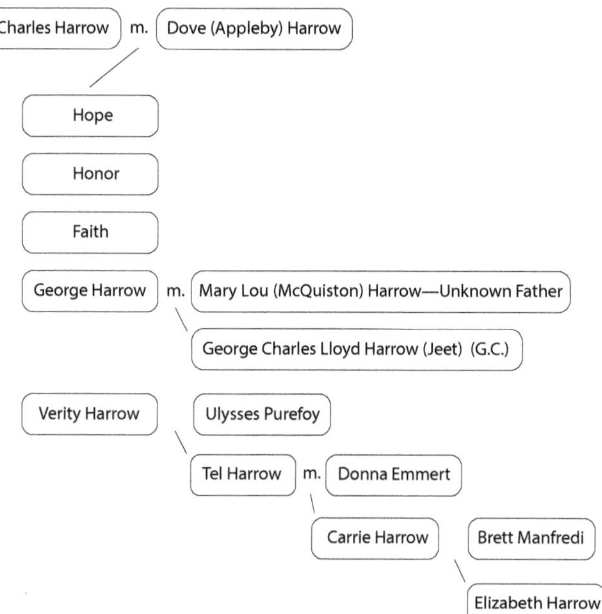

CHARLIE

He wore scarred leather cuffs, a pristine necktie, stovepipe boots rising nearly to his knees, and under the domed crown of his hat a pair of eyes impervious to surprise. These followed a clerk's forefinger tracing its way across a map very little littered with roads or place names. The finger stopped and bowed a bit as the clerk pressed at a particular location.

"Right here. This is where you'll find your corner post. Let me see your filing again. Yeah, that's it. This'd be your place." Then, ominously, "Filing sight-unseen, hey? Filing blind, like most of 'em do." Though a young man, the clerk breathed with some difficulty, his chest lifting, his nostrils flaring and whistling. Maybe a lunger. The land office smelled of ink and bone-dry paper, the clerk of witch hazel.

"I heard of it a long time ago," said Charlie Harrow. "Heard about it from a drover used to ride this country. He had some ideas about it, thought the dirt might be good around there."

"You'd go on a drover's word?" said the clerk. "You trust to luck?"

"Got no use for it," said Harrow, though he'd been known to bet on a long shot.

"You know farming?"

"Farmed in knee britches," said Harrow, still resenting it. "Farmed night and day for the old man. It's been a while, but I don't expect a man forgets." A farmer remained in Harrow's mind a man tied to something bleak and pathetic, and when this occurred to him Charlie nearly turned on his Spanish heel and returned to his roving, his homestead claim wadded in his pocket.

"You never wondered why that drover didn't file on this place if he thought it was so fine?"

"Never did," said Harrow. "Levon got himself strung up down in Utah back when they were still hanging their horse thieves. And what's it to you?"

"I like a sad story," said the clerk, "This is a fine place to hear 'em, too." As Harrow was leaving, the clerk added the little refrain he sometimes used to mock another honyocker out the door, to let him know the odds against him. "Forty miles to water," he said, "forty miles to wood; I'm gone to old Montana, and I'm gone for good."

"The hell with you, then," said Harrow. "Pomaded sonofabitch."

He went out of the office and walked knocking up the boardwalk, up the street to the mercantile where his team stood hitched, shifting from hip to hip. Harrow removed the feed bags he'd strapped to their noses, climbed up on the wagon seat, and drove out of town. As they passed the settlement's last saloon, he slowed a little, but then reconsidered and said, "Well, boys, the fun is over. We're men of parts now." And he drove on.

◊ ◊ ◊

If he could only survive in this. Under the blue maw of heaven, half his life already used in wandering, Charlie Harrow rolled onto that high benchland, a treeless prairie, to own a half section of it. Though this was some years into the 20th century Harrow's progress and provisions would have been familiar to any of several centuries past. Get up, Bailey. Get up, Ned. They needed constant urging to pull a wagon filled with hand tools, a single-bottom, moldboard plow, and sacks of dreaming seed. A butte loomed over the whole country hereabout, more god than temple, and of the shacks Harrow passed along the way it could be hard to tell those abandoned from those still in use. Approaching one of these he encountered a ropy man in overalls who watched him coming from a long way off, eventually raising his hand to shoulder height, palm out, a greeting as if he'd lost the power of speech, or maybe to warn him off.

Harrow asked him as he drew up, "Wouldn't have any hay for sale, would you, citizen?"

"Do I look like it?"

"I wouldn't like to say what you look like," said Harrow. "How you making it?"

"Bad. You'll see. My woman's long gone. Cow's dry. And the worst of it—I run out of chew about a month ago." The whites of the man's eyes were shot through with red veins, his eyelids lined bright pink. "You'll see, it's hard country."

Next, Harrow happened upon a white stone still bearing its chiseled **R** to mark the old cavalry route running from fort nowhere to fort nowhere now, and in their absence he heard pony soldiers, and Blackfeet, and buffalo, all of them sighing into the incessant wind and wondering, 'Who are you to own anything, much less this ground?'

Because he'd once thought he might have to kill his father, Charlie Harrow had been out west since '82, a year before his Adam's apple appeared, when, rather than accept another beating or any more berating from that endlessly unhappy old man, he had broken his arm with an axe handle and then before he could quite stop himself also broken one of his father's ribs, so young Charlie was gone that very evening from out of a Missouri county where the war was still constantly complained of and where the constable and several cousins desired an interview. Was he at any point moved by the many songs of that era lamenting homes long lost or times gone by? No. Charlie liked a jig or a reel. He was a traveler. Most often he'd worked as a mule-skinner, and riding behind and on the backs of generations of jacks and jennies, and over the course of thousands of short hauls, he had traveled from San Antonio to Telluride and back and all points in between and as far as the tracks of the Great Northern, so Harrow as he made his way onto Square Butte Bench that day was well accustomed to be diminished by big country. There'd been nothing so daunting as this, though, nothing to haunt him like a patch of earth by which he meant to finally measure himself or be measured. Humility was one thing; he meant in all events to be a freeholder.

Where he dropped the traces at last, he intended a farmyard, a future he'd staked about halfway between the Highwoods and the Missouri River where the weather swept in nearly always from some direction, blowing, but where there was also somehow a decent depth of top soil, good, ancient dirt that refused to be blown away. The sweeping, shelving topography of this ground kept its thrilling indifference always before you. Could a man farming alone in this country make it pay?

Harrow had never been much of one to yield to the situation, with odd result that he was about to found a family here, an estate.

"Rolled out that first morning and started digging a hole. Now, I trust a water witcher about as far as I'd trust a faro wheel, and to me one spot's likely as any other, so I just went ahead and started that hole, headed down for ground water. That was three months of digging would've killed a bull ape."

A hand dug well is a vertical shaft and must be wide enough to work in, and Harrow was not too deep in it before he was constantly climbing in and out to shift his burden; he built a headframe and windlass and rigged a way of harnessing his team to the hoist; still it was necessary to climb in and out of that hole many times a day, and the deeper he went, the longer the trip up and down, and he went down through dirt, then a sandy gravel, then through a shelf of rock, and Harrow made three trips up into the timber to lumberjack more shoring for the thing. Later he would recount these efforts by way of explaining just how petty it was of his family to complain of their alkali water.

"They say it's a shallow well. Wasn't shallow when I was down in it. I could look up at midday and see the stars from down in that well, and you're never real sure it won't fall in on you, and I never met anybody who wants to be buried alive. They say it makes bad coffee. I dug and cased this well without owing a penny or a favor for it, and to my certain knowledge that water has never harmed a soul, and my tomatoes love it, so I don't see where anyone should turn their nose up."

The digging of the well and the fruiting of his garden illustrated to Charlie's mind the benefits of sustained effort, the rewards, but the same tale more fully told might better be a parable on pride, for he had not asked for help in that hole, though he knew help was to be had for the asking, that he had neighbors in the same fix, that to dig such a hole alone was by far the least efficient way to do it. He dug on until late October, dug until it was done, leaving himself just enough time and material to throw up a rough manger where he and Bailey and Ned might winter. Breathing steam with the horses, and cold and hungry, Harrow was thirty-nine. That first winter on the place he knew a whole new program of injury and ache. Loneliness after all these years had finally tracked him down in Montana. He'd be years more alone, proving up that first homestead. A knuckleheaded teamster being slowly forced to learn the uses of cooperation, he'd joined the Farmer's Union, attended picnics and weddings, and Harrow had in time even given in and borrowed money from the bank, the serious farmer's inevitable partner.

Charlie Harrow was part of the land rush occasioned by passage of the Enlarged Homestead Act when tracts like Square Butte Bench, previously considered wasteland, were opened to new settlement by the very American expedient of doubling down. Under the Enlarged Act three hundred and twenty acres were on offer from the government to any wizard who thought to make the desert bloom, to find a living and live on it for five years. Land, so much of it, was the grand incentive and for most a hollow promise, for even among those who came to it equipped to turn miles of deep furrow and to outwait the whims of a fickle sky, the migrations of cut worm and grasshopper, even such hearty claimants as these usually went bust for the simple reason that it was a short growing season and a rum go. It was impossible. Still, there were those, and aren't there always, who stayed, who proved up their claims. Charlie Harrow. How?

Harrow the farmer was the very citizen for whom this bubbly republic had been conceived, a Jeffersonian hero, that canny customer happy with his small stake in things to put himself in the way of starvation or bankruptcy, or to run the risk of lying maimed in a field or of falling ill a long way from help if only he might do these things as his own man, to his own ends. Never indentured or jailed, still he'd yearned since earliest memory for more freedom, and even if he had in his time on the road been at no time a half hour longer in any location than he wished to be, his seemed a crabbed and constrained kind of liberty. It was the necessity of selling his labor to feed himself. Having known no circumstance but work he would never develop much use for leisure, but it was hard for Charlie to be told what to do and unendurable being told how to do it. When his only bank was his boots or his bedroll, he'd maintained a war chest with which he meant to eventually buy himself out from ever again being obliged to follow any-one's instructions or even listen very closely to their suggestions. Opinions were too plentiful in Charlie's opinion, and he already owned a complete set of them.

So where did he seek to buy his autonomy?

That spring he met at the rail yard in Fort Benton with Mr. Harold Loraas, factotum and representative of the Gas Traction Company of Minneapolis, Minnesota, and before the close of business that day Charlie, who at that point did not have even a hut, or any livestock to speak of, or much of anything else, owned eleven tons of fire breathing engine. He knew only approximately the workings of the wheel and of the lever, and Charlie had no previous experience whatever with internal combustion, but he became after an hour's instruction from Mr. Loraas the engineer on a land-crawling locomotive; he walked his Big 4 off the flat car and said goodbye to his life's savings.

Standing as he did between and just behind its driving wheels, he could see nothing to the immediate front of his engine, his view forward blocked by its great nose, its fuel tank, for this nightmare calliope burned kerosene, and he directed the thing by means of a small wheel equipped with a crank so that it might be spun vigorously, and by spinning it so, clockwise, counterclockwise, he gradually communicated his desires to the front wheels through a chain yoke. He towed his wagon with its new cargo of fuel, his team trailing behind that, resentful of having to follow and skittish at the unfamiliar noise. They went down to the river at three miles an hour, stalling only upon reaching the toll bridge and its toll taker, a man in a clean felt hat but with a worried way of crossing his arms high on his chest, who yelled up, "Mister, we'd both be in trouble if you tore up this bridge."

"She'll fit," said Charlie, "up-and-down, side-to-side."

"How do you know you won't mash right through the decking and drop into the river?"

"Shouldn't," said Charlie.

The toll taker made a show of examining the tractor with his head tilted well back. "This span ain't made for that kind of weight."

"Never know 'til you try."

"I know how cold that water is."

"If you wanted to be useful," Charlie said, "you could walk out there in front of me a way, help to keep me centered."

"No, mister, this is a good job, easiest job I ever had, but I only work for these people. I wouldn't dream of going down with their ship."

"All right," said Charlie. "If you're scared, stay back. Sure hate to swerve, though, take out some of your trestle."

"I ain't said you could go."

There would be costs scattered everywhere in the affairs of the Big 4; Harrow, with an extra dollar to the toll taker for his trouble and trepidation, crossed the shuddering bridge, first leg of a trip he'd have made with six hours in the saddle but which took him all that day and most of the night on iron wheels. When he finally shut the Big 4 down it ran on for hours in his ears, and like a sailor newly ashore he continued to sense a pitching underfoot even as he stood on solid ground. Charlie had never cared for machines. Charlie, however, would take a wrench as necessary to anything lying loose in any existence that offered itself, he would make the adjustment, and he now needed something irresistible. It was a question of scale.

His land had without cultivation grown grass these many thousands of years, and there were similar dryland farms in the vicinity growing grain, up to thirty bushels of wheat an acre. But how little like Missouri this country, how rare the rain, how utterly exposed his fields. Drought, hail, and infestation, it was an Old Testament proposition, Square Butte Bench, requiring at a minimum a surplus of faith. Harrow knew from his first sight of his place that he should not expect a cash crop from it every year, that he was prospecting here as much as farming, but it seemed to him that if he could timely turn and seed that whole three twenty, and if the good year of legend and of myth should then occur, then the processes of nature and simple arithmetic could make him rich. Wheat is a commodity like gold, it keeps, and it keeps its value. He calculated he'd need to bring in no more than one crop in three to go on.

The prairie with its many ways of suggesting that he was not necessary or welcome to it made him superstitious, yet here he came dragging a new twelve-bottom plow with his great machine, the shares rolling up brown dirt like frosting on a cake. Startled earth. Sod, when first turned, smelled unmistakably to him of regret, but he broke six hundred acres that spring, all of his and much of several neighbors' properties. He broke it, harrowed it, seeded it, immense farming, dawn to dusk on his irresistible tractor, dragging every implement he could hitch to his draw bar, and when his seedlings sprouted into the driest summer in a hundred years Charlie thought he heard the country rebuking him, and when the grasshoppers ate even those pale shoots to ground and lingered on to fling themselves against him so that he had to shield his face from them as he walked his shattered fields, then Charlie felt as one does among a plague of locusts, that nature was not too keen on him. His engine sat idle through harvest, or what should have been harvest season. In August and September there was a pall from forest fires in the west. Ash was in everything.

He built a manger for the horses and lived there with

them during his first two winters on the farm along with a cat named Beelzebub who kept the field mice out. First things first—he'd built the manger and a shed for his tractor before he built his shanty. Though he was at first obliged to buy hay to winter the horses, he bought no food for himself, subsisting in part on the sweet corn and beans and potatoes he was able to coax from his drought-stricken garden. In the fall he set up a salt lick to lure mule deer. A hip shot in those days, Charlie was known to harvest game birds on the wing with his .22, but he wasn't much of a cook and for as much of that dark meat as he ate, he never did learn to make it anything but gamy.

"Might be hard to swallow, but there was a lot to like in those hard times. Never went hungry, which is more than many could claim. I was awful honest because there was no one around to lie to, and I couldn't afford to lie to myself. Saw a good many seasons before there was ever much in the way of crops, or money, or any kind of complications, and every single thing I did was necessary. It's simple when you put the fruit of your labors straight into your mouth. But they call it the high lonesome up here. To be alone, day and night alone, that wore me out worse than anything. So, my family when they finally came along, they were more welcome than I could ever accurately say."

DOVE

She'd gone to some trouble to hang the classroom with pine boughs and bring in that festive, pitchy essence, but this was more than absorbed by the close stew of lamp oil, wool, and the horse apples imported on Mr. Lapotka's boots. Joyeux Noël? Dove Appleby's Christmas program. She'd got the coals banked too high in the stove, and though those assembled were just in from the cracking cold she had them sweating like thieves. Infants were chafing already, men's big voices barely contained in a room no larger than a proper parlor in any civilized part of the world. She wanted them there, didn't she? Dove's good fortune consisted of the current fashion dictating a skirt that tented from high on her hips to within an inch of the floor, a garment good to obscure the details at least of her hideous new walk. But she waddled. Passing through them to the head of the room, she rocked pretty raggedly from side to side, and what must they think of her? Since leaving the hospital Dove had not been very often or very much among adults, and she'd not yet assembled the personality she wished to wear as a cripple in their company. She recalled her recently whole self as a woman who didn't give a fig for anyone's opinion of her, but now if they didn't think her capable, she feared she stood in some danger of being thrown upon her neighbor's charity or upon someone's tender mercies. Dear no. Not at all. Pine boughs and ribbons torn from red rag. Chin up. Bright as a candle now.

"Everyone?" she said, her back to the blackboard, her ankle throbbing. "Everyone?"

As Dove began to thank them for braving such a fierce night, a babe in arms, the most recent of the earachy McQuiston children, cranked from whimpering into a full-throated cry, and, "Shush up, Wilbur. *Shush*" its mother could not console or cajole it quiet, and because Dove supposed the baby could hardly be taken outside or smothered, she thought to be calm and Christian and wait it out, but Wilbur wouldn't quit, and in time Miss Appleby began to think she'd mismanaged things, letting them all be held hostage like this to one child's showy misery. Her voice sounded childish, too, and too urgent when she pitched it to compete with the baby's. Dove delivered some remarks praising the cooperative moon for lighting their way to and from the school house tonight and promising those in attendance they'd be seeing a cast of proud students anxious to show off their talents, a group of born vaudevillians. She apologized once again for the lack of seating and asked that the taller gentlemen present move to the back of the room. The men, being men, jostled with each other for the honor of occupying the last rank.

So close. Their faces, the mothers' faces in particular, were often etched by a wind driven madness. Or leering. Leering? No. Dove knew she didn't present such a spectacle as all that, but under inspection she could not for a moment set aside the sense of being broken, of being perhaps inadequate to her sacred task. She stood before them with her hands having clasped themselves in that officious way she detested. "And so, may I present our school's second annual Christmas Follies and Benediction." Smiling as best she could, she summoned Mr. McQuiston who liked to wear a string tie and read from the Bible on such occasions.

She stood within the fumes of a fruitcake and soon enough McQuiston's preacherly cadences were making her even more seasick. What, Dove wondered, had the story of the prodigal son to do with Christmas? She was investing this event with too much significance, and Dove swallowed and swallowed and pledged herself not to publicly faint or regurgitate, vertigo sweeping her legs around under her like dust or seaweed. How much harder it was to make a favorable impression when a favorable impression seemed necessary. She'd let this silly program become a silly demonstration of her ability, her capacity to carry on. Her school was a fixture here, wasn't it? Dove Appleby would be as strong as necessary. Wouldn't she?

With little more than her fares in hand she had traveled by train, by stagecoach, and finally by foot into a place of taunting, receding horizons where she lay claim to a relinquished homestead already furnished with a tarpaper shack and a lofted pole barn. First, she'd faced those vistas down. Dove soon acquired her school building; briefly someone's home, it was another thing abandoned, and hers for the taking, and the good Mr. Harrow would accept nothing for mounting it on skids and dragging it to her location behind his enormous machine. Possessing a school, a barn, and a teacherage to live in, she'd set up shop, her notion to raise a cash crop of students on her homestead.

Three years now Dove had been regretting that the windows in her school building had not survived the trip and that she'd had to board them up. Sometimes a building needed to breathe. But this building and the school it contained had been sufficient if stuffy haven for a rotating dozen farm children, far flung, credulous prairie waifs, ages six to fourteen, many of whom, Dove knew, would see no formal education but in this or some other country school, their horses tied out back. There'd been little money in her teaching, but Dove ate like a queen as she was offered a piece of many a locally butchered animal and a constant stream of eggs and milk and, of course the wheat grown and ground right here on the bench. In return she'd given instruction in reading and writing, arithmetic, algebra, civics, history from the Greeks forward, music, French, anything wanted, really. She would endeavor to teach anything anyone was interested in learning, and Dove had discovered in this way how surprisingly much she knew, how quickly she absorbed those things she hadn't known. Still more surprising, and even more pleasing, she learned to tolerate, then to appreciate, then to need the nothingness surrounding her place. Had she not made herself essential here?

When she'd been healthy.

Fruit cake, an anonymous horror for the holidays. Probably very generous, very costly, but why? Fruit cake and pain. Her throat pulsed inconclusively. Pain was her problem. As of this twenty-second evening of December, Dove still needed her entire force of character to keep from grimacing or bending to her battered side. Though she'd never ride again, her injury didn't seem to otherwise prevent her from doing anything else, slowly, deliberately, that she'd done before. Except that she couldn't concentrate. It was the ache resident in her ankle, an ache radiating as far as her hip on a night like tonight, at a sudden change in the weather. Then too there were the twinges and catches and jolts traveling just frequently enough along her damaged ligaments to keep her constantly alert for them. She was hobbled most severely where she would least wish to be, in her mind, unable to think with any complexity about anything but how best to suffer. At this very moment her ankle hurt more than it had in the hour or two after she'd ruined it.

Did she want to deceive them, make them think she was the teacher she had been? Given time, Dove believed, she would be better, or she would learn to do better even if she hadn't healed. There was no reason they wouldn't give her that time. Who else could they turn to? If in the end her powers of mind were no longer up to the life, the responsibilities she'd chosen here, she'd be the first to know. Wouldn't she?

Dove thought it unlikely there was a drop of blood left in her head, she must be white as a pocket handkerchief. Mr. McQuiston, author of all those wretched children and his ugly piety, had now wandered into Leviticus—And he shall flay the burnt offering and cut it into pieces— At Christmas time? Dove had entirely lost control of the program; little Wilbur continued to howl; Dove swallowed and swallowed awaiting the blessed interval when both McQuistons might pause at once to breathe, and when that occurred, she rocked forward and said as conclusively as possible, "Amen." This was echoed round the audience in the same spirit, and Mr. McQuiston slunk away, looking directly at no one.

The next part of the program, as it happened, was also nothing to do with Christmas. "Let's start," Dove said, "with our very own Nick Savka and his popular recitation of *Abdul Abulbul Amir*." Withdrawn and usually a wall of a boy, Nick knew nineteen verses of the piece as he'd previously demonstrated at an open house and a graduation. He couldn't or wouldn't sing, Nick, and he wouldn't participate in skits with the other students, but he'd be a racehorse at the gate until she'd let him at his recitation. Mrs. Savka had boiled and starched her son's shirt for the performance; its collar cut at his neck causing his chin to twist constantly seeking a better accommodation, and with the delivery of the tin soothsayer at the penny arcade he said, "The sons of the prophet are valiant and bold," his overlarge farmboy fists pressed to either thigh, "and quite unaccustomed to fear." Nick droned through it, thrilling the widow Savka.

Dove noticed then that Mr. Harrow's cheeks were wet.

What could possibly be so tragic? She thought she knew him pretty well by then, or as well as a bachelor farmer might ever be known. Her nearest neighbor, he was her source for water, coal, and venison, and he'd even dragged the schoolhouse here. She held the useful Mr. Harrow in about the same esteem as he seemed to hold his beloved team, and though he had no children in the school he was certainly deserving to be invited to the program. Dove knew there would be food tonight, something always of interest to a bachelor, and the very last thing she expected was to see him weeping. Then she understood it for laughter, his shoulders working up and down, his eyes bright with tears and absurdity, and then Dove was laughing too, and both of them a little cruelly at poor Nick Savka. It seemed to Dove that everyone would take a turn tonight at somehow misbehaving. She was not sure if she'd seen Mr. Harrow even so much as smile before, and now they were laughing together. Now she had reason to reconsider some of the things he'd said to her in the past and to understand those things as sly jokes. Something had happened.

She introduced the Elizabeths, Misses Bell and Barnaby with their mothers' cameo broaches at their throats, little Betty Barnaby gap-toothed and lisping a little. They sang "Emmanuel" raising an audible lace, a harmony to lift the hair from a curmudgeon's neck, and Dove thought to see how Mr. Harrow was taking this part of the performance. Placidly. Inscrutably. Then, when she presented her living crèche, her cowlick Christ child, Mr. Harrow was immediately moved again to blasphemous tears.

Fruitcake, what a pungency. Someone, probably in Dove's presence, would be eating that thing. She tried to think of odorless food or of the continent of fresh air to be found beyond any of these slight walls, but she couldn't make herself feel much better, not even as she sang with the choir. Rejoice, rejoice. She was trying. It came upon a midnight clear, but not for Dove Appleby whose soul or something elemental had got enfolded in black felt, no light or air getting in. God rest ye merry gentlemen, but she *would* be dismayed, for Dove's ankle, in addition to everything else, had now locked as it sometimes did so that there was no movement in any axis and her whole lower leg was reduced to a tender stump upon which it was hard to balance or forbear, and here she was, trying to keep decent time for a choir of splendid children.

They so loved to sing. The nativity. Joy. Hope. Dove had insisted on all of it, and now with the choir not half through its portion of the affair she was in deep distress, surely teetering toward some mortification and not at all strong or confident or happy as she might have wished to be in this crowd, but Dove sang on. Then, pinned by her problem to a spot in the room, she observed the box suppers being eaten afterward and socialized as best she might. On the mend, Miss Appleby? Much better, thank you. If any of my four get up to their shenanigans, Miss Appleby, you let me know and I'll have my Jimmy turn 'em inside out. Those boys'll try and take advantage of anything. No, but, yes, and thank you, thank you, and finally, God speed, Dove got them out the door, not before catching Mr. Harrow's elbow and asking that he stay behind for a bit.

Given his years and weathering, Mr. Harrow could be boyish as necessary. He waited, expecting to be chastised, and when they were alone, he said, his better hat in hand, "Sorry, If I hurt that boy's feelings, but between him and that baby Jesus, I couldn't help myself. They had me going sideways."

"No," she said, "I'm the one to apologize, because I need your help, Mr. Harrow. Again. Never worry about

Nick. The boy is oblivious. He'd have to be with a mother like that." She told him about her ankle, how something in it, shifting bone, retreating tendon, something sometimes seized up so tightly she found it difficult even to move her toes. She admitted that this had happened to her tonight. Had he noticed how immobile she'd been for much of the evening? Did he suppose anyone had? Vanity, she said, had caused her to leave her crutch in her shack, never wishing to be anyone's Tiny Tim, or to suffer their pity on any account, but now she couldn't for the moment walk very well. Would he help her gather up the food that had been left? Would he be a shoulder she might lean on as far as the door of her residence? Twenty yards, but the path was in places polished slick and hard by two weeks of constant westerlies. If he could only just see her to her door, and avoid making mention of it, she'd never ask anything of him again. This was, of course, not true, but at least she was fairly sure she'd be done pestering him tonight.

Outside, the stars were piercing, the air brittle enough to shatter. There was for once no wind. Hairs froze in her nostrils. The others, that press of students, students' parents, and students' demon siblings were gone into a night as alive to sound as the interior of a bell, far enough gone that they were reduced to distant jingling at various points of the compass as they made their way home. "I thought I'd something to prove," she said, "but I've only shown myself an idiot. To have my families out in a night like this, out in a killing cold for a song."

"They'll all die one day," Mr. Harrow said. "Be about worth it to hear those two girls. Those two are dandy. Myself, I'd go anywhere they'd be pleased to sing."

"I should have waited for spring. Almost any pretty tune works at Easter. And, Mr. Harrow, if you do come again, to another performance, it *would* be better if you didn't laugh at the children. They try so hard. All of them. And what's worse, you had me going, too, and now I'm a little ashamed of myself."

"Nah," he said.

Her lamp was not lit, the fire long gone from her heater, and the moment Dove was unassisted she stumbled at her threshold. Mr. Harrow came in behind with his lamp, and now in short order she had seen him smile and laugh, she had taken his arm, and she had let him into her shack where in her absence several jars of preserves had quick frozen and exploded. The purposeful Mr. Harrow was someone in her imagination more engine than the engines he drove. She slumped on her rocker with the bad leg thrust forward like a pouting lip, and she let him fire her heater and light her lamp and set the room to rights. She didn't risk saying anything because she didn't want him to know how sorry she felt for herself. All she had for Mr. Harrow were her many predicaments, and these seemed constantly to multiply. She couldn't ride, couldn't walk any distance; she could barely hobble at the moment. Though not quite helpless, she lived in a place that could be fatally unforgiving of small mistakes even among the able bodied, and nothing stood between her and destitution but a dryland farm she had no means to work, and a tome detailing Babylon's first thousand years.

"How long does it last?" he said. "When your foot won't move?"

"Just a little while," she said. "So far. This is the longest it's tied up so far. Tonight."

"What can be done to help it?" Mr. Harrow fanned at the heater's grate and the new flame rose in it.

"I wait," she said. "That's all I've done so far. I wait, and it gets better after a while."

"What if it didn't?"

"It will," she said. "Or. Well, I don't know for sure. The doctor doesn't know. He's not sure exactly what happened in there. He didn't know if he should cast it, but he did, and now when it freezes up, that's the position it always assumes. Everything locks. It's very inconvenient."

If Dove Appleby knew nothing else that evening, things being so uncertain, she knew there'd be no return to Pennsylvania there to resume the care and keeping of six younger siblings who had by now no doubt gone feral for her absence; she could never resume care of her feeble mother, noble as that might be. Dove had put herself through normal school and saved for years to escape Pennsylvania, and now, if only as a matter of pride, there'd be no going home.

That night, of all nights, Square Butte Bench also fogged as her future. It didn't seem she'd be equal to it after all. She'd heard the lurid stories concerning women of her kind, homesteading teachers, a vulnerable species who tended in these parts to be poetically destroyed. Unconfirmed were the reports from Havre of two women who'd frozen while writing goodbye letters. Forgotten matches. True and verified was the odder story of the teacher found farther east in her nightgown having been tongued out of her bed then entirely out of her shack by a twister. Another confirmed fatality was the woman in Lewistown who'd simply been thrown from her horse, and, of course Dove had nearly accomplished her own demise with a riding cloak, a green-broke colt, and an especially windy day.

She feared no one calamity so much as the capriciousness of the local gods and how it made her so small. She was a speck in this endlessly visible world who might momentarily and whimsically be flicked from it. She didn't know how well she could hope to heal, but if she didn't heal substantially, she was no longer fit for this place; she hurt very much and had learned while being dragged that nothing at all can be taken for granted. Let the fire out in the grate, wear the wrong shoe for riding—these local spirits did not like sins of omission. She had seen her foot turned exactly the wrong way in a stirrup, her off foot kicking at it, and she'd heard herself screaming as if in a dream, and her frantic animal had heard it too, was urged by it to keep plunging on and on until she could make herself quiet.

Anything can happen. Skin and bone, she'd been told, are fairly quick to heal. Nerves and connecting tissue are stubborn. And slow. And often incomplete.

It was not by appointment, but she was expecting him when Mr. Harrow returned the following morning with burlap sacks of coal draped behind his saddle. He discharged these into her coal bin without dismounting, and before he could ride away, she'd invited him inside. Early in their acquaintance she had asked him to come in every time he'd dropped by to make some delivery or transaction, it was only neighborly, but then after many months of many refusals it had come to seem foolish, gratuitous to make the offer any more. This morning, though, she thought she'd try again, and she let him know, "I could give you some tea and—fruitcake." She hadn't flung the thing out onto the prairie. No self-respecting night creature was likely to come along and eat it, but perhaps Mr. Harrow—someone must find them edible. Something had changed. She'd seen him laugh. His were the patient eyes of a Basset hound, and he was old, and he had been so kind and unassuming as to not seem very virile to her, or even quite human, but since she'd seen him laugh, he had been restored or reduced to a man. And now he was getting off the horse he called Edwin to come in. He was bibbed and booted as a farmer and had a farmer's forward-lurching walk, a farmer's shapeless slouch hat, and—old—but she happened to recall in the moment that she had at times seen him ride like a vaquero. He was worn, but not worn out. How odd to find herself making such calculations about this unsuspecting man.

She might think of it, when inside, as her pretty cottage. Living in such open land, a snug enclosure was of great comfort, the very confinement of it. She kept her copper tea pot polished and lightly steaming on the iron hulk of her cook stove and heater. She'd lined a shelf with painted, lumpy crockery of her students' making, and she had thrown a nearly authentic Navajo blanket over her bed. Any guest here would have to know she was a woman who tried. How fine to have ground and a home of one's own. She had every reason to be proud. This morning, though, she happened to notice and be embarrassed by what close quarters her house made for the two of them, he having lately become a sort of stranger.

"You take cream in your tea, Mr. Harrow?"

"Don't know how I take it. Don't drink it, usually. But, sure, I'll try a dab."

"Mrs. Savka's Guernsey," she explained. "I've cream and butter coming out my ears."

He blew across it once and carefully brought his lips to the rim of her only piece of china, the cup she kept for visitors. "Why, that tastes like hay, don't it? Tea?"

"Sorry," she said. "I do sometimes keep coffee on hand. And, oh—honestly, don't. Please, don't. Just to be polite, no, you don't have to eat that."

But he chewed until he might finally swallow, and he said, "Must be quite healthy for you. That is the densest food I ever tried."

"I am so sorry," she said. "And I had the makings for

sugar cookies, too."

"I see you're getting around pretty fair again," he said. "You got that leg working right?"

She lifted the hem of her skirt and moved the toe of her shoe across a generous arc. "Hunky-dory," a term previously unknown to her mouth. Silly thing.

"You know," he said, "Miss. . . Dove. You probably hadn't better try it alone anymore. And neither should I."

Dove and her sixteen brothers and sisters had by turns turned their mother inside out, so Dove as a modern woman had found better uses for herself than to be bred like a cow. Behind her lantern jaw she reveled in a spinsterhood informed by the arts and elevated thoughts and the antique satisfaction to be had in her virginity, though that had been a condition awfully easily maintained. As a woman who'd kept her independence of spirit and her independent knowledge of the world and its workings, she was pleased to think that she'd become a little dangerous but was more often annoyed to think, to observe, that she was only troublesome, more trouble than she might be worth as a companion, and she'd gone along supported by the conviction that there wasn't a romantic bone in her bony body.

If at that time she'd any interest in marriage, she never would have thought of her neighbor that way. Mr. Harrow had preceded her onto the bench by only a few years but was as she found him there already a feature of the landscape, an outcropping of granite more suitable for a cornerstone than the flesh and blood uses of a husband; his proposal, until the day and maybe even the hour he made it, would have seemed bizarre to her. As it came, though, when it came, the idea offered a toe hold just as she was beginning to see how much she wished to climb out of herself if she still could.

"Be plain," she told him. "I should be sure of your meaning."

"Like you to be my wife. If it suits you."

"Why?"

"If you don't know, I doubt I can explain it."

"You are very kind," she said. "Or are you? What would you want of me?"

"Want? You are making this too hard. Can I call you Dove? Did you mind that?"

"You may. I should ask, though, you are aware of my—limitations? I am rather damaged goods, you know." He didn't know, and couldn't. She herself was unsure just how hurt she was. "Were you thinking of children?" she said.

"Reflects poorly on me," he said, "but I hadn't thought that far." He cocked his head to indicate that he was considering it now. "I wouldn't need any. If you didn't."

"And if I did? Need them?"

"As I say," he said. "You are making this too hard."

"We should both be sure you're serious. That is what I would expect of you. That you be serious."

"Jesus Jumped-up Christ," he said, "do I seem flibbertigibbet to you?" By way of courtship then he fixed those doleful eyes on her and continued wanting her when he couldn't be sure there was much left of her to want but her soul; thus Mr. Harrow contrived to be a devastating lothario.

"Charlie," she said experimentally, "I cannot marry for another year and a half. Couldn't marry anyone while I'm still proving up this place. I must remain the head of household. They're very particular about that at the land office."

"Eighteen months is about ten minutes, way time runs

by me," he said. "I could wait. If it's 'yes.' you're saying, I could wait. I guess I should've brought some jewelry to the deal, there's that ring they use."

"That wouldn't matter," Dove said. "I can see no purpose in that."

"Well then, what's it to be?"

"You should never press a woman so." Her cheeks bulged vaguely. She hardly ever spoke of herself as something feminine. "You must know that doesn't work."

"Oh?"

"I should have the chance to seem a little shy," she said. "A little shy, at least. And maybe thoughtful about it."

"Oh," and he was disappointed. "Well, with a thing like this, your first thought's usually the right one."

"I see," said Dove. "In that case, I think we can make an arrangement."

"Good," he said.

And Dove flushed, a warmth she would later recognize as the foreglow of lust.

It would have been futile and oafish to ask, so all through the trek of their engagement she did not ask but was left to wonder whether he thought her pitiable or just how enamored he was of her dowry. Their homesteads adjoined and would when legally entailed and combined make a property nearly worth owning in this country. Hadn't the landed gentry everywhere else been built by marriages of convenience? What an odd project, though, and how unlike her. Dove shortened 'Mr. Harrow' to 'Mister' by way of endearment, and he continued to call her 'Dove', and they were more often together after they reached their understanding, but the way they kept company was very little changed; nothing occurred between them that couldn't have happened in the lobby of a bank. If this was business, a dry partnership, then Dove thought she could and should be satisfied with it. Of late she'd come to understand she needed almost any solution to the groaning solitude, it had come to that, and here was a decent man with a going concern for a place and a wit that jumped up just often enough to surprise her. What more could she want?

As marriage loomed, she became more and more susceptible to impulses originating in her glands and not in her carefully cultivated brain. Assailed by these late-surging urges, and not sure that her intended was still of an age to share such enthusiasms, Dove, by and by, got anxious to know just how much woman she would be as a wife. Lo and behold, she was getting better. "Strong as a centurion," as she was given to say, "and every bit as pretty."

If they remained shy toward each other, they became as a couple uncharacteristically sociable, tracking the miles in pursuit of whist and cribbage games, visiting in her students' homes, often traveling north to mingle with some German Lutherans who had built a pump organ there and called on Dove to play it for them now and then. These were busy months, more promising seasons than any she'd known before, full of planning and preparation for a life larger than she'd previously let herself expect. Charlie doubled his house so that she'd not have to leave anything of hers behind when she moved. He expanded the school building and framed in new windows, and she liked him very well when he smelled of sawdust. A reputable pair, they were accorded the pleasant deference owed older, somewhat accomplished people, and it was against this respectability that Dove in very private moments sometimes imagined them as lovers. They were in these jarring scenes, as seen from a certain angle or in almost any light, repulsive—he wearing every minute of his hard years and with his hard, square hands always half clasped, and she of the atrophied calf and purpling toes, her big, square, bespectacled face and schoolroom ways. They were not a lovely thought that way, but not so grotesque as to end her curiosity.

Finally, early one summer morning when the winter wheat was up and green and bending on a breeze, they drove to Fort Benton where they were lucky enough to find the Justice of the Peace in his chambers arraigning two sneak thieves who agreed first to their guilt, then to pay their fines, and then to serve as witnesses to a wedding. It was, 'Doyou?' 'I do.' and 'Doyou?' 'I do.', and after the briefest vows permitted by law, Dove and Charlie shared their first kiss. She had anticipated somehow that he'd be salty, but her husband was so far almost flavorless.

"You're in it now," said the thinner of the criminals. "Congratulations."

Since Dove had been in Montana, she had been hearing of mountains arrayed just beyond her western horizon like truth for the nonbeliever, but, tied to her duties around the homestead, and hobbled, and poor, she had never seen them. When she happened to mention this to her fiancé he recoiled as if she'd admitted choosing to suffer some curable disease. "Never crossed the divide? That's no good." He told her he had a canvas tent and a Dutch oven. "We might as well just run off, don't you think? Go 'til we hit some high ground? Should be some wildflowers still out."

Dove had been dithering: About a menu—what to feed people? About a guest list—what to do about their German friends with feelings running so high against the Huns just then? About the ceremony—when, exactly? So here she was on the strength of Charlie's superior plan, a suddenly married woman following the sun in a chugging touring car, gasoline and kerosene strapped to the running boards, and odors of the countryside and buffalo robe and a cheese and a salami contending in her busy nose, and it was all so much, they were so very married. He had bought this motor car, she now knew, with her in mind.

The road, hardly more than wagon track after it turned due west at Great Falls, was in places so rutted as to seize their wheels and try and wrest the steering wheel from Charlie's hands, but he went on, patiently, relentlessly; Charlie had been driving one conveyance or another all his life and so would naturally drive on like this, but Dove had to ask herself—too late?—did she honestly think she could live day by day with so much energy? It was demanding even to be his passenger. They were not the kind of people to bellow over a motor or their rattling outfit, and they went on almost entirely given to their own thoughts, and the mountains when they raised them at last stood right up out of the plains, a green and blue palisade, a continental swelling, and to the north along this front a thunderhead was gathering to an impossible elevation, boiling, gathering power and radiance to itself, firing lightning from its base. Lightning, then with some initial reluctance, rolling thunder. To the south there was not a cloud in the sky, and to take in so much sky all at once, to see so much weather and in the same sweep of the eyes so much tilted land, it was surely the heavenly perspective. She had to value a man who would know the importance of bringing her to this.

At less than half the pace that an antelope would have covered the ground, they climbed a high, sage range, and it was that time of summer when twilight can persist for hours. Fading light saw them up into a pass and on a track twisting treacherously along the gravel flanks of a thousand sidehills. She had more than ceremoniously placed her fate in her husband's hands. With full dark they were still in the mountains, still driving, dependent on those pale headlamps. Her husband drove all night, and Dove spent some of this sleeping under her buffalo robe, but she was mostly awake with him. They never did escape the mountains. Sometimes in that journey a valley would open out before them, or a long, moonlit lake, but her main impression of the night was of the shaggy, hulking shadows of mountains crowding round.

They had a breakfast of brook trout at a five-stool café, a sunny little room with its mullioned windows. Their fish were caught just this morning, they were told; the meat was pink and firm and barely dead.

"I don't wish to complain, Mister, but I am worn to a frazzle."

Dove, who still thought something like a horsewoman, was also vaguely sorry for their automobile; he'd given it no rest at all. Charlie, looking quite as haggard by the morning light as she felt, drove on. They entered another maze of mountains, and these, being on the wet west side of the divide, wore a forest unfamiliar to her, a gloaming of red cedar and fir standing in tangled fern and berry bush, and down in so much vegetation the air was syrupy, and she wondered how long her curiosity might keep her awake. They'd not discussed a particular destination, and now, assessing the set of her husband's jaw, she understood that he was terrified of her, or of the marital bed—a tarp on the ground—and that if she didn't insist, he would keep driving. A day and a night and a day, and who knows how long he might go on?

"If I don't stretch my legs soon," Dove said, "I may lose the use of them. Can't we find a place to walk?"

They came at last to a meadow at the foot of a talus slope, and this was spread with a kind of blue bell, and Indian paint brush, and there was trillium in the shade.

He stopped beside the broad creek that cut through it and switched off the magneto. "This'd do, don't you think? Want to pitch camp?"

"It will do nicely," she said. "Where are we?"

"Not sure. Been a long while since I passed through this neck of the woods. But we're somewhere right off the Flathead, I know that much."

"This should be fine," she said. "First a walk, though. Before we do anything else. Will you walk with me, Mister?"

They couldn't keep pace with each other strolling the meadow with its hidden hummocks and deadfall, so they walked out on the road where their strides were still poorly matched and they struggled to stay abreast. Her husband, as her husband, was yet again a stranger to her. How often could this recur? How did married people converse? This was Charlie Harrow, had she expected a baring of souls? They hadn't tramped very far before Dove's dress, the dress she'd married in and never yet removed, was soaked with sweat and clinging to her back. The road ran them through one humid grove after another. She couldn't think of a thing to say to him until she was forced to admit, "I am vile."

"How do you? What?"

"I mean to bathe in that stream," she said, "muddy bottom or no."

The creek ran through the meadow and bent into a stand of shimmering birch and disappeared into a thicket of scrub oak and alder. Within this bramble Dove finally disrobed. Charlie stood with his back to her as if he were keeping watch though they hadn't seen another soul for hours or for miles. She sighed elaborately, removing her shoes. She exposed her whole knobby self. What was the protocol here? Marriage would make her remake the etiquette of every single thing. A bath. Something as simple as a bath. They had, in theory, everything in common, but he wouldn't look at her. Everything in common, and almost everything left unsaid. Carefully, nakedly she made her way through the brush and to the creek side. Along either bank a growth of violently green grass or sedge flowed downstream like hair; the bottom was a rubble of red gravel and rounded cobblestone, likely slick. Dove held to an overhanging branch with both hands and stepped into water colder than ice to the touch; the shock traveled up through her feet and ankles and she must have gasped because Charlie turned briefly to be sure of her. As simple a thing as bathing. Now she must somehow get clean in this painful water. Dove gave more of her weight to her branch and slowly it bent and lowered her until she was sitting on the rocky bottom, working very hard to breathe, so cold she burned, her pale flesh turning instantly pink wherever the water washed it, and she had already concluded she was clean enough when, silently, the first wasp came.

She thought at first that something had swum up behind and fanged her neck, its sting was so powerful. Dove shrieked, let go her branch, and this rebounded into the brush where it tore a gray paper nest from another branch, and the unhoused swarm was on her before she could scramble out of the water. Rock so slick, water so cold, and wasps, their stingers hanging heavy with that electric venom; stinging, stinging. She beat at them, then Charlie was there, swatting at them, and then she took his hand and he snatched her out of the creek, and they ran without stopping to gather up her shoes or clothes, pursued by insects so angry they burrowed into her hair to sting her at the scalp, so frantic they stung Charlie through his clothes or crawled down inside them to get at him. This was spastic running, with flailing and flinching, and she barefoot, tenderfoot. Her husband made the air so blue with a muleskinner's profanity that she could almost believe he had cursed the swarm into quitting them, but the wasps were silent, and so it was hard to know for sure when the attack had ended, and the newlyweds ran on until they were well winded.

Stripped, bruised, scratched, and swollen, Dove began to laugh before she had quite ceased to cry. Her groom was confused though he'd been warned that women could be hard to make out, impossible to predict.

"Did you see me running? Never a thought to that ankle." It was not like her to crow. "Running," she marveled. "I just ran, didn't I?"

"Yep, you were pretty quick. Are you. . .?"

"Fine," she wheezed. "Just fine. Don't you see? I ran."

"Like a little deer."

"That was quite a jaunt, wasn't it? And now I stand before you, relieved of my last shred of dignity. Can't you see how funny?"

"Not yet," he said.

"You can't have your modesty," she said, "if I can't have mine. We better make sure the little horrors haven't left any stingers in you—those can fester. Skin down, Mister."

Intending biscuits, she had brought baking soda; Dove used it to make a paste for dozens of small poultices that she applied to their stings. They were stung everywhere, the poison still humming in them. Carefully then, and tenderly, shyly, breath to breath, one thing led to another in the meadow.

◊ ◊ ◊

Sex was her first and only experience of the mystical, and she was glad to have married a stout man. Dove, once she'd tasted the animal thing, regretted her foolish chastity very much, and whenever time and leisure permitted, she would enlist her husband in a ceremony of long caresses during which they were completely unlike themselves, outside themselves, making those hideous faces, breathing in the other's ear. Gasping. On account of fifteen exquisite minutes a week Dove was almost continuously pregnant for years on end, and, plagued a little by that old-time religion, she would come to worry that her stubborn carnality, her pleasure, was the source of their sorrows.

Their first baby was due at the height of the epidemic when influenza was a pale rider stalking the hospitals, so Dove thought she would have the child at home as she supposed women had been doing forever, without doctors or anesthetic. That baby, a bumptious thing and frequent traveler in her womb, came early and so urgently that before Charlie could return with Mrs. Purdy the horrified neighbor lady who'd offered to help, Dove was already delivered of a slick blue corpse, a thing she accomplished alone, squatting over a bleached sheet she'd spread for the purpose. Hope, they named their daughter, an ancient looking thing as she appeared to them, and they buried her out in their recently planted shelter belt of caragana and Russian olive. Within two months Dove had, at her insistence, conceived again. Their next child and the child after that were stillborn under medical supervision at the hospital. Nurses there, assuming that the less she knew of them the better, bundled them off before Dove had properly even seen them, but she believed that these were daughters, too, and she gave them names—Honor and Faith—so that she might hold them in her thoughts at least, but this proved too hard to do without also wondering what may have come of them after they'd been whisked so efficiently away.

The Harrows were otherwise successful. In good markets and bad, foul weather and fair, people were always going under, sharp cheeked farm families suddenly seeking to sell out at any price so long as it would get them to town, any town, and Charlie hit like a hawk on these properties, and once he'd got the habit of acquisition, he went crazy with it and built a patchwork barony on and around the bench. A matter of scale. Huge machines and huge holdings. Such ground as he couldn't farm himself, he leased, and Charlie hauled grain and gravel, and Charlie shod horses and repaired various reapers, and it was the rare waking moment when he was not somehow improving their fortunes, so, while other families in the area, most other families were failing or getting good sense and moving on, the Harrows were installing indoor plumbing in the house and raising another barn. It seemed to Dove that they had got too much for just two people to share, or maybe she had only been seized by her mother's unreasoning need to breed, but whatever the cause she had come to long for a breathing baby; Dove had got pretty far in life without being much governed by longings, but now look at her. Something about this country—one wanted an anchor.

One sweltering afternoon Charlie was out in the farmyard, working under the bed of a grain truck at a repair involving a prolonged metallic hammering, a ringing that carried into the house along with Charlie's running commentary which Dove must pretend not to enjoy, and eventually she went out to him with a plate of corn muffins and a wry smile, and as she approached him, he lay on his back kicking piston like with both feet at something she couldn't see.

"Mister," she said. "Come out from under there. That is mad."

"Aw," said Charlie, "she'll ride all right, but you almost wish the potmetal sonofabitch would fall on you, put you out of your misery. I smelled you coming. Wasn't it just lunch?"

A hind quarter of the truck was raised off the ground, supported so far as she could see by nothing. Dove leaned down to see that her husband had somehow lifted the thing onto a cairn of stones he'd made for the purpose, and none too sturdily. "Mad," she said with more certainty. "Get out from under there. Please."

In an inverse crawl, on his back, feet forward, her husband came out to her. An irresistible old man who got up to such things all day, he stood; his hands wore luster-less black grease to the elbow. "I wouldn't be much of a hand for muffins just now," he said. "As you can see. Maybe you could ladle me out some water, though."

He'd brought drinking water in a steel pail from the house with a steel ladle, but he was so befouled he couldn't even drink without corrupting his water. Just above one brow there was a red slit situated in another smear of grease and from that ran down a gray tracery of sweat on his cheek. Dove wet her apron to wash this, and he stood patiently for it. She ladled him up some water then and the gratitude in his eyes nearly destroyed her. She held a muffin to his lips until he understood that he was to nibble it.

Thickly she said as his lips reached her fingertips, "I have an idea."

He held his greasy hands up, a pair of impossibilities.

"I can do everything," she said, and she could see he was shocked and intrigued by this.

"I," he said, his arms still raised before him as if he were being held up, his hard old heart racing. "It's too soon."

"You mean we shouldn't?"

"We probably should let you lie fallow for a while."

"I am not the good earth, Mister. A woman has only so long to be fertile."

"Well, I know I'd never use a brood mare this hard. You have to—recover."

"I am also not a mare," she said. She directed him to the shade and concealment under the truck, back to the danger she'd just made him quit, and she joined him there for an interlude she was to remember always and in some detail.

As the casualties mounted in her war with her body, Dove had finally begun to consider terms of surrender when she sensed something else alive in her; she determined at once to coddle and pamper this thing until it might live on its own. Dove paid close attention to her diet, her program of deep breathing and meek calisthenics and uplifting literature. She ate poems and green onions and rested a great deal with her feet up and was not much use as a farm wife. Charlie indulged her in all this, held her like a brimful chalice until, without incident, without much trouble at all, she bore them a boy. Seven pounds. Twenty-two inches. Their George.

Dove, as a mother, was still a sensualist and she carried her baby almost constantly throughout his infancy in one of several slings she devised as he grew; she explained the practice by saying it kept her hands and attention free to do other chores, but her real purpose was to keep that warm weight hanging near, his quicker heart beating close. She nursed him until he refused it. She talked to him as if he were a godly ear sent to hear every fluttering of her heart, and truly little George had a whole vocabulary of responsive gurgles, sighs, and grins. He would want down, though. All too soon he would want the use of his own lovely legs. He'd use them to run away from her.

CHARLIE

He had the boys in harness and they were already in the garden plowing before the birds had finished discussing dawn. Once, and not so long ago by his remembrance, birds had been about all that might be heard on Square Butte Bench, but Charlie Harrow had done more than his share to ruin that. He held by then clear title to two thousand acres and owned outright the world of equipment needed to sow and harvest and haul his crops to market, so in partnership with John D. Rockefeller and The Standard Oil Company Charlie had brought noise to his property and made money. He still maintained a team of geldings, though, for use in the garden, and this team got too little work to be very smart or very strong but they could plow an acre easily enough, and it was quiet but for the old soft symphony of harness creak and horse fart. He rode spring steel. Get up, Karl. Get up, Bill. Rounding the north end of the plot he saw George come running out of the house, terrified at having awakened alone in it; the boy had got his sun hat on but came stumbling and wailing barefoot across the field to Charlie who, feeling neglectful and ashamed, set him in his lap. They turned several more rows, one furrow at a time, the timeless way, sitting right atop the earth as it rolled up, and smelling it, and George was restored at once to high spirits and happy confidence. Geey up. Geey up. Charlie could not see how he'd played much part in the making of such a sweet temperament but was as proud of his son as if he'd built him molecule by molecule.

They grained the team and Charlie showed his boy how the horses were to be rubbed down with burlap sacking and a curry comb. The hired man came out from the bunkhouse at last and Charlie fried them some eggs, a pullet egg for George, and he thought to cut the boy's coffee with cream. "Dane:" he told his man. "While we're gone you might hang that barn door again and get it so it latches right. It'll rain later; rain all day, I imagine, and you never want to complain of any moisture, but see how it comes at the damndest, unhandiest times."

He bathed the boy and then himself in their porcelain, clawfooted tub, bringing hot water from the cook stove. Charlie, for reasons obscure to him, had determined his family should know luxury, and he had ambitions himself to one day, time permitting, soak like a pasha in this thing. He dressed them in their town clothes and they set out for Great Falls with a jack, a shovel, bags of sand, jars of milk, a tarpaulin and some blankets, and the rains came, and the Ford traveled as much side to side in the mud as forward through it; Charlie had constantly to manipulate the throttle and the spark advance to keep from overheating. The Ford, he'd discovered, had its own set of problems, not unlike a horse or a mule. Charlie was of two minds on motoring, but George loved a drive above all things, and to proceed at his father's preferred pace, a canter, would have killed him with impatience. Even as a toddler George was long and lean. He sat atop a pile of blankets the better to see out, and asked again from time to time, "New baby?"

"That's right," Charlie answered every time, but why so proudly? What had he done but wear down his poor wife?

They were three hours that morning just reaching Fort Benton where Charlie felt he'd already wrestled an anaconda. He stopped at a filling station to wipe the worst of the mud from himself because he had along the way helped to lever a fellow motorist out of the always beckoning ditch. The road beyond that was better, and he enjoyed the heat coming up through the floor from the exhaust pipe. The rain continued, a tapping on the canvas roof that seemed to leaven the engine noise. Somewhere around Portage Charlie slept briefly at the wheel and he woke to his son's laughter. They were well off the road, thrashing through raw prairie on a flat tire.

So, he should have started earlier. As they arrived at the hospital Charlie calculated that he was already too late, that some part of their return trip might take place in the dark. At night in the mud with babies and a fragile wife—though he was a much better father than his father had been Charlie sometimes thought he didn't quite have the knack of it yet. Until he'd turned fifty, he had given no more thought to raising children than to herding turkeys. He should have started earlier. The saplings along this street seemed not to have grown at all. The boy hadn't been back to Great Falls since his own birth, and town awed him; George was accustomed to his lightly populated circumstance and its humble structures, and as Charlie carried him into the brick immensity of Deaconess Hospital it was necessary to chuck him under the chin to close his mouth. "Last thing you want is to look the rube." In the lobby Charlie bought a cloth tulip from a society matron to support the Nurse's Aid Society. He held this in his free hand, intending to deliver it to Dove, but also to validate his presence and prevent someone in a starched uniform from throwing them out. His clothes were soaked through and muddy again; his boots squeaked on the polished floors. "Ready to meet your sister, kid?"

"New baby. Mama?"

"She's here too."

They passed through a corridor where patients had been cached along one wall in wheel chairs. People in white bustled by, going either way without a glance to spare for Charlie or his boy or the patients so dreadfully patient along the wall. The maternity ward was in another wing and sunnier. They were intercepted there by a flighty, pretty nurse who, when she learned his name said, "Oh, Mr. *Harr*ow, you must be bursting, sir, your little Verity is my favorite. I'm sure you can appreciate a lot of babies come and go through that nursery, but your granddaughter is such a precious little thing. So tiny. Can I get you a towel?"

"This is her brother," Charlie said. "He's never laid eyes on her."

The nurse gave them masks to wear over their mouths and noses, and when she was convinced that George could be trusted to keep his mask in place, she took them into a large, warm room with rows of white bins for babies. Just five of these were filled at the moment, and at the moment all the infants were asleep, bundles of blanket, their heads extruding like hairy raisins from their swaddling. Charlie would usually know within an hour of its birth if a calf or a foal was sound; children revealed themselves more slowly. His children kept him anxious and delighted.

Dove had had so much trouble making babies that it was not reasonable to assume this little girl was whole and uncompromised. He knew nothing about the child, and Charlie could not have offered one word of explanation as to how she differed from the others, except that she was his and therefore less alien.

"Well, kid, what do you think?"

"Baihty?"

"Would you like to hold her, Mr. Harrow?"

An earlier nurse had placed his daughter in his arms shortly after she'd been born, and she had seemed so insubstantial there that his heart had flown into his mouth; Charlie didn't wish to repeat that experience just now as he was preparing to carry the tiny thing off to Square Butte Bench, an increasingly bad idea. "She's asleep," he said.

"I don't think she'd mind," said the nurse.

"I've got my hands full," he said, though it was obvious that George, still astride his hip, wanted down.

Making his late rounds, Dr. Steiger, who had delivered George and Verity and all but one of their would-be siblings, joined them in quietly regarding the nursery's current residents whose faces worked without exception in bitter disappointment. Their admirers were careful not to wake them. Dr. Steiger motioned with his head for Charlie to follow him into the corridor. "He's turned out well," said the doctor of George. Dr. Steiger hadn't removed his mask, and his Barney Google eyes were like something up from the depths, considerably magnified by his spectacles. The man was prone to bear his bad news—there had been a lot of it from him—in a roundabout way.

"They were healthy," Charlie said. "I was told they were healthy when I left."

"Who? The little girl? Mrs. Harrow? They're fine."

"Oh," said Charlie. "Well. Good."

"George," said George.

"I remember," said the doctor. "And you've come on quite the sturdy lad, haven't you? But, Mr. Harrow, what you should know is that your wife will no longer be getting pregnant. She is no longer capable of that."

"But, she's healthy?"

"Yes," said Dr. Steiger. "Or, she isn't suffering from anything very specific. But she's not a strong woman. You know that."

"I know no such thing. She puts me in the shade. She's been told? About the?"

"She has," said the doctor. "Though I don't think it was necessary. To tell her. She already understood."

"And my girl is healthy? Our little girl?"

"She was small at birth," said the doctor. "She's thriving

now."

"Mama," said George, a statement and a question.

"Something else," said the doctor. "I've just come from Mrs. Harrow. She knows, she knew you'd be visiting today."

"Visit? We're here to take her home. It's been two weeks."

"She knew you were coming," said Dr. Steiger. "She's said not today. She can't see you today. She asked me to tell you."

"See us?" Charlie felt himself hovering over an emptiness. "This is her little boy."

"As I very well know, Mr. Harrow. Sometimes a woman needs a little time."

"You say she's healthy."

"I say she's tired," said the doctor.

"Too tired to see us?"

"Well—yes."

"What in the Sam Hill," said Charlie, "is wrong here, Doctor?"

"I really don't know," admitted Dr. Steiger. "Some of these things don't have names. Come back tomorrow if you can."

"Tomorrow."

George buried his face in the crook of Charlie's neck, and Charlie clung to and was clung to by his child. Stay away? His wife was stubborn in her way, but that way was hardly ever troublesome. Charlie could not imagine why she might want to avoid her son. George's lower lip trembling and trembling, but he never offered a suffering sound. Tomorrow? Charlie did not recognize his wife in this odd request, and now, to honor it, he'd have to defer asking why. She wouldn't see them? Down the rolling corridors, along the heaving sidewalk. During their succession of dead babies Charlie had become a kind of fatalist, having noticed that family life for all its benefits featured constant worry sometimes punctuated by the crushing reasons for it. The sudden vacancies of love: Death and every other thing. The Ford backfired when he stomped the starter. Charlie clung to the cotton tulip. "We better find a place to put up," he told the boy. "We'll take another run at it in the morning." His son's bravery could prove to be the one thing he couldn't stand. "What the hell, let's try the Hotel Rainbow."

Charlie's boots and trousers were still gobbed with the gumbo he'd picked up while changing his tire, so at the hotel desk he produced from the shank of one of those boots bills of larger denomination to address the Rainbow's desk clerk. He remained in his mind, if in no one else's, a gypsy, and Charlie liked to follow some of the old practices, he liked to lead with cash; Charlie, for as long as he had been one, had never entirely lost his disdain for farmers or for any citizen who couldn't up and leave at a moment's notice. A man kept money in his boot for bail or bad bets. "Two beds and a shower bath," he said.

"And will you be dining in, sir?"

"Your food any good?"

"Well sir, I've been around some, and it's the best I've had. Not only that, but we've got some new musicians coming in tonight. In the Palm Room. Quite something, they're supposed to be. Here we go—room twenty-eight. With a view."

"An orchestra?" said Charlie. "Could be we'll try that."

In their room George made a nest of plump pillows, lay in it, and went immediately slack jawed, his troubles escaping his gaping mouth. Little Mr. longbritches. Charlie, who kept finding mud on unlikely parts of himself, stood under the shower fully clothed, determined that he would be clean at least for tomorrow, whatever tomorrow might be. Stay away? The Hotel Rainbow, he concluded, must have a boiler in hell, for he rinsed and rinsed and never did exhaust the hot water, his for the turn of a knob, and he was very sure no Harrow before him had ever known such posh plumbing, and he stood under the water until it ran clear to the drain.

Then there was the problem of his dripping clothes. He wrung out his trousers, jacket, shirt, and socks, and draped them over the steam registers, cranking the valves fully open under them. His union suit, he decided, must dry in place, but it made for a very clammy rest, wearing it. Charlie listened to the sibilance of his son's light snoring, hoping for sleep himself, but he could not quit wondering after his wife. It wasn't too long before the room smelled like a shearing shed on a hot summer day; Charlie assumed the knock at their door was someone come to complain, that the funk had leaked into the hall, and he was more than reluctant to answer in damp underwear, but the knocking, though timid, continued. It was a man in a green jacket and sandy pompadour, the hotel's valet who wondered if the gentleman would like any assistance with his wardrobe.

"Gentleman? You're too late. Way too late, son."

"You think it's a good idea, sir, to leave your things on the manifolds that way?"

"Will be 'til they're dry."

"Yes, but. Could I at least do something about your boots?"

"Got some grease you could slather on? They been soaked today. Several times."

By supper that evening Charlie's town clothes were a suit fit for a misshapen child, riding dangerously high at the crotch, and bunching, and wrinkled. His boots, however, wore a high gloss, and he thought that hereafter he'd make better use of such services as he could afford whenever he was in town. They sat on tufted leather, at a linen table cloth lain with silver, lit with candle light, and what a companion in tidy little George who'd never until now known anything but a homesteader's augmented shack, and who was wide open for as much elegance and as many miracles as may want to happen. Charlie and son had hot buns and a watercress concoction with tiny forks while three violinists came in arguing with each other as they set up on the stand at the other side of the Palm Room. The Harrows received their orders of veal scaloppini while the musicians, still in dispute, were tuning. The ensemble played variations on a mawkish theme while George tucked in and ate like a full-grown field hand and sighed and sighed, nearly overcome with contentment.

And this would serve for Charlie's most persistent memory, the floor of his understanding.

"So, there I was with my firetruck nose, my alabaster head, and the unholy mess I'd made of my clothes. If ever a dirt farmer came to town. Least my boots got buffed up. Now, out on the road when I rarely had a pot to piss in or a window to throw it out of, I never gave a damn about that kind of thing, and I was too old and George was too young to worry about how we might be seen in good society. On my own I always used to go along pretty rosy and pleased with myself, but then I went respectable and ran into a lot of occasions where I wasn't sure how to behave. I'd purely cringe if I was to ever embarrass my boy, but I wouldn't have traded anything for the pleasure of listening to those fiddlers with George. My money spends as good as the next man's, and I came by it honestly—what I had, though, when you come right down to it, I had my hungry boy."

DOVE

Something more than a girl child had slipped out of her, and after Verity was born Dove was a dutiful mother but could be no more; she adored children she never held, for she found their attempts to love her back distasteful. Dove lacked the modern understanding of herself as a thing governed by hormones, but she was too modern to think she'd been cursed or invaded by demons, so she could only conclude she was sinning. Her sin was ingratitude. She'd been given so much. The country, the world it seemed was falling apart with depression and drought, and so many around them were doing without, living right on the lip of disaster; meanwhile the Harrows were always comfortable. She had a husband who capably saw to their comfort. She had children she believed to be an improved kind of humanity. Dove knew full well what she'd been given, but her demeanor never for a moment betrayed it. Dove endured her moods, the view from her kitchen window.

"Why did I feel so guilty? About everything? About nothing I could name."

VERITY

She is inhabited by each song and every sensation she's ever liked, but Verity Harrow can never recall last night's dreams or much of her early childhood. Who needs such details? She knows that her sleep must be filled with the same weird wanting her waking has always been, and that she has from the beginning been a guest at her own life. An anachronism in every era through which she has lived, Verity remains even now her father's daughter, her mother's stoic daughter, born and bred to not complain. Still, she has been heard to wonder in her old age, "How does a reasonable woman manage to squander her whole life playing a piano?"

She might well ask.

◊ ◊ ◊

In 1936, on the morning of her birthday, she went out to hang the day's wash on the line, a cracked and bowed copy of *Lorna Doone* lying concealed in the bottom of her laundry basket. Verity pinned up garments worn and washed by her family to near gossamer, and as these were lifting in the wind she ran away, a small escape. She ran, book in hand, tripping over her own endless legs as they ascended into her armpits, and tripping over the puppy Sir Francis who frolicked at her feet in the spirit of the thing. In the house Mother was fussing, for Mother had invited the Ragstads and the Malones to come by later and have cake with them. Verity was that rare girl who doesn't care for cake; she was agreed with almost everyone in detesting the loud Malones with their smeared and urine-reeking Bobby, but Mother just had to bring in the nasty neighbors, and Mother would certainly expect her girl to pitch in now and help make everything spic and span and delicious for their guests, and Mother had already decreed that Verity must wear her dress to receive company. So, there she'd be with her sharp shins on display for everyone's amusement. On her birthday? Preferring not to prepare for this dismal party or think of it at all, Verity ran to the barn and to the stall within it that had lately been her reading room. She sprawled on a pile of clean straw and sneezed and sneezed, and when she had finally with light slapping discouraged the puppy from licking her glistening nose, she returned to Exmoor where the farmers, though they farmed by hand, found time and energy to cultivate highwaymen and the large sentiments so little on display around her family's house.

Verity had at that time never personally seen a seaside or a moor; her notion of forests and waterfalls relied on descriptions of these features in books, pen and ink illustrations. To travel in the long-ago and far-away, to furnish any romance from her own unfurnished experience, this needed all her imagination. That fevered imagination, always her burden and refuge. She hardly knew what to make of herself without it. A girl, even a young one, must from time to time visit her mirror, and this is what Verity had seen in hers that morning: A plain, skeptical face framed in a page boy bob of brown hair and looking back at her with her father's sad eyes. She wore her brother's supple, hand-me-down boots, his hand-me-down blue jeans rolled twice at the cuffs and secured to her with a strap wrapped half again around her waist and hanging loose at the buckle; she wore a linen halter that Mother had made for her, her bone white shoulders flaring out from it. She did not take a tan. Though she was only rarely confronted by her appearance, her sense of herself was always with her, no more satisfactory than that face, and so she found it necessary to ride whenever possible, to ride out on her bicycle, one of the horses, some improbable story.

Now, these were hard times and she was just worldly enough to know it. Children of her acquaintance sometimes went hungry while she had never missed a meal. She had friends from school who slept four to a bed with their siblings while Verity famously, infamously, had a room of her own. She was thought to be spoiled and was not entirely patient with her own discontents. But look out the door of that barn. To the south you'd see the butte, of course, and to the north the Nelson's tiny windmill, and nearer down the road Mother's old, listing school. And in any view, in any direction, there'd be dirt or grain in season. "Goddamned, wind-soaked prairie," as Father had once in her hearing called it, and she was cast adrift to idly paddle on that brown sea in hopes of some more detailed and various shore, a place more like those she'd read of in books.

"Veeehr-itee" Mother's call, a quavering thing. Next, she'd ring the dinner bell, tap it just once—ping—to bring her daughter in. Another little sprint, then Mother there at the door of the house, fists on her hips. "Miss Houdini," she said, "whenever I need you for anything, poof, you're gone."

"Chafe me not, sweet Mother, and I'll vex not thee. My duties were discharged and I only sought an hour's repose."

"No," said Mother. "Before company comes, you'd better just stop it. It makes people uneasy to hear you talk that way, and you know it does. *Nooo*, keep that dog out. Can I possibly get you to do some dusting before? There are other books, dear, better books. We don't speak that way; I doubt anyone ever spoke that way, so please, for today, will you quit? Must you always play at being strange?"

"I shall do thy bidding," said Verity, "as ever."

"Verity—now. And you'd better have your bath before

the men come in from the fields. Well, come *on.*"

A girl for whom monotony was a near constant and almost unbearable, she was not skilled labor, and her every menial chore added three or four hundred pounds to her body weight. Verity's family and most of the men who worked for them seemed to simply become whatever they were doing at any given moment, their labors as natural and necessary to them as breathing. Verity had not acquired this common knack; she freshly resented doing dishes, for instance, three times every day as a more or less heartbreaking waste of her time. Mother feared she would fall into all kinds of depravity if she failed to make her bed in the morning. At least the feather duster gave Verity an excuse to moon around, but there was nothing that interested her less than whatever slight advantage might be gained from using it, and she dusted, dreading that dress and the party soon to come with its conversation concerning, undoubtedly, weather and people's ailments.

The Harrow house contained by then many corners, the original shack having been extended end to end and side to side, built a room at a time as rooms were needed. One of these alcoves contained the piano Charlie had bought to surprise his wife in hopes of improving her spirits. Abramovich & Son, Chicago, Ill. The prairie Steinway, it was an upright hulk of cherry wood and cast brass, reputed to stay in tune, if necessary, on the back of a wagon. Dove had played it a handful of times only to discover that she'd lost her music too, that where the piano was concerned, she was just one reluctant mechanism bothering another. After that, when she was induced to play, she played so grimly that it had been a very long time since anyone had asked her to do it, and so her daughter knew the thing not as an instrument but as big furniture, a shrine of dark wood and doilies, the family's photographs set out on top. Many of these pictures were of times before Verity's existence. Father in a smithy's apron at an anvil. Mother under a boxy hat, with a diploma and a fountain pen. Father and Mother together, solemnly wearing corsages and posed standing for some reason about six inches apart with their hands behind their backs and leaning slightly forward in eternal anticipation. George was there as an old-fashioned baby wearing a frock his little sister would cause him to long regret.

So much life had gone on without her, before her. This was a world complete before she'd arrived in it, completely stocked with brave, productive people, and that was the problem, wasn't it? She had no idea of herself as anything more than a minor disruption here. Verity lived with family whose doings were generally essential—she who could barely boil an egg and was only a little useful and only when forced to be.

Blithe spirit, Mother sometimes called her in those days, to be nice about it. An elder Verity is less charitable toward the child she was. A writhing wretch, wasn't she? A planet without a sun, or in search of one. If only she'd been more curious, or curious sooner she now thinks, she might have had a childhood as a prodigy. Maybe not. But she is of two parts, Verity, she has been two people, and the first of these was a knob, a brute, a non-musician who was banished on that birthday almost as if she'd died.

Her mother's only hobby was a collection of stones she thought interesting, and shards of colored glass she'd found and washed and set out for display along the piano's faceboard. Verity had seen this clutter so much, so often, that ordinarily now she didn't see it at all, but she was obliged to remove it to the piano bench to dust it and to dust the somber surfaces under it, and she was aggrieved by the idiocy of dusting rock, demoralized by Mother's small, sad passion, and so in a bit of a snit Verity seized the pegs at the front of the faceboard and rolled it back on a long brass hinge grown stiff with disuse.

There stood the keys in their elegant rank where they had been wanting her touch; patiently, impatiently they'd been awaiting her in the dark.

CHARLIE

"You'd think by living with people you'd get to know 'em. You might be wrong there. Those women—hell—I'd come in the house for supper some days and see where they didn't even know each other, didn't know themselves, see how it nettled 'em. They did what they needed to do, and everything was kept running right, but I thought they sunk a lot of work into being nettled. Had no room to say anything about it, though. Me, of all people. George. He had every motor on the place ramped up and running hard, which was good for the operation, but in him, too— in him it was that hurry, and you know there's some of that in every young rooster, there's supposed to be—but I did wonder. They kept me wondering. That wondering, that's what I bargained for."

DOVE

She likes it," George said. "You can sling her around, get her up on two wheels; long as you don't tip over, she's fine. Good American steel, she's built for anything. See—."

Dove would never adjust to these new velocities. Sliding onto the main road, her son waltzed their big automobile around like a cow pony, and she was already exhausted with tensing and bracing herself, "You could give us a bit more warning," she said, "before you do those things."

"There's only a few more corners between here and town," George said, "and you know where those are."

"Fine, but no more jumping. I don't know what those men were thinking when they built this road."

"It's just a little dipsy-doo. You have any idea how much power you'd have to generate to get something this heavy off the road, Mother? Even a quarter inch off the road. Other than that, she'll do about anything I ask her to."

It was hard to check him. These rides with George juiced her sagging heart, and it was nice to know she was not entirely immune to a thrill. Careering along, spraying gravel in their wake, her stomach lurching up and down. Dipsy-doo. Probably best not to encourage him, though. "We've plenty of time," Dove said, "and no matter what you say I won't be convinced this automobile can—I am saying, *please*. There's a long day ahead of us."

"We're so heavy," George assured her, "we've never actually got off the ground."

"Yeah," said Verity, "but *we're* flying around in here. When you hit those humps, we sure as hell pop up in the air."

"Young lady," Dove said, "we are going to town. Will

you embarrass me there with your ugly talk? That is so unlovely in a girl your age. Any age."

"Poor Mother," said the girl. "What children she's got."

"Well, we don't get to town very often, and I'm not certain you *do* know how to behave. I've neglected your social skills terribly. Particularly yours, Daughter. You don't have any so far as I can see."

"George is pretty charming, though. He didn't turn out too bad."

"I'm only saying, *dear*, that you don't need to seem common just because you live on the land."

"If Father ever talked in public. . ."

"Father is not a young lady."

"What a thought," George said. "Dad—a young anything. I can't feature it. So, it's all right for him to cuss? Because he's old and wise?"

"Because he's your father. I certainly hope you two don't plan on ganging up on me all day, take turns being difficult and muleheaded."

Dove considered herself a preposterous old woman and dressed as one. She wore a shapeless velveteen hat trimmed in faux violets and netting, and she was herself shapeless within her cotton dress. What a thing to inhabit, a body. The spritz of rose water on her wrists sometimes smelled to her of decay. Wearing her special shoe, her brace, and her stately misery, Dove sat beloved and quaint at the center of the back seat so that she might see between her children and watch the road come hurtling at them. Her boy was an early master of short, interesting journeys.

Great Falls smelled irredeemably to her of doctoring and the stockyards, and she came to town as rarely as she could, but her doctor required regular visits of her, and Dr. Gorman's office was their first stop of the day. She sent the children off to the music store so that they wouldn't have to wait for her. "There should be plenty of time if you don't dawdle. They usually keep me a while. But don't let her dawdle, George."

Dove checked in with the receptionist, a woman new to the office, who told her that the doctor was running behind as usual but confided, "He's so darn thorough." Dove thumbed through magazines advising women what to do with their spare time and what they might fashionably wear. Her own interest in fashion was as always academic, but she did entertain hopes that her daughter might one day move on from dressing in just anyone's cast off rags.

"Mrs. Harrow?" said a funereal nurse. "Come on back." Dove was then left to fret in a room with an illustration of a curved spine for which she felt some absurd sympathy. The exam room was kept cool enough for hanging meat. She'd let herself become overwrought, and Dove was relieved when the nurse returned to take her pulse and blood pressure and to weigh her. The nurse listened to her chest with a stethoscope she thoughtfully warmed first with her breath. Dr. Gorman dispensed with this nicety when he applied his own stethoscope a few minutes later. The doctor palpated the glands under her jaw and kept his fingers hooked there to examine her face as if he intended to paint it or she might attempt to escape his gaze.

"Not good, Mrs. Harrow."

"No?"

"How's the leg?"

"I may need a new brace soon," Dove said. "This one doesn't seem to fit very well anymore. What a wreck. What a project I am."

Dr. Gorman had not released her head or ceased to look in her eyes. "All I can advise is rest, young lady, but I can't advise that too strongly. It *is* a matter of life and death, and this isn't the first time I've told you. It's all up to you, and I truly wish it weren't." Orange flakes in his earnest blue eyes, he was accustomed to be obeyed in all but the most important things.

Dove liked her doctor, wanted him to think well of her. "My goodness, I'm doing as little as humanly possible now. I'm inert. My family is too protective of me. Boredom can also be fatal, you know."

"No," said the doctor, "it isn't. But I can tell you for an absolute certainty that these attacks, or even the inhalant I've got you on could be. Fatal. If it happens too often, if you use it too much. All of this is very hard on your heart."

"I suppose. But what isn't hard on a woman's heart?"

"You're still young," said Dr. Gorman, "and could still enjoy. . . You're still young, or could be if you took care of yourself."

"Young?" she said. "Doctor, I think you've earned your fee."

Her children were in the waiting room, luminously healthy. Dove floated to them on the strange liberation that seemed to come of Doctor Gorman's pessimism about her. "In the pink," she said. "I'm to get back in harness, I think. No excuse for being lazy anymore."

"Harness?" Verity didn't like the sound of it.

"And what about a nice luncheon," Dove said, "In fact, I think I'll insist on it. Did you find something you like at the music store, Verity?"

"They had *Scalar Exercises for Two Hands.*"

"You already have that," Dove said.

"This," Verity said, "is volume two. With modes."

"Dear God."

"They told me," Verity said, "they couldn't fix my metronome, but they'd sell me a new one. So, I said, 'maybe.' If I sold some eggs or something."

"Enough of your broad hints, Daughter. I swear, we're not in town two hours before everyone wants something. To buy."

"Lunch," George said.

"Yes," Dove said. "But first things first."

George was then a week away from graduating high school, and Dove hoped to find a suit with sleeves long enough to cover his wrists, something he could wear to commencement that wouldn't make him look like a tent pole. If she must give her children over to the world, she wanted them to look like something. Dove hated rites of passage and they seemed to be happening very often now. She'd been overstimulated. A buttery spring sun dappled the streets through trees newly in leaf, and their sedan purred along enjoying the luxury of pavement; Dove felt for once rather powerful herself.

"She's not coming in there with us," George said. "This is bad enough without her making fun of everything."

"Yes, dear," said Dove. "But imagine how we'd regret it if we bought something she didn't like. How we'd have to hear about it." To Verity she said, "You will have to keep your remarks to yourself. Please."

"And your funny looks and everything," George said, "you can hang onto those, too. Whatever you've got con-cocted, don't do it. So, let me get this straight—I have to get my sister's approval before I can buy a suit?"

"Yes," they said in unison.

"There," Verity said. "That's it there. It's the men's wear place, George. *Haber*dashers. Park!"

"Maybe after we're done here," Dove told her girl, "maybe we can find you something you'd like. To wear. New. The girls are wearing their hair longer again, thank goodness, and you're getting to an age where you may wish to pay more attention to your appearance, and maybe. . .

All right, I'll say no more on the subject. But I honestly don't know what you're trying to prove."

Should any little sound bounce forth there were rows and rows of thick garments to absorb it, a hush in the shop. There was a bouquet of pipe tobacco and cedar in the air, and in this atmosphere even Verity was subdued. Dove sensed things here had been settled a long time ago in favor of a different class of people. Considering the position of a woman's chin to be critical in such situations, she drew herself up to address a salesman who glided to them through the clothes racks and who was quick to assure her that George's problems were not problems at all, that he'd hang clothes on tall, thin people all day long if he could. He glanced at Verity who seemed heartened, and who said. "Fred Astaire. We've seen him."

The salesman was everywhere with his sausage fingers and his tape, mapping George like a new continent, and George, a shade darker for these attentions, stood with his legs spread, his arms wide, crucified without a cross. Dove seldom had a chance to examine her boy like this when he was not in motion, occupied or preoccupied. Six feet three in his stocking feet, he was taller by half a head than anyone in her family and taller than any Harrow that Charlie could recall. George had never yet weighed more than a hundred and fifty pounds, but these were arranged on his frame like a system of oiled cables operated by reflexes he constantly challenged. Dove knew that she had been told very little of the risks he liked to take, and she liked to maintain a certain ignorance of them. He'd trained an auburn wave to crest on his head, his eyes were colored in accordance with the situation; he was glorious when the rest of their little family were just short of homely, and if her son could be very silly, especially in his sister's company, grown men were already coming around to consult with him on crop rotation and to have him weld for them. Her boy, so handsome and so full of useful knowledge, and more than that, so full of sweetness. He is not ready, Dove thought.

"These shoulders," remarked the salesman. "I wish they'd send us some mannequins with shoulders like this. Things drape so good on a frame like this." The salesman glanced at Verity again, saying this, his eyes full of puzzlement. Dove thought he was trying to flatter them, and he seemed unwholesome, but she told herself she was becoming an old woman who'd lived apart too long, that she couldn't read the subtle cues folks in town knew so well. She didn't wish to be a suspicious yokel.

A man in a dun uniform came into the shop, tucked his cap under his arm, and made straight for them, and when the salesman looked up at him, he said, "Do you think you might be able to do some alterations for me? Today. I'm leaving tomorrow. Going back. It's not much. I just want it taken in at the waist. The jacket. You can't change it very much. Regulations." The intruder had trouble acknowledging anyone's presence but his own; when he did, he inspected them with flat disapproval.

The tailor straightened, clamped something in his lips, removed it again, and said, "Sure. Slip it off. I can see from here what needs done." And to George, "You can lower your arms, son. Bear with me a minute while I help this gentleman." He left them with the soldier.

In any gathering of two or more men at that time there would be talk of the war. Even some women seemed infatuated with the subject. Dove understood she'd been foolish to think they might get through a day in town without once encountering the popular conflagration. She only hoped she wouldn't hear anyone speak of it, as people often did, as a sort of sporting event, speak of it so that she wanted to put her hands over her ears and scream.

It was Verity, of course, who broke the thick silence that settled between the Harrows and the soldier. "You've a got a lot of medals," she told him.

"These aren't medals. Just badges. I haven't earned any medals yet." His chest seemed to swell in anticipation of decorations to come. He asked George, "Your eyes any good?"

"He can see three miles," Verity said. "See little things three miles off. Can you?"

"You a college man, then?"

"A farmer," George said.

"Farmer? Lucky guy. You'll miss the show, probably. Must be nice to be necessary to the war effort." The soldier, his hat clamped under his arm, could not seem to decide if he should feel sorry for himself.

"People must eat," Dove said. "There are plenty of soldiers in the world, young man. Too many, if you ask me."

"I'm not a soldier. I'm an airman. It's off we go into the wild blue yonder for me. Ever hear of an airman with a blister? I'll let Boeing or someone do the heavy lifting, thank you very much."

"You fly?" George asked him.

"Like a bird," said the airman.

After returning the airman's jacket, free of charge, the salesman sold George a silk suit over Dove's several reservations. "Warm in the winter," claimed the salesman, "cool in the summer, and it wears like iron. That is what you wanted? Something for year around? Isn't that what you said?"

"It's terribly shiny," Dove observed. "Isn't it?"

"That's the style now," said the salesman.

Though Dove could not refute this of her own knowledge, neither could she believe him. "Verity?" she said, "We haven't had your opinion yet."

"Why not?" said little sister. "We just have to hope no one mistakes him for the Tin Man."

"Well," George said, "I *do* like it."

"We wouldn't have to make a single change to it," said the salesman. "He could wear it right out the door. Might be the only suit in the store you wouldn't have to come back for. No alterations at all. Hem up those trousers, and away you go."

"Yeah," George said. "Why don't I just wear it? Hear that? Hear that sound it makes when I move? How are you supposed to top that?"

"You can see it's cut along the bias," said the salesman, closing. "A very nice feature."

She would deny them nothing today; Dove wished for once to be lavish and, heedless of any expense or trouble, to show her children a memorable day. At a downtown diner George had pot roast, Verity a finger steak, and Dove experimentally ordered a watercress sandwich from which she took one dainty bite.

"You're tired, Mother." George had already mentioned going home.

"I am not tired, and I don't intend to be."

There were milk shakes all around, and the Harrows discovered cheesecake that afternoon, and Dove realized too late what a job of work it would be to carry this meal around in her stomach; she came very near to dozing in the booth.

Gently, George prompted, "If you're still set on taking us to that movie."

"I am," she said. "I promised. How often will you graduate first in your class?"

"We'll have some time to kill before the show," George advised. He had recently acquired a wrist watch.

"Well," Dove said, "why don't we buy that metronome,

then? Take us back to the music store, why don't you?"

Dove was ordinarily of very little use to her daughter; the child would take no direction, and why would she want guidance from a woman she'd known only as a mope and a scold? An old cripple. As a girl, Dove had herself been pressed into the running of her family's household, and she knew what that drudgery was, and she suspected it must be even worse for Verity who was a very bright candle, probably too bright for her own good. Dove was never sure if she feared for her daughter or feared for herself. When Verity suddenly decided on that piano one day there had been a chance for a connection between them, something they might have shared in the way that Charlie and George shared farming. Dove showed her the books that had come in the piano bench, and a bit about how to decipher them. She touched and named twelve notes and showed her girl how the pattern repeated, and Dove should have known even then, when her normally inattentive girl instantly made all this information her own, that this was to be more than an hour's enthusiasm. It began at once, the painful learning, and because she relied on Verity for nearly everything, Dove had no choice but to be patient with her. One day as dutiful Mother she'd even sat down to play for her girl the very first piece she'd learned by heart, a minuet, and Dove wasn't twelve bars into the thing before she felt it poking holes in her soul. This would be her very last venture to the piano, and after that Verity was entirely on her own, a Harrow about it, relentless, and soon she'd taught herself more of music than Dove had ever known anyway.

On leaving the music store for the second time that day, Verity happened to notice a card pinned to a corkboard, advertising piano lessons by Egmont Milhouse. Reasonable rates. There was a Great Falls address. "We should look this guy up," Verity said. "We still have plenty of time to kill."

"Daughter—now why? You've got your metronome, dear. You can't expect to be coming into town all the time for lessons. Even if he accepted, you. You've so many bad habits, and he may not even. . ."

"Mother. Gee. What could it hurt to just talk to him? Maybe he could show me a few things, save me a lot of time. Answer some questions. Tell me what else I should be doing. You want me better, don't you? Whatever I can do to get better. You're the one who has to listen to me all the time."

"We're trying to enjoy ourselves, Daughter."

"I bet George could find it with his eyes closed."

"You won't let this go now?" Dove said. "Will you?"

On the civic grid of Great Falls, it wasn't too difficult for George to navigate them to 118 3rd Street South, but as they neared those coordinates he suddenly realized, "Oh. Know where we are? This is the colored section."

"Colored?" Verity disliked the distinction, or didn't understand it. "How do you know?"

"Everyone does," George said. "It's where they live, their part of town. I think that was their church we passed. It's no secret."

"I didn't know," said Dove. "Not that I had ever inquired. How disgraceful, though. But maybe they prefer it. To live together. They have their own church, so." She appraised the neighborhood. "Neat as a pin, isn't it?"

"Of course, they'd prefer it," George said. "Wouldn't you? You'd want to have *some*thing that was your own. Which is why it might not be the best idea for us to be nosing around."

"The guy left his card," Verity reasoned. "That means he wants us to look him up." They had passed through a neighborhood of trim cottages and into a section of buildings dedicated to more obscure, more purely urban purposes. "That's it right over there. That has to be it." A large cube of bricks, once a warehouse, now advertised itself as the Alabama Chicken Shack on the first floor and, in neon tubing, the Ozark Club above.

"Well, we're not. No," said George. "That's a night club, and it's not night. I'm very sure they don't give piano lessons in restaurants."

"You don't know everything," Verity said. "I'm going over there and see, long as we're here. This is the address he gave. Well, *stop*."

"It's the easiest thing," Dove said, "to just let her satisfy her curiosity. I almost wish we hadn't eaten lunch already. Do you smell that chicken?"

Verity put her question about the piano instructor to the man running the chicken shack, a cotton haired old man as tall as George and twice as heavy, who pointed to a location straight above him and said, "Try Leo." He didn't seem to like them very well.

On the street again, the Harrows confronted another door, this protected by an awning. Verity pushed at it, and George said, "No. That's the Ozark Club."

Verity pushed through. "Yeah, I can read, too. It's where he said to go."

"No. That's no place for you. Or you, Mother. Or me, far as that goes."

"Sort of on your high horse, aren't you, dear? I believe where we should and shouldn't be going is still for me to determine."

"No," said George. "What I mean is. They entertain here. All *kinds* of entertainment."

"That doesn't sound so very awful," Dove said.

"Mother. Mother. What I'm. . ."

"Okay," said Verity. "The guy said to go up there." She pushed through a second door that opened onto a long, steep stairwell.

"Mother," George cautioned, "look at those stairs."

"I'm sure I can manage," she said. "Better that than stand squabbling in the street. Verity, you take the lead and let me latch on to your belt. George, you follow behind us, and up we go."

George, who had heard stories, was not about to let his curiosity show in this company. "Remember," he said, "it was me who said it was a bad idea. I bet they're not even open. I hope not."

"When did you become such an expert on the Ozark Club?" Dove asked.

"You hear talk," George confessed. "Now I guess we'll have our own stories to tell, won't we?"

They rattled up the tight stair well, and Verity banged through the door at the top of it. They were familiar, a little, with dance halls, but not with saloons. A history of the room was published to their virginal noses before their eyes had adjusted to the dark. There was burnt tobacco, and grain alcohol, and a memory of sweat, and a stronger one of the disinfectant the swamper had used that morning in his mop water. Eau-de-this and that. Verity, still in the lead, led them to a semi-circular bar and the men standing on either side of it; the nearer of the two wore an elegant ensemble including a long watch chain and a fawn fedora, and for all the Harrows knew, they were hardly ethnologists, he might have been a sleek Eskimo. His voice, even as he challenged them, lilted in tones they were not accustomed to hear. "Lost your way?"

"No," said Verity, "we meant to be here. You wouldn't be Leo, would you, sir?"

His cigarette depended from a fist he'd enlarged some

while campaigning as Kid Leo; smoke curling up through slant light. He was amused. "Who's asking?"

"Sorry. Bad manners. Again. I'm Verity Harrow, this is my brother George, and this is our mother, I guess she'd be Mrs. Harrow. We're trying to find a guy, or I am. We're not from here."

"You don't say," Leo said. "What do you want with him, this guy you're looking for?"

"Piano lessons."

"I told her, sir," George said. "I told her this was a night club. And. You know."

"So, are you?" Verity asked. "Leo?"

"Verity," Dove corrected, suddenly aware of how long she'd been standing by mute.

"Egmont Millhouse," said Verity. "That's who I'm really looking for."

The man behind the bar was in shirt sleeves and had been funneling one bottle of liquor into another and suffering a tongue lashing from the boss as the Harrows came into the barroom; he'd been relieved at the interruption. He gleamed black even in the dimness and possessed, even when being harassed, much physical grace. "Egmont?" he said.

"You remember him," Leo said. "That rusty cat used to come around, try and sit in with the band sometimes. One night he was creole, another night he'd say he was something else. The boys'd run him off pretty fast. One thing he never was, was any good." And to Verity. "You didn't miss a thing with Egmont. Guy was worthless."

"You don't know how I'd find him?"

"Don't know *why* you would," Leo said. "Last I heard he got booked on some charges, extradited somewhere. So, he'd be long gone. Nobody's missing him, either."

"Thank you, sir," said Dove. "You've been very helpful.

Now: May we *go*?"

"I wonder," said Verity, "Could I try your piano for a little bit?"

"*Verity,*" said Dove.

"I know how to play," she said. "And you never said, are you Leo?"

"*Verity!*" said Dove.

"I must be," said Leo. "If you say so, Pistol." He nodded toward the bandstand, the house piano. "Have at it. You couldn't do any worse by it than Egmont Milhouse did."

"No," said George again. "I mean, sorry, sir, but once you let her get started, you just don't know."

"You play any ball?" Leo asked.

"A pitcher," George said. "I throw junk, but it usually gets 'em out."

Leo seemed to approve of this, but he had to add, "About those vines, man, they tell you that was sharkskin? If you wore that suit in here during regular business hours, you could get cut. They'd take you for a pimp, cut you up. That suit's a hazard."

Dove thought that she and this Leo might see eye to eye on a lot of things.

Verity stepped over a short picket fence to mount the Ozark Club's band stand and address its piano. Untended cigarettes had left brown images resembling a host of caterpillars on the woodwork. The keys were as variously colored as the teeth of a poorly kept mouth. She made one pass up and down them and stopped and touched the A immediately before her and the A two octaves hence and she announced, "Those are not in tune with each other." She touched them again. "Hear?"

"Verity *Harrow*. I'm sorry, sir," Dove said. "I'd like to shirk responsibility and say she was raised by wolves, but. . . we just don't get out very much."

"Not up to your standards, Pistol?"

"Not quite," said Verity. "Mine plays true. Every note. My piano at home."

Verity by then could play beautifully and even tranquilly, and sometimes when the house was asleep, she could be found doing just that, her head bent low to the keyboard, so Dove knew her daughter might, if she chose, soothe the savage breast, but that was a choice she rarely made by daylight. The girl was prone to execute scales, arpeggios, and etudes as a sort of digital close order drill, and the accelerating precision of these performances could be brutal for the idle listener.

"See?" George said when she had treated them to some of this.

"Dear," said Dove, "this is not how to repay a courtesy."

Leo, whom Verity would one day know as Leo Lamar, lit another cigarette, drew from it, and said, "You need to find you some nice old lady to give you lessons. They'd go wild for that, but here. . ."

"Wait. How about this?" Verity's left hand began to roll independently in the bass cleft, her right stabbed at syncopations, a loping vamp, and then she used it to approximate a horn section coming in.

"One O'clock Jump," said the bartender. "Absolutely."

"Just when I think I've seen everything," said Leo Lamar. "My, my. Your girl can swing, Mrs. Harrow. How'd that happen?"

Feeling antique, Dove made an antique gesture, pressing her hand to the flat of her chest. She shrugged.

"Kansas City," Verity said, still playing. "We get a program. Right weather I. Dial it in. Kansas. City. But. You'd know. Count Basie? He's? Isn't he really a negro?"

"All *right*," said Dove, "we've taken up enough of these gentlemen's time," and she chivied her children out of the Ozark Club.

Their open natures were fine for most uses around the farm, and in fact Dove gloried in her children's innocence, but she knew it was none of her doing and only a function of distances; they'd lived a long way from temptation and from what Dove by then considered the spectacle of mankind defiling itself. Year by year, however, it was a shorter and easier trip to town, a trip made more often and for less reason. The world must come pouring in all ripe and provocative. She would see them harden, no doubt, see the soft petals of their blooming curl inward protectively, but they would always remain children of a sort. Her children.

"Mother?" George had caught her in the rearview mirror. "What now? We can't go to the show if you. What's wrong?"

"Joy," she said. "It's only joy."

"Joy?" Verity wasn't having it. "Well, that's no way to do that. That does *not* look like. . . Oh, *please*, Mother. And especially not at the showhouse. Try not to do that if you can help it."

"You're not tired?" George asked her again.

"Not at all," Dove lied.

GEORGE

He avoided popcorn for fear of greasing the suit he now detested, that fabric whispering stupidly against itself as he edged his way to his seat. George promised himself that in the future, in the very near future, he was going to quit plunging into things this way. As manly as decisiveness might be, perhaps he wasn't just the man for making snap decisions, and maybe even a bit of a boob in his gaudy suit and his beat shoes; George was suddenly anxious for the houselights to come down. Mother tried to take them to a show every year because it was as close as they'd come to experiencing theater, but George felt perfectly fresh off the farm, as if the movies were entirely new to him. Having turned eighteen in the winter of Pearl Harbor, he was raw and ardent and terribly susceptible to the spell of the pictures.

A sprocket rattled somewhere above them. A fanfare swelled into a march. The March of Time. Their faces turned as one, as moon worshipers toward the newsreel. There were bad incidents in Burma. Nazi armor was shown slashing through Christmasy fields, bewildered peasants standing by. Fat black arrows sprouted on a map of Eurasia showing the Axis progress there, but now it seemed, 'They've picked a fight with the wrong party. They'll wish they'd never messed with Uncle Sam.' A girl with her hair done up in a bandana claimed she'd found a message in a bottle down along the Gulf Coast. 'RSVP? Well, who knows, folks. Maybe. With a little luck.' For the camera she flung it back into the ocean. Dogs were caused to prance at a dog show. A terrier posed solemnly near a wreath with its happy owner. 'Best in class, best in show. This pooch is tops, ladies and gentlemen, but what a dog-eat-dog competition.' The March of Time loosed its final fanfare as the credits rolled over the last half century compressed into a rush of grainy but luminous scenes. In the next short Abbot and Costello sold war bonds. The cartoon feature then retold the story of the three pigs so that this time all three pigs prevailed, smug little buggers, and even the straw house, cleverly reinforced, resisted the wolf's worst huffing and puffing. How funny, the frustrated wolf. George had little filter against any fancy fiction, even a cartoon, and music, even music that he disliked, moved him, and he was not accustomed to sugary drinks. It would be very hard to keep from squirming in his seat during the hours of *Pride and Prejudice* he was about to endure to appease his mother.

It was a bad time to come of age. Some of his friends were already gone and the rest were hot, or claimed to be, to go off to this latest crusade; the war loomed necessary, inescapable. George couldn't decently wait beyond next harvest season to throw in, and he knew he'd do his bit, but not without reservations. Through the years the Harrows had employed several men who were the refuse of the previous war and who would live and die in bunkhouses or boxcars. The former doughboy Red Stipe explained how they'd got that way one afternoon while they were waiting out a snow storm in the Harrow bunkhouse. "Once you've seen a man blown apart," he'd told young George, "you're never the same. When you've seen 'em splattered by the dozen, then, brother that's another story. Evacuate your bowels, and your patriotism and esprit de corps and every other goddamned thing flows right out of you, turns out it was all shit anyway. My country 'tis of another boss who stiffed me on my pay, and I don't believe in nothin.'"

This time it seemed there'd be no trenches, still George did not want to be blown up or shocked into a lifetime of nervous tics and nihilism and, as he was prematurely set in his ways, he thought he might have a problem with army discipline. Called, he would come, but against his better judgment; George resented the war as a practical matter. On that score it was hard not to be a little bitter, that young men were still being sent off to learn the same old lesson the hard way. Still, George was hungry to see some new country, some new anything, and this bright curiosity shaded into an unmentionable fascination that might not mind a little peep into the abyss as well. The young yearn, everything depends on it, yearn without knowing quite what is wanted, and George at eighteen swirled round himself-what else is new-and he sat between his mother and sister, determined to take in and savor everything. It was his job.

Attention Young Men

Another march blared, and there was the now familiar insignia again, a star on outspread wings occupying much of the movie screen, and then a long shot of sky empty but for wisps of cloud, then someone sounding like someone's friendly uncle, claimed, "This is a classroom." Into the picture nosed a flight of stripe-tailed army trainer planes. The announcer said that young men between the ages of seventeen and twenty-six, healthy and patriotic, might apply to become air cadets. George had always assumed they'd want a lot more in the way of credentials before they'd let you anywhere near their airplanes. Qualified, he felt a warmth spreading through him. A squadron of low-winged monoplanes had been filmed from above and behind as they flew just over an expanse of tall sand dunes, a squadron with its shadows flying just ahead of it, shadows leaping from dune to dune—maximum dipsy doo. "So, remember that number, fellows," said the announcer. "Here's your chance to find out what it takes and learn from the best." Now the squadron was high in the pewter sky again, and one by one its airplanes chandelled up and out of the picture, up and away from the enthralled viewer. George had the number by heart, so much so that he would never in his life forget it: 607 Custom House, Philadelphia, PA.

◊ ◊ ◊

A shaft of light fell into that country church and across Lt. Harrow, burnishing the bars on his shoulders. His eyes were brown for the occasion, a hastily arranged marriage to Mary Lou McQuiston who stood with him at the altar, the same sunbeam glorious in the coils of her hair. She'd been weeping since her sister Betty had handed her a bouquet of dandelions to carry down the aisle, but even blotched and pink, especially blotched and pink, she was a girl you'd want to swallow whole, a pulsing confection. She wore a dress with a busy pattern of tea roses tied in blue ribbon, the best the McQuistons could do for a wedding gown on such short notice and a dress that could not be improved upon for George's purposes, unless by removing it.

Not everyone, of course, approved the union. Of all the moves he'd made to upset his family lately, marrying Mary Lou was as they saw it, as Verity described it, "*The* most boneheaded thing you could possibly do. I know that girl. We were in the same class room for years. She is *dumb*, George."

"Come on, V. You think everyone's stupid."

"She's in a category all her own," said Verity. "Have you talked to her? Can she talk? Would you want her to? What does she know about anything outside this county, or anybody outside those people in their nutty little church? What does she know?"

"Well, what does she need to know?"

"Not that much," said Verity. "Looks like. She'll bore you to death, and sooner than you think. It is not too late to wrangle out of this."

"She's probably developed a lot," said George, "since you left school."

"Duh-veloped." Verity would not be won over.

Mother had taken him aside more than once in the dozen days since he'd announced the nuptials, and even in the face of what was for her an emergency she disliked speaking ill of anyone, but, "I've known the McQuistons since I came to the bench. Lloyd and Thelma. They ran their first batch of children through my school, poor things, and they're. Or at least Lloyd has always been. They're *grim* people, dear. Now, your Mary Lou may be a perfectly lovely girl, *but*."

"She could be," George had admitted. "I wouldn't be at all surprised."

His father, once he'd been made to understand what was going on, had given George the same look he'd given the hot little Ford George had bought to use during his leave, and George was grateful that the old man so rarely resorted to speech anymore, that would have blistered. The army also did all it could to discourage marriage among men awaiting orders to combat, the formula being that if the army wanted them to have wives, wives would have been issued. Fine. Right or wrong, hell or high water, he was marrying Mary Lou, and there sat his family all in a row, grieving.

Verity, together with George on the island of the farm had invented an existence there as an inside joke, a conspiracy of whimsy, and she supposed all too accurately that no one would ever amuse or be amused by her as her brother had. She was also prescient in thinking he'd soon have reason to regret Mary Lou, but what good was that?

What good was knowing? Mary Lou with all the gall in the world had asked her to be a bridesmaid, and when Verity refused, citing her limited wardrobe, Mary Lou asked her to play the wedding march, but when Verity tried the piano here she'd found about every third hammer defelted, dead, so she was left with nothing to do but watch the wedding with her fists clenched.

Dove, meanwhile, considered this the ruin of her life's signal accomplishment, the wasting of the apple of her eye, and it was perhaps the hardest thing yet to have a son so terribly careless of his gifts. First, he'd signed up to be slaughtered—now this packet and her obvious little charms. Dove's efforts to steer her boy away from these disasters had only succeeded in convincing him that she wasn't proud of him. She was too proud, if anything, but she had been a grown woman when the Wright brothers were at Kitty Hawk, and aviation had not progressed in her mind beyond suicidal novelty. When one heard of airplanes in Montana, it was usually something about falling out of the sky. Nothing would do, though, but that George must become a pilot, and one day he was simply gone. Letters came at intervals to keep them informed of his triumphs. He'd got through basic, whatever that was. He'd been accepted for pilot training. He was a pilot. He was promoted, an officer. He'd done very well in the army, and Dove's dread had finally subsided to manageable weight, and she'd allowed herself the luxury of believing George was somehow charmed when the telegraph came: BAD LANDING. LONG LEAVE. KILL FATTED CALF.

He came home handsome in uniform, militarily erect in the corset he wore for his sprained back, and Dove resisted every urge to press her argument, even with such good evidence so fresh, and she made not a single mention of the fate of things that go up or how littered myth and history were with mangled dreamers who'd convinced themselves they had a special exemption from gravity. No. Too late for that now. Her boy would be returning to the army soon enough, flying again the moment they let him. "It's fine," he told her. "We're human beings. We can do any dang thing we put our minds to, Mother, including fly. Nothing like it. You get that third dimension going, your up-and-down, throw that in, and you're *flow*ing, if you know what I mean."

She only knew that her son would be making no use whatever of her hard-won wisdom, that she was no match for his compulsions.

Charlie was stone deaf by then and often preferred it that way. Neighbor McQuiston had always been a blowhard. The Reverend McQuiston, mail-order sonofabitch that he was, had taken it on himself to marry his daughter off to George here in the church he shared with several other scratch gravel congregations. Many a sad and sadly specific prayer had gone up toward heaven from this location. Not one of the Harrows had previously set foot here. McQuiston, a halo of his spittle all around him and the ancient grievances to goad him, had hijacked the ceremony to deliver fire and brimstone, and old Lloyd was just the ass to hold a captive audience like this right to the end of human endurance as they shifted cheek to cheek on those good pine benches that were supposed to be all the true believer could ever want by way of comfort. He went on and on, Lloyd; the man had always been a piss poor farmer and looked to be no better at this trade. His flock were mostly his children, children he'd actually sired, and you'd know them anywhere as his because he'd bequeathed them that odd complexion, faces like the underside of an orange rind. Their noses ran perpetually and when gathered up like this they produced snot by the pint. Of the whole rabbity bunch, George had got the pick of the litter at least. She was the youngest of them, Charlie thought, a berry of a girl, ripe to bursting, and she'd be good for about as long as a berry, too. She seemed to know she'd hit the jackpot even as old McQuiston continued his hollering at them. Charlie, more immune than most to a sermon, but just as miserable, passed the time looking around. The building was visibly out of plumb; just sitting there he could see it listing maybe ten degrees to windward, rising cockeyed out of the floor, and he enjoyed thinking of its eventual collapse.

Mary Lou, grimacing through those tears of joy, thought, 'Preach, Daddy. I can stand it easy.' She happened even to hear some of it, a thing she liked about some old geezer telling Pharoah, 'Let my people go.' 'Preach, Daddy.' He was punching her ticket out of Egypt right now. 'Wear yourself out.' She'd be done with Daddy's claptrap soon enough, and getting George Harrow in the bargain, and it had all happened so quickly, so unexpectedly and so much better than anything she'd expected. Hurry, Daddy. The last thing she wanted as Mrs. Harrow was to have to worry if every other thought that passed through her head was a sin.

Lloyd McQuiston needed forty minutes to pronounce them man and wife, having never mentioned love, not even in the vows. Honor and obey. This was their fifth date, and this marriage was for George only one in a whipsaw series of big surprises.

◊ ◊ ◊

Shortly after he'd finished the advanced stage of his pilot training, George, who had lately moved up in the world, was lounging around one morning in Bachelor Officers Quarters when Captain Couture came in looking for someone to ride shotgun with him while he wrung out some newly delivered twin engine trainers. George volunteered. Couture had been his instructor through much of this stage of his training, and Captain Couture, an almost serene survivor of his own combat tour, was golden; George was interested in everything the man did in the cockpit of an airplane. They took up three successive Cessnas, flew them into empty patches of Sonoran sky well away from the airfield and auxiliary airfields, and threw them around, allegedly to be sure there were no bugs in them before they fell into the hands of new students. Stick and rudder men. Boys in a boy's wonderland of Uncle Sam's airplanes, burning Uncle Sam's fuel, and full of roll rate and rate of climb, and, 'watch this,' and working up an appetite with a full day of aerobatics.

Last flight of the day, coming in on final approach, gear down, flaps down, wheels just feet off the runway, Captain Couture's head suddenly twisted left as if he'd been punched from the other direction. "See that? Off to my nine?"

"What?"

"That light. That flash."

"Where?"

Couture flinched again, rared back on the yoke and tromped the left rudder pedal. He caught just one throttle. The Cessna flared, rose nose high, lost all its airspeed, twisted, fell off to its side, and ground looped nose down onto the runway, the whole thing occurring in a kind of slow motion that let George know in advance that they were going to hit but left him no time or room to take the controls and recover. They hit. Firetrucks were coming across the tarmac next he knew, and George hung obliquely from his seat belt; his torso from pelvis to ribs was a single sensitive knot. It was all that was wrong with him, as far as he could tell. Captain Couture was collapsed just beside him, lying on the cabin's bulkhead, "Ah, fff. Aah. Aah. Thigh. Fffff. Fuh. . . it's my thigh."

"I'll need help to get you out of here," George said. "You think it's broke?"

"Yeagh. Oh, yeah. It's ahhh. You see that. The light?"

"Light?"

"Came right at us," Couture insisted. "It. Twice?"

"Must have missed it, sir."

"No. It. No, you would've. Just before. Aaah. You would've. No? All right. I. All right."

"I can try and get you out of here," George offered. "If you want. Be kind of clumsy, but. We should get you unbuckled anyway."

"No, they're here. They'll get us. No fire."

Doped fabric over wooden spars—the thought of a fire in this airplane was an unhappy one.

"Listen," said Couture, as if George had any choice. "That was, uuhgh, a joke. Right? About the light. When, mmmn. . . they debrief. It was mechanical, all right? Gear snafu, right? No light. Forget that."

The following morning Lt. Harrow remained at attention even when Col. Mangan told him to be at ease, it was the only posture that didn't cause sparks in his enraged lumbar. Col. Mangan inquired after his condition, and George said, "I'm fine, sir."

"The flight surgeon disagrees," said the Colonel. "You've seen Couture?"

"Yes, sir. He's still doped up. I guess they worked on that leg quite a while."

There was on the Colonel's desk a small, gilded globe and a picture of his lumpy wife. In the heat his face resembled a McIntosh apple. "That's the only reason he's not here. That was a brand new airplane, Harrow. Who was flying?"

"Sir?"

"You got this far in the program," Colonel Mangan noted, "so I know you're not stupid. You won't like how this goes if you try and play stupid with me, Lieutenant. Who was flying?"

"The Captain was flying, sir. On approach."

"Then what happened?"

"We were just about to touch down," George said. "Nose came up all of a sudden. We fell off, caught a wing, and I guess we nosed over."

"The nose *came* up?" Colonel Mangan asked.

"Yes, sir. Very abrupt."

"It just *came* up."

"Up," George explained, "then off to the side."

"And how did that happen?"

"Fast, sir. They should take a look at that elevator."

"Couture was one of your instructors, wasn't he?" Colonel Mangan was old army, a career cavalry officer on loan to the Air Corps who considered foolishness the defining feature of the aviators in his charge. "You ever hear things about him?"

"Things?" said George. "No, sir."

"What was your personal impression of him?" the Colonel asked.

"Best pilot I've. . . Nobody's easier on the equipment."

"We think a lot of him around here," said the Colonel. "You don't know what he's been through."

"No, sir."

"He's a hero, you know," Mangan said. "Couture. So, Harrow you'll be getting a convalescent leave out of this. They sent along a six-week light duty chit from the infirmary, so you're no good to anybody around here. No sense in the army feeding you while you're useless."

"I could fly right now. I'd just as soon. . ."

"Could you pull somebody out of an airplane, Lieutenant? Could you run across the tarmac if you had to? Tell me you don't like home cooking. Just write out your report, and be sure and mention that thing about the elevator. Write up a report the same as you told me, no more, no less. And we'll get you on a train."

George had by then been assigned to train with a B-17 squadron, and that meant he'd be going to the air war over Europe, then the deadliest theater of operations, a meat-grinder from which it was about an even shot he wouldn't be returning. It was a circumstance that rendered his family so impossibly dear to him that he didn't know how he'd face them while he was sorting through his dread, and with most of his fellow trainees he shared a preference to get a crew formed up, and get over there, and get the thing decided one way or the other. No use in going home where in idleness your terror might catch up with you; why risk making some display of it there? But an order is an order, and home George had gone where he was alter-nately mistaken for the boy he'd been last year or a hero, as if he weren't confused enough. He would spend much of his time alone in the car he'd bought coming in on the train, a traveling salesman's panting steed. "Boy howdy," the parts man had said, "that V-8, you'll know just what to do with her, young fellah." George had changed the coupe's spark plugs and cruised, his orbit never arcing far from home, but far enough—down to the Missouri Breaks, up around the base of the butte; he cruised the Harrows' and their neighbors' ground, a farmer again, nicely intent on dirt. Big Sandy, Coffee Creek. He startled antelope out of coulees, stars out of the night sky, and he cruised, and he couldn't quit it though he knew his absence from the house hurt and puzzled his family. How to explain it? He could not stand their imploring eyes. Everything will be fine? Won't it? George had come to an unsettling understanding in the moment just before they dented that airfield down in Douglas, a realization late in coming because he was the kind of brassy lad who must be convinced of a truth long obvious to everyone else: Certain things, forces, lay outside his control and beyond his capacity even to anticipate. Captain Couture's light, the look of him before and after their wreck. George inventoried in the aftermath and saw that he was often at the mercy of fate, and this was not the state of mind he wanted to take to war. When his sole duty lay in resting and restoring his back, he could only drive. His back, at least, soon felt fine, and he drove reciting check lists, winning old arguments, singing tunelessly, attempting to locate some new and serviceable bravery.

One day he came upon a pedestrian, a rarity in that country. He saw her as he topped a small rise, walking directly away from him, about a quarter mile off, and even at this distance and vantage he knew her at once for Mary Lou McQuiston—her hair, that happy hue, the never tarnished penny. Her walk also distinguished her as he came closer, and if he hadn't given this girl an instant's thought in a very long time, George was surprised at how specific and numerous were his memories now. That prissy walk, her arms nearly straight at her sides, her feet with a seeming distaste for the ground. She was a bobbysoxer, and her hips wore blue jeans artfully. She didn't turn to him until the car was very nearly upon her and even then without much interest. George rolled up beside her and rolled a window down. "Hey, Mary Lou. You headed somewhere?"

"No," she said suspiciously. "Oh, *George*. Sorry, I didn't. I thought you were off in the war."

"Not quite," he said. "Not yet. You're just out walking? You still live in that same place? You're miles from home, aren't you?"

"Yeah," she said neutrally. "I can never keep my shoes nice."

"Hop in."

"Really? Gah, this is darling. Our car hardly ever runs, and there's tons of us in it when it does. Oh, but where were you going?"

"Anywhere you want," he said.

"Yippee."

It would never occur to Mary Lou to momentarily consider his difficulties, not when hers so entirely consumed her. They had never been more than slight acquaintances, but it seemed she'd been saving up her shoes and all the other fragmentary details of her tragic existence to share with him in a steady torrent, and the beauty of her problems was that they were not his problems, and George relaxed right into them. Her eyes were too pale and too incurious, but, oh the spray of freckles across that bobbed nose, and, oh, that bowed mouth. Her hair, very fine, flew around her face like spun sunlight.

"I couldn't believe it," said Mary Lou, "when Verity dropped out. They had her play the piano at assembly, so. Then my daddy kept giving me such a hard time about staying in Geraldine, staying in the dorm. And algebra. Mr. and Mrs. Wexler. Joni Tingstad. I mean, why did I even need to be in school, what was I getting out of it? But, gee, Verity was *smart*. And she dropped out before I did. She used to be kind of mean sometimes. But they all were. I *wanted* to flunk, you know? But *home*? That's awful, too. Now I tell 'em I'm out praying, and maybe I am. I'm not doing anything else. But my poor shoes. I just wish I had more stuff to think about. Even school stuff or anything. I wouldn't mind knowing. Something. Hey, wanna go to Lewistown?"

"What's in Lewistown?" George thought of grain elevators.

"How would I know? You said anywhere, but if you don't feel like. . ."

"Lewistown it is." George executed a one-eighty that left them pointed in the desired direction, wreathed in their own dust. Mary Lou squealed appropriately.

They stopped along the way for Mary Lou to tell her mother they were going to dinner, the purpose she used to explain their journey. On their arrival the good reverend had slammed out the back door, but Mrs. McQuiston, a mound of a woman butchering a lean, wet chicken, was ecstatic for the plan. "But you oughtta get fresh first," she said. "Take some time and warsh up before you go."

Though Mary Lou was the last of the babies raised in this house, it still smelled somehow of the many children raised in it, the vestiges of diapers and cabbage soup. "No," she said. "Gotta scoot. Don't we, George?"

Their leaving was joyful as a jail break, and George discovered at once that Mary Lou was good for any amount of speed. He put his foot into his V-8 and flung the little car down the roads. He took her to Lewistown, some stockman's eatery, and fed her a pound of steak.

"Aren't you hungry?" she wondered.

"Not that hungry," he said.

"I never asked, how long 'til you have to go back?"

"Thirteen days," he said.

"Somewhere," she said. "You've been somewhere already. Else. But that's quite a bit of time. Left. We could have a lot of fun in that amount of time. I bet you know how."

"Sure," he said.

"If you want to," she said.

"Might as well."

"You don't know what it is to be poor," she said. "Not really."

He had noticed a zig zag pattern to her thoughts. Evasive action?

"We could really have a good time," she said. "If you want to."

"Why not?" What could be dangerous in this conversation—what did she want?—but the other fear, the usual fear he'd set aside. Here in company with a girl and her steak he could forget all that.

They drove into the foothills of the Big Snowies and followed a long gulch up to a secluded prominence from which they might watch a sunset settle into the sage rolling out below them, orange then magenta on that horizon. Conversation soon failed, but not until Mary Lou confided, "Tell you this: I am happy." Twilight on her peach cheeks; her lips tasted of beef and butter, and before she let him up for air again Mary Lou had made a whole world in the front seat of his car, upon which they were both much better traveled before they'd finished, spent, content, coated with each other.

George took her home by way of an isolated stock tank with its cold, artesian water slicked by algae. When they were clean again, Mary Lou regained her voice. She told him once more that she was happy. "Not usually, I mean. I mean right now I am. Some of the girls wanted to go in for welding. They said Seattle. I wouldn't care for that. But stenography. Now. In a big city. A *big* city, where nobody knows who you are or anything about your family. I'd like to go where it's just me. No family. None of mine, anyway. Cafes everywhere. Dress nice. I'd probably smoke. Then I could be happy all the time. Nice stockings."

"You're a city gal at heart?"

"I don't know. I must be something. It's . . . My house?

Glaah. My people? They're. If you knew. If *I* knew how a person, a broke person, went about leaving. You're lucky, you get to travel. My house? Gee."

She kissed him so lavishly when he left her off there that they almost failed to say good night at all. George went home to the bed that had seen his whole childhood, where he could not sleep and where it seemed there was only one available certainty—he would not die a virgin. He tossed and turned until the morning light, and the heart wants what the heart wants, as do other urgent organs, and by dawn he'd convinced himself the only honorable thing to do was marry her. He'd taken advantage of her and wished to do so again and again while there was still time. In this situation, how else might an officer and a gentleman proceed?

His bunk was the only reliable warmth he'd found this side of the Atlantic and George quit it reluctantly. He shrugged a sheepskin flight jacket over his pajamas and went out into the company street to splatter the quiet before dawn. The latrine at the back of the barracks would at this hour be a foul ammoniac cocktail of last night's nervous pissing. All for nothing. They'd know by now. If crews were going out today, they'd have been roused by now, so this was the easy hour of reprieve in the barracks when they might let themselves sleep deeply, but George remained too much the farm boy ever to return to his bed once he'd left it. He dressed and dry shaved in the dark, tied his shoes by feel, and went out of the barracks again through a goofy symphony of snoring. Sleep tight, babies.

Gauzy, beckoning squares of light, the mess hall's windows floated in the near distance, in the fog—fog on the continent, too?—and England's morning smelled sodden and green. The cooks had only begun making breakfast, a porridge in color and effect like Portland cement, but there was an urn of chicory-fouled coffee, and George drew off a mug of this and sat alone in the dining hall, a newly emancipated man listening to someone far back in the kitchen singing "Amapola."

Having lately memorized it, he did not reread the letter in his hip pocket. She had written:

> Dear George,
>
> Here is the news from the home front. Mother is rolling bandages with the Red Cross ladies and it is a nice social outlet for her. Father and I went to an auction yesterday to see about buying a grain auger. Mary Lou was there. I couldn't get a chance to talk to her. She is still pregnant.
>
> That is about all from here. We are all fine but miss you. Be safe as you can.
>
> Your sis

The letter in its upper righthand corner contained a date, its most neatly and legibly inscribed part, establishing that the 'yesterday' of the letter was more than eleven months—he'd counted it out on his fingers and once with the aid of a calendar—since George had last been with his bride. *She is still pregnant.* He was allowed to draw his own conclusions, and the only reasonable conclusion also explained why Mary Lou's correspondence had dried up a few months before, right in the midst of a pregnancy she'd seemed so proud of at first. She had suggested naming the baby for his grandfathers if he were a boy, or Lloydene might be pretty if she were a girl. Lloydene? *Still pregnant.* George wasn't even the first man in his squadron to be jilted by the girl he left behind, but he reckoned he must be about the happiest cuckold in the whole sad history of romance.

She had made him promise to write her every day to say at least that he loved her, and George, once he'd mentioned the white cliffs and Piccadilly was reduced to filling pages of airmail paper with columns of 'I love you,' which was at this point a rote and dutiful lie. He could not begin to love his wife at this distance, not the mere idea of her, and he had been glad for the press of duties that kept him from thoughts of his marriage, and he was just as happy that his doings were mostly things not to be discussed in any detail through the censored mails and that his thoughts were mostly too technical to mean anything to her anyway. So, he had written, 'I love you,' faithfully once a day to fulfill the promise and perhaps in the pale hope that it could be made true by repetition. He doubted she'd detect anything inauthentic in it, even when he sent his fake sentiments by the dozen. His one hope lay in thinking that maybe when they were physically back together she could make a believer of him again. But then her letters, when she'd still been sending them, came to him, and they followed a depressing formula with one piece of gossip, one garbled platitude, and some childish overstatement of her own supposed love. Her x's and o's and exclamation marks were eventually a mild hellscape for him. It wasn't as though he hadn't been warned. Her heart was dust. How had he not noticed? She claimed to love him more than God in heaven, for God sakes, so Mary Lou's pregnancy, when he'd first heard of it and when he'd assumed he was its cause, had seemed the seal of doom, and he'd been afraid he'd make a poor husband and father if his heart weren't in it, and, as near as he could tell, it wasn't. He should not feel this way, but George dreaded getting through what he was getting through only to be returned to Mary Lou and what looked to be a long slog of a life with her.

She is still pregnant. The pain of her infidelity was gone in fifteen minutes, a charred nest from which he felt his phoenix soul lifting; he could hardly sustain hard feelings toward Mary Lou who had, after all, given him everything he ever asked of her, and who seemed a universally generous girl that way, just following such instincts as she had been given to follow, and now she'd given him the greater gift of letting him off the hook. Responsible to neither wife nor baby, he'd be honorably down the road. He had two missions to fly; when those were over, or soon thereafter, he promised himself he'd find another carefree existence like boyhood had been.

When the mess hall began to fill with other early risers Lt. Harrow rode his bicycle to the Nissen hut that served for the bomb group's briefing room, his knees flaring out from the small machine like alternately flapping wings. Corporal Hughes, RAF, was there under her steel wire hair; militarily square from the shoes up, she stood at a map of Northern Europe about twice as large as a billiard table, shoving an icon across it with what might have been a shuffleboard paddle. She acknowledged him as Leftenant Harrow, and he asked her, "Who's winning the war this morning?"

"Mother nature," said Corporal Hughes.

"Does the fog ever lift?"

"We like to think not," she said. "Isn't your aircraft still disabled, sir?"

"It is. We're at loose ends for a while."

From within the small deference due to George's rank, Corporal Hughes regarded him as a distraction from her work, whatever that was. "Well," she said summarily, because in war there is no innocent information and can be no idle curiosity. Command did not like their pilots to know anything more than they would need to know for their immediate future, and if they weren't flying soon, they weren't very welcome in the briefing room. The danger, George supposed, was that he'd get drunk in a pub and let some German agent know what the weather over Germany was doing. "Well," he also said, somehow foolish in this woman's presence. "Thought I'd try and pass some time. See if. But. Okay, then. See you later." At least he had remembered not to call her ma'am. He rode his bicycle back to the barracks.

He considered himself well trained, but there was no way to prepare for the waiting. The crew of the Dirty Dora had been in England quite some time by Eighth Air Force standards, much of it waiting for their aircraft to be repaired or decommissioned entirely and replaced. They'd been used as Luftwaffe bait in their earliest missions and returned to base remarkably shot up. Thirty-three of thirty-five missions, and many miracles had been needed to get them this far. Command had been crowing lately about Allied air superiority, but George and the boys were still flying well above any breathable atmosphere, breathing canned air and wearing electric underwear, delicate systems for combat conditions; and there was no noticeable shortage of capable enemy, and always a few incompetent colleagues, all trying to kill them. George could without dreaming, without even closing his eyes, see airplanes twisting out of the sky in flames, parachutes descending into ground fire. In a fight, when he was busy, George would note these events almost in passing, it was later, in febrile remembrance that they became so terrible.

George found Lt. Loberg in sole possession of the dayroom, the bombardier compactly sunk into the cushions of the room's best chair with his flight jacket spread across his knees and an old, page-sprung edition of Punch spread across that, presently being ignored. Economy and moderation would keep him from loading or lighting it for hours yet, but Loberg's meerschaum was clenched in his teeth, and his lips formed around the stem as if insight might be drawn through it. The bombardier fancied himself a philosopher, a condition exacerbated since he'd bought this pipe. He glanced up from his latest ominous thought and said, "I've been thinking."

"Well, quit it," George said.

"You know what a marshalling yard is?"

"A primary target," said George. "Target of opportunity. Quickest way to cripple their railroads. Et cetera."

"But what we call that," said Loberg, "we call it a switching yard in America. Know what my old man does for a living?"

"He's a railroader," George recalled.

"Yeah, he's a switchman," said Loberg. "Old Ed's not a real go-getter, so he's never climbed too high in the organization. Works the switching yards. Always has. Always will."

"Oh?" George had never hastened his bombardier toward any conclusion but a bomb run.

Loberg pulled at his pipe which, though dead, reeked sweetly of burnt leaf. His cheeks had been deep tanned coming up in Carpentaria and frost bitten in flight so that they were patchy red and pale; his eyes were set in them like an owl's. "I've been thinking about German Ed," he said. "That poor shlub down there who never had enough ambition to actually hurt anyone, he's down there trying to buy his supper the only way he knows how, and that's the poor, dumb cluck I'm dropping my five-hundred-pounders on. Me, I'm accurate. Never been praised so much for anything in my life."

"Yeah," said George. "But we sure give 'em a fair shot

at us. Lot more of us get smoked than anybody on the ground. As a ratio, anyway."

"So, it's fair?"

"They started it."

"They did? German Ed did? Some school girl gets caught in a firestorm? They started it? The babies and nuns we want to starve into submission? What if it is fair, does that necessarily make it right?"

"Stop thinking," George said, "and that's an order."

He arranged himself with his feet under the brazier that feebly sought to heat the room, and George attempted *The House of Tudor,* a sober study that had been circulating through the bomb group at least as long as he had, and he was well asleep by the first beheading. He twitched into and out of a dream of Renaissance conspiracy and woke to find that Lt. Loberg hadn't shifted, had moved hardly at all and was only awaiting the return of his audience. "What in God's name are we doing here, George?"

"Don't know who I'm here for, exactly," George said, "but it wouldn't be Him."

"Amen," said Loberg. "But what I mean—*here.* Hanging around the airfield."

"Us?" said George. "What are *you* doing here? If Dolores knew you had a long pass and didn't come and see her, you'd be in trouble, I think."

"I'm not fit company," said Loberg. "For Dolores or anybody else."

"No?" George might have vouched for this, but didn't.

"I'm a mess," said Loberg.

"I inventoried his things," George said. "Been trying to think of a note I could slip in with 'em. Something for his mother."

"Saying what?"

"Just something," George said, "from somebody who

actually knew him."

"But what?" Loberg pressed. "Tell her he's dead, which she already knew by the time she gets his stuff?"

"Dear Mrs. Swaney," George mused, "of Potlach, Idaho."

"Tell her we loved him, too?" Loberg offered. "Loved him."

"Who knows how she'd take that? I could tell her we thought an awful lot of him, at least. Tell her how good he was at his job."

"Shit, George. Letter she'll get from the Colonel probably says that much."

"I could tell her he didn't suffer. That might be important."

"He didn't suffer *dying*," Loberg corrected. "But remember how scared he'd get. I used to just ache for the guy."

"Good at his job," said George. "Scared as he was, he did it anyway. Did a perfect job for us. Arnie was my idea of real brave, but you'd have to go into all the details to really explain that to her."

"He was good to have on those cheek guns, too," said Loberg. "Just yelling at 'em, 'Come on. Come on.' With Arnie, it wasn't just suppression fire. Arnie knocked 'em down. 'Come on. Come on.' Tell her he was responsible for those swastikas painted on our nose, confirmed kills, closing speeds at five hundred miles an hour, and, blam. Man. Our wild man on the nose— and that's why we loved him, among other reasons."

"Too complicated," said George. "That's more than I'd know how to say. Thought I might mention how funny he looked all scrunched up at the navigator table. How he never missed a coordinate. We knew where we were at all times with Arnie."

"Tell her," said Loberg, "how funny he looked without his face."

"Stop it," George said. "You better stop it, Dale. We can't afford that until we're done here. We've got these people we have to get through this. And we're going to do that."

"Sure, we will," said Loberg. "Don't worry about me, I'm good to go. I'm fine. We should've gone to Bath with the guys, but who could stand to see another goddamned ruin? Sit in the damn, stinky water. But his *face*, George. That's a person's whole personality. When it's gone, that's it. Dead-eye's dead, and I mean he was erased. Brains in his lap. Spend any time with a corpse, you get the general idea—we're a cheap cut of meat with a little juice running through. Spring a leak, and that's all-she-wrote. Did I feel his spirit hovering around? Nope. He was just. But do not worry about me. I am fit to fight. I am ready. Let's get to killing. We're on borrowed time, anyway, buddy, and somebody else pays the interest. I am ready to go. We have to be, don't we?"

They had been particular friends, George and Arnie Swaney and Dale Loberg, since the crew had formed up for training back in the States. None of them college men, all hailed from obscure and presumably fly-blown corners of the West, and they had enjoyed in each other a studied lack of polish, appreciated the almost sly competence they seemed to also have in common. How far they had come to demonstrate once and for all time the earth-shaking capacities of the common man unleashed. Handy hicks they had come out of pure decency to lift a tyranny off the suffering world, and their friendship and confidence in each other had been the nucleus of a fine, proud air crew that had got through all these raids and several ruined bombers without suffering a casualty in the ranks. Until now. Dear Mrs.

Swaney. So sorry about your boy?

George pretended to doze again, eyes closed, heart closed around what seemed a great betrayal. Where was his grief?

As with so much in the war, friends were ill advised and inevitable. Better not to be too fond of anyone so much in harm's way. But how not? Living as they did from combat to combat, they had arrived at their respective secrets pretty quickly, an intimacy unprecedented for all of them. It was so clearly a temporary time, why not be frank? But their secrets had proven generally laughable by light of day, things only a country boy would ever bother to conceal.

Arnie Swaney's hidden life, for instance, consisted of having lapsed into jack Mormonism, and being a little less rough and ready than his family might desire, and he hadn't yet told that family of his plan to make his way with numbers and Uncle Sam's help through school and into a profession that would lift him out of the woods, out of the sawmill, and into a profession where he could reasonably hope to keep his fingers through his entire career. Certified Public Accountant, licensed and bonded. This mild aspiration, or its mildness, was all his shame. It seemed his people would think it womanish, his wanting to work inside, warm and dry. Arnie Swaney had never rhapsodized of home, but often spoke with great definition and desire of where he was going next, though he'd never been there. Arnie saw himself far from the Panhandle, and far, far, far from the whining saws, married to a blond in a place where the larger trees were confined to parks. He was aimed at a neat, comfortable neighborhood that did not resemble Potlach. He had wanted it so much.

So George had been privy to the deeper operations of his friend's life, and Arnie's death yawned open, especially regrettable because George knew that in dying young his young friend had died so unfinished, so unrealized, and it should have been brutally sad, but George hadn't really got through his first and still most eminent thought about it: Not me—that rush of relief that Arnie Swaney had been sacrificed to the menace that might as easily have claimed them all. It was disappointing. He was not friend enough to even briefly cease to appreciate that he, George Harrow, had been spared.

"Dear Mrs. Swaney. If I told you what a wonderful guy he was, would it make it any easier?"

DOVE

A bulbous green car stood in the farmyard, the plume of dust it had pulled up the road still hanging in the strange, still afternoon. She had come out of her pantry to greet the men in uniform who'd knocked at her door; their insignia signified nothing to her, but their bearing said one of them outranked the other. Dove's first instinct was to offer her hand, her hospitality, but she could not unclench either hand from that jar of pickles, couldn't in her confusion even open the screen door for them. "Mrs. Harrow?" said the taller man, the self-important one. "Mrs. Charles Harrow?"

"Yes," she managed.

"Are you alone here, ma'am? Is there someone who could. . .?"

The other soldier looked stricken. He held a triangular bundle of fabric, a small black box balanced on that, and, less conspicuously, a scrap of yellow paper. Western Union.

◊ ◊ ◊

She lay briefly in brine and broken glass before the soldiers lifted her out of it, but in those moments so much occurred. She would soon have reason to regret that the news didn't outright kill her, but as she lay on the floor she reviewed her life as those dying are said to do, not its scenes or incidents so much as all the seasons of her sensibility; she felt that awful surge of humility that had come of walking into this country, more profound than a thousand Sunday sermons; she heard children who'd never drawn breath come babbling of other planets; and all in a rush now she felt how through the years the great wide open had come to invade her insides. There had been so little left of her to carve out, but it was a completely hollow woman now that the kind soldiers helped to her chair.

◊ ◊ ◊

Her son had been the essential soul. This was true for Verity and for Father, too—their George was the yeasty boy who gave rise to what was best in them. A comfort, a gift of a boy. For Dove he had been—and such a lot to heap on a young person—the entire justification for the pain of living.

Something about a rocket. Explosions in mid-air over enemy territory. No remains.

"We lacked the means and even the inclination to try and comfort each other. I'm afraid we're that kind of people—too terrified of the empty gesture. I've been crippled that way, too. But what could you say? What could a person possibly say that wouldn't ring hollow? How could you be sincere in anything now, or risk one additional feeling?"

VERITY

It was that week in June when in the fields along the Jefferson River the year's first cutting of hay lies freshly mown and raked into windrows to cure; driving into Twin Bridges, Verity was grateful for the green of this harvest in her nose. Anything kind to the senses. The town was, like most towns she knew, a row of brick store fronts briefly lining the road to somewhere else, a place to buy gasoline. She asked a young man at the Texaco station, pimples and grease rag, for three and a half dollars of high-test and for directions to the orphanage. "You just need to stay headed toward Dillon," he told her. Washing her window, he kept glancing around inside the car for a glimpse of the bundle he assumed she must be delivering, and he asked her, "Check your oil?"

"Get lost," said Verity.

Her idea of orphans and of the places where orphans were kept came from Charles Dickens, but she found Montana's state orphanage set on grounds a millionaire might have coveted, that river full of trout running by, and the orphans she saw around the campus seemed at least as well fed and full of purpose as farm kids anywhere, awfully like herself, really, and the sympathy she'd concocted to face this occasion was already proving useless. There was a tall building that with its wide veranda and turrets seemed the most likely place for official things to occur, and she went into it, into a large, battered, musk-smelling room where a small boy under a tall crewcut was seated on a stone bench, swinging his legs under him, the anxious pendulum.

"Hi," said Verity. They regarded each other, measuring. "Where would I find the boss?"

The child shrugged, and they continued for a long

time to stare at each other. Finally, a distracted woman in a denim jacket emerged from a hallway to confront the boy on the bench.

"Now." She said. "Gilbert. What don't we do? What don't we ever do?"

The boy's shoulders drew up around his ears like a griffin's wings. "Put our fingers there," he said.

"Where?"

"*There*," the boy insisted.

"Go on," said the woman. "Try to be useful today. To somebody. This doesn't get you off work." As the boy scrambled out, the woman turned to Verity and said, "Yes?"

"I'm here for a baby. I believe it's all arranged."

"Oh, for Georgy?"

"Yes," Verity admitted.

The woman's nose was lavender and expansive. Her manner changed at once; she chose to brighten. "That's just fine," she said. "I think I'd heard he'd been placed. I'd better find Mr. Boyle, I guess. He'll be in one of the dormitories now, I'm pretty sure But, in the meantime you might as well get acquainted. The nursery is right here in Main."

The building contained much curvilinear wood, a curved stair well, and silent echoes. The small woman led Verity up to a room that proved circular as they entered it, the interior of one of those turrets. There was a girl in a chair, reading a book by the milky light of a leaded window. As they came in, she let the book into her lap, a long black valley in the homemade skirt that appeared to be uniform with the orphan girls. There were two cribs in the room and these also suggested local manufacture with their crudely joined, very tall railings. On the floor of one of these cage-like affairs sat a baby with his legs splayed. He was only just old enough to have mastered the impenetrable countenance Verity had just seen on the boy on the bench, the orphan stare. The baby seemed to look right through them.

"Beth," said the woman, "this is, oh, I'm sorry, I forgot to get your name."

"Verity. It's Verity Harrow."

"Oh? So, then you'd be. . ."

"Verity," she said. "That's all."

"Oh. Well," the woman in the denim jacket said, "She's supposed to be picking up George today, so I thought they should, I don't know, maybe get to know each other a little bit. But let me go find Mr. Boyle. I won't be long, or try not to be."

Then it was the three of them in the round room, the orphans examining Verity with the unembarrassed, unimpressed curiosity of house cats. Their stillness, especially the baby's, was hard to bear, and Verity made a show of looking around the room, appreciating it. "Pretty fancy," she said, and it once had been, the builder's idea of a cozy garret, a showcase for the plasterer's art, an antique light falling into it. The girl with the book was only a few years younger than Verity but remained very much the little orphan girl, enormously buck toothed, watchful. "Beth," asked Verity, "didn't she say?" The girl affirmed it with a tight nod, and Verity caught herself before asking her how she liked it here. She thought to ask instead, "You take care of him?"

"I'm in the nursery most days," said the girl, "when there's babies here. Which they try not to have. Very many babies. They're not set up for it here. Now I'll have to go back to the dairy again."

"Sorry," said Verity.

"It's okay," the orphan girl said. "The little ones get adopted out pretty fast, usually. Little white boys, they go fast if there's nothing wrong with 'em. Been here myself, on and off, since I was seven." It seemed she thought the reasons for this would be self-evident and obvious. "So," she said. "You gonna be his mother?"

"No," said Verity.

Then a floodgate opened in poor Beth, and Verity was suddenly become a confidante, and Beth said that she didn't mind the work at the dairy, and even kind of liked the cows, believe it or not, and even most of the boys down there. She then described in details she seemed to savor several sordid offenses committed against her by the other boys, the bad ones. "So, what would you do?" she wondered.

"Me?" Verity said. "What would *I* do? You better ask some of the people here. Some of these people here who could maybe do something about it."

"No, but what would *you* do?"

"I'd go to these people," said Verity. "The staff, I guess they are. Talk to them. Tell them."

"Yeah. But what if that wouldn't work?"

"Don't ask me," said Verity. "Pick up a rock. Brain 'em. Find yourself an equalizer. It's a barn—run a pitchfork through their foot. See, you really don't want to ask me what I'd do, 'cause chances are real good I'd do the wrong thing. You should talk to somebody who's—maybe, well—*here.*"

It was not an answer the girl wanted, so she went quiet again. Even her glasses had a homespun look. They waited, the three of them, for the next big shift in their fates, and where could Mr. Boyle be?

"You think he's all right?" Verity asked the girl.

"How do you mean?"

"He doesn't move much. Hasn't moved since I've been here." More to the point, he hadn't taken his eyes from her face.

The girl Beth spoke to her little charge in the same manner she probably used for the cows. "You're all right," she said. "Aren't you, Georgy? Kind of a odd little bugger, for sure, and you'd have to say your head is awful round, but you'll grow out of that." Then to Verity, "But you should have got an older kid, some kid who could work for you right away. But. He's sure not fussy, tell you that. About the closest I ever got to having any privacy around here was being up here with Georgy. You'll go hours at a time and never make a peep, won't you, baby? Oh, he's, he's all right, I think. I mean, he don't fuss *at* all. I guess you know, they won't let you take his blankets or anything. That stuff stays with the home. For the next one."

Mr. Boyle came at last. Summoned from a distant field, he'd begun to sweat or be aware of sweating the moment he got inside, and he came into the nursery wiping his face with the back of his arm, no-nonsense fashion. A bureaucrat in a cowboy hat and with his acquired belly draped over an old rodeo buckle, he saw at once that Verity could not be the Mrs. Harrow he'd been speaking with on the phone. Verity was quick to say she was *Miss* Harrow, only her daughter, and her chin swerved to direct the conversation out of the nursery, and she explained once they were in the hallway that she wasn't sure how much the little boy might understand of what would be said between them.

"Mrs. Harrow couldn't come?" Mr. Boyle asked.

"She died," Verity said.

"Oh. I. Sorry to hear it. Condolences. She seemed like a fine, cultivated woman."

"Yeah," Verity said. "So, that's why I'm here."

"For? You thought *you'd* take him?"

Verity saw that this man somehow held all these children in his affections; he must be a superior person. "That was the idea," she said.

"How old are you?"

"I'm of age," said Verity. "Believe me."

"You must know it's not quite that simple," said Mr. Boyle. "We couldn't just hand him over to you. Your mother was the adoptive mother. It's not like you'd inherit the child."

"You can't hand him over to her, that's for sure."

"That's not my point," said Mr. Boyle. "Would you be caring for him, then? Had you given that any thought? That's a lot of responsibility to take on."

"Oh," said Verity, "I gave it plenty of thought, and that's why I. The thing is: I promised her. Promised I'd come get him."

"You know what it takes to raise a child?"

"Not exactly," said Verity. "But some of the women around home who've managed it—it can't be that hard. As I say, I promised."

"And I admire your determination, but it's not that simple. Was she sick, your mom? She never mentioned it. I knew she was older, but."

"It probably slipped her mind," said Verity. "Being sick was fairly regular for her."

"Well, I'm real sorry for your loss. But I'd probably better try and get a call through to the County Attorney. See where we're at legally."

Verity dug in. "My father's on those adoption papers, too. And he's still alive."

"Why isn't he here, then?"

"He's farming," Verity said. "This time of year, we couldn't both be off the place all day. So, he sent me down."

"I should call him, at least."

"Wouldn't do you much good," she said. "He's deaf as a post. Never used a telephone in his life, far as I know. Even when he could hear."

"That promise," said Mr. Boyle. "You have to know that isn't enough. That wouldn't be near enough reason to take this on at your age."

"It'll have to be," said Verity.

CHARLIE

He shared his idleness with the red headed boy. Always careless of himself around beasts of burden and whirling machinery, Charlie had never expected to go on so long; he should by now have successfully worked himself to death but had instead outlived his bareknuckle West, nearly all his acquaintances of old, and most of his family; he was outlasting even his senses. Trapped in an alien shell as hard and gnarled as a walnut, he was too stiff most mornings to do anything more useful than build pots of coffee and sit in the kitchen watching or being watched by the red headed boy. Charlie did not consider this easy duty. His memory, for better and worse, was the one thing unimpaired in him, so he often repaired in his mind to old times to ease the tedium of today. He might kill an hour remembering by name, and fondly at last, every animal that had ever kicked him.

The boy looked up from his picture book, his horrid, pallid lashes flicking, and when he saw he'd caught Charlie's eye, he chalked MILK on his slate board. The boy had never seemed especially precocious to Charlie until he'd learned from Verity this trick with the slate board, the words necessary to describe his needs, MILK PANCAKE HANKY. He was very little trouble, too little trouble for a boy child, so far as Charlie could see. Because the kid was still too short and too slight to break the rubber seal to the door of the trembling box, Charlie got the bottle out for him. Their milk came from someone else's cow these days and was cream-poor for Charlie's purposes, but it kept so cold in the trembling box that it beaded the glass as he poured it. Given his choice, the kid would subsist on this blue milk, and when Charlie was in charge the kid was almost always given his choice. Little bugger asked for so little. But there were those endless eyes of his, a wanting. The kid had some McQuiston in him, in his coloring; fortunately, he'd come without their twitching mannerisms. He was too calm if anything, and so heavily freckled and weirdly watchful, and red headed, and for as much time as they'd spent alone together this way, Charlie had never learned to comfortably endure the boy's gaze. It was even worse now that he knew the kid wasn't stupid. They kept silent company.

The trembling box was hooked to a wire. The cook stove, hooked to a wire. Within the improvised walls of this old farmhouse a copper vine had grown. Verity's kitchen was equipped with any number of electrified whirligigs, and if Charlie had never heard any of these small appliances in operation, still he imagined them shrill. With so much time on his hands his imagination bent idly; his heart, if he wasn't careful of it, tended toward various sorrows. Dove was gone. George was gone. He no longer knew the workings of his own farm, and the daughter who'd never wanted any part of it was trapped in what was left of his best intentions.

Shortly after George died the Harrows had learned that Mary Lou had been turned out of her own family's house and that she'd gone off somewhere to have her ill-timed baby. Many months later there was a call from the orphanage concerning a certain George Harrow. There had been no divorce, after all, and Mary Lou in her crowning outrage had delivered the poor mutt in a charity ward where she hung a princely name on him, George Lloyd Charles Harrow, and listed real George on the birth certificate as the misbegotten baby's father. Mary Lou had then dragged the thing around for a while, through various charities, churches not her father's, before finally surrendering it a bit malnourished to the state. Charlie learned of all this through notes from Verity that had to be writ large and came in no coherent sequence. Dove, a big-eyed madness on her since she'd lost her son, and mortally frail, insisted that they take the boy in, adopt him, and Charlie watched his wife and daughter argue about it. Spared the details of the dispute, he assumed Dove would in time come to her senses. A sensible, dignified woman, his wife, and they'd all relied on her for that, and she'd always before righted herself whenever her heavy emotions threatened to run away with her. But she pressed and pressed at her bad baby idea until she somehow prevailed in the argument by dying, and so they had done this poor boy the poor favor of taking him in when no one left living on the place really wanted him there.

The red headed boy. None of his fault, but there he sat, penance and penitent with his picture books and their dragons and matadors and skiffs of prose—the child seemed to read some already. He was intent on something. Red headed boy, companion to Charlie's vast old age, and at different ends of their respective lives they'd adopted about the same strategy for getting through it; islands of self-contained self, they circled round each other like electrons in that tiny kitchen. Charlie had come to know time as an illusion, his yesterdays, some of them more than half century past, returned with more particularity than the present, perhaps because he'd been better equipped in those days to take things in.

It would have been '95 or '96, and he must have been broke, because he'd taken a commission to haul hides from an abattoir to a tannery down around Cheyenne, and the butchers did not scrape those hides very well at all, and they'd leave them stacked under the sun for him, and one morning he picked up a particularly reeking load of this, the air not moving a lick, and Charlie was just two miles down the road and through that stillness before he wanted reinforcements; he came to one of those slap-up saloons so common along every roadside; Charlie tied up, swaggered in, and he asked the barkeep for a shot and a beer. What a place, daylight leaking through the walls, not a spittoon in sight and snoose spattered everywhere on a floor of rough-sawn planks. But the barkeep said, "No. Find yourself a bath and burn them clothes you're wearing, then I might consider selling you a drink. Until then, it's get-out and stay-out." Where Charlie would always prefer to come back sharp at an affront like that, here the man had the truth on his side—Charlie stunk of rotten meat, and it made it hard to be but so clever, so he slunk out of the saloon where he encountered the same drunk he'd seen coming in, a man sitting disconsolate on a stump, a young man who didn't look like he'd make an old one, he'd been used too hard and looked like he'd lately been in the wrong yard with the wrong dog, his pants legs all shredded round his ankles, and Charlie happened to remark how they were awful picky about their custom in that saloon for an outfit selling busthead, and the drunk complained at how the barkeep had called him a mooch in there, which was, unfortunately, more of the truth, and what could he say, and Charlie, to make him feel better told the man he looked like a good old waddy, and the drunk said sure he'd been a cowboy, but the distance between busted up and flat busted was about a month. He said the worst of his troubles would be fixed, though, once Charlie got downwind of him with that wagon. Charlie felt very well for the moment—if all he really needed was a scrubbing—so he flipped the drunk a silver dollar he could not afford to give.

Charlie in his deafness tends to remember scraps of ancient conversations. He remembers that the drunk had offered up his wisdom by way of thanks, had said by way of parting that a man might as well surrender to the grand design. In those days Charlie had believed that only the work of his hands and his will were inevitable, so his final word to the rounder had been, "Bullshit."

But he'd come to wonder now: "Can you ever get your way? This whole family has been stubborn as hell, but I don't see where any of us got our way, exactly, or even figured out what it was. Not for lack of trying, though. Wasn't for lack of trying."

ULYSSES PUREFOY

Since he'd been stationed at the edge of nowhere, Ulysses Purefoy had decided to experiment with himself; he never left base without his horn and a hipster hitch in his walk, and whenever he was not in uniform he affected a purple beret. Daddy-O. Purefoy would not have attempted these stylings in Rochester. If he bent a note back home or tweaked a rhythm it had happened by accident or on the sly. The foxtrots and waltzes he let drip from his honeyed trumpet in Minnesota had always been so well received, but in the wild west, in Great Falls, Montana of all places, he'd gone frontiering, and the new erratic, ecstatic jazz was to be his music here, maybe even his religion.

Some years earlier good citizen Leo Lamar had solved the harrowing hours after church by throwing his Ozark Club open to Sunday jam sessions, come-one, come-all. It was soon a tradition, a near cult, with airmen like Purefoy and Sergeant Otis with his mournful clarinet coming in from the base, and students brash and bashful from the halls of the high school; there was a mail carrier and his fiddle, an albino saxophonist who worked at the power-house, cowboys would sometimes appear with their guitars and accordions. Chick singers, of course. Purefoy hoped for those wondrous days when elements of the Ozark's house band sat in, serious, professional people with taste and technique and currency in what was then current on 52nd Street. He preferred players who stretched him, but even when Purefoy found himself as sometimes happened in a crowd of three-chord Johnnies, he was still among folks who shared a desire to shed the banal for a while, who were inclined to appreciate Ulysses Purefoy in his quest for the sublime. Purefoy tried hard to avoid having duty on the day of rest, and he approached these sessions at the Ozark Club with a hot sense of occasion. His small renown among this cow town's exotics was the only thing that made his time in the Air Force tolerable.

One sunny Sunday afternoon in September he stood in the good barroom gloom with his back to the bar, thumbs hooked in his suspenders, and he'd been declaiming on the bebop glissando when in walked Verity Harrow. She came straight for him, looking straight at him, her denim shirt buttoned to the throat and at her wrists, her big brown hands hanging out. It seemed she cut her hair with gardening shears. Straight for him, her gaze steady on him as if approaching a fight, crazed thing. Purefoy glanced down; her brogans advanced, sounding on the tiny dance floor. He was further startled when from just behind him Leo Lamar hailed the apparition, "Long time no see," said Leo. "Glad you could make it in. These things've been dull and tame without you."

"Summer," she said. "Been summer on the old farmstead."

"Pistol," said Leo Lamar, "here's a cat you oughta meet, cat we call 'Up' for short. Ulysses, if you please. You two are after a similar style, I believe, both trying to sound like those heroin addicts."

Purefoy sensed the approach of another, odder detour from the beaten path. He could not easily meet her eyes. She smelled of straw dust.

"So," she asked him, "you play, do you?"

Purefoy mumbled, stuffed and suddenly humbled, "I do." With an authority about her that would wear weird in a girl of any age or color, she reminded him uncomfortably of his grandmother. She commandeered the piano then and began touching chords amounting soon enough to 'Don't Blame Me.' Purefoy twisted his mouthpiece in and joined her, and at first he caught himself playing sharp, playing flat, playing behind the pulse she kept so impeccably; he'd had every reason to think himself a gifted balladeer, but she made him nervous as no other audience. It was the quality of her listening. She heard everything. He ruined the first tune they tried together, but she said the moment they finished, "Again. I'll count you in from the top this time."

Though it was to be some time before he would know her as anything but Pistol, they were intimates almost from the moment they met. She told him that first day that she'd had no experience of playing with other musicians except for the sessions she was able to make here at the Ozark Club. She said she owned just six record albums and played them under a cactus needle to keep from wearing the grooves off, and that for the rest of her repertoire she relied on an unreliable radio signal, sheet music that she could never be sure she was playing correctly, and the fumes of her own cracked brain. Purefoy said that was all right. They both knew she was better than all right. She'd quote from Bach or anyone else, and her gift included few social graces, but he could tell she was very glad to have met someone at last with ears to fully hear her, to bear witness. Those Sundays thereafter when he found himself crewing on the flight line he would pine for her, wonder if she'd made it into town that day, and this was long before he had ever guessed they might be lovers.

Because they had obligations elsewhere and their days weren't their own to schedule, their chances to play together were few and sometimes far between. On those chance Sundays when they were both free, their encounters had been full of songs they wanted to try together and with fending off lesser musicians who were trying to intrude too much on their thing, and no time whatever had been wasted between them in small talk. He'd known her through several seasons without knowing her given name or any other detail you might expect to have of the slightest acquaintance. Suspecting she came of some fierce situation, he required no further particulars; she could be his prophet come out of the wilderness, and leave it at that. Pistol. One day, however, Purefoy needed a way back to base, and it happened she'd been the only available ride, and so it was that he had come to ride in the rattling cab of a grain truck, a coffee can half full of fencing staples clamped between his feet; their progress between stop signs had her constantly shifting gears. "Our car just went kerflooey," she said. "I think the coil's gone bad, so I'm down to driving old Bess 'til I get it fixed."

"You live out of town?" It was hardly necessary to ask.

"About seventy-five miles out," she said.

Seventy-five miles. A hundred and fifty round-trip. Purefoy felt he owed her something on that account, felt he was obligated to ask at last after her name, at least, the name her mother would call her, and when he had it, he further inquired, "Verity? You a church girl? You come from one of those colonies out there?"

"Chops like mine, and you think I'm a Hutterite? Do I *look* like a Hutterite?"

"I don't know," said Purefoy, and he didn't. "Maybe. Maybe one who ran away. Some of their women escape sometimes, don't they?"

"Oh. An escapee."

"It's just that name," he said. "You have to admit, it's a very churchy handle you got."

"But, a *Hutter*ite?"

"How am I supposed to know," he wondered, "*who* might be living out there?" In truth he didn't know what to make of her, and until now, except for her musicality, he hadn't spent a lot of thought that way. She was about as feminine as angle iron, and until now he had vaguely and conveniently thought her a lesbian, but it didn't seem she was beyond taking feminine offense. "You drink coffee? I should buy you a cup of coffee, at least, before you drive all the way back."

The country was at that time sustaining wars hot and cold, rocketing prosperity, and a domestic hysteria so severe that the mildest eccentric in the most unlikely backwater might be mistaken for a threat to the American way of life. Discretion being the better part of valor, Purefoy had limited his circuit in Great Falls to those spots where he could be reasonably certain his jive manner and wardrobe would be reasonably welcome—the Ozark and the pool hall; he wasn't about shoving his act down anyone's throat, so he was not well or widely acquainted with this town. They chose the Treasure State Café only for its broad parking lot. They went in, and its windows were spread with crystalline fields of condensation, its walls paneled in knotty pine; beef stock and chicken broth simmered somewhere on the premises. It was Purefoy's idea of a comfortable establishment, or might have been but that the companionable click and clink of diners dining fell away to near silence almost the moment they appeared, and instantly Purefoy began to throb with the old familiar caution and resentments. Making their way to a corner booth, they passed behind three crew cut huskies lining the lunch counter with their jeans cuffed, sleeves rolled. These were broad-backed, glance-exchanging louts, and one of them, Purefoy was very sure, said something that included the word 'jungle.' A lop fingered short-order cook set a plate in the window from the kitchen, and with a small man's special malevolence stared at them and stared at them until they'd tucked out of sight in their booth. Ding. "Order up." Now that they'd got sealed off from it, the life of the café could be heard resuming around them. Was Purefoy imagining this? "Squares," he said. "I'm out there keeping the Russians off 'em, and this is how they want to act? Know what Leo tells me? Says it's illegal to be Chinese in this town. Among other things. Says his daddy happened to be a Chinaman."

"You know 'Now's the Time'?" she asked him. "We should try those changes if we happen to think of it next time."

"It's just," said Purefoy, "I get awful tired of this." He spread his hands, palm up to indicate that by 'this' he meant everything.

"Try being female," she said. "And ugly. Then see how it goes for you. If I worried about what people thought of me, man I'd be. . ." She warmed to the subject, "We raise wheat, and we raise barley, flax, and rapeseed, and anyone who doesn't like it can certainly kiss my rosy ass."

We? Rapeseed? For such a direct kind of gal she did preserve her mysteries. Purefoy had thus far taken her for a celestial music box, but now, face to face in the strange privacy of their booth she did him the strange favor of looking right at him, of seeing him it seemed. Her eyes defined her, and it was just as well, for her other features were ill sorted, a mug large, bony, and frank, but inescapably now a woman's. They waited for the waitress. "How High the Moon," said Purefoy. They waited for the waitress. "I've never seen you at the club," he said. "At night. You ever come in when it's jumping? Have drinks or anything?"

"No," she said.

They waited for the waitress, knowing the waitress had seen them. "You should try it some time," he said. "People are free there. They don't care *who* you are in there, long as you pay your bar tab."

"It's all I can do," she said, "to get away from the place for this long, for these Sunday things."

Waiting, Purefoy had gotten hungry. "See," he said, "this is why I spend so much time at the enlisted men's club, playing dominoes. But, you really should try and get in to the Ozark some night. Hear their band. Doubt they'd let you at the piano, but they're sure worth a listen. A hot ahn-sahm-boh, you know. They've got a groove going, an understanding. Some very tuneful cats. And, like I say, people can be free in there. Be who they want."

"Oh," she said, "I can be who I want any old time. Can't help it. It's being *where* I want. That's the ding in my deal. Sometimes I'd like to be in San Francisco, for instance. Or New York, far as that goes. New Orleans. Rio, fruit basket on my head."

"Yeah," he said. "A person does get jammed up against reality. I know I'm not playing near as much as I'd like since I've been in the Air Force. Can't in the barracks. Can't even play my records much. There's always some caveman around, wants to make stupid remarks, try and defame Dizzy Gillespie. I can't afford to get court martialed over a fist fight, but, man, it's so tempting."

"That's one problem I don't have," she said.

"What problem?"

"People I need to punch," she said, "or at least they're never handy when I do want to hit 'em. Unless I come to town."

"I think," said Purefoy, "it's the two of us together. They think we're. . ."

"'Wildwood Flower,'" she said. "Don't laugh. You can have quite a bit of fun with that one."

"I've played every corny thing there is," he confessed. "Used to work in a dance band. I'm sure we played "Happy Birthday" a million times. You try to tell yourself it's not what you play, it's how you play it."

"You think?"

"Well," Purefoy qualified. "Kind of. But when I get out and get back home, I'm going to have me a trio, a quartet at most. Start gigging right away, and *no* birthday parties, unless it's for royalty." It occurred to him even as he said it that this might be taken for an invitation. To what? She made quite a point of being bound to something here. She'd also made quite a point of making herself a hell of a piano player. "Now they've got me starving," he said. "You think they'd have some pumpkin pie?" He leaned out of the booth and into the line of sight of their waitress, and she saw him and turned away. Purefoy raised his hand, the cavalry officer halting his column behind him, the executive hailing a cab, and still from the corner of her eye the waitress ignored him. He retreated into the booth again. "This might be a dead end. Usually it's not this. They think we're, I don't know."

"What about you, though?" she said. "They ever let you away from that outfit you're in?"

"Leave," said Purefoy. "I get a certain amount of leave every year. I'll use that to go home. They give out forty-eight-hour passes all the time. Probably one a month, or so. But those are kind of a cruel joke. Here. Where you gonna go from here that doesn't take at least a day to get there and a day to get back? So, I'm king of the bones. Stick around base, make a killing playing dominoes. Do my hitch, get out, go back home. Put together my trio. Some of the guys will hop on a transport plane, they get a pass, just to ride somewhere. But what's the point in that?"

"I'd like to get up there once and try it," she said. "I hear it's fantastic up there."

"It's like a bus ride," said Purefoy. "Bus without windows."

"You ought to come out some time," she said.

"Out?"

"To our place," she said. "Home of the true piano. I'm much better on my own piano."

She had promised him, and she seemed a person who'd make good on her promises, that if he came out to the farm, they would be able to play as much as they wanted, anything they wanted to play, any way they wanted to play it. There was no one to object or butt in, she claimed. "It's my only advantage," she said, and like much of what she said, this suggested several things to him. Purefoy had carried her number for months in his wallet until boredom and his curiosity got the best of him, and he called to tell her, "They owe me a pass, so if that offer is still open—and if you can come to base and pick me up Friday morning—or you could pick me up, uh—I don't know how else I'd get to you. But if. . ."

"Right there at the gate?" she said.

"That works," he said.

"Packed up and ready to go?"

"What would I pack? I mean, I could probably get my hands on some. . ."

"We're on a party line," she said. "Your horn should be all you'll need. What time?"

And now here he was under a dominant sky, a few cirrus clouds snaking through it, apparently lost up there. They drove and drove toward her farm, and Purefoy could not shake his sense of this as hostile country. There was too much of it. Out where it seemed he could see to the Arctic Circle he found he didn't care for the view; the farther they traveled the less he could think to say to her.

"Does madame burn?"

"Cook?" she said. "I have to. We'd starve if I didn't. But the boys, they sometimes act like they'd prefer it. Starve to death. You should see some of the looks I get. I make a decent loaf of bread, though, so there's always that if you feel your ribs caving in. I mean, I *like* what I make, and you might, too. I like to try different things, you know."

Boys? She'd mentioned these boys before, but Purefoy had never pressed her for more detail, and she hadn't offered any. The boys? And who might they be? They'd be white, anyway, and he thought the half-wild Verity Harrow—Pistol, as he'd known her—could very well lack an understanding of what it could be for him to try and mingle with white folks. In their home? Since they'd crossed that frail bridge over the river it seemed they were driving away from everything, and Purefoy had entirely lost his bearings until something she'd mentioned in passing began to loom before them—Square Butte, and no mistaking it, a landmark, thank goodness. Maybe he'd stumbled into the real deal.

Ulysses Purefoy had always expected that his woman of mystery, should he ever encounter her, would be a little more attractive than Verity Harrow, and not so pale, and that the setting would be less surreal. Purefoy had never, however, worked with a musician anything like her, and an hour or two here and there wasn't enough to realize what they might do together. She had such big hands for a woman, and she favored big, wide chords with room in them for dissonance. She had her own prairie chick style, an uncorrupted way of playing that drew unexpected things from him. They became as they played a whole greater than the sum of their parts, his horn a golden eagle over her fruited fields of grain. But what else might be involved? What had he gotten into? Purefoy preferred not to think about it.

When they came at last to the farm there was in the farmyard an enormous towheaded man in coveralls lying face down on a swayback gray with its lead hanging slack to the ground. Both creatures were entirely at peace. In the door of the farmhouse stood a boy in a coonskin cap and a pair of sunglasses that covered a third of his face; shyly he raised his hand to them. Even behind those glasses his eyes had the quality of a portrait on a wall; Purefoy felt them tracking him.

"Swede," said Verity Harrow. "Goddamn Swede. This'll happen when I don't give him enough to do. He gets the blues. Mother's idea of Christian charity, and here we're still stuck with him."

Purefoy helped her help the big man off the horse and toward what turned out to be the bunk house. She explained the smell of him, "He makes his own apple jack. You know how much apple jack a guy this big has to drink to get this snockered? You're a sad case, aren't you, bud? You'll be out of whack for days now."

The man mumbled his regrets in what might be the language of his youth or might just be mumbling, and when they had him settled, he looked like he might be bunked in for the winter. It was an isolate monk's cell, the bunkhouse, with a small, homemade approximation of a Franklin stove, an enamel wash bowl and pitcher. Reading glasses, a stub of candle in the lid of a fruit jar. A Farmer's Almanac. Purefoy did not find the man's funk in any way surprising. What a brutal life.

The strange child still awaited them as they came up to the main house, anxious to make some announcement, and Verity introduced him as, 'Jeet.'

"Jeet?" said Purefoy.

"It was his idea," she said. "Jeet," she said, "this is Ulysses, or you can call him 'Up' if that's too much to say."

"Ulysses," said the child precisely. He pointed to their barn, or as Purefoy was soon to understand, the scene then occurring somewhere behind it. "Rob got out," the child said solemnly. "Charlie went after him."

"Rob," Verity Harrow explained, "is our other nag. Rob Roy. Charlie is my father." She hoisted the little boy onto the back of the gray, and they went to see what to do about the wayward horse, the wayward elder, Verity complaining all the while about the nonsense horses brought into their lives. They rounded the barn and there a buckskin capered in its fresh freedom and a very old man was advancing unsteadily toward something in the field; the old boy carried a neat little carbine at port arms; what hair remained to his head was fine as a baby's.

"Oooh," said Purefoy.

"It's all right," said Verity. "He tells us he ran his own shooting gallery way back when. He's still a great shot."

"Oh?" said Purefoy.

"He can't hear anything," said Verity, "but he still sees more than you'd think he would."

"You tell him I was coming out here?"

"Yeah," she said. "Oh," she said. "No. He's after birds. Long as he had to come out here anyway, he probably thought he might get us some birds."

"It's guts," despaired the little boy, "just only guts and feathers."

"Those upland birds," said Verity. "Father feels we have to eat 'em if they feed on our grain."

Then, as they came into the periphery of his vision, the old man wheeled to them, rifle at the ready. "Sage hens," he shouted.

These Harrows were white as white could be, except for the old man who was mahogany, and Purefoy was so far out of his element here that he'd circled back around and reentered it. Folks is folks, he told himself rather plausibly, and these folks were strange folks indeed; he felt somewhat at home.

While preparing them beans, and some unimaginably complex cornbread, Verity took a call from an herbicide salesman and made one to a trucker apparently in her employ; her end of the latter conversation made mention of a tire, and Beatrice would you please get off the line, and Monday afternoon, and absolutely no more excuses, meanwhile Purefoy idled most familiarly in their parlor, a very small room, with the silent ancient and the silent child who did not wear his glasses indoors, but who was, with or without them, eerie. The old one, Purefoy suspected, had taken the visitor's measure at once and was therefore indifferent to him. But who knew? The old cat wasn't saying, and didn't seem to feel the need, and more power to him. They had, like Papa Bear, Mama Bear, and Baby Bear three chairs, each with its own light, its own pile of books and periodicals. Their radio resided in a beautifully burled cabinet. When switched on, Purefoy would later learn, its tubes glowed warmly within it, producing also a warm little hum.

"Her piano," said the little boy at last, as if to offer it to him.

Purefoy looked into the alcove containing Verity's piano; there were pictures set out on top of it recounting her people who, it seemed, had been hunkered down out here for quite some time. Many of these pictures were of people no longer present. Way, way out here—no wonder these people were as they were—A person did not have to worry about making idle chat on this farm.

The shellac was worn through to bare wood where she sat her piano bench, and sure her instrument would be a lot more companionable than the people she lived with. Purefoy understood now why she had seemed so like his grandmother—women with too much to do, they radiated impatience, the personality of a staff sergeant. Regarding that bench polished raw, Purefoy had another feeling about the woman, another sense of her. This was where and how and why she'd got so good, and the thought of it made him sentimental.

He had come to play, Purefoy, and now he really wanted it, but maybe she had promised more than she could deliver after all. Her time was obviously not her own. And she had promised him time, hadn't she? World enough and time?

◊ ◊ ◊

"Carmine," said Purefoy, "I'm going to rip this phone out of the wall, you keep sending calls back here." The phone line into the embalming room was another executive decision on which he'd not been consulted. "You're sure they're not calling for my dad?"

"I *always* make sure," said Carmine, melodious even in distress. "This woman is so pushy, Mr. Purefoy, or you know I'd never ask: But, can you take it? Please?"

Purefoy peeled off one rubber glove. There was a click, and the receiver became a sea shell conveying a sense of ocean into his ear. He hung up and waited, leaving his naked hand naked. The phone rang again.

"Sorry. Sorry," Carmine said. "It's these buttons, I."

"Relax," said Purefoy. "Just relax, and aim for the one that's lit up, and mash that one. Take a deep breath and." Click. That distant sea again, but then a voice as well, "Up? You there? Hey, Ulysses?"

"Verity? Verity Harrow?" Odd, to hear himself say that name. He'd never used it much, and not at all for a long, long time. Not aloud.

"'Fraid so," she said. "Howdy. How've you been?"

"How'd you find me?"

"Called information," she said. "I'm quite the detective."

"Oh. Sure. But you didn't call the house, did you? My residential listing? Or, heaven forbid, you didn't call Senior's number?"

"Just here," she said. "Just the mortuary."

"I didn't mean to," he said, "I mean I have wondered sometimes. About you."

"Looks like you fell into the family business after all,"

she said. "Funny how that can happen."

"Turns out death is quite a bit more popular in Minnesota," said Purefoy, "than progressive jazz. We get most of the darker people in the area, so that's a nice steady business." He bled the dead for his handsome living now, and who begrudges the mortician his prosperity, and Purefoy wasn't usually shy about his work, an honorable profession, but her voice had taken him right back to that vacancy in him, the hole left by a young man's abandoned vocation. "So, yeah," he said, "I am the heir apparent to the funeral director. It's easy, once you're used to it. Pays for a house, my Buick, my boat, little runabout I take to the lake. Yep. Comfortable as *hell.*"

"Sorry to call you at work," she said. "You in the middle of something?"

He'd been sewing a mouth shut, a job he might have cited to end this conversation, but, "No," he said. "How often we get a chance to catch up? I mean how *have* you been?"

"Good," she said.

"Your father? Charlie?"

"He's older," she said. "If that's even possible. Older all the time."

"Little Jeet?"

"Not so little anymore," she said. "Duck-to-water down at the schoolhouse, so he's doing dandy."

"Yeah," said Purefoy, "but, really, what about you? You. . .?"

"Oh," she said. "No. It's just me and the boys. Harrow farms. Piano. I'm noodling away like always, my own audience. Good thing I'm a devoted fan, I'm my only audience, which is kind of galling, but. You playing anywhere?"

"No," he said, a sort of understatement. Purefoy had long since let his lips go soft so that he couldn't tolerate his own tone. He no longer even thought to listen carefully to a song and went months on end without thinking to regret it. But he had his regrets, and here they were, where, apparently, they'd been percolating in him, and he did not like his tone of voice, either, describing himself, "Square as a cardboard box these days. Pure Purefoy, one of Rochester's res*pec*table so-called negroes. You should see my lawn."

They'd had a half dozen weekends together on the farm during his last year and a half in the Air Force, and Purefoy had been at times so excited as to set all other considerations aside and talk of places he knew that might book them in the Twin Cities, of recording studios, of Birdland, why not? They were that good, he'd often thought, or could have been in time. They'd be like no one else—her mind and his technique—look out. The heart of the night was her best chance to play, so they played while the world slept, played all through the American song book, and once they'd played a single tune all night long, and Purefoy entered a bubble in that nook, that little house where they might be for a while be only a song, a song in the making, a single living thing.

They played each night until he was groggy. Verity Harrow never seemed to tire.

After they'd passed several such nights chastely Verity would tell him, "You know, you don't *have* to sleep in that sleeping bag. If you don't want to. I know I'm not that. . . or sleep in that chair. That chair dang near cripples you."

Unsure of the implication, he'd said, "I wouldn't want to ruin anything."

"Ruin?" she said.

"A good thing," he said. "We've got a pretty good thing."

"I guess," she'd said. "But I could sure stand to be ruined a little, if you don't mind."

The prairie chick. Mother of invention. She had invented a vernacular, and it fit him like nothing he'd know again. But her life, their lives, were not their own. It had ended, as they had always known it must, and she and all that he'd had with her had long been swallowed by that emptiness out there.

"I'm glad to hear you're still banging away at it," he said. "To play: That's the important thing."

"Sure," she said. "Anything to keep the bats out of the belfry. But that's not what I was calling about. I decided here lately I'd probably better let you know you've got a son."

"I," he said. "Sons," he said. "Two of them. And I'm married, Verity."

"I was fairly sure you would be by now," she said. "Congratulations. But I'm talking about a son with me. That we had. That last time you were out. I guess that rubber didn't do the trick. So, you're up to three now. Sons."

He had the used the Sheik he'd been carrying in his horn case since he was sixteen. For emergencies. It had smelled of valve oil, Purefoy now recalled. It had failed. He had failed. "I'm married," he said.

"You said that," she said. "Don't get wound up here, Ulysses. I'm only letting you know. You never intended, so I've never meant to ask for. I don't know. I finally decided you should at least have the choice. If you wanted to know him or not. But it was my idea up until now not to trouble you about it."

"Trouble me?"

"I took you by surprise," she said. "I know, I kinda sprung this on you."

"What am I supposed to . . . do?"

"Nothing," she said. "Probably easiest all around if you just stayed out of the picture. But, like I say, I thought it should be your choice to make. I'd come around to that point of view."

"He, he'd be—five?"

"Just turned six," she said. "Maybe I waited too long. I'm not suggesting I handled this just right."

"You don't know," said Purefoy, "what you've done."

"Made a baby," she said. "A nice one, I think. Around here we don't seem to bother about the usual formalities, but we wind up with some pretty good boys."

"Yeah but, Verity, this baby'll live in a world you don't know. You don't have the slightest idea what it'll be for him."

"The future?" she said. "Or—oh—that." Not that they'd failed to notice, having revealed so much flesh to each other, but their respective complexions was one topic they had never got around to discussing. "Well," she said, "between us, I guess you could say we made an Italian or something. Don't worry. I mean, he's beautiful. Be better looking, I bet, than either one of us."

"What's his name?" said Purefoy.

"Tel," she said.

"That's some kinda cowboy name, or?"

"Short for Telemachus," she said. "I didn't want to hang that whole thing on him, so I called him Tel."

"What?"

"Telemachus," she said. "Ulysses' boy? Don't you even know your own poem, man?"

"Yes, I do," said Purefoy. "Know that bitch inside and out, and you don't, and that's my point. You don't know."

VERITY

She followed her headlights north through Nevada desert about as barren as the looming moon; how good of the boys, she thought, to bear with her this way. Tel slept in the back seat. Jeet, another night person, rode bolt upright in front, hoping she might let him drive for a while. She'd had so little sleep recently that no amount of blinking would scrub the grit from her eyes, and Verity fiddled and fiddled with the radio dial, rolling it over a twitching medley of static, a steel guitar, static, an Okie selling redemption, static, an ad for Quaker State Motor Oil, an ad for Brylcreem, static, and the Everly brothers faintly urging them to, 'Dreee-eam. Dream, dream, dream.' She switched it off, and then there was just the rush of tires on blacktop, of wind through her wing window. They crossed counties this way—eighty-five miles an hour, ninety, and the stench of resignation stayed strong in that well-ventilated car, but Verity didn't mention it, nor, for miles on end, anything else. Home? Homeward. There was certainly no hurry about it, it would be waiting for them when they got there, but she seemed to need a certain amount of speed tonight. Speed for its own sake.

"At least," Jeet said at last, "we got to stick our feet in the ocean, see palm trees and boulevards and everything. From now on, when I read about that stuff, I'll know exactly what it is."

"They get no winter," Verity said. "No winter down there. So, who knows? Couple years without snow, you might decide you miss it." But she knew that she would never really come to want the cold, no matter how long she'd been removed from it.

Jeet, bored with the long night and his longer adolescence, renewed his case for a turn at the wheel. "Empty," he said. "It's just nothing out here. Can't be more'n about a car an hour coming at us."

"I must prefer it that way," she said. "Back in the big empty, huh?"

She was explicitly not his mother, Verity, but they shared a bad restlessness expressed in many wakeful nights and sometimes in long drives with and without destination during which they'd discovered they both suffered chronically from the idea that someone else, somewhere else, was being who they should have been. They understood themselves and each other as people misplaced. If Jeet had not a drop of blood in common with her, still Verity had shaped him in her way; if she wasn't his mother she could easily and maternally enough tweak his gut with just that note of defeat in her voice. They blasted along through a landscape of gravel and sand blanched by the gaping moon. Prickly pear everywhere, cluttering the ground.

"You know," Jeet said, "I hate it back home. Hate it even more now."

"Nah," she said. "That's no way to talk."

"Some day," he said.

But when? And what? And what now? There he sat wearing his freckles in their thousands, with that orange thatch on his head and another fringing his poor, pink penis. Fate had equipped Jeet Harrow altogether cruelly. His eyes were so sensitive to the glare of fair weather that he'd been sporting smoked lenses since early childhood; his skin could singe at the first touch of wind or sunlight and often burned with embarrassment when he was indoors. Commonly mistaken for a coward, he'd been in more fights than anyone he knew, but he had never become very handy with his fists. Who wouldn't turn inward? This series of unsuccessful fights had successively split his lip so deeply that he'd be a bit of a harelip henceforth, and he'd swallowed a tooth to leave a hole in the middle of his already fugitive smile, and as of that evening his wounds remained at a voluptuous, yellow and gray stage of their healing. Not yet, he thought. Not yet. Jeet was and must always be the red headed boy, but he was young enough then to think that when the time was ripe, or when he was, he would somehow escape himself.

◊ ◊ ◊

"It's time," she announced one day. "The boys were called to the superintendent's office, where she told them to gather up anything they wanted to take from the school, said they were leaving, said she'd boarded the horses with the Jacques, and packed the car, and fifteen minutes later Geraldine's grain elevators were receding in their rearview mirror. "It's time," she told them. "Cripes sakes, it's 1962 already—if we're ever gonna do it, better do it now before the bastards can get another chance to blow us all to hell."

She had been talking about Southern California, brought it up several times of late: What would they think about selling out and moving to the Los Angeles area?

Jeet, who might have volunteered to colonize Mars at that point, was all for it. He had read his Raymond Chandler and knew LA to be full of beautiful and dangerous people, guys and gals with gats, and depraved and quirky people, and Jeet felt that in the City of Angels anyone, just about anyone, should be able to fit in. The gold coast, a promised land—sure, what a thrill. Jeet went south all agog, delighted.

Tel, who even then loved the farm above everything, had loathed the idea of leaving it, and pouted when they left, but it was not in his nature to do so for long, and when he came around to the adventure was as wide-eyed as anyone. Tel, as a boy had that gift of letting everything wash over him, of taking it all in, and he'd developed a big appetite for California too.

And Verity couldn't remember when she hadn't wanted some indefinite something else, something on the other side of what she had before her.

First she'd been obliged to her ailing, failing mother, whose standards, however, never did decline and who wanted the house kept just so. Obviously, someone had to cook, and put up the canning, and bake the damned bread, so Verity had got crusty early on and fiercely efficient about slamming through her chores so as to turn her thoughts as soon as possible back to the ethereal and return her fingers to the keyboard. She was known as a girl for an array of quirks and strange interests, and it was while still a child, a dutiful child, that she'd become a night specimen, a hard thing for a farm girl and a terrible thing for her family who might be called upon to sleep with a hundred consecutive verses of 'Honeysuckle Rose', her improvisations edging into their dreams. "Such a Harrow," Mother had said of her girl. "They *do* go on. They're possessed, I often think. Is it any wonder I'm always so tired?"

When George went off to the Air Corps, it also fell to Verity to serve as Father's translator. It had been some time by then since Charlie had clearly heard his own voice, and his speech had become blurred, unmoored, and whenever he spoke at any length he'd begin to shout. Unable to hear if he was saying quite what he meant to say, Charlie could too plainly see the confusion and alarm his shouting caused, and it was a rough way to do business, and so Charlie had recruited his children, George, then Verity, to speak for him. With this additional duty, high school became impossible for her, and Verity had quit in spite of Mother's pointless protests, and so it happened through happenstance that Verity had become by turns a house frau, then a farmer, and she sustained herself in this by thinking it would end with the war. Then George died. How you gonna keep 'em down on the farm? Just like that. And Verity had grieved more than his dying. So much for Verity Harrow in the hallowed halls of ivy, in library stacks, and concert halls. Goodbye to that idle young woman considering rainy days through rain-streaked windows in coffee shops and garrets, reading notes from a wise lover. She'd meant to walk philosophically under shade trees. In those days she'd gone so far as to imagine some new venue in which she herself would become more elegant or at least less absurd. But then George had died, and long after he was gone, and after Dove and Charlie were settled into whatever reward awaited them in the plot down the lane, Verity remained her mother's creature, her father's voice, and she was still indentured to the good return to be had from working that ghost ridden farm.

Also, she'd acquired the boys along the way.

What she thought of as her life had been doled out to her in the wee hours, and when Verity admitted that she had become by day a tired, red-eyed, sharp-tongued horror—this trip was suddenly afoot with very little planning; the time had come for the impulse of the moment and her artistic temperament to be given their due, so she greased the Plymouth and they flew south that winter, a bird of turquoise tail fins. There was a bag of apples, loaves of sliced bread, and some potted meat to be eaten in the car, and, apart from the urging of the fuel gauge or someone's bladder, no reason to stop, and the thrumming of the motor crawled up inside her until her body hummed in harmony with her machine, and the miles scrolled by in the windshield like the pages of a book demanding to be read to the end. Verity drove them right into a milder climate. Windows down in December, they breathed in fragrant exhausts, and with her misfiring nerves and tired eyes beginning to play tricks on her Verity learned to drive the freeways. Negotiating asphalt and stucco cities without any open ground between them, towns defined only by name, they'd got deep into an ant hill in which it seemed to Verity she was the only ant not knowing where to go. She'd become so fuzzy headed she couldn't accurately calculate how long she'd been at the wheel, and rushing around three and four abreast with a world of fellow motorists she remembered that there must be more to any journey than simply going. There must be an arriving, too. She'd gotten woozy enough to be a little dangerous.

"Huntington Beach," Jeet read a billboard, its blood orange sun sinking into the sea.

Tel read them the sign's lower half. "Surf's Up," he said. "That sounds pretty good."

"Sure," said Verity. "Let's try that."

The Del Mar Motor Court seemed as likely a place as any: Salt Air! Kitchenettes!! Free TV!!! Clean and Comfortable rooms by the week and the month. Vacancy. Their room contained two large and stony beds, a television with rabbit ears, a sink, a hot plate, and the animal and chemical musk of sad events. Verity sent the boys to the bodega around the corner to buy some groceries while she transferred their things, as many as possible, from a pile on the floor to dresser drawers, but she hadn't half finished the job before she tried to rest her eyes, fell asleep on the bed, and was at once back on the freeways where dream motorists merged at her from either side and surged all around. The boys giggled to find her in this twitching condition when they returned from the store. Jeet slipped her shoes off and folded the coverlet over her.

Day and night were the same in that room with the curtain drawn over its picture window. She woke but for a long time didn't move. Jeet was sprawled on the other bed, reading a Gideon's bible by the mustard light of a bedstead lamp; Tel lay facing the other way, belly down, feet scissoring absently at the ceiling, watching Daffy Duck on the muted television. Verity's arm was numb under her. Heavy with guilty love, she spent a long time in unaccustomed meditation, not moving, and when she did move, she regretted it, the odd posture in which she'd slept trying to make a permanent claim on her. What the hell kind of California was this?

"What time is it?" she finally asked them.

"Thursday," Jeet said. "We ate all the food, but there's a Pepsi left if you want it."

"Wooo," she said, gingerly swinging her feet off the bed. "Now you know why I never nap."

Tel bounced up. "We're *starving*."

Verity showered and changed clothes and they went out to walk the last several blocks to the edge of the continent. Along a nearly idle street they encountered an Aztec looking woman and a girl with a similarly proud nose selling tamales, tacos, and exotic soft drinks from a cart. "Hungry," the girl declared at their approach. She pointed to each of them in turn and said, "Fifty, fifty, fifty." The girl shook her head as if at some shameful situation and she made a bowl of her hands and placed it over her stomach or the place where her stomach might have been if she'd had much of one. On the cart there was a propane burner, and on that a cauldron containing a pig's head looking up at them from a froth of burbling scum.

"What is it?" Tel said.

"Well," said Verity, "it's food, anyway."

"Mom," Tel said. "No."

"They're out here trying to make a living," Verity said. The cart was parked in the lee of a fat palm, a meagre wind break where the wind must blow all the time coming up the street from the ocean. "Heck, you've had tongue before, so this should be pretty. . ."

"No," said Tel. "I would *never* eat that. Remember?"

Jeet stood quietly by, trying to master his rising gorge.

"New things," said Verity in conclusion. "Might as well get used to 'em." She handed the girl a dollar bill and two quarters, and the girl replied with a tamale wrapped in corn husk and wax paper for each of them and by opening three sweating bottles of a sweet brown beverage. Meanwhile, the woman had begun to build tacos, a one-at-a-time operation. She lay a thick tortilla on a sheet metal dome to warm it, then with tongs and a long tined fork she tore strips of flesh from the hog's jowls and these she folded into the heated tortilla to which she added a red sauce, pinto beans, chopped cilantro, onion, and radish. She squeezed a wedge of lime over this construction and handed it with some ceremony to Tel.

"Mom," he said.

"Oh, just try a bite. It won't kill you. You don't want to embarrass these gals, do you? Hurt their feelings?"

"I might not mind," said Tel. "Did you see what she. . .?"

"A *bite*," Verity said.

Tel closed his eyes, closed all his senses as much as possible, put one end of the thing an inch into his mouth, tore off a morsel with his teeth and chewed furiously, but he had no luck keeping it off his tongue and soon enough he'd tasted it. "Oh," he said. "Oooh. . ." He tore off another, bigger bite. "It's de-*lish*-ous," he said. "O*kay*."

The older woman tried to give the next taco she built to Jeet, who held his palms up.

"Aw, come on," Verity said.

"I've had enough," Jeet said. "I'm not hungry," the pure truth of the moment. "That other thing was plenty for me."

Verity and Tel soon understood they'd bought all the tacos they could possibly eat, for as soon as they'd finished one either the woman or the girl would be pressing another on them along with soft but urgent Spanish. Jeet stood by, looking down, looking off and away from the hog's ravaged face, and the girl, regarding him with a showy distaste, tried to return a quarter to Verity, but Verity said she wouldn't dream of it. This was a bargain, she said, a rare treat for them. They ate and ate until the woman was finally convinced they could eat no more. The woman, a thick black braid trailing down her gingham bosom, put her hands on her hips to take satisfaction in a job well done, in Tel who was grunting or sighing little exhalations, part joy and part distress; red sauce and grease ran from his wrist to his elbow. "*Cariño*," the woman said, adoring him.

Jeet, feeling he'd been his queasiest little self so far and far less than bold, took it upon himself to lead the way to the beach then, and when he reached it, he spread his arms panoramically and declaimed, "The biggest thing in the world."

"What?" said Tel. "What is?"

"That ocean," said Jeet. "That's the Pacific Ocean."

"Mmn," said Tel.

"And here we are," said Jeet importantly. "Looking at it."

"What's that blob?" Tel said. "That big green thing? That slimy deal. What is that? Wanna touch it?"

"You can lick it," said Jeet, "if you're so curious."

"Come on," said Verity. "Let's take our shoes off and walk down to the pier. Sand's nice, huh? Ever think we'd be goofing around barefoot this time of year?"

None of them was accustomed to go anywhere but to bed unshod, and so they minced down the strand recording three sets of tender tracks, and the waves washed up and receded, hypnotic as open flame, leaving a foam lace on the sand and speaking to them, that same word incessantly, 'reeeh-laaahx—reeeh-laax,' and as inlanders they were astonished to see how many sea shells the sea threw up on the beach. Pebbles and sharp shells. There were young men, some of them blue with cold, riding long boards on the waves. The Harrows collectively caught their breath when one of them rode his board right through the pilings under the pier. He was not killed.

"Now, that's for me," Tel said. "I've got to try that."

"You can't swim," Jeet reminded him.

"I haven't even tried," Tel said. "But I bet I could do it. *Fish* swim, so how hard could it be?"

Her senses refreshed perhaps by their walk, Verity noticed upon their return to unit 17 that its walls were infused with mold and that behind one of them the couple in 18 were conducting a very audible affair. Their names were Jack and Tim and they were vigorously then unhappily in love with each other, and even when Tel was allowed unfettered access to the television's volume knob the couple's exertions next door continued to mingle with the roar of gun play.

"We'll have to do better than this," Verity said.

"I like the beach," Tel said. "Quite a bit. And that food we had. We get three teevee stations just clear, and couple more fuzzy ones. It's all right here."

"I'd be fine, too," Jeet said, "if I had something else to read. About had it with these prophets. Prophets and shepherds and who slew who. I don't see where it's about God at all."

Tel used his best, most wicked grin on her. "It's kind of icky, Mom, but you'd have to admit, it's very funny, too."

"Poor guys," she said. "I mean, I don't want to know that much about *anybody's* romance. And you boys shouldn't be. . . Shouldn't. . . Well, I think we can do better."

They went out again and returned to a hole in the wall

they'd passed by earlier, Bedrock Books. A very fat and yet very delicate suspendered clerk sat near the store front window, surrounded by displays of magazines, Chiclets, and cigarillos. The clerk balanced a transistor radio on his shoulder, listening impassively to basketball scores and then the call of a horse race, and he didn't seem to mind or particularly notice the Harrows loitering among tilted stacks of books in the back, partaking freely of his wares. After an hour of this Tel selected the six Superman comics he hadn't already read on site, and Jeet, using his own hard-earned money, bought *Henley's Practical Approach to Ventriloquism, Life on the Mississippi, The Confessions of St. Augustine*, and several packs of clove chewing gum. Verity, wanting information more than entertainment, came away from the Bedrock with a trade paper, and the Thomas guide to the streets of Los Angeles County.

The next morning, they formed another expedition, Verity driving the Plymouth again, Jeet as navigator with the Thomas guide in his lap, and Tel the hyper-excited passenger sliding from side to side in back. "Hollywood," he sang, "duhn, duhn, duhn, duhn, duhn, Hahl-eeh-wood."

"*West* Hollywood," Jeet said. "It's in West Hollywood."

"That must be where they make the shoot-cm-ups," Tel concluded. "I could probably get a job as an Indian kid. They could dress me up in buckskins."

"I think," Verity said, "we must have landed in the wrong part of town, down there by the beach." She would soon discover that no matter where she was in Los Angeles, she was twenty-five miles away from where she needed to be. So much rushing around, so much seething humanity, and how fertile this ground must have been before it was all paved over. But there were several million pairs of ears here and some chance of an audience, and this was the place to look, she thought, if she was looking to be heard.

Jeet directed them to 817 Vine Street, a boxy white building of depressing modernity that seemed to Verity a soulless abode for any kind of union hall much less Musicians Local 47, but once inside she liked the waft of floor wax and the nice cacophony leaking from the doors of a half dozen rented practice rooms. There was in this mix an oboe working its way through scales in minor keys. She stopped at the glassed door stenciled **BUSINESS OFFICE**, and told the boys, "This looks like the ticket," and pushed into a room with filing cabinets lining one of its long walls and windows all along the other. There was a woman at the windows gazing out and down to the street as if she wished to escape to it. A bank of telephones, a maze of blond wood cabinets, and the woman at the window was alone with all of it. Built like a professional wrestler with a coil of wheaten hair spiraling from the crown of her head, she turned to them and sighed, and came to the counter on a pair of extremely high heels; the name tag riding her ruffed blouse said she was Mrs. Scapelli; her expression suggested that here at last she was met with a form of eccentricity she could not abide. "Can I help you?"

"Came to see about joining your union," Verity said.

"Vocalist?" said Mrs. Scapelli. "Chanteuse?" she said drily.

"Never so anyone could hear me. I'm a piano player. So, what do I need to do?"

"You pay an initiation fee and your first year's dues," Mrs. Scapelli said. She seemed to think this would end the conversation.

"That should be fine," Verity said, "if it means I can get work."

Verity was given an application, but this amounted immediately to a list of problems. Address: 17, Del Mar Motor Court, Huntington Beach—only very temporarily.

Phone: Verity didn't know it, and it would soon be useless anyway. Musical Education: None. Ensemble experience: None. As Verity was considering all this, Mrs. Scapelli asked questions pertinent to completing a referral card. "Style?" she said. "Or styles?"

"Style?"

"Of music," said Mrs. Scapelli. "What do you play?"

"Oh." Verity consulted the boys. "What was the word?"

"Eclectic," Jeet offered, "I think that's what you said."

"Nuts," said Tel. "Crazy style."

"Well," Verity said, "I'm serious. Serious about it."

"I see," said Mrs. Scapelli, disapproving. "Sight read?"

"Some things," said Verity. "Some things I have to figure out. I'm self-taught."

"Doesn't sight read," Mrs. Scapelli said and wrote.

"I can play anything by ear," Verity said.

"That's fine," said Mrs. Scapelli. "But we can't very well send out two musicians for one job, can we? Somebody to play the music so you can hear it and then play it? That wouldn't make much sense, would it? Our members are professional musicians. That means most of them sight read. Anything. Everything."

"You telling me those dues'd be a waste of money in my case?"

Mrs. Scapelli advised, "Membership does provide some insurance coverage."

"If I wanted insurance," Verity said, "I think I'd probably just go to an insurance agency. But I'll be back. Get my situation figured out, and I'll be back."

"Fine," said Mrs. Scapelli.

"Would you take a check on a bank out of Fort Benton, Montana? Take a while to clear, but it'll be good."

"Shall we worry about that if it becomes necessary?"

"Oh, I'll be back," said Verity. "Be reading like

Paderewski, too. I'll be all brushed up on that, too."

"Well," said Mrs. Scapelli dispiritedly, "that's the spirit."

Verity was well accustomed to the fumbled first impression. She was odd, she knew, and often abrasive. Jeet could also be odd in his contained way, and Tel, poor thing, was odd by association, and the three of them together were a collective abnormality, a strange formulation of family. No one knew quite what to make of them.

Mrs. Scapelli had softened a little, and she said, "You aren't by any chance a beatnik, are you dear?"

Verity considered it. "May*be*," she said. "Maybe that's what I've been all along, now that I think of it. You boys beatniks?"

"I'm not," Tel said.

"I could think of worse things," and Jeet touched his sunglasses thoughtfully.

"Jazz?" Mrs. Scapelli inquired.

"Well, yeah," Verity admitted. "More than anything else. But I hate to bring it up. Kind of spooks people when you bring that up."

"Not here," said Mrs. Scapelli. "It's a real infestation around here." She thought it a pretentious music, and ugly, and Mrs. Scapelli thought this young woman from Fort Wherever rather fit the bill as she dressed and carried herself like a longshoreman, and wasn't it just like these jazz people to take something plain but perfectly serviceable, a song, one's person, and ornament it or strip it down until it was unrecognizable and unlovely. "Good luck," she said somewhat sincerely.

Out in the hall again, Verity was now intimidated by the hell clamoring from those practice rooms—professional musicians, and all of them banging at their tunes, their arpeggios staccato and legato. "Sheesh," she said. "Big talker, me. I better not show my face in that place again anytime soon."

Sensing something had gone amiss, Jeet asked her, "You still want to try that other place? That club you mentioned?"

"Of *course*, we do," Tel said. "Let's *go*. Marilyn Monroe. Geeze, it's Hollywood, who knows what's out there. What if they're making a chariot race today? Would you want to miss that?"

Verity was sweating unseasonably as might be expected of the pilgrim having advanced on bloody knees to within a few blocks of her personal Kaaba, her Shrine of Guadalupe. If the boys should happen to guess how giddy she was right now, she was afraid she might forever lose any authority with them. Could she be trusted? Not necessarily. "As long as we're already in the neighborhood," she said.

The Manne Hole, had been, as much as anything else, what had caused her to throw everything over and to leave the farm entirely in the hands of hired help and interrupt the boys' education. She was behaving, she thought, as foolishly as a normal woman might for the sake of a man. It had been in her mind since she'd read of it in the summer issue of Downbeat; never intending to, she'd retained large parts of the article verbatim. *It's a howl. It's a phenomenon. It's a mecca. In the two short years since Shelly Manne opened his club down on beat Cahuenga Boulevard, it has become the pot where West Coast jazz is cooked and the stage where East Coast jazz is imported. What's new? That's the question now being answered every night but Monday at the Manne Hole.* This account had tickled every hunger in her. It had been sounding hourly in her head since she'd first read it. "Long as we're this close," she said, "we might as well get a look at it. See where it is at least."

There were along the way shops selling plastic masks of movie stars, pot metal six shooters, and other garish trash, and the sidewalks were populated by pamphleteers, panhandlers, and tourists, some of whom had turned menacing at the discovery that any glamour in this town was by invitation only, and no one in their crowd was being invited. "Crummy," Tel said. "This can't be it. Are you reading that map right? This can't be it."

"Here," said Jeet. "Right here. This is where we turn onto Cahuenga. I'm taking us right to it. See? Cahuenga."

"What are those?" Tel asked. "Are those. . .? Is that guy wearing *shorts*?"

"Bermudas," said Verity. "It's a style."

Some misguided soul had clad the front of the Manne Hole in weathered wood, an effect not rustic but contrived in a brick and mortar neighborhood, and the club, just one city lot wide, crouched between other low, skinny buildings, and Verity was so disappointed at first by this small and possibly silly reality that she nearly drove on by, but Jeet said, "Here it is," so proudly.

"Did you think it was this dinky?" Tel asked as she parked.

The club was closed at that hour, and she couldn't have gone in with the boys anyway, not to a bar, but Verity stood on the crusty sidewalk out front and browsed a history of performances that had been published by stapling successive posters to the barnwood wall. These were plain notices, most of them, a name or names and a date or dates. The names, as she read them, made her sweat again.

"Why's everything so crummy?" Tel wondered.

"Bill Evans was here," she said. "Just last month."

Jeet would later recall hearing something in her voice, later remember this as the very moment that set a whole chain of events in motion.

She drove them back to the Del Mar and they walked from there to the beach again to lunch on breaded sand dabs and watch the waves for a while. The boys ran on the sand; Verity paced on it. Returning to the room, she bought a salami, some soda crackers, and crystals they could use to make fizzy water right there in the unit, and she said, "You don't need to do this like a pack of wolves. You could make it last a while."

She bathed then, and bathed some more until Jeet was rapping on the bathroom door, and wondering, "You okay in there?"

"Oh, fine," she said. "Trying to get clean. I needed quite a soak." She came out in gabardine trousers `a la Hepburn, she hoped, and a silk blouse of cowgirlish design, yippee-ti-ye; it was the debut of clothes she'd owned for years. Her toes burst in astonishment from open toed pumps that were also making their maiden voyage. Still more striking, Verity had concealed the geometry of her self-inflicted hair cut under a blue head scarf.

"Mom?" Tel recoiled.

"What do you think? Too much?"

"Not at all," said Jeet. "But it is different. You are. Or, I mean—looks fine."

"I'm going back to the Manne Hole," she said. "Thought I'd go back. They've got this gal coming in tonight, this Alice McLeod, and I don't know her, but she's their headliner, so she'd have to be pretty good. So, I'm going back in. You two'll be fine on your own for a while."

"You should look like this all the time," Tel said, composed again. "This is actually way better, once I'm used to it."

She waited until she was in the car to apply her lipstick, a new acquisition, and, working in the rearview mirror by the light of the dome light which her head nearly obscured, and with no prior experience, she thought she did a creditable job of smearing her lips with it; but that shade, the red associated with emergencies, and it was so much glossier on her face than it had looked in the tube. She felt ridiculous but was going to Hollywood, and where else would a person go if they were looking to guild the goddamned lily? Lately she'd been asking herself, 'What's with the boots and the dungarees?' Lately, Verity Harrow had been thinking that maybe it wasn't entirely necessary to always celebrate her lack of a cute personality or a turned-up nose.

Though often alone, she was rarely so lonely as this. She came too early to the club. The Manne Hole was no bigger inside than the Ozark Club had been before it burned, and the California club was even more crowded for containing a small kitchen. As many tables and chairs as possible had been crammed into the space between the bar and the knee-high bandstand, but at that there was seating for two dozen patrons at most. Verity the businesswoman wondered how the proprietors made this proposition pay— she'd paid no cover charge—and Verity the fan wondered, 'Bill Evans played *here*?' She had learned two of the man's early albums note for note and had assumed without thinking much about it that he must have a horde of a following and need a large hall for his audience anywhere he might play. There were other names on the posters outside that were almost equally exalted in her estimation, and it was so hard to associate them with a small room that looked to have been decorated by a dull teenager. She'd come a half an hour before the evening's scheduled performance to be sure of having a good seat to see this Alice McLeod, headliner, piano player, so Verity was waiting alone with the bartender who assured her that people would come straggling in, all in good hipster time. To satisfy an old curiosity and to pass that time, Verity asked for a mint julep. Bourbon and sugar. Her mood swung this way and that. At nine she was still alone with the bartender, beginning to think a mistake had been made, but there was a nice baby grand on that little stage, so this must be right. "I'll take another," she said. "You can skip the sugar and mint and just give me the whisky." If she got loopy or lonely enough, she thought, she might just climb up there and play that thing herself, her specialty, after all, playing to an empty room.

Three couples arrived as a group, variously hued people generally somber as a panel of judges coming into court. Verity's first glance caromed off the men's tight trousers. To the shoes, then. The women had tottered in on those popular spikes that thrust them up and forward and sculpted their calves, a fashion on par for Verity's purposes with Chinese foot binding. The men's shoes were merely impractical. But no. She hadn't come so far to stare at people's feet. Look up. Wordlessly, as if by prior design, the group shoved three tables together so that they might sit behind them, shoulder to shoulder and face the stage. Their heads seemed large. This could be an effect of the small, nearly brimless hats the men wore, or of the women's lofty hair-dos, or of the whisky Verity had been drinking. Nothing of consequence had happened yet, certainly no music, and Verity the untrained celebrant was already drunk.

A chattering blade of a man from the new group came back to the bar; all but writhing in his delight with himself, and he said, "Gerald, please tell me you've stocked Courvoisier at last. I have been clinging to that hope."

"We are," said Gerald, "just barely beyond selling sandwiches here. And Mr. Manne does the liquor order when he's in town, as you very well know. So why do you have to come in and work me over about this, Pinewood? I happen to have some decent champagne, though."

"I like browner things," said Pinewood from out of his small, neat skull, his eyes active all the time. "All right, your house scotch. We'll go high yellow at least. Make it six, and six soda backs. They can drink what I drink, if I'm buying. Or seven, Gerald, why not a lucky seven? You can set this lady up, too. See if it improves our luck."

"Thanks," said Verity. "You're—what was it? Pinewood?"

"Was," he said, "and is."

"Well, thanks," she said, and she told him her name, front and back, and shook his hand, which seemed to amuse him. Those quick eyes passed over her again, and she saw his curiosity entirely satisfied, his strafing interest moving on already, but Pinewood, bless him, had referred to her as a lady, which was novel enough, and Pinewood's date was staring daggers at them, and Verity could never remember having inspired jealousy in anyone, and what an unexpected thrill; in years to come she would come to think it pathetic how often and fondly she'd call to mind this fun misunderstanding.

The club's custom came dribbling in, and now she was lonesome in a crowd. They did seem so expectant, but did they have to breathe down her neck? Did every last one of them need to light a cigarette? Drinks in either hand, Verity claimed a chair so near the stage that she might have propped her heels on it. She waited, drinking, thinking she was fundamentally a thing of vast sobriety, a child of the great wide open, and she did not feel well. Pinewood's voice could be heard at intervals above all the others. She heard him complain of, ". . . another ofay organization." Still no songs. But then, and suddenly after so much waiting, there were men on the stage, Shelley Manne himself, and his men, and with that big piano, a standup bass, and a full drum kit, and horn players standing side by side, they fairly filled it. Manne, drumsticks and brushes in hand, explained there'd been some mix up with Alice at the airport, but that she was on her way, and into the otherwise respectful silence Pinewood said, "Ofays. See, I knew it."

"So," said Shelly Manne, until then. . ."

Fresh drinks continued to land on the table near her elbow; Verity wanting no distractions, could not be bothered to find or thank her benefactor, but she did absent mindedly drink the drinks. Once begun the playing sounded in her chest as much as her ears, and the very motions of the players vibrated into the stage, and through the floor, and up into her feet. She listened with her whole being. How rare for Verity Harrow to be so pleased with herself, but wasn't she a fantastic audience? She heard chord changes bouncing from Greece to Africa, felt polyrhythms shivering through her, and before long she'd got brutally smitten by the tenor man, a trim fellow in a trim suit. A wedding band round his finger. But what a mind. What a horn. They were all so wonderful, and to hear them playing near and in concert, in sympathy—precisely why she'd come. Precisely why she was alive. She was here. On the scene. Verity was inclined to love everyone, and her heart was a pump well primed for the arrival at last of Alice Mcleod.

In the length of her neck and the grace of her carriage Alice Mcleod was a second coming of Nefertiti, chic in an apricot sheath. Unannounced but not unnoticed, she flowed in, and the room parted to make her a path to the bandstand, and the band stopped like a dropped egg. Shelly Manne came out from behind his kit to offer her his hand. She took it, stepped lightly up, and whispered a seeming secret into the drummer's ear. His face tried several expressions before settling on one of triumph, and he raised her hand as if she'd won a prizefight. "Ladies and gentlemen," he announced. "Alice McLeod." He paused for their applause, and then he milked it, his headliner's hand still aloft. When the clapping and hooting faded, he said. "We've hit a little snag tonight. The fellows Alice usually plays with couldn't make it out of Detroit this morning, her erstwhile band, but ladies and gentlemen, with your kind permission, and if Alice agrees, we'll carry on in the fine tradition of the Manne Hole, we'll make like humanity and improvise. May we be your ad hoc side men, madame, the Men and I?"

Alice Mcleod did not suffer speech to trouble her serene demeanor but serenely touched the back of the young man on the piano bench who relinquished it at once, bowing to her with his hands pressed together. The young man stepped down from the stage and claimed the chair nearest Verity's, and Verity, never previously exposed to any kind of fellowship, felt quite encircled by piano players, people ogling each other's hands. The young man, whose work Verity had admired when his back was to her, she now saw had a great deal more to recommend him. Just beautiful.

Alice Mcleod played a swooning version of 'How Are Things in Glocca Morra?' Her fingers seemed to draw the keys up as well as depressing them, her hands to stroke and caress her lucky instrument. A woman playing. A woman's playing, sweet not saccharine. Verity leaned into the performance, her forearms on her thighs, her slight decorum abandoned. Eventually Shelly Manne ticked in on his hi-hat, taking things up tempo tic by tic, and the other players joined one by one, and Shelly Manne juked the beat until they'd made the tune a big Calypso, but it was still somehow Glocca Morra, and Alice Mcleod's technique remained perfectly fluid even in service to a jumping arrangement, and she led them on a detour through 'Lester Leaps In' and back out again to Glocca Morra, and all the while there was rapture on Alice Mcleod, her face the perfect expression of Verity's feeling sometimes when she was playing well, an expression Verity herself could never conceivably express.

Alice Mcleod stopped eventually to ask for water. "Would someone be so kind?" she asked. "No ice."

There was murmuring, and a flurry of glasses being passed forward. Into this interval Verity Harrow slumped happily. She had at some point forgotten how to naturally breathe, an excess of sighing having broken that rhythm. The young man beside her was sighing also, her handsome hero of a piano player, but then Verity heard him say, and she was sure she heard him say under one such wheezing breath,

"Fucking bitch."

◊ ◊ ◊

The memory, her most recent one, was on her before she'd opened her eyes—she'd been a sudden fountain of chewed sand dab, whiskey, and bile, vomiting on his shoes. Verity woke at day break on a day bed in a furnished room, misery slouching through all her senses, and through throbbing eyes she gradually understood the lump on the floor to be the young man whose name she didn't know or had forgotten, though Shelly Manne had at some point announced it—sleeping there where he'd made a pallet for himself. Sleeping like a prince. His foolishness hadn't involved much alcohol. "Hey," she said. Why whisper? They were alone. She was trying to wake him. "Hey," she hissed.

He rolled to her, not rising. "What?"

"Can I use your phone?" she said.

"Phones?" he said. "Wouldn't have one."

"Say," she said, "I'd pay you five dollars for a tube of tooth paste right now, or even just a couple squirts from one."

"Make it a thousand," said the young man from the floor, "and you've got yourself a deal." He rolled away again, and with his back to her he said. "In the bathroom.

Toothpaste, baking soda, anything you want in there. You can even use my toothbrush if you'll throw it away. There's a pay phone down on the corner by the drugstore. Other than that, could you please leave me alone? We're a long way from noon, man."

Lipstick had spread across her cheek nearly to her ear; she looked quite the cadaver in that mirror, in his clinically lit bathroom. Was that her liver complaining? Had she hurt herself? In cupped hands Verity scooped water from the faucet into her mouth, enough of it that she nearly caused another round of retching. She was not sound, but terribly, terribly sober. Having gargled something vile, she took some of his aspirin, and swallowed until she was sure she would keep them down. Oh, the damages. She wetted a washcloth to scrub herself and wipe at her defiled clothes. She found and cleaned the young man's shoes. She washed the wash cloth. There remained then those stains on her evening she couldn't wash away.

But hadn't it started with him and his nasty remark? She remembered a point in the evening when the room, the Manne Hole, and the night generally had begun to slowly wheel around her, and then he'd said that thing, and she hadn't known what he meant exactly, or to whom he was speaking, and it was obvious no one else had even heard him, but she'd heard, and she hadn't liked it, and because she was drunk or because she was Verity Harrow she couldn't let it pass, and she'd challenged him. "*What?* What did you say?" The sheepish downsweep of the young man's eyes further infuriated her, and she'd said, "Well, fuck *you.*" This everyone had heard. Everyone within earshot. Everyone in that club. And they'd turned to her, open mouthed, as if she'd said it to each of them individually, and what a still moment that had been. Then the carousel had accelerated.

He'd been kind, or maybe it had just been the bum's

rush, but he'd followed her out into the night air, and as she fixed on a semi-distant street lamp and inhaled the improbable weather, the young man had turned apologetic. He explained, "I get a chance once in a blue moon to sit in with those guys. And I was, tonight, or I thought I was, holding my own. You okay? I mean musically. I was on fire, man. Then *she* sails in all transcendent, and Boyo's chopped liver again. I'm an envious little turd sometimes, but. You sure you're all right?"

Verity was well enough to think him handsome again. "You were good she'd said. "You were fine."

"I didn't mean—Or I probably did. A person hates to be so ugly."

"It's all right," she said. She understood nothing if not envy, and how quick and fickle her shifting sympathies. She was suddenly ready to forgive much in this sunkissed athlete. "There are some things," she said, "you don't need to explain at all. Not to me."

"You have a way home?" he said. "Other than driving?"

So, they had gone off in his car. Quiet in his car. And up the echoing stairs to his room. And then she had vomited on his shoes.

◊ ◊ ◊

Scrubbed, Verity slipped out of his building into a morning still mercifully touched by dew. Suffering, she waited on the corner for the drugstore to open so she could make change and use the pay phone. A nearby bird sang a three-tone tune that was new to her, and she made a point of breathing deeply, deliberately; her flaring nostrils may have had some part in attracting the cruiser that rolled up beside her—black and white, POLICE. The officer riding shotgun asked her, "Enjoying ourselves?"

"I'm not enjoying anything," Verity said.

"Working then?" The patrolman seemed mostly sinew. "We on the job this morning?"

"We? Ah." This cracked her grin. Sure, she'd look the part, her toes still hanging out of those ridiculous pumps, chilled and gray now. Sure, she'd be looking chancy as any hooker. "I think," she said, "you could safely call me a tourist here. But thanks for asking." The law rolled on, the joke subsided, and Verity was sad again. A certain sadness hung over this town like clouds of swamp gas. To think of the poor people still lust ridden and prowling the streets at this hour of the day.

Her fist finally full of dimes and quarters, she made three calls from a fish-smelling phone booth, one to information, and two to the impenetrably stupid desk clerk at the Del Mar Motor Court who could not or would not understand the switchboard and patch her through to line seventeen, and who claimed he might be fired if he left the desk to deliver a message.

Verity returned to the young man's building, two floors of long brown bricks crowned with a plaster frieze and cornice. It would not be as easy to enter as it had been to leave. Met with a brass plate and a line of buzzer buttons, she tried the door: No go. So, the nine buttons. One of these, she hoped, might gain her entrance, but which one? There were brackets under the buttons for name cards but just two of the tenants had made use of them: O.O. Ombuteh and Caroline Yee. Verity could only touch buttons randomly then, she'd never noted the number of the young man's room; thinking to work her way systematically through them, she pressed number nine. A burst of dental drill came through the speaker and then, almost at once, "Oh, hello," a wobbling voice, feminine and gentrified.

"Sorry," said Verity. "Sorry to disturb you, ma'am. I got a wrong. . . I made a mistake."

"Oh," said the old woman. "Are you sure?"

"I'm looking for someone else."

"Of course you are," said the old woman.

Verity tried the number eight button, waited twenty seconds and tried it again.

"Yeah." It was him, the young man. He was unhappy.

"It's me," said Verity. "The gal from earlier."

There was another buzz, but she had not been prepared to thumb the latch, so with her pride wadded like wet cotton in her chest—what an incompetent—she buzzed back. "Could you do that again?"

He buzzed her in. The stairwell was tiled and again quite resonant. Rounding into the second floor hallway, she saw that he'd left his door ajar for her. He lay on the daybed staring at his ceiling as she came in.

"Morning," she said.

"Bewh," he said. "Don't I know it?"

"I know I'm being quite a pain," she said. "But I need you to tell me how to get back to my car, where to catch the bus. Which bus to take, you know."

"Tell you?" he said. "We're in Glendale."

This meant nothing to her. "I don't even remember how far it was. I wasn't navigating that great."

"If you'll wait a while," he said, "I can drive you back over."

"Got some boys," she said, "probably wondering what's become of me. I better not wait."

The young man groaned and passed his hand over his face as if to conform its flesh to its bones. He didn't appear to have been that much damaged by the night. "Boys?" he said.

"My boys," she specified.

The young man groaned again. "All right, just let me try and get this crick out of my neck."

"Can I apologize for everything all at once?" she said. "The yelling. The trouble. I'd sure be happy to buy you some gas. I didn't really mean to yell at anyone."

"You sounded very sincere to me." The young man sat on the day bed, the heels of his hands set on the edge of it as if to push up, but he stalled there, his chin lifting slowly up and down. Verity did not take this for agreement. Except for his shoes, he wore what he'd worn last night. His clothes were miraculously unwrinkled. He'd not even loosened his tie. Blond. In this light, clearly blond. For having passed a rough night on the floor, he was still such a pleasure to look at. "I'll probably cope," he said. "You said I was good, and that has to be worth something."

"I liked your whole outfit," she said. "Everybody in it."

"It's not my outfit. Russ Freeman had the flu. I was moping around as usual, so they said I could sit in."

"You were still good," she said. "You guys had me going way before Alice McLeod came in. You were very good."

"Now you're talking," he said. That angular jaw, his dimpled chin moving slowly up and down.

"You're better than me," she said. "Tell you that much."

This brought his eyes to her at last. "Than you? What are you? You play?"

"That's why I'm here," she said.

"Here?"

"In the city," she said.

Verity excused herself to drink at the bathroom sink again. There was ceremony in it, a cool cleansing that came of scooping water up in her hands. But that damned vanity mirror. What could she possibly mean by that haircut? All those horrible haircuts? What would possess a person to sabotage her own appearance? Into her hangover crept a sense of injustice. Were these the thousand-yard peepers she presented the world? No wonder she was lonely. She'd been hiding from herself for so long up on Square Butte Bench, telling herself she was only too busy, and now she was an old woman intruding on a young man's room, but that room reassured her some when she got a good look at it. He must be every bit as strange as she was, he must easily match her eccentricity for eccentricity. Sweet and sour. His air was thick with ginger as the alley behind a Chinese restaurant; chow Mein noodles crunching underfoot. There was nothing here much resembling a table or a chair, for furniture there was only the day bed and the big hassock at its foot. There were enough wires, knobs, and gauges in the young man's stereo system, Verity thought, that he might have used it to send up a space shot with a live monkey. He had hundreds of albums in their fussy plastic cases, a whole section of venerable 78s. Dehydrated and in heat already, Verity also suffered a certain lust after those records, she would have loved to hear some of those records, but again—no time. The young man knelt near the hassock, a crusty leather item pretty obviously retrieved from the street on which there was a dusty copy of *The Naked and the Dead*, and, nearer the young man there was a tray that had recently served as a packet, a much creased square of wax paper piled with white powder. From the cuff of his sock the young man pulled a short length of straw. He offered it to her. "You want?"

"What is it?" she said.

"Whites," he said. "Dirt cheap. I crush 'em up for my convenience."

"Whites?" she said. "And what's that?"

"About thirty-five cups of coffee," he said, "all at once."

"I like my coffee black," she said.

The young man shrugged, lowered to address the powder, and using both nostrils in turn, he sucked it off the wax paper tray. With an air of resolve he rocked back on his heels, his pupils already smaller.

"Gee," said Verity. "Will you be okay to drive now?"

"Okay?" he said. "I'm Juan Manuel Fangio. At Le Mans, man. And I know *all* the surface streets."

He kept his high-mileage Eldorado in an underground parking garage across the street from his building, safe behind a rolling steel door. She didn't remember the rigmarole with chains and pulley from the night before, nor even his car particularly, though when he drove it up into the light of day it proved glorious, those chrome cones advancing like warheads through a vast chrome grille, a big cat of a car purring along on its whitewalls. The young man drove it up to the street, parked, and skinned the canvas roof back from his great, creamy sedan as Verity was ratcheting down the steel door. He pointed skyward, "You don't mind? A little fresh air?"

"I'll take as much of that," she said, "as you've got."

They rolled out reclined on blood red leather, the young man talking up a storm. Compelled by his drug or by something to explain himself, he said he lived on an allowance, imagine that, and that he relied on his membership at the three country clubs where he hustled golf, which had become, he admitted, a little tedious by now. She wondered what happened if he lost. He never lost, he said. He said he was a focused person, a person who went down wormholes of concentration. From ten to nineteen his focus had been golf; he said he could get around any course with four clubs, that he carried his own bag, that he walked the course, a point of honor. But it was time consuming, he said. The young man said he was in a hurry because he'd never touched a piano until he was nineteen years old; he rather despaired of it. "You start so late," he said, "and you look around at all these cats who played in the cradle. They're natives, they're naturals. Me, it'll always be a second language. The Soviets are right about this. Start 'em early. Get 'em before they've even learned to think. Rachmaninov, right from the start. You start so late, you're always scrambling to keep up. Meanwhile, down in Bel Air my golf swing is absolutely grooved. It's tawdry. They line up to be skinned. They make appointments to lose to me, and, except for actually taking their money, and I mean seeing them count it out in my hand, that kind of golf is drudgery anymore. But you thought I was a musician, didn't you? I've made up for lost time, don't you think?"

This, she thought, would be a good time to ask, "How old are you now?"

He complained of being twenty-eight, and truly he was several years older than she would have thought. Tan, and not parboiled like the boys back home. A kind of well-kept man who slept in if he wanted. So, he was not so terribly young after all, but still fresh, and how luscious, and awful, and urgent to ride with him, and when they found her Plymouth settled on its hubs and differential case, looted in Hollywood, Verity's despair was considerably tempered by the thought that at least she wouldn't have to say goodbye to the young man just yet.

"Now what?" he asked her.

"I still have to get to those boys," she said.

"And they're?"

"In Huntington Beach," she said.

"Why?" he said, verging on despair himself.

"No reason," she said. "It's where they happen to be."

"Huntington Beach," he said. "Is that where you're from?"

"Montana," she said.

"The mountains," he dreamed.

"Nah." Unexpectedly, unaccountably proud of it, she said, "We're more open-country people. High plains people. I mean it, though. I'll owe you a whole tank of gas. Believe it or not, I don't usually inconvenience folks. That's not what I do at all. It's embarrassing."

"You get embarrassed?"

"I guess I do," she said, "when I need help. Name's Verity Harrow, by the way, and I'm hardly ever this useless."

He said that she might call him Otto, or Otto Two, or Otto Rieber, Jr., but never, never ever, was she to call him Junior, to do so would end their friendship. His left wrist draped negligently upon the power steering wheel, his right hand pranced on a phantom keyboard playing the frantic melody to 'Fascinatin' Rhythm,' which he vocalized, a lark in the morning. Verity might just as easily have reached right over and touched him, and she went so far as to think of it, but she didn't touch him. Poor guy was just trying to be kind.

"Where do you play?" she said. "If there's no piano in your room. You must play every day, don't you?"

"Encino," he said summarily.

"Where's that?" she said. "I know none of these towns out here."

"The other direction," he said.

"Sorry," she said again.

"Don't worry," he said. "It's always in the other direction. Every day. But that's where they hold my baby hostage."

Everything he said extended the dimensions of his strangeness, and she fell for him in sympathy as well as desire. Verity considered letting herself be overwhelmed.

"So, you get it?" he said. "This music thing? Say you play yourself?"

"Maybe," she said. "It sure gets me. I *thought* I played. Now I've seen people who *do* play, I feel like maybe I piddled around too much, lost some ground. Feel like I should have got after being serious about this a lot sooner. I was actually a much better improviser as a dang kid."

"Music," he intoned, "is the prayer that answers itself in its utterance."

"I'd have to agree," she said. "Who said that?"

"Who?" he said. "I did. Just now."

"Well, for Pete's sake," she said. "That's pretty good."

"Prep school Latin," he said. "Years of that killer-diller grammar; I can turn a Ciceronian phrase, but it turns out there's not much call for that on the open market—probably a good thing I can drive a golf ball out of sight. The bastards have to pay me for *some*thing."

Victim to an unaccustomed crush, she felt in Otto's presence always at risk of acting the fool; Verity tucked into a plush corner of his Cadillac and let him talk, and he was gabby, and he soon revealed his chief complaint with the world and another possible basis for their friendship: They were both of them entirely terrified of being mediocre. By coincidence or not they happened to have met when they were facing an identical crisis. "A person would like to be heard," Otto said. "But you'd like to be worth hearing, and you get to this point as a piano player where you're looking at the piano player you want to be—that truly nimble cat, some real dream weaver, and you're looking across maybe another ten thousand hours of real hard work. And you wonder, did I wait too long? Am I too old to be really good? To be, you know, splendid the way some people are?"

At the Del Mar, faced once more with the impossible prospect of saying something like, 'See you around,' Verity was relieved, felt she'd got a reprieve when Otto said, "My turn to ask if I can use your phone."

"Sure," she said. "If you can get out. I had a heck of a time trying to call into it this morning."

She unlocked the door of Unit Seventeen, cracked it, knocked on it, and said, "Everyone decent in there?" The flickering of a television in a dark room. 'Stay tuned!' and a tinny tune.

"Mom," Tel said factually.

The boys sat at the end of one of the beds, hands in their laps as if they were being chastised. "Well," said Verity, hoping to accomplish her confession in one breath, "Got too drunk to drive home. Tried to call, but. Boys, this is Otto. He's been saving my bacon. Another piano player. And I, I don't know what to tell you. Everything all right here? Shall we get some breakfast? Geeze, you could grow mushrooms in here." She drew the curtain open, a sort of feminine flourish, she hoped. Let some light in. That light and a slightly new perspective showed her Jeet's newly bulbous, freshly discolored lips. "Ooonh," she said, "What happened now?"

"He got hit again," Tel said. "We went out for a walk, and some guy hit him."

"Some guy?" she said.

"We were just out for a walk," Tel said.

"Buddy? He just walked up and hit you?"

"Oh, he said some things first," Tel offered. "About how he looked. How Jeet looked. About his hat and everything. His glasses. And Jeet tries to ignore him, tries to go around him, but the guy just has to know, 'Who do you think you are?' Then it's—Blammo. Right in the face. As usual."

"Man," said Otto, "I hope for your sake you're not a trumpet player."

Poor Jeet, sitting there for all the world a kicked dog, for some reason contrite, and that and Verity's suddenly impossible guilt and the sheer unfairness of everything prompted her to say, and she'd remember and regret saying it forever, "Jesus, Jeet. Can't you ever duck?"

He smiled, but hideously, brokenhearted.

"Yeah," said Tel. "Something else, too, Mom. You might

want to pull that curtain back. We might be hiding out a little bit."

"That's pwetty dwabatic," said Jeet.

"So the guy," Tel recalled, "looked like he was gonna hit him again. He was making those moves. So I picked up a rock."

"A bwilliant thwow," Jeet was appreciative.

"*And*," said Tel. "the guy goes down. Right down. I mean, I dropped him. We did make sure he was breathing and everything, though. Before we left."

"He blehd a biht," said Jeet.

"Wild west show," said Otto. "You people are a lot of fun."

"You know," said Verity, "I keep making the same mistake, thinking this day can't possibly get any worse. Golden State—my ass."

◊ ◊ ◊

His goosed neurons filling him with light and optimism, Otto scooped the Harrows up as a boy might claim a box of abandoned kittens. Their things didn't half fill the trunk of his Cadillac. These people were obviously not travelers, but they were traveling light, and their circumstance and remarks gave Otto to understand they'd made themselves refugees on a whim. This fascinated him. Though Otto knew a good dose of amphetamine made him dangerously susceptible to fascination, he thought he may as well roll with his better angel for a bit and savor the irony of it, for he was typically no one's savior. As he drove them back through the city, away from the beach, the woman and the sunglass kid went enigmatic, suffering in silence or something, but the young one, the one they called Tel, was alive as hell, actively digging the car, the scenery in town after town, the flowering moment. This Tel spoke his every satisfaction, and he and Otto were soon pals, partners in enthusiasm. It was Tel who eventually thought to ask, "So where *are* we going? Now?"

"Encino," Otto said again. "The Rieber compound."

"I feel," Tel observed, "like a criminal on the run. It's great."

1989 Porfurio Drive was the terminus of that street, the final groomed property in that neighborhood beyond which the desert resumed in a canyon filled with grease-wood and coyotes. The street ended at a stucco wall, a wrought iron gate. Otto punched a code into a steel box, the gate swung open, and they proceeded into a contained landscape offering an olive tree, native-maybe-plantings, and a scattering of stunted, japanesy pine strung with foil. The house was an inn-sized Tudor half-timber, a place that in its big, cheerful, expensive artifice seemed like the California Verity had in mind as she'd come south. Some glamour, finally. She regretted there'd be no need to use the brass knocker on the front door, a lion's hinged head. Otto used his key.

A gate, a key, so much security was impressive to people who'd never locked a door. The boys by then had most unusually passed most of a day without a bite to eat; their stomachs having churned through the morning's excitement they were ravenous, thinking almost exclu-sively of their hunger, and the big house only looked like a disappointment to them. It did not smell of food as had so many places they'd passed along the way. In the foyer their party startled a sparrow of a woman in a servant's long white apron, and Otto only managed to say, "Carol, this is. . ." before the woman disappeared into other rooms. Otto was amused briefly, then inspired. "Hey," he said, "they didn't drain the pool this winter."

They moved as a nervous knot from the foyer into a

formal dining room where, still clustered, they stood at the head of a gleaming table that was long enough to seat a threshing crew, but the room had certainly never known a use so prosaic. The house was a museum or a shrine to its inhabitants or to itself. That long, walnut table with its upholstered chairs. There was a china hutch containing a green and gold service, every conceivable piece in duplicate. There were banks of thick white candles, not one wick blackened. Occupying much of one wall with its own dedicated lamp was a picture of a little boy, a younger Otto presumably, wearing short pants, a bow tie, and a blameless expression. The present Otto seemed quite as uneasy here as any of the Harrows. As a group they leaned toward a wall with French doors, toward the veranda beyond and the pool beyond that, but they were still waiting to follow Otto's lead that way when Carol returned with her employers.

Otto made introductions, a jumble of names that left the strangers he'd thrown together even more uncomfortable with each other. He briefly hinted at the Harrows' difficulties and then he said, "Well, I'm off."

"This," asked the elder Otto, "is how you treat your guests? You would abandon them for a game?"

"Hundred dollars a hole?" said his son. "Oh, certainly. Prepare to roast a haunch of walrus upon my return."

He'd said something about a tee time over the phone back at the Del Mar, and Verity had thought he was speaking of a *tea* time, and she had even been looking forward to it, and now she felt idiotic, and now, suddenly, he was gone with everything but the clothes on their backs riding in the trunk of his car with his clubs, his tam o' shanter, and his spiked shoes—his absence so sudden it left a considerable silence among those he'd left behind. At last Mrs. Rieber said, "Not, Mrs. Rieber, please. You must call me Hedwig. And he does not *haff* to play golf. This is a misconception."

The Harrows had fallen into a well of loneliness at the end of Porfurio Drive, made a soft landing in the southland after all, and Verity with her father's aversion to owing money or gratitude was not a natural foundling, but what choice in the matter? They were taken in, taken up, for the Harrows were presently in need of almost everything, and the anxious people they'd found knocking around this mansion were possessed of a nearly desperate generosity. Within half an hour of their arrival Verity and the boys were installed on patio furniture round the pool, a pool they would all one day remember as if they'd seen in it the source of the Blue Nile, and there were sandwiches built of rye bread and ham sliced nearly transparent, and linser torte under whipped cream, grapefruit plucked right from a tree in the household citrus grove, Viennese coffee. Carol Padilla, sweetly fluttering, brought coconut butter for the pale visitors who then let themselves be melted under a pale winter sun, even Jeet who greased himself thoroughly for the experience.

At peace already with that morning's stoning, Tel declared they'd entered, "Heaven. Or better, it's *living*. This is how everybody should do it, huh?"

Mrs. Rieber, a big shouldered and gimlet-eyed woman, invited them to take a swim, apologizing that the water wasn't heated, but saying also that she was using it herself every day to be invigorated. Benjamin Franklin, she said, was known to every school child in Europe as the man who had pulled electricity from the sky and invented the lightning rod, and, she said, as they probably already knew, Benjamin Franklin had taken a cold swim every day of his long life.

Verity apologized in her turn for having arrived without any swimming gear.

"We haff," said Hedwig. "Effrything. It is too much.

Effrything, but not used. Never used; it is too much."

"But the other thing," said Tel, "we can't swim."

Challenged, Hedwig drew herself up and challenged Tel, "You are a strong boy, yes?"

"For my size I am."

"You are tough?" she asked, wrapping her gray braid round her head. "Maybe a little?"

"Maybe," Tel allowed. "A little."

"Can you stand the cold?" she asked him. "I was physical culture, you know. I can teach you, if you can stand the cold. This is the finest thing for the blood, for the circulation."

"How to swim?" said Tel. "Well, sure, ma'am. I could just wear my pants in."

"No," said Hedwig. "We haff the professional wear. For freedom in moofing. You must wear the suitable thing."

When Tel and Hedwig went into the house to dress for their lesson, Mr. Rieber said, "My wife is a Jewess."

"Oh?" said Verity.

"Is that?" said Jeet. "I mean. . .?"

"A non-observant one," said the elder Otto. "I myself am a non-observant communist. We've been foreigners all our lives, somewhat unwelcome everywhere, but in America, at least, a man's home is his castle, so we become invisible here and offend no one." He had a story to tell, Mr. Rieber, and obviously very little chance to tell it. Verity and Jeet lounged and listened; the man's delivery was courtly and soothing, his life perhaps instructive.

Otto, said that when he'd been young Otto, he and young Hedwig had discovered each other in Salzburg at a chaste mixer arranged by their hiking clubs. They'd been striking then, Mr. Rieber claimed, and this was easy to believe because they had remained so well formed these many years later, so well provided with hair and easy limbs.

There were other, more important commonalities, though. Their fathers, as it happened, had both been out-of-favor civil servants for the Hapsburgs, posted to the empire's punitive backwaters, and so the young people had passed their childhoods growing up within a few whistle-stops of each other in Bosnia, acquiring the Turk inflected accents that would dog and corrupt every language they might subsequently speak. Young Otto and young Hedwig, for all their long-limbed elegance and mountaineering prowess had both been held in some suspicion by their fellow hikers, a rosy cheeked, usually uniformed crowd. There was then in Austria already a whiff of doom about her lineage, his political sympathies, and so, having sniffed the foul wind, they married and immigrated to America, he to be a ski instructor, she having something to do with Sonja Henie and with ice. Sun Valley. It was the Austrian Alps again, but without Nazis. It was Idaho. "We were so thrilled," said Mr. Rieber, "to make an American baby. The world was our oyster with a child."

Tel pranced out, joints all ajangle, caramel in his trunks, and Hedwig, padding barefoot behind him reminded Verity of Otto the younger, the woman's stride was like her son's. Otto's way of walking, and Otto's way of talking had been too much in Verity's thoughts, and it was well that the boys were fed, but she was still hungry in her way, still sick, and sick with longing. She reclined at her apparent ease, her sweat smelling like a distillery in a coconut grove, but what fine weather, what mild air, and in the pool, Tel had somehow involved that severe woman Hedwig in a frolic. There was splashing and laughter, and those watching poolside were envious, if not enough to brave the water themselves.

Jeet's thickened face had been frowning round the question he finally got the cheek to ask. "Sir, did you say you were a—*communist?*"

"I am," said Mr. Rieber mysteriously, "my father's son."

Jeet was not satisfied, nor was he, so far as he knew, his own father's son. "But. I mean. You're not. . . not like Kruschev? Those Cuban guys?"

"I rarely bang my shoe," said Mr. Rieber. "And I do shave every day. But, yes, I still believe Herr Marx was correct in almost everything. Of course, this was not something I admitted so freely when Senator McCarthy was conducting his inquisition. I knew friends in those days who were deported, driven from business, some of them were the purest capitalists, impeccably greedy people, but they were also ruined. So, I was circumspect; in any event, who wanted my opinions?"

"But, *really?* A communist?"

"Who has become," said Mr. Reiber, "everything he despised as a young man. It's not so terrible after all."

"Isn't it against their rules to get rich?" Jeet said. "Unless you're the dictator or something?"

Elder Otto was amused and flattered by the lad's curiosity. "Rich man through the eye of a needle," he said. "Wealth," he said, "everyone seems to frown on it for others and want it for themselves. One notices that Mammon's temples are everywhere and everywhere crowded. No—we are comfortable, and, I think, safe at last, and in the end, there is no good reason not to accept one's good fortune. But my library still has its copy of *Das Kapital,* Marx still explains things better than anyone else. I am good with numbers, however, and took no vow of poverty. When in Rome, or in Los Angeles as the case may be, all in the march of history."

"You have a library?" Jeet surrendered entirely to awe.

"You might enjoy it," said Mr. Rieber.

"Look," Tel called from the pool; he splashed across

its width using his newly acquired stroke, Hedwig behind him, saying, "Breathe—and breathe."

The day waned in that sad winter way and they shared a supper of spare ribs and kale and cress, and the boys ate as if they'd spent their lives until now always unsure of their next meal. The Riebers had cocktails while their supper was making, Verity another fresh squeezed grapefruit juice. She didn't smell particularly human yet but was beginning to feel better. After supper, Tel and Hedwig found a basketball game on the Rieber's television. The others retired to another room where Mrs. Padilla lay a fire against the chill while Mr. Rieber spoke of her as if she weren't there, "Carol's family operated a quite successful truck farm before the war," he said. "Near Sacramento. Unfortunately, her father and brothers were killed to a man. They went back to the Philippines to fight the Japanese, and—killed to a man. Her mother died of heartbreak. So, we're her family now." Carol Padilla, who had yet to utter more than a word or two in their presence, seemed pleased to have all this known; she'd seemed pleased generally to have them in the house, though the Harrows meant more work for her.

"We're famers, too," Verity told her.

Mrs. Padilla fairly beamed to hear it.

"Also lost a brother to that war." It sounded, Verity thought, like she was complaining when she only meant to commiserate.

"Farming?" Mr. Rieber wondered. Verity had been introduced to him as a musician.

"They wouldn't call me a farmer back home," she said. "Might call me a book keeper or maybe a female dog. I run things. It's real, real rare for me to get on or under a piece of machinery, but I run things. We raise grain. Some years a lot of it. I keep buying ground. Personally, though, I'm not what you could really call a farmer. Any ten-year-old kid can bend a wrench or smell the weather better than I can. Or at least Tel can. I'm more of a . . ."

"Business person?" Mr. Rieber suggested, welcoming her to a conspiracy.

Tel and Hedwig came in from the television room, and the boys arranged themselves on the floor in front of the fireplace, and as if the pop and crack and dancing flame weren't narcotic enough, Mr. Reiber took them layer by layer through Henrik Schliemann's excavations of Troy, told of civilizations piled one on the other. Tel was the first to nod off; almost as soon as he did, Mrs. Padilla was there gently guiding him to his bed. There had been no discussion or any mention of the Harrows spending the night. There had not, for some reason, been any mention of the younger Otto. Where was Otto? Mrs. Padilla then collected Jeet. Soon Verity drifted into a dream that was recollection as much as anything, in which she was mutely screaming, "Fuck *you*." Mrs. Padilla rescued her from this and led her upstairs to a carpeted bedroom with its own bathroom, its own shower. "You rest now," she instructed. There were towels on the bed, lotions in the bathroom; Verity found her second wind and had an ecstatic shower. She slipped naked between the sheets, unwilling to foul herself again with her clothes. The texture and taste of the night air here were new to her, as was the texture of their linens. For a person who'd known only the house her father had built with a hammer and a handsaw, this house certainly served as a change. What kind of place was this with so many uninhabited rooms, so many empty beds? Where was Otto?

Her next slide into sleep was a considerable journey; she slept profoundly.

Somewhere in the middle of the night she heard, and she was only gradually aware she wasn't dreaming it, "Montana. Hey, Montana." He was in her room. In the

darkened house; a startling and then a promising development as she woke to it. Was he hoarse when he asked her,
"Did you see it?"

"See?" she said. "What?"

"No one showed you the piano?" he was outraged.

Verity had something else in mind. Here he was. Here
she was. The dark was deep and convenient around them.
"I didn't ask to see it," she said. "But you can show it to me
if you want. In the morning."

"Yeah, come on," he said. A dark room, a dark house,
an almost disembodied voice. A nice voice, along with
everything else.

"Well," she said. "I'm naked as a jaybird here. So. You
mean *now*?"

"Get dressed," he said. "I'll be out in the hall."

She would have said no to this, but she wasn't yet very
articulate, and he'd stepped out so quickly. It had been the
work of a moment for him to get her fully worked up and
full of impossible possibility, and now he was waiting in
the hall.

He took her to a room containing his piano, a piano
bench, and a window seat lodged in the eyebrow dormer
she'd noticed from outside—this would be the uppermost
room in the house. Otto touched the ceiling that descended
to within a foot of his head; he gestured to walls hung with
a kind of quilting. "Insulation," he said. "Got my five in
tonight, and I'll bet you didn't hear me much, did you?"

"No," she said. "But I wasn't hearing much of anything.
Five? Hours?"

"It's my daily minimum," he said. "It's not really enough,
but I make sure to get that much, anyway."

"Time," she said. "That's what it wants, isn't it? Almost
all your time."

"Time and attention," he said. "But I'm a compulsive

guy. Try it."

"Play?" she said. Though she was no longer groggy, Verity's hands remained tremulous for untended desire. This seemed an audition and a very poor time for it. "You," she said.

"No," said Otto. "I'm done. Real strict about that. When I'm done for the day, I'm done."

"Look at this thing," she said. "Extra keys and everything. It's like a cross country bus."

"It's the biggest Bosendorfer," he said. "Ninety-two inches. Try it."

It was something of a ship in a bottle, for it didn't seem possible that this vast piano could have been got through the door to this room even in pieces. An expanse of gleaming black lacquer, a box of long, taut strings. Verity sat to it. She had, after all, wanted to be heard, and here were the most discerning ears she was ever likely to encounter, the finest instrument she'd probably ever touch, but she was for once reluctant. Her fingers were aflutter, and it had been days since she'd played a note. Rather than demur completely, she played a gymnopodie. The ceiling and walls might be damped for sound but the parquetry under her was perfectly hard, and her very thoughts seemed to well up from below and pulse through her. Some finesse was needed to keep the Bosendorfer from overwhelming the French pastry she'd chosen to play. This piano wanted Beethoven, enormous rooms, and yet this piano was a ride on a responsive cloud. She let the last lugubrious chord ring and ring; this piano, in this room carried the momentum of a runaway freight train.

"Great," said Otto. "You're all ready for your first recital. "Get with it, man. Why don't you check the action? Bang on it, baby. That's what it's for, or hadn't you noticed? We've got this world in here to ourselves."

He smelled, she thought, of peaches. They'd be peaches out of season.

◊ ◊ ◊

More or less marooned to the compound, they lodged with the Riebers in the week it took Verity to have the Plymouth retrieved and rebooted, and then, when Hedwig learned of Tel's imminent birthday she insisted that the Harrows must stay on so that she could throw the boy a proper party, which as it happened would consist of the veranda strung with crepe paper streamers, and of conical paper hats that no one but Hedwig would wear, a three-tiered cake littered with marzipan bunnies, a catered lunch, and not a single guest from outside the household. Tel opened two packages, neither of them from his own family, who looked on feeling cheap as he delighted in the snorkel mask and the swim fins the Riebers had given him.

It had the feel of a fool's paradise, but after that the Harrows stayed on out of inertia and in the grip of an implacable generosity, and Verity did not recognize herself in the shameless guest she became. She'd fallen ill with the vague wishing that seemed a contagion in this climate. Every day one of the Riebers, the elder Otto, or Hedgwig, and even Carol Padilla, now grown less shy, would draw her aside to confide how very, very happy they were to have the Harrows in the house, and to urge them to stay on as long as they liked. "You are such an improofment in our lifes," Hedwig claimed. "A breath of fresh hair."

While it might be supposed that lonely people, when they happen to encounter other lonely people, should be the solution to each other's problems, Verity saw at once that it might not work that way where she was involved, and she could never be convinced that she wasn't abusing the Riebers' hospitality. She had to pitch a hissy fit just to be allowed to pay for the Harrows' share of the groceries. Her reasons for staying, though, remained for quite some time more persuasive than good sense, or her customary independence, or her countrified delusions of decency. For Verity there was that Bosendorfer and the man who came around every day—every night—to play it. Her obsessions heretofore had strolled along in the languid rhythms of farm time; in California she had the sense of looking through a window of opportunity that might at any moment be shuttered. Looking at what? For what? Until she sorted this out, she did not allow herself to wonder too hard about what made them so weirdly welcome here.

Perhaps her hosts had fallen in love with Tel, a common enough occurrence in those days when her son was such a bloom of a boy, such a sweety. Under Hedwig's tutelage, Tel was not only swimming but had soon learned to do backflips into the deep end and handstands on the lawn. Hedwig would engage him in a fierce form of badminton that involved a strategy of driving the shuttlecock straight at an opponent's chest. Carol Padilla took the boy into her kitchen where she taught him to make adobo. At home Verity had stayed firm against having a television, but there were three magnificent sets in the Rieber household, and Tel had constant access to at least one of them and to the many channels they received; he could and did watch *The Twilight Zone* in Spanish, and Jai Alai matches, and cartoons.

Jeet would each morning share the LA Times with Mr. Rieber on the veranda; reclining side by side on chaise lounges they exchanged sections of the paper and their views of its contents. Jeet was not accustomed to the pleasure of having his views consulted. They read, and talked, and drank carafes of coffee in the mild morning air, and all this compared most favorably to the cold up north, to his

Junior year at Geraldine High. Between mornings, between meals, Jeet would burrow into the library, into a capacious leather chair where he might imagine his face intact and even handsome and breathe the fertile musk of a book filled room. He read what Mr. Rieber considered to be the best English translation of *The Odyssey*; he read a signed edition of *Kidnapped*. For Jeet this glimpse into the perfect situation could only be too brief, and while Jeet also felt they might be taking advantage of an excess kindness here, he had felt a bit like that for as long as he could remember, and he was used to it.

Otto Two had told her to bang on it, so she did. She played him 'Our Delight' in full vigor which made for a small earthquake on his monstrous instrument. Then, to show him that she could also be sensitive, she played 'Nardis,' and these renditions impressed him enough to make him nervous and snippy with her, and he'd said, "Yeah, I know those tracks, too, what are you, a human tape recorder? It's an improvisational art." Even then, even when he was being small, she liked him far too much and thought she might well cause herself some trouble about it, but that thought, and the thought of the boys being out of school and of the farm probably going to rack and ruin in her absence, all those thoughts taken together weren't enough to make her leave that huge piano, that harried man. "Bang it," he'd said that first night. When she'd done so, he'd said, "You can play this as much as you want. Whenever I'm not playing it, you should be. You're not bad. You could do something."

Verity didn't much want a patron or any kind of mentor, but she did adore that he let her so much at that Bosendorfer. When Two learned of her determination to improve her sight reading, he produced movie scores, lead sheets, and transcribed solos; it seemed Two had inherited an odd version of his parents' generosity; equally mixed in his regard for her talent was petty jealousy and a real desire to see her succeed, and Two, in addition to being such a swell specimen, seemed quite as confused as Verity and about many of the same things, and they understood in each other the one thing they understood of themselves, that need to reach the music, the call of it. So, Verity, after she had reconditioned her lower back and her mind so that she might profitably spend long hours on a piano bench, began to get better. Even when she wasn't playing, she liked to sit in the window seat under that eyebrow dormer, and she'd look down at the blue pool, her son frolicking in and around it, and she'd look out over the wall and a hedge at the sere hills behind them, and she'd glance back at the music in her lap, making it sound in her head. She got better quickly this way, much faster than she'd imagined possible, and she began to regain as an improviser some of that dash and elan she'd had as the girl who let nothing stand in her way. She was off, reclaiming the musician she'd once been, aimed at the musician she wished to be: This world to ourselves. What a luxury. She was getting better, which she had thought was the whole point of this experiment, but now she was getting better for him, which really shouldn't be the point of anything.

One morning Mrs. Padilla summoned Verity to the front door, saying a visitor awaited her there; Verity approached the foyer expecting a mistake or something worse. The visitor was an older man, as freckled as Jeet but wearing those freckles on a much darker palate; he also wore a houndstooth sports coat that doubled the natural width of his shoulders. He offered the most exquisite hand Verity had ever seen, his elegant fingers. She took them lightly.

"Mr. Murray?" he said.

"You are?" she said.

"Well," he said. "Yeah. Didn't Otto tell you?"

"No," said Verity. "Tell me what? I mean, I don't see him all that often. We don't, uh—not too often. You mean? Which Otto?"

"The hustler," said Mr. Murray. "The young one. He didn't tell you about the lessons?"

"You want lessons?" she said.

"I *give* lessons," he said. Mr. Murray's eyes were of a color she'd seen previously only in cats. He wore nicely draped slacks, an elegant slouch. "He didn't tell you, man?"

"No offense," Verity said, "but I don't think I need any. Lessons. I wouldn't even know how to do that."

"I have been fully remunerated, and I had my prime excuse to get out of Watts this morning, so I'm good either way. It's up to you, miss. I have been paid."

"Miss?" she said. "Paid?" she said.

"Yeah," said Mr. Murray. "Otto. Paid in advance, which I do demand from any kind of hustler. What's wrong? You scared?"

"Scared," she said. "No. Otto? Hm. What I should have said—I probably do need some lessons, I just don't know what kind. There's probably a lot of things I could stand to know."

"You and me both," said Mr. Murray. "They still got that big, beautiful battleship upstairs? If nothing else, I'd like to visit her for a while if I could."

They played then, turn and turnabout, Mr. Murray laying out an eight-bar package, then yielding the keyboard so that Verity might duplicate it. When she succeeded in this, he moved on to twelve-bar sections of greater complexity, and when she successfully repeated these, he stood behind her calling out various chords, requiring her to play them in two or three different voicings. When she faltered in this, Mr. Murray would show her what he meant with those hands of his which had got their beauty, it was now revealed, because they were so alive, enlivened by genius. In an hour the brilliant, possibly seedy Mr. Murray had opened a number of musical doors to her. He spoke of patterns, shapes, tonal coloration, and in such a way that it all made good sense to her. It was the most instructive morning of her life, and Verity told him so, trying not to suggest how little she had expected of their session.

He asked her, "Who you playing with now?"

"No one," she said.

"Need to find you some people to play with," he said.

"That," she said, "could be the hard part. Seems like everybody I've met down here is another whiz bang piano player."

"You'll be all right," he said. "You got it. Just keep working on those voicings. Remember the neglected sixth tone. You know what the Chinese say?"

"I doubt I do," she said.

"If you would be wise, first you got to know the names of things. G flat minor, first inversion, second inversion, third inversion, etcetera. Seems silly, but it keeps you sorted out. Helps you remember what you did. You got to call up them combinations, see?"

"Believe it or not," she said, "I think I do."

"You get to a point where there's *no* wrong notes, where you're just too hip for that. You're pretty close, I think."

◊ ◊ ◊

Tel insisted she watch with him, and he was well within his rights. "It's edu*cation*al television." He'd found that special channel. "So, you should watch. Mom."

From its corner it commanded the Rieber den, a

rotund screen in an oak cabinet right at home among plush and brass appointments. On the floor before it, chins in their hands, they watched a documentary, a reenactment of the fate of the Cargo Cult. Poor, snaggle-toothed islanders out in some Pacific fastness, doing or not-doing what they'd been at these millennia past. Then all at once the Seabees have swarmed their island and built a landing strip on it, and a great bestarred bird swoops in and discharges little khaki demigods from her pregnant breast. Gifts are distributed, gewgaws, crates of engineered army food, and the natives hysterically round eyed, round mouthed throughout the whole exchange, genuflecting a little, and much dialogue is had, none of it understood. Then, suddenly, the great bird rounds up her generous chicks and flies off, never to return. The Seabees melt away. The islanders though, the Micronesians, the Cargo Cult, do continue some generations later to keep that landing strip cleared. With stone tools. They worship the unopened rations as religious artifacts. In the final scene, there they stand in their rough clearing, scanning the sky.

"Oooh," said Tel. "That is *sad*. I'm not sure I even wanted to know that. Wanna try some Loony Tunes?"

"People believe what they want to believe," Verity said.

"Was that the lesson?"

"Don't mislead yourself," she said. "That's what I got out of it."

For having put them into the wind, look what comfortable luck they'd blown into, but some next move loomed, and with it at last some hard self-assessment, and Verity Harrow had known all along that she lacked the look and the disposition to ever be much in the way of show biz, and that as a performer she might expect a poorly paid career in church basements where her sound could well enrage an otherwise meek audience. There was studio work, but as she now knew there were also squadrons of studio musicians, conservatory trained, well connected people, and all of them undoubtedly more sociable than Verity Harrow. She did not, in sum, see how music might feed them, how she could continue to justify the time she was investing in it.

She had been managing the farm by phone and had run up the Rieber's phone bill like the national debt, and when she offered to pay it, Mr. Rieber said not to worry, that he would expense it out on his taxes. He also told her that if she was good with numbers, and he was sure she'd be good with numbers, then he could show her an easier business, one requiring no more than a dedicated phone line and a rolodex. He said he bought and sold empty promises and that his business was brisk in markets bull and bear, and though his offer was sincere and a little tempting it bore some taint of moral risk. Promises? Easy money? If the business involved any kind of deception, she knew she'd be no good at it.

What was she doing here? Waiting for that rare bird Otto Two to descend again, and she was a woman not especially well suited to this kind of pathos and didn't like it; she was beginning to not like herself very well despite all her progress in the piano room. What did she want? The next move—and she'd begun to want that quite a lot. She recognized this particular, heavy suspense from the last month or so of her pregnancy, so it seemed that unavoidable next move must be coming right up.

Eventually Verity understood that the paradise at the end of Porfurio Drive had been built with Otto Two in mind; there was quite a lot of palpable and unrequited longing for him about that house, a house he visited daily, almost never having contact with its inhabitants. Two. So lovely to look at, and limber of limb and wit, and stuffed with art and surprises, but chief among all his charms and the thing that made him irresistible was his sheer unavailability, that glossy, mad shell he wore. He came almost always late at night, and though the night was also familiar territory to Verity she would never consider bothering him in his work. She saw him then, when she saw him, on those few occasions when he came by day or early evening and bolted upstairs to the piano room, and found her playing there. He would listen sagely while she finished playing whatever she'd been playing when he came in; he would listen with his hand over his mouth, and making an intermittent sound part sigh and part groan that signaled, she liked to think, his approval. He would listen politely and say nothing. She, also courteous, would then surrender his piano to him and retreat to some other room or to poolside.

For as wide a swath as he had cut through her life, and continued cutting through her thoughts, she had spent a very small amount of time in the man's actual presence.

One morning shortly after her morning with Mr. Murray, Verity was wandering around a composition that had evolved out of her name-that-chord exercise into a clever thing with a life of its own. Otto Two happened in. He assumed his posture, the listener, the thinker, and he made those sounds of his. It was her piece, after all, and hers to end as she pleased, so she played on, elaborating the thing to extend the moment. When she ended it at last, Two did at long last remark her playing.

"Shit," he said.

"What?"

"I was afraid of this."

"Oh?" she said. "Afraid?"

"You're smarter than I am," he said. "I kind of suspected it all along."

"Be serious," she said.

"Serious?" he said. He was never otherwise.

"It was Mr. Murray," she said. "He came by. That guy is great. Thanks, by the way. Made me feel like getting out and seeing some acts. I meant to see some music down here, anyway. Got any suggestions?"

"You think Copland's corny?" he said.

"Don't ask me about corny," she said. "I like the Carter family. Copland?"

"Aaron Copland?" he said. "Rodeo?"

"We don't rodeo," she said, "except by accident."

"No," said Two. "The ballet, the tune. Feel like seeing the symphony?" He hummed a few bars of it, and she remembered hearing it in the background at a grain elevator, hearing a wobbly transmission on the airwaves back home.

"Sure," she said. "If you'll let me buy the tickets."

She didn't initially think of it as a date, but then Mr. Rieber found her in the dining room with her Thomas Guide, plotting her route to the Philharmonic Auditorium, and she explained why, and when Mr. Rieber reported the pending event to Hedwig and Carol Padilla they came clucking round, Hedwig with an emerald broach suitable for wear at a coronation, and Carol Padilla with a scent she said she had no use for anymore, a perfume so rich it had once been intended as part of her trousseau and her dowry, and to be nice Verity dabbed what soon proved an immodest amount of it on, and she wore her best clothes, those silly clothes she'd worn so unsuccessfully to the club, and here she was nearly all the way through dating age having never been on a date, unable to determine if she was on one now, and headed downtown looking like exactly the idiot she was and wearing that inscrutable Asian reek.

There was some predictable trouble about parking that she had failed to predict, and she was late to the hall, less than surefooted in her shoes, and there he stood awaiting her on the sidewalk outside the auditorium. A bowling shirt among the evening wear, that golden boy. He ran his hand through his crew cut, but patiently. A nice man, she thought.

"Sorry," she said. "I guess I didn't figure in the. . . well, anyway, where's the box office?"

It was the symphony, he explained. People paid by subscription and some through advanced ticket sales, but there was no box office. Verity took this to mean she'd screwed the whole thing up, but Two assured her she hadn't; there was at one entrance to the hall an enormous man in the maroon livery of a toy soldier, the palace guard; Otto approached him and pressed something into his gloved palm and the man furtively ushered them in, then they were dashing along the dreamy thick carpet, up a vaulted stair and to the very rear of the uppermost, rearmost balcony of a hall filled with thousands of impossibly handsome people. Verity would have preferred to be sweating less visibly, but it was very warm where they were and they'd come at just less than a sprint.

How quiet that throng. Somewhere someone coughed and the acoustics in the hall were such that it carried everywhere, like an omen, then pure silence with the conductor's lifted baton, and then it fell and ranks of brass fanfared, and tiers of strings, call-and-response, and tympany, and this guy Copland, Verity thought, must be about the most optimistic person in the world to write such a piece, and he must be from way up country because he'd painted a big existence occurring out in the open somewhere, a tune that against all odds succeeded in making her homesick. The Philharmonic fired up and, though she heard it from the furthest, hottest reach of the chamber, and though she continued sweating liberally, her battered vanity was gone.

Subscribe? Sure, she'd sign up for this if she lived here. *This* was the high life, and no doubt about it. This sound, this collaboration.

But the music ended, as it does, and then they were back on the sidewalk again, and what next? Verity was about to make herself ask him when he said, "You know how to get to my place from here?"

"I'll follow you," she said.

He drove in as stately a way as the freeways would let him and used his turn signals to make it easier for her to follow; still, to follow him needed all her attention, a good thing, too, else she'd have been burned alive by randy thoughts. His place. She'd been there before. What did people do? How did they approach each other? If she hadn't cracked these commonplace mysteries yet it seemed she never would, and if Two should truly understand her for what she truly was, and nearly all she was at the moment, a slavering, horny old hag, well she'd scare off her feathered friend once and for all—wouldn't she? Or something. She didn't know.

He assured her it was safe to park in the street, that his was a safer neighborhood, though he once again secured his own car underground. They went up that echoing stair. Sweet and sour his room. Sweet and sour sauce.

"You like ginger ale?" he asked her.

"Sure," she said.

"Anything else?"

"No," she said. "That's plenty for me."

He had an old-time ice box with no ice in it, but it kept the pop cool at least. He poured it into cloudy glasses. He had fat pretzels, a cheese in a wax rind. When all this was dispensed, they were confronted with the fact that neither of them had ever learned the art of conversation, never even heard what they considered artful conversation, so they sat silent, she on his secondhand hassock, he cross-legged on the floor.

"Red Garland," he said. "Been on a real kick lately." Tenderly he placed a record on his balanced turntable, tenderly and with deliberation he placed his diamond needle on its spinning edge, and the quintet in question played them a blues long enough and so heavily sexualized that it seemed to constitute a complete affair. They said nothing. Nothing to be said about it. Through that tune, that record, another round of ginger ale, and then another Red Garland record they said nothing, until at some point Verity was beginning to think that if she couldn't think of something to say it would be impolite of her. Also, though she was truly fond of Red Garland, she was pretending to listen a lot more intently than was really possible. What to say? I'd like to touch you?

Maybe Two sensed then that she was about to embarrass them both to the hollow bone, and he said, "See? Like him. You've got it."

"We're both self-taught," she said.

"But not that," he said. "It," he said. "A person's got it, or they don't."

"Well, thanks," she said. "But you too. I think you're better than you think. Doesn't matter when you started, where you were. It's its own thing. And you've got it yourself." She didn't wish this to be heard as flattery.

Then they were quiet again, a real interlude with no music playing to cover it.

"There's about five hundred ways I could got lost between here and Encino," she said at last, "so I better get headed back."

"Can you wait a minute?" he said. "Just a minute."

The flat, smooth planes of that face. "All right," she said. "You mean? All right."

"Just a second," he said, and Two went into his little bathroom and closed the door behind him, and more than a second, and a good deal more than a minute passed. She heard him run water into the sink. She heard this several times. Wait. When he emerged at last, she was breathing heavily and stinky with anticipation and hoping she hadn't completely misread things. Wait. How long she had waited. But now. Here he was. Two.

Jaw slack, his eyes huge with fear, something he desperately wanted to say had got so thick he couldn't force it from his mouth and he was reduced to a sort of mewling.

She began to see things, spectral things, darting counter-shadows in the dark, the highway throbbing at times before her. "I just go," said Verity, "until I'm a hazard, don't I? That makes it your turn, bud. You better not drift off, though. You sure you're wide awake?"

Jeet was sure and said so. He'd been waiting for this, to take control of just anything. He drove them through a dull stretch of Utah. Verity was unable to sleep even as a passenger, and they rode along with Tel dreaming in back, giggling, snoring, sighing from time to time.

"It's not like it was your fault." Jeet said at last, "You just happened to be there when it happened."

Logic was as usual small consolation. The blame for the stroke Otto Rieber Jr. had suffered in the bathroom of his apartment might fall on that powder he liked to snort, or to bad luck, or even to the young man's sheer intensity, but Verity had been there to see that first fear in his eyes, and Verity had been the one to drive him by the most roundabout route to the hospital, she not knowing where to go and he unable to tell her except by a confusing suite of gestures, and it had fallen to Verity to call his parents with the news. Now she could not avoid feeling that she was abandoning him and not too coincidentally just when she'd ceased to find him attractive, his face melted on one side, his mouth full of mush.

Otto was in Encino now, in that room at last that had been preserved so long for him, there among the trophies, pennants, and found treasures of his childhood, a few doors down from the lovely piano his lovely left hand no longer knew. He could be heard howling from time to time, and his mother was unable to entirely conceal her satisfaction at this turn of events. Hedwig, despite herself, was happy. Elder Otto and Carol Padilla shuffled around still shocked, their ears cocked for that next howl, and the Harrows, as you may well imagine, left this situation as if shot from a canon the moment they decently could. And that was California.

JEET

Blasting north, Verity asked her ward, "You know what the worst habit is? The worst habit you can have?"

"Doubt?" said Jeet.

"That's not a habit," said Verity. "Or maybe it is. But I'd say self-pity. And that's a hard one to avoid, because a lot of people are sort of entitled to it. Got every reason to feel sorry for themselves. Doesn't mean they should."

"You think that's me?" he worried. "Do I do that?"

"You might," she said. "I know I do. Have to tell myself to snap out of it sometimes."

"Is this advice you're giving me?"

"My advice," she said, "probably doesn't look like it's worth much right now. I did get better, though. Wanted to get better, and I did, and pretty fast, too. So, there's that. Got back a lot of what I lost over the years. Creativity. You can't take that for granted." She had in her possession Otto Two's last words to her, written with his serviceable right hand in big block letters on a sheet of Rieber Co. stationery, his demand: YOU PLAY. "Know what I think we might do?" she said. "I might wall off that piano when we get home. I plan to stay at it now, keep putting in the time, and I don't want to drive you boys crazy."

"You would have by now," Jeet said. "If you were going to. We don't even hear it anymore. We'd probably be lost without it."

"I doubt that," she said.

"You're lucky," he said.

"I am?"

"To want it that much," he said. "To have a talent. A person should be good at one thing at least. A lot of us aren't. Me. What if a person wasn't ever very good at anything?"

"There's no excuse for that," she said. "At least there wouldn't be for you."

Something was building between them. The more Verity wanted sleep, the less it wanted her.

"I don't complain," Jeet finally claimed. "I never do."

"No," she said, but warily.

"There's some things," he said, "Back home. I have to admit, I hate 'em. Really hate 'em."

"It's not for everybody," she allowed.

"No," he said. "I don't mean that. I don't mean the farm. The *farm* farm. The work or any of that. That's okay. But. Well, you know when Louie hit me? You know what that was about? He was saying we were related. He said I was related to all the McQuistons."

"That's why he hit you? Because he thought you were related?"

"I said some things myself," Jeet confessed. "I didn't think Louie was quite that quick. But this isn't the first time. People dropping hints. And I do look kind of like 'em, which is bad enough. But. I mean, I know I came out of the orphanage, that your mom adopted me and all. But. What I really hate, really, really hate is how people back home seem to know more about me than I do."

"They don't know squat," Verity assured him. "About anything."

She'd told him thus far only that he'd been named for a fallen hero, and even this the better part of the truth wore on him as an assignment. George Harrow. Jeet had never felt equal to it. He remembered nothing of the orphanage and hoped he never would, and sensing it might be ugly territory he had until now cultivated a careful lack of curiosity concerning who had named him and when and why, but these questions had got infected in him at last, and tonight was the night when it must finally be asked, "Who am I? If you know."

"I do," said Verity. "And you do, too. You're the guy who stands up in his shoes every morning."

"Yeah," he said. "But not that. Not philosophy. I'm talking about. . . I am *not* a McQuiston. Am I?"

"You're a Harrow," she said. "You are now."

"Yeah. But obviously there's other. . . By blood?" Louie had been his classmate, but there were McQuistons everywhere in that community, slumped at the edges of every ball game and ceremony, pale people known to breed like rabbits, generally fat or frail in form and rarely well made, and worse, if Jeet was any judge, they were people pale of spirit, too. "*Not* a McQuiston. Please."

"Maybe," she said. "A little bit. Your mother would be aunty to most of those little bastards."

"Would be?" he said.

"Is," she said. "Somewhere. Far as I know. Mary Lou. Maybe you've heard of her."

"My mother?"

"I guess the cat's out of the bag," said Verity. "Might as well let you in on all the gory details. You're probably old enough to handle it now."

"The cat?" said Jeet.

◊ ◊ ◊

The day he turned twenty-one Jeet converted all but fifty dollars of his patrimony into traveler's checks; he treated Rude and Rudnik to tomato soup at the 4-Bs and to rounds of boilermakers at the Ox, and when the bar closed and his friends drifted off, he sat in to a backroom poker game with the same three players clicking chips through the deep of the night and a mortally bored dealer with no better place to be. Jeet was about even money in the game when at dawn on the first full day of his majority he walked through the slush on Higgins Avenue and down to the train station, frequently touching his hip pocket to feel the passport there, thinking he should find a better way to secure it. This valley's winter morning, sepia and gray, industrial stench and woodsmoke under a lid of clouds and the usual chill from the Hellgate. Carrying his funny money, a bag for his clothes and shaving gear and another smaller but heavier bag for the books he considered essential, he boarded a train to Minneapolis with connections to points east. So long, Missoula. His only discernible regret upon leaving this once beloved town was the fishing tackle he'd pawned here, and he hoped his clothes wouldn't hold whiffs of the card room or the pulp mill.

Jeet was going. as the young are given to go, elsewhere to remake himself, and in this he had the advantage of sudden wealth that was his through no fault of his own and of starting this new personality almost from scratch, for he was then a collection of naughts, no one's son, no one's boyfriend, not quite a college graduate, an apolitical atheist, a man without trade or vocation or, until recently, much in the way of ambition. He subsisted on books and poker. But what of that big wanting? That had to count for something. Didn't it? If he could find some way to express it? He couldn't be entirely without substance. Could he? Air brakes chuffed explosively, releasing, and the engine took hold, and the train slid clacking past the round-house, into the canyon. He tried his dogeared copy of *The Stranger* but couldn't for motion sickness read more than a few pages at a time. Jeet intended to be a hearty traveler. He meant to go until he'd left it behind or found it. It? He intended to become someone with more accurate thoughts, clearer intentions. With this in mind, he pulled the collar of his Loden overcoat up around his ears and leaned his head on the rocking glass. Mountains, high plain, prairie. He slept fitfully all the way to the Dakotas, and every nap seemed to yield an entirely new landscape. So far, this was exactly his notion of what travel should be.

He was soon to encounter himself in almost every public place, that forlorn seeker who litters most bus stops and lunch counters, often another starkly dressed young man, also moody and of no particular use to anyone, and Jeet found it unpleasant to discover he was such a cliché, to witness in other people his own obsession with self, but Jeet had more justification than most, perhaps, for being so lost in himself. What's in a name? Quite a lot if you've been stuck with George Charles Lloyd Harrow, a given name he never spoke and never fully used even on the dotted line, a name that was a drama fully cast with heroes and a kind of villain and that he, Jeet, viewed from a bemused distance. All these men mentioned in his name, even the loony Lloyd, were men of larger capacity than he thought he'd ever demonstrate, so he would continue to be merely Jeet, the name he'd given himself in the time when he had been so much with old Charlie, a name that made an obvious shape of his mouth, a word the old man might recognize on sight.

Charlie had been almost mummified by the time Jeet knew him, a stillness on him usually only interrupted by the rare bark of his laugh. What was so funny? No one else, no one living, was ever let in on the joke. Jeet had known from forever that Charlie, as he'd been instructed to call him, was the source of almost every material thing in their world, including even Verity, and as the hours rolled by, the years eventually, Charlie remained always a Jovian presence to a child already unsure of his welcome, for Charlie would surely know at a glance a boy's every failing, and Charlie might easily guess a boy's every foolish thought; in those days Jeet's conscience wore weathered flesh and sat right there at the kitchen table with him. Who wouldn't keep his head down? Fortunately, there was almost always something, if only yesterday's Tribune, to read in that house. Charlie had loomed over Jeet's formative years and so when Charlie was gone his absence was to leave a permanent hole in Jeet's understanding of things, and Jeet would never in life presume to call himself Charlie, or Charles, or even Chuck.

And Lloyd? Here was a name come from someone with whom the orphan actually shared some blood, his mother's father whom he knew only as some kind of religious nut, and the man most responsible for fouling Chouteau County with so many unhappy McQuistons. Kin be damned, Jeet wanted nothing to do with that pinkish crowd and less to do with that turd of a name. Lloyd: Absolutely not.

And that left George, and George was so far beyond him.

Bathed in the light and warmth of a dying sun, real George, original George was for Jeet the probable high point of civilization, though all he really knew of the man came from a drawer in a filing cabinet that also contained crop insurance documents. There was a baseball trophy, fake gilt chipping away from a statuette, TIGERS inscribed on its base; there was a diploma and a graduation picture and another photo of the young skipper with his young crew assembled around him on a runway and smiling for all the world carefree, but with that runway running off behind them toward a vanishing point. In hindsight Jeet thought real George already wore in these pictures the excess nobility and the thick, dark shock of hair that marked him for a doomed hero. There was a sort of jewel box that contained Lt. Harrow's Distinguished

Flying Cross, a device with a four-bladed propeller. There was an accordion file stuffed with all manner of materials from the war department, including the telegraph announcing his death and official accounts of Eighth Air Force actions, every one of them it seemed involving heavy flak, heavy losses, and these, taken all together, could be stitched together as an account of the combat career of the Dirty Dora; they must have been a crack crew, for they'd flown thirty-five such missions, encountering the enemy every time, and they had returned from all but one of them. Jeet liked to imagine the adoration that crew must have heaped on original George, the boy who'd grown up nursing equipment to the end of the row, the end of a harvest, and whose tender willfulness had got his people back to safety so often they must have come to expect he'd one day also bring them home. According to a citation commending one such instance of valor:

> Flying in the top tier of the formation, Lt. Harrow's aircraft was set upon by a pack of Focke Wulfs, which the crew beat back with sustained, concentrated fire while successfully delivering their ordnance, but not before their aircraft had much of her vertical stabilizer shot away and also lost an outboard motor to enemy fire. Constantly cross controlling, Lt. Harrow flew his badly crippled machine through the crosswinds that had developed over the channel and returned her to his home airfield with less than two hundred pounds of fuel on board

and no loss of life to his command.

◊ ◊ ◊

Demigods had preceded him, and Jeet could see he might never be more than a quiet little man with his quiet little interests. Verity, in finally opening the grab bag of his personal history, had done more to inform him of who he wasn't than who he was. Coming back from California that night, when he'd finally asked for particulars, Verity set it all out for him, a tale of a half-wit, faithless mother named Mary Lou, now vanished, and of her own half mad mother and the promise she'd extracted. So, this was the story of how he'd come to be, and no wonder the sense of abandonment he'd always worn as his soul's hair shirt. She'd done him a favor, really, Mary Lou, when she chose not to lug him through whatever shabby life she must have led, and who wants to be anyone's badge of shame, but it was not much good, either, to be such a completely inadequate replacement George. Verity told him that she'd meant to change his name after she picked him up at the orphanage, thinking he might prefer a name that was his own rather than that of a father who was not, except for legal purposes, his father, but then she had learned of the many benefits due to the children of soldiers killed in action, and she thought the boy might as well have those benefits. Good old Verity had saved nearly all the money the government had given her to raise George Harrow's son. The moment that fund became available to him, Jeet kicked his education, a tame and aimless affair so far, into its vivid phase. 'This will be me,' he thought. '*Live*,' he thought.

◊ ◊ ◊

No one comes to Morocco to be rained on, but mischance and foul weather had been themes in his travels; Jeet had contrived to rent a house on what must be North Africa's wettest highland during her wettest season. On clear nights he might climb the ridge behind his village and see a faint radiance, possibly Tangier beyond the horizon, but there had been very few clear nights among those dripping with rain, certainly more rain than he'd ever seen fall on Montana. He lived by chance too near the mosque where the muezzin's wail, at first electric to his ears, had now in its repetitions driven him to the conclusion that time was not passing in this village at all, that it had stalled in a loop. His days here were nearly identical.

Though he'd been traveling without much intention, this had been an unintended stop. On his way to the Sahara, or so he thought, he'd caught a ride with a truck driver of his very slight acquaintance on a truck piled with brassware, but there had been a misunderstanding or a change of heart, and the truck driver, who had claimed to be going down to the desert, took them instead to his own village in the Rif mountains, and there the truck driver quarreled with a man who carried a curved dagger, and then for reasons Jeet didn't comprehend, the truck driver lost the use of his truck and was obliged to leave the village afoot. Hot-footing it. Jeet did not follow.

They were Berbers in and around this village. Along the indifferent roads that led to it, Jeet had seen many southfacing fields of resinous hemp presently at full height and in full flower, a circumstance that might not favor the appearance of a stranger in the area. Playing ronda in the city's cafés he'd learned enough of their dialect to count to twelve and to name the four suits of a Spanish deck, but Jeet could not think how these terms might help him explain his arrival here, and though he'd gone native to the extent of shrouding himself in a djellaba he knew he'd never briefly be mistaken for a tribesman. As usual, but more than usual, he did not belong, and he was considering all this in the village square when a brazen child, an entrepreneur wearing one of those small black fedoras that the gypsies favor came straight up to him; the boy pointed to his own chin, touched his own chest, and said in a reassuring way, "Youssef."

Upon determining that Jeet carried the right kind of currency, Youssef immediately took charge of his existence and for a few dhuram got him a one-room house and a carpet for its earthen floor, the sum of his furniture, and there Jeet repaired, sitting, kneeling, crouching, reclined, rarely out of arm's reach of the little oil burner that he used to heat water for his tea, another of Youssef's bargains. The windows were few, narrow, and set high in the walls, but by their meagre light Jeet read at last St. Augustine's confessions having carried them with him for years, the last printed matter in his knap sack, and now that he'd finally got around to the saint's account of himself it seemed all worn out. Augustine, so Jeet had heard, had practically authored an age of faith and was a very big deal, but the age of faith had long subsided anywhere Jeet Harrow lived, and he simply wasn't buying anyone's exaltations, nor *inshallah*, nor nirvana, nor any of that other hoohaw one heard of on the road. Five times a day the call to prayer left him unmoved. When he finished the Confessions there was nothing left to read, and there he was, lounging on that carpet, on a dirt floor, within those thick, earthen walls, and even the small dome above him was formed of mud brick, slowly blackening with the smoke from his oil burner.

Youssef had sold him the burner, a spouted tin tea pot, two heavy cups, a wooden sebsi, and the long stick to clean its stem and keep it drawing freely; the clever young entrepreneur had created a steady market, for now he'd be making daily sales to the Nazarene of fresh mint, kif, and hashish. The pale one also wanted majoun whenever it was available. Jeet would lick that jam right off the leaves it was delivered in and settle in to his mild hallucinations.

Though he'd made himself essential, young Youssef made no kind of companion; he could not be induced to try his hand at ronda as he could not see the point in playing any game he might lose. He did one day reveal his heart's desire by imitating the reedy howl of a Berber flute, imitating it so well perhaps he no longer needed the actual instrument. Beyond that, they had nothing to say to each other. The delivery of goods or services and payment for them all came about without conversation. Among these services, Youssef arranged for his widowed aunt to keep the stranger fed. The woman came, timid at first, but soon enough it was each morning with her stout knock, and tattooed chin, and hennaed hands, couscous and figs for Jeet's breakfast, and often something that sounded awfully like scolding, and in the evening she'd bring him a steaming tajine and another reproach. Was she angry? Her carping ways were just as well, he thought, for she was a young widow and extravagantly beautiful, and he was prone to disastrous loves. He was rarely hungry but found himself eager anyway for her visits. At least the shrew knew of his existence, and that was something. How long? How long the rain? He was never to learn the woman's name but would remember always the patterns on her hands, the particular tinkling of her every ornamented movement.

Do not, he instructed himself, fall in love. Where was he? The end of time, very near the end of his inheritance. He had discovered in his journey of self-discovery that he was bad with love, bad with women, bad with money, and terrible whenever he tried to manage any of these things in combination.

◊ ◊ ◊

He'd started frugally enough. Jeet had shipped on a freighter out of Baltimore. A non-member of the Seaman's Union, he'd been relegated to working the ship's galley, but it got him to Europe at no cost save the seasickness he suffered in those long, mid-Atlantic swells. Antwerp. And he'd got through Belgium without going crazy, but by the time he reached the Rhine he was tired and thought he'd treat himself to a nice hotel, and within the week the Deutschmarks were flowing, for in addition to eating well and drinking well, he found the simple expenditure of money bought him quite a lot of panache here on the continent, and so he spent like a sheik. He bought an Alfa Romeo, of all things, in Berlin, of all places, a car curiously dimpled in its sheet metal, but with a straight frame and a wonderful price. Also in Berlin, in a gallery on the Hibbenstrasse, Jeet met Hjordis, Valkyrie art student from Oslo, her glacial eyes consuming everything, including, incredibly, Jeet Harrow. He nurtured the theory that maybe he was okay here, not so funny looking and possibly even an enigmatic figure under his broad brimmed black hat in a German art house, and he made so bold as to approach her. Apple cheeks, blond braid on her shoulder, a big, fashionable milk maid. Not shy, not the kind to look away.

"You like sports cars, ma'am?"

In very good English Hjordis made it clear, as she would continue to do, that she'd escaped her home to study everything. She was interested in everything. She was a long way from home, she emphasized, and free to do exactly as she pleased.

"Me too," he said.

They went out from the gallery and cruised the city, top down, their noses running like fountains in the winter air, laughing pitilessly at those poor, greatcoated border guards posted along the wall. Something about proximity to a Marxist paradise made them giddy, and most of their time together was to be a tour of the Eastern bloc, Prague, Warsaw. They loved to be so out of place, to camp in dismal hotels knowing they could always leave. They reveled in border crossings, sex, and such history and art as was left to these ancient places after their recent wars and occupations. The sudden couple cruised in the Alfa Romeo and laughed and laughed in a sort of frenzied callowness, and Hjordis would prove to be every bit the athlete she had first seemed, distinguished in endurance and agility. Jeet bought these adventures for them with his always useful, always negotiable traveler's checks, and though he well knew he hadn't bought Hjordis's abiding love, he gave himself to her body *and* soul, and in France, one night in Besancon, she strolled out of the picture along the old Roman wall, hand in hand with one of those other interests she'd mentioned.

Jeet drank his way down through wine country. Given his history in romance, it was very easy to think he'd just experienced his whole love life over the course of a few weeks, and there would certainly never be another Hjordis. That weepy, inescapable French music. He didn't speak French. He didn't speak anything that didn't get him sneered at here. Where was she now? Why those accordions everywhere? Accordions weeping through loudspeakers in public places. Wine was their water in France, but it remained wine to Jeet, and he remained drunk until one night in a pass in the Pyrenees he drove into a snowstorm almost indistinguishable in color and texture from a Basque shepherd's flock, which he also drove into, and he left the Alfa Romeo crumpled in the mountains having somehow avoided all those sheep but not a venerable oak, and having made a drunk's charmed passage through the accident he walked away unharmed. He told himself to snap out of it and hitchhiked into Spain.

In an old Mercedes full of monks, he rode south. Monks, or priests, or they must be something religious with those elaborate collars, and they were obviously men who'd spent much time together for they'd developed a strange way of speaking to each other, their own fluid language containing almost no consonants. The conversation in that car was a high wind through dry leaves, and it was soothing enough until one of them laughed. They laughed often, and Jeet thought there was something ugly and heavy in their humor, and then for some miles he entertained the suspicion that these holy men had all been jilted too, and that was the sad explanation for how they happened to be jammed together in this car. A bota of sherry was in circulation, and each time it passed him Jeet said, "No grossyawss," and there'd be more nasty laughing. They passed through country that reminded him of Wyoming's Gas Hills where he'd worked one lobster red summer as a chain hand on a drilling rig in a landscape of gravel and dust that really didn't bear repeating. He was offered vermouth and he was offered absinth; the celebrants were drinking straight from the bottle. "I wouldn't dare," he declared, for it was desperately close with monastery musk in that swerving Mercedes; at least one of the brethren had bathed in cologne without bathing.

Their pilgrimage or vacation took him as far as Granada where, as Jeet just happened to know, Garcia Lorca lay still undiscovered, undisturbed, fertilizing his imagination. Here was a wonderful place where poets were so influential they needed shooting, he climbed to the Alhambra, a thing manmade more beautiful and serene than the mountains surrounding it. Fine. But then he'd seen it, and then he was moving again, moving as if his life depended on it, and before the day was out, he was out of Granada, headed to Gibraltar with a Japanese tourist in a rented Citroen.

Africa. Well, why not? Another continent for the price of a ferry ride.

Some months later someone at a party was to tell him that Tangier was where wanderlust went to die, and by then Jeet was himself proof of the proposition. He was considering staying on permanently. At least half the people in that town, nearly all the foreigners, were on the run from one thing or another, usually themselves, and he found it comforting to be among so many other fugitive souls. For less than it had cost to sleep in a French hostel he lived near the beach in a cottage with maid service. Everything was within walking distance, and he walked everywhere, and along the way to most places he would at some point find himself lost in a maze of streets so narrow they were always in shade—streets with mystery doors, populated by burros, domesticated birds, monkeys, and people accustomed to expressing themselves entirely with their eyes—streets that wound their way eventually to a plaza, a fountain, a prospect of Europe across the blue strait. When he wished to speak English there were the clusters of Brits and Americans, Aussies and the like, people passing through or living in and around the old International Zone, and many of them maintained a sort of bohemian open house, perpetual parties, and the people at these parties tried on ideas like a rich woman in a dress shop; the talk was of syndicalism, existentialism, Dada, liquor, the beginning or end of civilization. Happy or sad drunks. Jeet came to prefer the cafes, though he often had no idea what was being said in them. In the cafes he would have a hand of cards as long as he wanted to play, and there would be as much tea as he wished to drink, as much kif as he wished to smoke. He'd landed in a culture that provided nicely for its wastrels.

Jeet was taking his ease one day in the Café Meziane, and was three pipes into that ease when a man appeared in stockman's boots, his jeans rolled at the cuffs and a kerchief round his neck, and just in case anyone had failed to appreciate the old-time cowboy duds he flung a big 'Howdy' at the first startled Muslim he encountered. Though he would have been full grown for some time, the man had not yet adjusted to his full growth or left his adolescence behind. With him was a young woman as trim and self-contained as he was shambling, a Frenchwoman Jeet supposed, the gamin with her pixie haircut, and capri pants, and shoes that were hardly more than ballet slippers. Her expression remained one of complete indifference or incomprehension all through a heated exchange between the cowboy and Thami the Meziane's manager; her expression never changed as they were ushered out the door, the cowboy saying, "Well, that's just fine by us. Daphne wanted a place where she could get a drink anyway. Ah-reeeh-vwaaah, asshole."

Thami hustled directly to Jeet's table, his palms pressed together in front of a brocade vest that matched his brocade cap, apology in his eyes, and Jeet imagined the manager would try and explain the kerfuffle, but Thami had come to say that Jeet's welcome was also worn out, and he too must leave, and when Jeet asked why Thami lifted his palms outward and made a small, vigorous waving, meaning undoubtedly, 'enough is enough.' The manager repeated something Jeet thought at first was Arabic but then understood to be Thami's bubbling version of 'Yankee go home,' and Jeet, his slight patriotism slightly ruffled, his feelings slightly hurt, left the Café Meziane vowing, as if anyone would especially want him back, never to return. He soon came upon the cowboy and his companion eating flatbread at a stall, and he told them what had transpired, and he asked the cowboy, "What on earth did you say in there?"

"Bastard wanted me to take off my boots. They should be glad I didn't. My feet. No. Not for public display. Used to ride motorcycles. Hill climbs. And, yes, there's hills in Kansas if you know where to look. My feet? Ruin a person's appetite. Guy should've been grateful I didn't expose him to that. Guess he wasn't, though."

"That's all right," Jeet said. "I think they were just looking for an excuse to kick me out of there. I'd been really skinning 'em at cards lately." And he'd been taking, maybe, a little too much pleasure in beating them at their own game.

The young woman's expression was still fixed, but now that he'd got closer to her Jeet saw she was no dullard. He felt uncomfortable under her gaze. "Wichita," she said, "can't you buy this man some camel's milk or something? A piece of meat? Some consideration for getting the poor fellow expelled from his club." She spoke in those highly modulated tones the Brits would call plummy, a small, imperious Englishwoman.

"Come on up to the house with us," said the cowboy. "I've got everything they've got at that café, and you won't have to listen to their horseshit music."

Wichita with his knack for making quick and useful friendships had somehow managed to meet Dutch doctors, man and wife, and he'd arranged to caretake the bungalow on the Mountain where the doctors expected to retire. This was a neighborhood elevated in prestige and altitude where Jeet had never previously ventured. They climbed out of the stink and clamor of the Medina and into air carrying scents of eucalyptus and pine. Not much talk was possible walking in the heat of a hot day and up a steady grade, but even then, before they knew each other at all, they had begun to form a cabal, a little league of the dispossessed, people who by instinct will recognize each other anywhere. When they came to know more specifically what they had in common it would be that they were all elective outcasts, dreading home.

The bungalow sat on its own prominence and from its small terrace, seeing but not seen, shaded by poplars, enclosed by plantings and wrought iron, they had before them a city of white and tan and rose walls marching down to the seas, both the city and the seas shimmering that afternoon in the heat. It was cooler on the mountain with a breeze from off the Atlantic. "See?" said Wichita as if he had promised this. As Jeet and Miss Dobb settled in rattan chairs, he quizzed and tempted them. "Daphne, you want anything in that rum? You like coffee, partner? We've got coffee'll knock your socks off. Got sugar, got honey, got bourbon, comes right down to it. Kentucky bourbon. No? Hashish? Got the local and some Lebanese blond. Just a second, I'll roust Rahim, get him up off his ass and get us some coffee built."

Suddenly alone with Daphne Dobb, Jeet suddenly understood that he was in love with her, poor sap. She would have been terrifying enough if he weren't smitten. Jeet made a great show of considering the scenery and eventually managed to say, "This is quite something,"

"This?" she said.

"The whole, uhm, panorama. . . The, you know."

"I suppose," she said.

Still witless, but with some calculation he asked her, "You live here, too?"

"I don't *live,* anywhere," she said.

"What?"

"Or should I say," she said, "—-occasionally. I stay here occasionally. Professional guest, don't you know?"

"Oh," said Jeet. "He did not know. Not yet. Not exactly. And now he didn't want to know, but of course he would, in due course, find out. These were to be his people now, his flamboyant pals.

Wichita, as it turned out, was only Wichita in Tangier but would be Ted Tollefson again upon his return to Wichita, there to eternally run his father's feed lots and lease his father's equipment to the oil patch and rub shoulders with the crème de la crème of Central Kansas. In Tangier Wichita shuddered at every mention of this future. He would have very much preferred to be his hell-bent-for-election grandfather and not the boy raised in privilege and private schools, but born too late what could he do? In Tangier he could at least act the big American roustabout and swagger around a city that didn't know any better. His family had recently ceased to subsidize him in the hope of forcing him back into the fold, and, accustomed to having and spending money he was always in need of it, forever scheming, but because he was frank and funny about it, his scheming wove right into the fabric of his charm.

Daphne Dobb was also living by her wits. Deeply, ironically English, she liked her dram of rum with breakfast and again at tea, and she rarely failed to drink the Queen's health. She explained herself as the end of the family line, "We're Royal Navy, darling. Have been since before Trafalgar, since we were Daubissons and terribly froggy. I'm afraid this third daughter, though, this latest

Dobb is as inconsequential as they come. Adrift, as the Blue Admiral would say."

Jeet was not usually inclined nor usually invited to fall in with new people this way, and it may have been the good air, or the views, or the various intoxicants, but it seemed awfully easy to get on with them, to accept their acceptance. Once he had met them it was all he could do to prevent himself from climbing to the Mountain every day and making a pest of himself at the bungalow. By the end of his first visit Jeet understood that Wichita and Rahim, openly affectionate and jealous of each other, were the couple of the household. This meant, or so Jeet hoped, that Miss Dobb was a third wheel and only a guest after all. He knew that among the expats of Tangier nothing morally usual should be assumed, but whatever her arrangement here it hadn't touched her much. He was often alone with her on the terrace while in the bungalow Wichita railed at Rahim or other of his associates, fierce negotiations in commercial French and scraps of the local Arabic that the cowboy seemed to need as much as Jeet needed his dangerous chats with Miss Dobb.

These conversations with Daphne had their military parallels, Jeet sending out his sappers to tunnel under the castle walls and Midshipman Dobb directing her canon. Perfectly hard on herself she could afford to be a pitiless thing and her remarks could rake like grapeshot and dismast a fool in a hot instant. Simply to avoid this fate seemed to Jeet a kind of triumph, and to be safely serious he found himself talking too much about "the farm where I grew up" as he always called it, the most serious thing he knew. In time he relaxed enough in her presence to form a coherent thought, to express it, but she would always be a smoky-eyed risk. Courtship, or siege, or whatever this was, she remained a constant thrill, a walking contradiction, the steel cutie pie in an off the shoulder jersey and a plum scarf. He wondered if she'd be warm to the touch. For weeks he wondered, until the wondering was almost unbearable. This campaign was like any other, after any number of strategies and any amount of maneuvering the issue could only be decided when someone risked everything to see it decided. Jeet had not yet screwed his courage to that sticking point. He regretted his freckled, battered face more than he had in a long while, and behind it he kept himself at bay by thinking in platitudes. 'Casual,' he thought. 'Keep it casual. Easy does it. She's only tolerating you.'

And if he did confess himself, what could he say? 'I live in dread of things you might say to me, and it makes me so alert, so thank you.' 'You're adorable.' Most of what was true was better left unsaid. And for what should he ask, if had guts to ask? What did he want of her? Could we hold hands? Take off our clothes? Twine our souls? So far, he hadn't even dared to ask her away from the Mountain for a drink. As she went on about her St. Bernard and her Corgi, now deceased, and about Uncle Bertie at the flower show, Jeet didn't think she'd noticed how he'd reached a quivering impasse. She had no idea how near he was to doing or saying something calamitous.

Or maybe she did know.

One day, curled in her rattan throne, she leveled a look at him and asked, "What do you *do*?"

"Do?" he dissembled. Until that very moment it had never occurred to Jeet to feel guilty about lying idle so long. "Oh," he said, "one thing or another. I've always had some kind of. . . even if it was just mucking cards. Lumber yard. Oil rig. The farm, of course. I was a student."

"I mean *now*," she said. "What are you doing here, that is when you're not chatting me up?"

He thought this had taken a bad turn, and Jeet said, "Oh. I guess you could say I do no harm. Like they tell the doctors. I mean I've always. . . Soon as the money runs out, I'm sure I'll be working at something. But."

"No," she said. "Your time. How do you fill your days?"

He didn't fill them so much as note how they evaporated here. "I, well I had been playing a lot of cards until recently. I walk." This sounded like an old man's wan regimen, and he knew the world's opinion of a reader, but thought he may as well admit, "And I've been reading. Even more than usual. Been reading Proust."

"In the French?"

"Just a translation," he said. "I'm from Montana. We don't use discouraging words or French up there."

"You're not angling to be some dreadful intellectual, are you?"

"Wouldn't be the worst thing," he said. "My nose is always in a book, anyway; be nice if I could arrange to get paid for it."

"With no French?" she said.

"Nope. No French. No Latin. Just. . . When my money runs out, I'll be. . . something. But working, anyway."

"If the things weren't so astronomically expensive," she said, "and heavy, I'm sure I'd read more. There's a mystery on everyone's nightstand. Potboilers, that's my life of the mind."

Jeet had caught a glimpse of himself as an indolent man and had expected for one very bad moment to be dismissed. "You should try the lending library at the American Legation," he said. "It's free."

"Proust?" she said.

"Yeah, but also Mickey Spillane or, or I think I've even seen some dog books on the shelves."

"Dog books?" she said. "Now I've convinced you I'm

an idiot, haven't I? And it is the American Legation."

"You could be my guest," he said. "Though it probably wouldn't be necessary."

"But if I should fail to return a book, what then? Diplomatic incident?"

"I doubt anyone would even notice," he said. "It's quite an informal thing. And free. I mean there's nothing very new, usually, but I've found plenty to read."

"You seem rather apologetic about it," she said. "You shouldn't apologize."

"Reading so much? Well, I'm an okay gambler, but other than that, reading's about the only thing I'm good at. But what's it good *for*? Doesn't seem to lead to much but my satisfaction. Where I'm from, you're supposed to be a little more productive than that. I expect that's about how it is everywhere. Once you're out of grade school you hardly ever run into someone who tells you to go sit in a corner and read."

"You should take me, then," she said. "To your library."

"Take? Oh, sure. That'd be fine. Sure," he said. "Any time."

"Tomorrow?"

She would know just how he was hearing this, for by now a half dozen shades of surging pink would be competing for dominance on his face. He could not be appropriately calm and was physically incapable of being discrete. "I guess," he said, "I could probably squeeze that into my schedule."

"Are you up and around by ten?" she said.

"I can be."

"The breakwater," she said. "That's near your house, isn't it? We'll meet there."

Only very much later would he think to notice how quick she had been with the details of that rendezvous.

Vastly overstimulated by the bare thought of a date to the library, and not even a date so much as an appointment, he'd slept very little and been up very early to pace his cottage, then the beach, then to arrive at the breakwater an hour before he was to meet her there. He stood sweating lightly under the hood of his djellaba, behind his shades, humming with sleeplessness and the sprawling, pulsing activity of the port, and steeling himself for the big disappointment. How, with no exact expectations, could he be disappointed? Easily. Almost inevitably. He waited, telling himself again and again, 'We're going to the damn *lib*rary,' and even that was uncertain until she showed.

Finally, she came along the footpath under the wall of the Casbah, prancing more than walking. Wearing a head scarf in deference to the local scheme, she was otherwise dressed as a young Nazarene woman, relatively naked in her slacks. She came to him with her dancer's strut and a quick, frank smile, and he thought, 'If it's only this. If this is all I ever get.'

By way of greeting she said, "It's broiling already. One glorious day, I swear, I will wear the practical shoes of a practical Wessex woman," and she continued with no pause in her step to walk out onto the docks, and he fell in beside her. Were they to be tourists together, taking in the sights? Fishermen were shaking out their salty nets, scavenger birds wheeled low overhead, a barefoot boy ran by them with a sand shark slung on his back, the giddy thief glancing rearward with no one in pursuit. Boats were tied in places three deep to the dock, many of them in some state of repair or disintegration and less than seaworthy, but nearly every hull was brilliant as the plumage of a tropical bird; it was so obviously Africa at dockside. Daphne Dobb, however, was not out for a stroll; she took no noticeable interest in anything, including Jeet, and walked so purposefully toward the end of the dock that it seemed she meant to walk right on out to sea.

But she'd been intent on a certain boat, the dullest in the whole flotilla under its blistered, dark blue paint, tied up alone near the end of the dock, a motorboat with a single coil of rope on its duckboards, a turbaned man kneeling in the bow singing the worst song Jeet had ever heard; he'd be a member of that local cult that liked to sing itself insensible. Miss Dobb crossed her arms and looked down at the turbaned man, making her displeasure as specific as possible without speaking, and when this failed to have effect she yelled, "Out!" Still the turbaned man sang on, and Daphne, nearly under her breath, hissed, "Out! I said out, bloody wog. Not yours. It's not yours anymore."

At last the turbaned man climbed out of the boat, eyes and moustaches drooping, song ceased, and he turned his powerful back to them and walked away under the weight of his misfortune. "Not his boat," said Daphne as if this one fact should satisfactorily explain everything.

"Is it yours?" Jeet said.

"It's in receivership," she said. "In hock. The man missed his payments."

"He owed *you* money?"

"No, no," she said. "Friend of a friend. Of a friend. One of Wichita's tangles—I'm not even sure. Do you know motors? You must."

"I. Well. Not intimately. I could gap a spark plug if I absolutely had to, get the water out of a fuel line. If I had tools. I can usually get 'em started." Jeet wanted to prove useful.

Daphne asked in maternal pride, "What do you think of her?"

"Well," said Jeet, "I'm no water person." The only boat

he'd ever been on had tried to kill him with her swaying underfoot. "I take it you like it?"

"She's so sleek," said Daphne Dobb. "The most beautiful lines."

"Cut of her jib, huh?" Even through a landlubber's eyes it was clear to Jeet that in this Daphne Dobb was delusional. It was a craft he might have trusted for use on a very shallow pond, old, and small, with a peacock lace of leaked fuel swirling around her in the water.

"I have a proposition for you," Daphne said.

She wanted him to go into business with her. Import, export. She wanted him to buy the boat. Wichita, she said, had connections on the beach for hashish, and on the high seas for watches and perfumes, and Wichita knew which Moroccan officials to bribe and how much, and she had managed to convince him that she could navigate this lucrative circuit in the dark, and she thought she probably actually could do it because there were some colossal boobs in her very own family who'd got around the horn and back. Duty free merchandise, the dark of night. "A fabulous opportunity, don't you see?"

"Mmm," said Jeet, hoping she was having her little joke with him. "Still want to see about the library?"

"Would they have charts?" she said. "We'll need to try and understand the current through the strait. The tides and everything. See, darling, it's only a matter of putting our heads together and being creative, and—voila! — we're in the chips. What a perfect lark."

Many if not all the flaws in her plan were obvious to him at once. Jeet didn't swim, couldn't read the map of the night sky, and he had never operated a boat or even ridden in one so small. She gave him to understand that they'd be going out on the big water to deliver the hashish and receive their incoming booty from a ship anchored, briefly, well out in international waters. They would be running without lights in violation of maritime law and in the middle of the busiest shipping lane in the world.

"So," she said, "we'll be wanting something nimble, won't we? A clever little thing just like this."

"But you know these things? How to patch the leaks? How to find your way around out there?"

"I coxed for the heavyweight crew at school, boatload of massive dykes. We cleared out many a pub, I can tell you, the girls and I. But that would be my seagoing experience so far—crew, a trip on the Queen Mary, the channel ferries. I'm a girl, you know."

He knew and only too painfully—this girl factor was the only one to recommend the nightmare she was suggesting. If the worst that should happen was their failure to turn a profit from this caper, that still meant his investment would hasten and not delay his return to the states and to some workaday situation there—not what he wanted at all. He'd been living close to the bone to avoid it. So far as Jeet knew, he had no head for business or for crime. "This boat?" he said. "*This* boat?"

"She's my little bobolink," she said, so fond of it. "Are you on board, matey? Barbary Coast; it's just the thing, don't you think?"

She was so relentlessly inspirational, Daphne, that Jeet found himself exchanging traveler's checks for pesetas within the hour, and before noon they were at the Hotel Atlantide, meeting there by prearrangement with a Señor Espinoza who was evidently delighted. Jeet bought the boat from him. Jeet was being carried right along. They celebrated with sangria. Jeet and Daphne hiked back up to the bungalow to inform Wichita of their progress and for further celebration. Later, though, somewhere in the middle of his second consecutive sleep shorted night, Jeet's pleasure plunged as he pictured them swept out to sea, pulling fruitlessly on a starter rope, or lost, or swamped under some seaborne colossus whose crew would never so much as notice them as the propeller chopped them to chum. On sober reflection, Jeet remembered that he didn't even like getting wet. Surely, there were easier ways of making money.

The following morning, they met at the same time and place, Jeet arriving early again in order to repeat the pleasure of watching her come to him. They took possession and took stock of the boat. Jeet lifted the duckboards out and found a bad depth of standing water lying above her keel. "First thing," he said, "we better get a siphon hose."

"Is that necessary?" she said. "Boats just leak, don't they? Skin breathes. Boats leak. The natural order."

"Mmm," he said. "I'm not so sure about that. But I am sure I wouldn't want it to leak too much." Jeet understood then that he'd only begun spending money. They went to the Medina where he bought a metal coffee can, a set of metric spanners, and a djellaba for Daphne to wear. It was good in all weathers he told her and served also for a disguise with the hood up. The best garment ever. She bought herself a pair of sunglasses and said, "Now we've a uniform, darling." Jeet even happened on a compass offered for sale in a basket of random items, and they were to remain unreasonably devoted to this instrument for all the good it was to do them out dancing on the waves.

They returned to the boat and began bailing the water from the bottom with the coffee can. The barefoot boy from the day before came along and was soon insisting that he take over the work. He didn't need to insist for very long. The boy would also find and apply some pitchy caulk for them. He had appointed himself ship's deckhand and would not accept the coins Jeet offered him, and when Jeet pulled the outboard motor awake and Daphne guided the boat away from the dock the boy froze in the posture of a faithful dog and didn't move from it until he had watched them all the way out of sight.

"Tears, darling? I'm happy, too. But let's not go overboard. In any sense."

The boy on the pier stood watching them out of sight, and Jeet Harrow knew just how he felt.

◊ ◊ ◊

There were no life jackets to be found in the Medina and none to be seen around the docks, Muslims being, apparently, fatalists by faith. Inshallah—no life jackets. Finally, just before that initial cruise, Jeet mentioned that he couldn't swim and that he would like at some point to maybe find some flotation.

"Brilliant," Daphne said. He didn't know how she meant this, and nothing was clarified when she added, "Fucking brilliant, Mr. Harrow."

The motor he'd bought was a surprise, a bargain, eager to run and powerful. Jeet was also surprised at himself when he took almost immediate command of the vessel. A necessity. Daphne had no finesse with the throttle, which she kept wide open, and if left at the helm wearing that weird, wild grin of hers, it seemed pretty likely she'd ram the boat to splinters on the first rough water they encountered. It was purely a smuggler's boat, painted to merge even in daylight with the sea, and powered to be too fast for her own good. Then another surprise—Jeet seemed to have some facility for driving her. Anchors aweigh! Once underway with a badly muffled motor and the propeller wash and the hull pounding the water, it was impossible to talk, so Daphne the navigator simply pointed where she wanted him to go. She devised a set of symbols for her small fists to show him if he was to go fast or slow, to port or to starboard.

Arrangements had been made. They were to have only this one shake-out cruise to determine if the boat was sound and to find by daylight that nasty little bay between Tangier and Ceuta where they were to make by dark their first connection. There were to be exotics rowing that night in rowboats laden with hashish round the rock anvil of Isla de Perejil. It was all arranged. A certain time and place, a clear night. Then out to sea where they had only to stay on an imaginary line drawn between the peak of Mount Sidi Moussa and the Rock of Gibraltar, and there about midway on that line they were to find a trawler lit like a Christmas tree and waiting with another species of contraband for them.

"It's all designed to be uncomplicated," Wichita had told them. "Set up to be simple as possible for you. They know where to be and when to be there, so it should be easy."

Time was of the essence. Tangier was mad just then for a wrist watch or for almost any time piece, and though Jeet and Miss Dobb were about to go into the business of supplying that fad, duty free, and though they would come into possession of hundreds of them later that night, neither of them presently owned a wrist watch, because of, as Daphne explained it, "The infernal ticking." A watch was the last piece of equipment that Jeet, very reluctantly, bought. That night, if all went according to plan, they should have watches in their hundreds and return to port reeking of gasoline, Estee Lauder, and Chanel, the very essence of illicit prosperity. It was only a matter of being in the right place at the right time, and how odd it would be to go from having no schedule at all to keeping such a strict and compelling one.

It was such a brazen operation that Jeet sometimes wondered why they bothered to do it at night. Much of the coast they followed to the Spanish zone was populated, all of it heavily traveled, and from the beginning it was clear that their best concealment lay in hiding in plain sight, as if there were any choice. Only in the rocky cove behind the Isla de Perejil was any privacy assured, and there Daphne Dobb produced from her vocabulary of gestures a ring she made of her arms as if she were embracing a barrel and by which she placed their order with some floating representatives of the forty thieves who very quickly offloaded many ten-kilo bricks wrapped in printed sisal.

Riding lower in the water the smugglers then headed out to open sea where the currents of the Mediterranean and the Atlantic conflict. The landmarks they used were more than sufficient, always in view, and in any event their route ran closely parallel to that of a ferry line, but to maintain a heading, any heading in a small craft was no small thing out here. Going north they crabbed with their bow about fifteen degrees west of their direction of travel to compensate for the inflow from the ocean, all the while bouncing on random chop.

But it happened that he was sailor enough, that Daphne had French enough. They made the necessary transit and exchange. After only three such expeditions, Jeet's expenses were already recovered, and they entered an intoxicating period of pure profit. Stars above, twinkling ships below, aromatic cargos—they were in business. Wichita claimed it was the high season for their trade and said they should expect to be going out at least every other night so long as the weather held favorable; Wichita never did explain just when or how the weather might be expected to change.

Too tired between trips to spend much of the money he was making, Jeet was soon awash in francs and had begun to take what miserly satisfaction he could in the state of his bank account; goaded by a nearly satiable greed he found his life of crime in some ways too like a regular job and almost welcomed those occasional moments of liquid terror to refresh the thing. Mostly, though, it was to be hours upon hours of mutely pounding over open water in an open boat, all those nautical miles. Driven, they rode together, they rode apart. Hour upon hour, night after night, and even on their return to the dock there was no talk between them, only the growling, the residual ringing of the motor in their ears. A taxi would be waiting. It was all arranged. They would load their loot in the taxi and take it for deposit at the Hotel Atlantide, a portion of which Señor Espinoza, had converted for use as his warehouse, and from there Daphne would continue on in the taxi, on up to the bungalow on the Mountain, and Jeet would hike home to his pipe and his beckoning bed. It was become a job of work, more or less honest labor, and the money was good, but whatever Jeet had hoped might happen with Daphne Dobb wasn't happening. He was no longer visiting the Mountain. They went out at night and stared into the wind, and what else could he do? Stare at her all the while? Study her to his heart's content? No. They were so often and so little together. They were driven, alone. The money was good. He remembered from time to time that money had not been his first purpose in all this. To work with her, and to be trusted in this way by a flinty thing like Daphne Dobb should be entirely satisfactory, but it wasn't; he wanted more, and what more he wanted remained unclear to him, and he thought it very likely that he would at some point do something to upset their profitable partnership.

All the wanting was wearing, too. Many of his days were consumed with patching the boat. While he knew well enough that theirs must be a short-lived operation, he had fooled himself into thinking they were the kind of people who suffer no illusions and that he was not being led through it like a bull with a ring in his nose.

One night as they were coming sluggishly out of the bay and away from their meeting with the hashish merchants an isolate light began to appear intermittently along the headland to their starboard— Jeet, having lately ditched Proust for the Hornblower books had acquired some seagoing jargon to help him make sense of what was going on out here. The light shone briefly at long, seemingly random intervals, and gradually it separated from the headland. It looked to ride low on the water and to be nearer them every time it appeared again. A boat, no doubt, and a fast one. Jeet struggled to calculate how coincidence might explain why it had launched just then from that rocky shore, why its course seemed so determined to coincide with their own. But no, it was coming for them—a light/notlight apparition, nearer, nearer until they could hear it, too, mingling with their own racket, and then by starlight make out its shape even when it was running dark, a boat smaller than their own and much quicker at the moment. Jeet shared glances with Daphne Dobb, no need to shout about the obvious, and he continued on toward the trawler as there wasn't a better line of retreat, and he continued to entertain the possibility that he was mistaken until the light came again, this time shining in their eyes; Jeet happened to think of Amos Davis jacklighting deer back home. Just before he was blinded, he'd caught a glimpse of the other boat's crew, two men in spare rags, and they'd be serious people, for it was cold on the water at night, sometimes very cold, and these men were lean as whippets. And then they were alongside, one of the wretches swinging a small anchor by a length of rope, intending it apparently for a grappling hook. There was a short, bright sound in the general uproar; the man suddenly reconsidered his business with the rope; he then reconsidered everything and fell into the sea. Daphne Dobb held one of those sleek little pistols the Nazis use in the movies. The man at the tiller turned hard away from them, but Daphne shot him, too, and he rose off his bench into a writhing crouch, and she shot him again, and he fell over the tiller so that the pirate boat, still running full out, began to describe a tightening circle round its outboard motor. Daphne tossed her pistol into the water and with her now empty hand still in its pistol shape she pointed to the trawler. Press on.

While those pirates had not so much as put a hitch in the schedule that night, those pirates when they floated up bloated, flotsam and jetsam now, may or may not be fished from the sea, and they had at least succeeded in providing Jeet Harrow a better understanding of mortality.

That night after they'd finished dropping their goods at the Hotel Atlantide, Daphne asked if she could stay with him, and Jeet didn't think this carried the usual implications. She'd probably be wanting to talk, talk about what had happened. But, no. She didn't want that. Under her djellaba there was suspended another pistol hung by a cord, and on her chest a field of bruises suggesting both weapons had been hanging there, banging there, these many nights past. Then they were lovers, or at least she would stay with him for the remainder of each night after a run, and she was as might be expected a fierce lover, but within that there were fragments, flitting bits of tenderness that were more than he'd ever hoped for. He suspected, though, that her favors were given to keep him interested in the project, for he'd lost nearly all his enthu-siasm for smuggling.

The weather changed, bringing nocturnal fogs that seemed to blow in from the Canary Islands, and because that fog robbed them of their landmarks, their essential navigational tool, there were no runs to be made. During this interlude Jeet holed up with Horatio Hornblower in the West Indies and his earnest adventures, and Jeet smoked kif and wondered horribly, constantly what Daphne Dobb might be doing at any given moment. After a couple of days of such wondering he headed up the Mountain and to the bungalow where Rahim told him that Wichita was off somewhere being entertained by a rich woman and that Miss Dobb had claimed she was going to Zanzibar, which may have been a joke, but she had taken her things, all of her things, and she was gone. She'd been complaining, Rahim said, of boredom. And now she was gone.

◊ ◊ ◊

Jeet marched down the mountain and signed the boat back to Señor Espinoza. In a fog he caught a ride with the lamp merchant, the man with the brass laden truck. In a fog Jeet found himself in Yousef's village, waiting out the rain in an empty room with nothing to read and no one to talk to, and that much introspection would scar anyone. He was, against best advice, against the way he was raised, feeling sorry for himself, laying up taking drugs and longing for a legitimacy he was in no danger of achieving. Snap out of it.

So Jeet decided he must be headed home, but not before there was another little Arab mix-up that got him rerouted through the desert after all, and instead of Tangier he found himself in a garrison town, a sullen oasis, where, as he was waiting for the first camel west, he had a bout with dysentery. Al Whereveritwas lay under a sky with terrible implications, an absolute blue, and its air by day was like breathing flame, and at night Jeet lay in his hammock freezing, shitting dust, thinking this was it for him, and wishing he'd lived a life worth dying for.

TEL

There were eruptions of special grace from time to time in her family line—her brother, her son—and Verity lived in fear that the world lay in wait to feast on such shimmering creatures.

"No," she said.

"It's a done deal," Tel said.

"No," she said, "it isn't. You still have to pass some kind of physical, don't you?"

Jeet, as usual, was quick to take Verity's position. "She has a point," he said. "There's supposed to be a lot of ways to get your heart racing, screw up your blood pressure for a while. Maybe you could convince 'em you're nuts; how hard would that be?"

They were gathered round the hallowed old kitchen table on the occasion of a Thanksgiving, and Tel had waited until now to tell them both at once that he had enlisted in the Marine Corps. That's what he'd been doing in Great Falls the day before. "It's just two years," he said. "It could've been worse."

"How?" Verity said.

"I kind of freaked out." Tel plucked a small, invisible orb out of the air. "Geeze. Somebody pulls a ping pong ball out of a cage, and, whammo, there you are—you're number eight. Selective Service has your number, and your number is eight. Now you're waiting for that call, and you know it'll be coming any old time. Maybe I kind of panicked, but I just wanted to get it over with. The suspense was already getting to me."

"No," Verity said, though she no longer had the power to forbid her son anything, a power she'd used very little when she'd possessed it; her pretty boy had also been a decent and reasonable child who seemed to know what to do.

"Just happened to be a marine hanging out in the hall at the recruiting center when I came in," he said. "I keep wanting to call him Sergeant Trichinosis, which isn't quite right. Nice guy. He tried to get me to go for four years so I could have some technical training, said they might even make me a photographer. But I held out for two. Two years. I'll be back farming before you know it. You'll barely have time to miss me."

"No," said Verity.

"There's a million deferments," Jeet said. "You could have gone to school. Graduate school. Law school. Stay in school forever like I did. Been years since anyone thought this war was a good idea, but it just keeps dragging on, so a short-term deferment's no good. You need something to last as long as necessary. I'll bet we could still get you into school somewhere."

"Too late," said Tel. "Besides, that sounds even worse than the military to me. Too late for deferments now."

"You'll have to follow orders," Verity said. "Did you think of that? You go with those people, you don't get to decide for yourself anymore—about anything—including what's right or wrong. Did you ever think of that?"

"Not exactly. Or maybe I did, but not right when I was doing it."

"That's a contract" Jeet said, "Those papers you signed, they're some kind of contract after all. Gotta be some holes in 'em. I'll take a look. Guess we could chop off one of your toes. I mean, what exactly were you thinking, Tel?"

"Other poor guys have had to do it. I'm trying to do the honorable thing. I don't know—my duty? You're not supposed to like it. If you did, it wouldn't be a duty. Anyway, those recruiters were telling me Nixon's pulling us out. Pulling us out of the north, and that's the marines, so it's supposed to be an excellent time to be in the Marine Corps. Anyway, you don't get to pick your wars—which war you want to fight in. I don't think it works that way."

"Shit," Verity said. "Honorable. Honorable? Shooting up rice paddies? Getting tropical diseases?"

"Well, I'm gone," Tel said. "Told 'em I'd go, so the way I see it, now I have to go."

A farmer farming, a singer singing, he'd been happy then; according to Jeet and Verity he'd been happy from birth. Tel sometimes still remembers that sunny self of long ago and in remembering is ever reminded that nature gives no guarantees.

On graduating high school his friends had drifted off to the service, to college, to populated places outside Chouteau County where jobs might be had and squalid young marriages maintained. Tel got no farther than Geraldine where he rented a shack and had the luxury of tending his own and only his own eccentricities, and from which he went right on farming Harrow ground. His mother handled the business, the books and the taxes, buying and selling, hiring and firing, those operations Tel didn't like so much, leaving him the bloody-knuckle, dusty-teeth end of the operation, which he loved, the banging on balky equipment and knocking around in country whose every season, every seasonal event he knew by scent, by the particular caress of the wind on his skin; he knew weather, he knew wheat, and in a community of farmers he was already esteemed a fine farmer.

Singing on and over machinery, on and over his mother's playing, he had also developed a massive voice, and while still in high school he'd caught on as the lead vocalist in a band that called itself Torque Wrench and now toured the bars of the Hi-line and southern Alberta every winter. Tel was assured of a warm welcome in Canada or in any of those many bars where he could only legally be as a member of the band; his voice was a three-octave horn rich as Mexican chocolate; he'd inherited his parents' precise hearing. On the road he was forever being reminded he was handsome and often asked to serve as a warm place in the north country. At home he was never by choice alone and never under any circumstance lonely. He had loved to farm, loved to sing, and wanted for nothing so far as he knew.

Lately, however, his contentment had begun to wear a little thin. The sap was up in him and conditions were ripe for a wrong impulse to prevail. He was ripe, apparently, to bursting. He knew this for a mistake even as he was making it.

◊ ◊ ◊

They had told him he'd be shipping everything he wore or brought with him back home, so he wasn't wearing very much. With a few hours to kill on New Year's Day before catching his first flight anywhere, Tel walked streets named for minerals and the states of the union. He wore tennis shoes and a fresh crewcut, hair not as short as it would be tonight, but not much use against the cold. No hat, no gloves, teeth chattering in cold so sharp it seared his lungs to sing, but he sang anyway.

"Hot fun in the summertime."

Butte had made itself ancient in its hundred years, eaten a deep hole in itself, and was suffering this morning from a hangover. Newspapers and candy wrappers swirled in the wind, in that cinematic shorthand for desolation.

"I cloud nine when I want to," he sang.

"Ooout of schooohl," he sang.

"County fair in the country sun, and everythaang

is true-oooh—ooh yeah." He sang. He sang the whole family Stone—alto, to tenor, to Sly's rumbling bass, this was a vocal parlor trick that had really wowed them in Medicine Hat and Havre. A songbird then, his song the answer to everything.

Mile high, mile deep. It seemed awfully futile; Butte with its cold whistling down off the pass and up from the bowels of the violated earth was far too cold for an under-dressed fool of a boy, and Butte could be a little ominous of a winter's day. If you let it.

"Hot fun in the summertime."

The several benefits of being Corporal Harrow included never having to pull guard duty, a privilege more than offset by the days and nights he spent just outside the apartment where his commanding officer had stashed a girlfriend, his job to sit in Captain Burnham's jeep and keep it safe in a larcenous neighborhood not too far removed from Suckahotchie Alley. This part of Koza, built entirely of poured concrete or cinder block, was uniformly gray and smelled of the benji ditches running through the back streets and of strange cookery. In Okinawa, for all Tel knew, someone near at hand could be boiling octopus or kelp—snacking on it. On Gate Two Street or somewhere off in the neon-lit part of town a band of sequined Ryukyans was playing 'Smoke on the Water,' and they must be rattling the walls, for the anthem pulsed almost undiminished these many blocks to reach him; Tel hummed along for a while, but this too proved boring. The night air clung to him; he'd become greasy in his recently starched utilities and had only his sleeves to mop his face.

Almost everything Tel detested in military life had

been predictable—had been predicted—and he knew he was not particularly entitled to his outrage, still he felt misused. He had managed this enlistment so far with a bare minimum of personal inconvenience; Corporal Harrow did not pull guard duty, rarely stood in formation, never suffered an inspection, and he was allowed noteworthy liberties with regards the length of his hair. Hippy Harrow was said to be, and not too ironically, the most powerful man in the company, typing orders in the air-conditioned comfort of HQ, orders that Captain Burnham did not usually bother to read before signing. Even with these vaguely pimpish expeditions into Koza and to other amorous or shady locations, Tel's duties were hardly more than irksome anymore.

He was a hunt-and-peck man, an office pogue serving in the catbird seat as his commander's de facto adjutant and tour guide. Lately he had come to know a number of men who'd only lately come from hell, and so he felt small to chafe so much at mere silliness, but he was a Harrow through and through and doomed to fit poorly in any kind of organization. There was a hot nerve running through him that got inflamed the moment he found himself at anyone's beck and call or was required to attend on any superior's orders, especially those orders emanating from people he considered dolts. On ceremonial occasions, the Marine Corps birthday, the Fourth of July, Tracks Company could expect to stand at parade rest under a tropical sun and hear speeches concerning freedom given by men who'd never in their adult lives drawn a free breath, lifers who fancied obedience far more than seemed proper to Tel Harrow. Six months to go. Six easy months as an NCO, but the taste of the high and dry and of good cold seasons was already in his mouth. Home. He was a Harrow. He was a farmer, son and grandson of independent operators, and to be otherwise now seemed almost intolerable.

At last Captain Burnham erupted from the stair well of the apartment building, the girlfriend still attached to him, the pair of them raising a ruckus that instantly produced sets of eyes in many neighborhood windows. The girl, a person exquisitely delicate of form and feature with a liquid cloak of hair that swayed with her every exertion, had got hold of the back of Burnham's belt and was trying to dig in her heels to impede his departure and was shrilling some demand over and over in a Japanese or jaybird dialect, and Burnham, who was at that point in his career almost constantly guilty of conduct unbecoming an officer, dragged her along behind, declaiming in a parade ground voice, "Many yen, many, many yen, Akiko." A half back in high school, Burnham executed a distantly remembered twitch of his hips, freed himself from her grip, and sprung into the passenger's seat. "Hubba hubba, Harrow. Let's book."

Tel worked all the way through the Jeep's pathetic gear box getting around the first available corner, then observed, "She got you again, sir. This one's nasty."

The Captain touched his cheek where three freshly inscribed lines ran parallel, one of them originating very near the corner of his left eye. "That's what I love about her," he mused. "She's so direct. There's none of this beating around the bush with Akiko." The marks were reminiscent of this country's brush painting, as if at one stroke she had rendered on his cheek a series of waves or cirrus clouds, but in vivid red. "Straight forward," said Burnham, "that's how I like 'em. If she ever got busy with that butterfly knife, though—whooh. That *could* be bad."

"She doesn't seem to need it, sir. There have to be some calmer women around."

"You've seen her, Harrow. There aren't many of those."

"That might be a good thing, sir."

"Naha," said Burnham, changing the subject. "You remember how to get to the docks, right? And stop at a drug store somewhere." He would apply antiseptic gel and pancake makeup to the parting gifts she'd given him, it was nearly routine now. He must like it. The girl had slashed him pretty often, but was overwhelmed with joy whenever Tel returned the Captain to her, and to the neutral observer this couple was so obviously a wreck gaining momentum.

One of the homesteader sayings Tel's mother had beat him over the head with was, "If it's worth doing, it's worth doing well." Tel did not think this was necessarily true of his present job.

Though he had been trained as a grunt, a ground-pounding rifleman, Tel had somehow been assigned to an armored battalion on Okinawa, an outfit whose various units maintained, repaired, and even occasionally operated tanks and self-propelled guns, lobbing their huge shells at targets floating out on the ocean. In these ranks there was endless use for a hand like Tel Harrow and his long familiarity with the big wrench, the welding torch—but, no—he was posted instead before the steel-frame Remington typewriter that was to serve daily and implacably as his enemy. Tel's talents did not then include typing, and he had no idea how he'd got this of all jobs. In this sink-or-swim situation, however, he soon developed a savage technique in which his forefingers flailed at the keys like a marimba player's mallets. Everything in triplicate. His manual was the best machine in the office for pounding through these forms. Working right under the noses of his executive officer and the First Sergeant, Tel had become proficient enough to remain invisible, and he had expected to keep his head down and type for a year or so and be done with this nonsense.

One day, though, walking across the grinder toward the PX, he happened on the Captain, and the Captain's driver, and the Captain's jeep which was just then refusing to start. Tel diagnosed vapor lock, and told them a short wait should fix it, and from that moment forward he was for the Captain's purposes an expert in all things and wise far beyond his years. This was only the first of many quirks the Captain was to reveal to him, this instant and unshakable faith in his abilities. Within a few months the Captain was essentially to cede the day to day operations of his command to his clerk typist, and PFC Harrow pounded out various fates and directives on his Remington and became Lance Corporal soon enough, and then by meritorious promotion Corporal Harrow. Meanwhile the Captain pursued a range of extracurricular activities in which he thought his young genius should also play a part. Tel did his office work and served also as the Captain's personal mechanic and driver, and eventually as they cruised the length and breadth of Okinawa in that breezy jeep, the man's confessor.

"I've gone Asiatic," the Captain would say. "I must have. Otherwise, why would I be here?"

His professional prospects, his past, the unfairness of it all, Captain Burnham spoke of these things in a pressured way that the speaking never seemed to relieve, and certain phrases came round and round again, prayers on a prayer wheel. He was fond of saying, "The oak leaf will never land on these shoulders, Harrow. I am not armor, I'm supply, and you know, you just know this shit encrusted company is where they send careers to die." 'They,' as Captain Burnham used the term, meant the Marine Corps, and by extension the United States of America. He identified hypocrisy everywhere and in everything and had for his own reasons chosen to confide his many suspicions to Corporal Harrow. "Oh," he said, "I ran the dogs through the barracks like a responsible CO. Drug dogs, hmph. Practically the first thing I did. But the fix was in, wasn't it? Or the dogs were dogs, I don't know, but that's just what they did, they ran right on through. You never saw so many delighted troopies in your life, Harrow. They couldn't believe their good luck. So, fuck 'em. Who am I trying to save from themselves? Fucking lepers."

Tracks Company as the unit was more formally known had in fact been the last assignment for its last several commanding officers, an outfit too far to the rear that was somehow always home to an inordinate number of knuckle draggers and had long been rife with booze, buddha stick, China white, and fights with or without reason. "Tracks," Burnham would say. "They can jam whatever they want in their arms, kill themselves however they feel like doing it for all I care. Know how much a go-getter like myself makes in the World, a man who moves merchandise? Beau coups, Harrow, and name your industry. I don't know why I'm not already gone. I would've made a wonderful field grade officer, though, tell you that—but nevah happen now, G.I."

Captain Burnham, for all the good it did him, knew himself somewhat, and he often admitted, "I've got this love/hate problem." His chronicle of himself usually began in sixty-three when, loving his country without measure or moderation, he'd enlisted in the Marine Corps right when the whole Indo-China thing was looming. Was it his fault he'd been stationed at Marine Barracks Treasure Island and billeted in supply? He hadn't asked for a soft thing. So, Burnham put himself through San

Francisco State taking classes at night, and in the process young Burnham, regulation haircut and all, did happen to spend his share of time sitting cross legged on floors in the Haight and the Tenderloin, drinking wine, smoking weed, saying 'man' with bizarre frequency, and he'd made his trips down the shattering rabbit hole with Mr. Owsley. Burnham graduated college in the spring preceding the Summer of Love—remembering it he would roll his eyes and say, "Ell—Ess—Dee, the pure stuff. Now *that* was beautiful. Acid always got such a bad rap. My first mistake, I should have stuck with the counter culture. We all should've. . . Ambition. Plans for the future, feather your nest and so forth—those people were laughing at that, and I thought at the time they might be onto something. Those merry prankster types were a lot happier than I've ever been."

Burnham had dutifully gone to OCS, and then as a freshly minted lieutenant to Viet Nam where, still in supply, he was to serve two consecutive tours of duty without, so far as he knew and discounting backfires, hearing a shot fired in anger. He had managed a great depot from which he distributed materiel to Marines and ARVN alike, and the Vietnamese he supplied operated within the ancient laws of supply and demand, and Burnham found it impossible to escape their gratitude. This secondary income was not, of course, taxed. "I'm holed-up in the compound, watching old movies on Armed Forces teevee. Sumo matches. I was making rank, making book, and investing in the dream, Harrow. That was my war."

The strand in his story that jabbed him most painfully was a girl who'd become a woman over the course of these episodes. Berniece, whose name came always with a dollop of vinegar, had been his high school sweetheart, then his long- distance lover, and then the long-distance fiancé who had believed so whole-heartedly in him. Berniece, who now owned, ". . . she *owns* not rents," as Burnham would always specify, the most beautiful beauty parlor in Boise. "College girls? Mormon girls? Got any idea what they'll pay to achieve that natural look? And whose idea was that in the first place? Whose money put her through beauty college? I'm sweating my ass off in my room with Humphrey Bogart and fifty boxes of Girl Scout cookies, and I'm buying her the Sunrise Salon, and I'm thinking she'll be happy, I believe I have every right to think she'll be real happy with me, and I'm living like a *child* in Vietfuckingnam, and I get home and she tells me she doesn't think she can get over what I've been doing over there. What I've been doing? Getting people their refrigerators? Their fans? Their ammunition, yeah, but. I mean, come on, I'm a warehouse guy. She can't get over it, though. But what she can get over, and she *did* get over, believe me—she's perfectly fine with that beauty parlor even when I tell her it's the spoils of war. She can deal with that. No problem. *Mrs.*—Berniece—Pitcairn. Fuck her also. Fuck 'em all, Harrow, far as I'm concerned."

Burnham could and often did work himself into a froth reminiscing; the Captain had failed to make some critical adjustment. "Then," he would say, concluding with the most recent outrage, "they send you to the rock. To Tracks Company. And you don't know bugger-all about armor, or heroin, or anything else you might need to know. And it's bad. I may have to try out one of these ancient gook philosophies."

Okinawa by Tel's reckoning must lie exactly between the devil and the deep blue sea. The Captain's complaint was more longwinded and detailed than most, but its thick cynicism was standard issue among the marines of

Tel's acquaintance, a trait that made being among them as wearisome as treading water in boots. Who here did not feel somehow betrayed? They were, for one thing, the sons of fathers who'd gone to a perfectly righteous crusade, and now the war of their own time was a mortal and moral mess conferring little benefit or honor, and few of those who'd been to this generation's never-declared war would ever forgive the world for allowing anything so pointless to go forward, and serving side by side with them were those marines who hadn't got to the war, and who'd been convinced they were born to fight and were now sorely disappointed at finding themselves still oceans away from any actual hostilities, playing the tedious charade of the garrison soldier; and there were of course the inevitable marines who were marines only by way of evading jail, or debt, or matrimony and who had found in the Marine Corps the worst possible refuge from life's little annoyances. They were people marking time at a duty station a long way from anything relevant, a situation that left them collectively convinced they'd been hoodwinked. And how must the Okinawans feel, their narrow homeland clogged with these lumbering roundeyes and all their insane equipment? A dense undergrowth had grown up on heights once plowed by naval gunfire, unexploded ordnance still lay in their ground. The place was haunted by an ill spirit and, to a northerner's nose smelled everywhere of sweet rot.

At least, Tel thought, he had no one but himself to blame. He'd somehow come to understand that he'd come to this ugliness goaded by an ugly curiosity. At least he was no longer curious.

◊ ◊ ◊

Monsoon to the max someone had called this weather.

Rain lashed the roof and the windows so heavily that any talk was impossible inside the office, so Tel used the break in the interrogation to type some things in his in-box. Since the Captain's arrest, Corporal Harrow's standing in the company had fallen far and fast; he was the residue of a corrupt regime. His relationship to his typewriter remained the same, though, and for once he was grateful for the monotony of it. The office was presently empty except for himself and the men from CID, a gunnery sergeant and a warrant officer who wore their white-striped helmets indoors because they were under arms, and who, because they had nothing better to do while the rain bore down, patiently watched him type. Since his fall from grace, Tel had been told he could expect to stand Corporal of the Guard almost continuously until he rotated back to the world, and it happened he was serving in that capacity now. And now he was a suspect or something. Suspect. Corporal of the Guard. A bottomless tray of typing. What else? Stay busy, he thought. Four months, he thought. A little too busy at the moment. As duty Corporal, Tel was himself armed with a .45 that he was not technically qualified to discharge. The CID men wore .38s in shoulder holsters. Sidearms. They'd just gotten started on an edgy conversation when the rain interrupted them. At last, and with a great ripping suddenness the rain stopped; its absence was a sound unto itself.

"I've got guys walking guard under this," Tel said. "I should go see if they're all right."

"No. Let's just finish up here." The warrant officer had a badger's build and approach to his work.

"Aye, aye, sir. I, I doubt I'll have much to tell you, though. And you never said—am I in trouble?"

"Well. . ." said the warrant officer. The gunnery sergeant stood rocking slightly with his arms folded, certain of some outcome.

"If I did anything wrong," Tel said.

"Did you?" The warrant officer's nostrils were active in an otherwise stony face. "Do something wrong?"

"I didn't think so. Not *real* bad, anyway."

"Real bad?" said the warrant officer.

"We weren't using that jeep for, oh for strictly military purposes, sir. I knew that. But I. I was just a PFC when. . . Is this a thing where I shouldn't talk. Incriminate myself?"

"How do you feel," the warrant officer wondered gravely, "about national security?"

"I'm all for it," Tel said, "but who isn't?"

"That means," said the warrant officer, "you want to help us." His eyes were slightly mismatched in color, a spectacle effective as a hypnotist's watch.

"Yes, sir," Tel said. From the moment he'd stood on the yellow footprints in San Diego he had determined that he must feign total obedience so long as he was in the service, it seemed the only way through, and it had not escaped Tel's notice that feigned and actual obedience produced exactly the same result, and at moments like this he got an awful glimpse of his battered will.

"Let's not have any more of this shit about the fucking jeep, Corporal. That is if you are truly interested in avoiding trouble. What was he doing?"

"There was the girlfriend," Tel said. "A couple girls, actually."

"Corporal," said the warrant officer, out of patience. "You don't owe the guy anything. And let me give you a little tip—we already know what he was doing. We set him up. This was a sting."

"This? Sir, I'm still not sure I . . ."

"The *tank*, Corporal?"

The sergeant rocked on his heels, enjoying himself.

Beefy law enforcement.

"Oh," said Tel. "Oooh." The warrant officer had at this point answered more questions than he'd posed. "You should know, sir—the Captain was sort of losing his mind."

"And?"

"Wouldn't that make a difference?" Tel said. "Some kind of difference?"

"In what?" said the warrant officer. "Just tell me what you know, Corporal, and quit fucking around."

Tel then commenced the account that he hoped would illustrate his point or satisfy the investigators that he wasn't holding anything back. He started with that final evening at Akiko's, then the Captain's odd, idle mention of the Teahouse of the August Moon. But that wasn't where they were going. He'd been directed to a shanty down by the docks in Naha, a place they'd been before. The same man had answered the door on both occasions, a small, sunken cheeked Asian man, Tel could say no more because he'd had him in view for under five seconds altogether, both times in bad light. He'd stayed as usual with the jeep while the Captain went inside. And the Captain hadn't been there for long. Captain Burnham had a number of associates with whom he shared little or no language, and his communications with them usually amounted to an exchange of scraps of paper. Tel did not know what was on these slips.

"You never asked?" The warrant officer's tone suggested some shame should attach to such a lack of curiosity.

"No, sir," and Tel rounded right back to his story. "So, on our way back to base he asks me—the Captain—if I can drive a five-ton. I'm sure I can. They're just four-on-the-floor, pretty simple. He wants to know if I can pull a trailer, and I tell him I can. How about a *heavy* trailer? How heavy? Around fifty tons, he says. And that's when he started mentioning this tank. He's telling me he has to get rid of a tank before the Inspector General comes around. The company has a tank it's not supposed to have in its inventory. Captain said it makes no sense *not* to sell it. Do I have any idea how much steel there is in an M-48? And, by the way, do I think I could drive a tank? I tell him I've run a Cat, a D-6 if it's anything like that. I think that's when he told me he loved me. I mean—see what I mean? You could tell he was losing it.

"And I did try and bring up all the practical problems. Like—wouldn't we need some paperwork to get it through the gate? Nah, he says. Says it'll be down on Kin Blue beach. And I ask him—I'm supposed to pull this thing off the sand with a five-ton? Sure, he says, no problem. What about a flag car, crossing guards? Don't need 'em, he says, at three in the morning. He tells me I should have my firewatch get me out of the rack at 0200 the next night. I'm supposed to meet up with him behind the motor pool.

"But the other thing he's saying—he just keeps saying Teahouse of the August Moon, and after a while I know it doesn't mean anything, he's saying it 'cause he likes the way it sounds. And he's wanting to sell this tank in the middle of the night down in Naha, and I have to admit, I was kind of relieved when you guys came and got him."

The Captain had also seemed somehow relieved, handcuffed as he was and framed in the door of his office between these same two agents. Beyond relieved—delirious. The Captain's eyes had rolled in the Groucho Marx manner and he reverted right back to the call of the shitbird, the lingo of the enlisted man he'd once been. "Secure," he squawked, his final order, which would like so many others be ignored. They led him out, the Captain, sharp creases running the length of him, glistening Corfam shoes, and a big bowed neck ascending into a high and tight haircut that flattered him so. The CO of Tracks remained a poster marine to all appearances even on the occasion of his arrest, his loss of command. Except, of course, for the madness in his eyes.

"There was never any tank," the warrant officer said. "Think we'd let that idiot get his hands on a tank?"

"I wondered about that, sir."

"And the Chinese guy was ours," said the warrant officer. "From Plano, Texas. He got that accent from Charlie Chan movies. Your captain was a real easy mark."

"Chinese?"

"You didn't know? He was selling, or thought he was selling a tank to the Chinese."

"No, sir," Tel said. "I didn't know that. The *red* Chinese?"

"He never really pressed Tex for that kind of details. Just wanted to know if it was a cash transaction and what kind of cash would be used. It was the easiest set-up anybody ever set up. Burnham ran right into it. Lot of morons in this man's Marine Corps, Corporal, but I believe your captain takes the cake so far."

Tel resolved in the moment that he would for the rest of his life steer clear of anyone so obviously courting disaster. They were just too assured of success. "Sir, he wasn't thinking straight. I did know that much. But. Whew."

"Let's talk about these people you mentioned. Those other people he'd been talking to."

"Yes, sir."

"Who were they?" the warrant officer's upper lip wore beaded sweat.

"Who?"

"Aw, now, Corporal, I thought you were finished fiddlefucking around."

"Well, it was just everyone, sir."

"Everyone? That's helpful. That helps me a whole lot. How about some names?"

"I never got their names, sir."

"They didn't have names on their uniforms?"

"Didn't have uniforms. If it was service people, Americans, they were always in civvies."

"For Christ's sake," said the warrant officer. "What base?"

"It was always off-base somewhere."

"All right then. What *kind* of people would he be talking to?"

"All different, like I say. The Captain was a real friendly guy. He stopped and talked one day with an old man riding a water buffalo. Just friendly. But what I should probably tell you about is the book. The Captain had a big ledger book. Kept it in a locked briefcase. I think it all had to do with the book. Find that, and it'll tell you a lot more than I ever could."

"He never told you what he was doing? What these little meetings were all about?"

"No, sir." And truly the Captain had been remarkably mum about his current doings, considering how often and volubly he visited his past and his future.

"You didn't wonder?" The warrant officer seemed astonished, disgusted. "You didn't think he was up to something hinky?"

"Well," said Tel. "Not *China*. I sure didn't think it was anything like that. I thought he was probably loaning people money. I'm not too familiar with things like that. I'm a . . ." Tel was about to say 'farmer' but decided not to cheapen the fact by using it in this way. He felt pretty cheap as it was. "The thing is—he was really having some kind of breakdown, sir."

"He'd been greasy for years," said the warrant officer.

"Oh. But am I in trouble?"

"You did what you were ordered to do. Right?"

"Right," Tel said, ashamed.

"Asked no questions?

"No questions," Tel said. He'd also gone well out of his way at times to avoid overhearing those suspect conversations.

"Then why," the warrant officer asked, "would you be so worried?"

"Well," Tel said. "If it was something wrong—I mean, not *if*, sir. I really didn't know what was going on."

"And thought you better not find out. Were you going to help him steal that tank?"

"I was hoping he'd come to his senses," Tel said. "That's why I was so glad when you showed up. I mean, I felt bad for him, but. I don't know. I'm wondering, though, and this may be kind of technical—is it even possible to steal something that doesn't exist, sir? Legally?"

"Conspiracy," said the warrant officer, as if the word explained everything. "You're a big part of that, Harrow. What you just told us."

"Oh?"

"Yeah, congratulations. We got all we needed, so thanks."

"Needed? For?"

"Flush his ass," said the warrant officer.

"Oh. And I? I'm. . .?"

"Jack down, Corporal," said the warrant officer. "Stand down. You're okay. You did your bit. I told you, you gave us what we needed."

Perhaps Tel did not appear as relieved as he should have. He had been terrified that his time in the Marine Corps might somehow be extended by this mess. But he had pitied Captain Burnham almost as much as the Captain had pitied himself.

"Relax," said the warrant officer. "We let him cool his heels in the brig for a while. Now we'll let him know what we got from you, and where he's at—give him a chance to resign his commission, which the douche bag will jump at. So, Captain B goes home, gets elected to Congress, no doubt, and we all go on our merry way. Bing-bam, thank you, ma'am. It all comes out in the end, see?"

"I think so," said Tel.

Never previously a church goer, and never to be a sincere one, Tel had let himself be taken up by the First Reformed Bible Baptists, among whom the Bible was little in evidence. There was on base a Reverend Fuqua who, tall, gaunt, and jaundiced, looked every inch the malarial missionary, but who had a funny little electric clavichord and a powerful need to sing; he operated his church out of one end of a typhoon-proof barracks as a glee club as much as anything and required few professions or demonstrations of faith from his parishioners. His sermons were mild and quick, and as a matter of policy he would say, 'Let us now bow our heads,' no more than once per meeting. Mrs. Fuqua, an Okinawan woman, was pleased to cook for the small congregation she called her boys. Hers were unidentifiable meals taken, probably, from somewhere in the sea and savory enough when drenched in soy sauce or daubed with wasabi. Mrs. Fuqua, desperate to please, would with a reflexive nod and a quick, "Hi!" affirm anything anyone said in her presence.

The singing, the food, the whiff of wholesomeness, Tel was glad to have stumbled into the Reformed Baptists as a welcome break from a barracks teeming with hopheads, and malcontents, an alternative to the ville and Koza with their gauntlet of scams and well-aimed temptations. He'd quickly got his fill of dens of iniquity. Bringing in the sheaves. Might as well. He'd joined an incredible choir.

It was at church that Tel met Braxton Carde, though both were from Tracks Company and having arrived there within a few weeks of each other had lived not fifty feet apart in the same barracks ever since. Their friendship finally came about when Pastor Fuqua touched a single key on his machine to prompt ten strapping young marines and a navy Corpsman to hum A 440, and they became an instrument sufficient to rattle the glassed walls of a cathedral, and even within this powerful choir the voices of Tel Harrow and Braxton Carde were distinct, larger, truer, more confident than the others, and there was a certain resonance between them, a thing heard usually only with siblings, the same unexpected voice in two vessels. Later, walking back to the barracks, Tel even joked, "You aren't by any chance from Minnesota, are you, Carde?"

"Tennessee," Carde was emphatic. "Goodcorner, Tennessee, and that's a *long* way from Memphis." He said that he came of a similarly named church back home. The something or other something Baptist, and back home they were more serious about their worship. "My people would run this Fuqua out on a rail and get somebody to *test*ify. What's the use in a half-spooked preacher?" Carde was rock ribbed in his faith and tiresomely certain about everything, and yet he was to be the only close friend Tel would make in the Marine Corps. That voice. Also, Carde was the only black person, apart from himself, whom Tel had ever really known.

Tel's black father was a fact he'd let lie dormant until he'd got to the Marine Corps because there were so few facts to attend it: A black mortician in Minnesota who once played a mean horn—his father had never been especially real to him, and this was an absence so complete he'd never noticed it, or so he'd let himself believe. Tel himself was not black, not literally. Weathered, maybe. Until he got to the Marine Corps and encountered the way these things were reckoned—and that they were reckoned so much—Tel had not understood that by common understanding his black father made him a black man no matter what he himself looked like. He had only lately encountered the term 'passing' or had any reason to believe he might be guilty of it. And this seemed unfair. He'd never signed up for so much confusion. Tel often imagined himself on the prairie, on a piece of equipment dragging a cloud of dust. Alone.

In the meantime, though, he thought friend Carde might be a chance to learn something of himself, the unacknowledged part. He and Carde sang in church but had soon found that to sing in the barracks or near almost any aggregate of their fellow marines was a sure invitation to a fistfight, the prettier the tune the more provocative. So, because they were neither of them scrappers, they passed most of their free time like most everyone else, sitting footlocker to footlocker talking of times to come, the lives they'd renew upon their return to the world. Carde, bless him, was not interested in the more usual preoccupations, cars and beer and drugs, and he was not given to the common and casual discussion of killing that made Tel so uneasy among his fellow killers, and Carde might easily be forgiven his enthusiasm for his religion and for the soon to be booming real estate market in rural

Eastern Tennessee. His speaking voice was sonorous as his singing and rolled out like Martin Luther King's, but another subject Carde seemed to avoid was race, though that discussion was always right around them and often hot. After they had known each other quite some time, Tel decided that if he was ever to learn anything of blackness from Braxton Carde, he was going to have to bring it up himself, and there was never going to be a seamless way to do it, so one day he plucked the topic out of thin air, "Maybe I should have mentioned it before," he said, "my dad's a black guy."

Carde, all right angles even to shape of his head and his hairline, was inclined to skepticism. "How black?"

"That," Tel admitted, "I couldn't say."

"Ah," Carde said knowingly.

"It's not like that," Tel said. "He's supposed to be a pretty decent guy."

"That you've never met?"

"Well, no," Tel said. "I was an accident, I guess."

"No one," said Carde with the usual confidence, "is an accident."

"Or everyone is."

"I'd keep it to myself," Carde said. "These *brothers* around here, they love to call you a country nigger. Next time I hear. . ."

"You think it's all right?" Tel asked him. "To not say? Not mention it? You wouldn't believe some of the things white people say when they think it's just them."

"I have a pretty good idea what they say," said Carde. "What they think. Whether they're Christians or not. What color is a man's soul? It has no color. That's how we look at it in Goodcorner."

"That seems right," Tel said, relieved.

"Of course," Carde qualified, "Goodcorner *was*

eighty-nine percent black on the last census. That information comes with certain property listings down south."

Braxton Carde seemed to feel he had little in common with many of his urban counterparts. He had no use for anyone who kept a pik lodged in his hair or who wore the leg of a woman's nylon over his head. "These *brothers*," he'd say, "spend half their lives shaking hands. See each other five times a day, and every time it's the whole whoop-de-doo thing—hand jive? I don't know. It's childish."

Tel clung gratefully then to his colorless, odorless soul and to his four-square pal. Sure, they longed for the heart of the heart of the underpopulated country where the benign point of view was so much easier to sustain.

The guard shack did not much alter the temperature or even the humidity in the weather out of doors, and as shelter it offered only sultry shade. The room where Tel spent most of his sixteen-hour shifts as Corporal of the guard contained a steel desk, empty but for a two-way radio, a steel chair, a single window overlooking a near prospect of concrete wall, and a haunting calendar now three years out of date and offering an even more dated illustration of a toothy woman wearing her blouse tied up at the midriff to make a mechanical marvel of her bosom, and with one palm gracefully upthrust she seemed to be offering both herself and the red Impala she leaned upon— **Going my way?** Jeff Norton Chevrolet - Keokuk, Iowa. Tel's fall from grace in the company had coincided with the rainy season, and now he was assigned oceans of time on guard to make up for all the duty he'd skated out on when he'd been Captain Burnham's pet. His duty as Corporal of the Guard devolved under the rain to nothing more than changing post every four hours and between times trying not to fall asleep in that brutal shack and risk a court martial. Tel read 'The Godfather' three times, every Louis Lamour in the PX. As he approached his discharge date, time became a physical thing, a glob that would not flow as it should and congealed to a dead stop when he was on duty in this room.

In Tracks Company guard duty was usually a punitive thing and especially so on a holiday, and while Tel had no part in drawing up the guard roster, he was charged with being sure his miscreants, his select shit birds did their job, and their job was hellish, and there was really no way to monitor them out walking in the rain with their scatter guns slung barrel down under rubber ponchos that served in that climate for a portable steam bath; two troops must perennially walk the company's perimeter, round the armor park, and the shop with its tall bays and cranes and hoists, round the company armory, all of it about as subject to attack here in Okinawa as it might be to collision with an asteroid, and two snuffies bored nearly unconscious in the suffocating heat but with cold, wet feet, two marines with their weapons slung barrel down under wet rubber sheets and their shotgun shells in their pockets would be about equally well equipped to deal with either event, and the whole point of guard seemed to be its miserable pointlessness.

Thanksgiving, and Tel was once again in the guard shack. Right around fifteen hundred hours Carde showed up to say he'd been to Reverend Fuqua's sermon, and he couldn't say why, what a bust that was, and he'd been to the chow hall's version of Thanksgiving dinner which had brought him nearly to tears, and not in a good way. "I'm no cook," he said, "but even I know you don't try to make stuffing with moldy bread, and you need to stuff it into something that looks a little bit like a turkey or at least some kind of bird. It's disgraceful. I meant to bring you something, but I can't see you'd want it."

"I'm lucky," Tel said. "Grew up on my mom's cooking, so I'm pretty tough. I even kind of like that canned cranberry goo. They have any of that?"

Carde was a walking hymnal, and they sang 'All People Who on Earth Doth Dwell' that day, not because it was Thanksgiving but because they had the privacy in the guard shack to do so, and because they always sang it when Carde had any choice in the matter. He'd said of the tune, "In the book there's no time signature, not even any bar lines, and I think that means you're supposed to emphasize every note." It was a style of singing, a hammering optimism for which Carde was well suited. For as much as they'd sung this song Tel had only lately learned the lyrics with any confidence, for they were full of antique turns of phrase and iffy advice, and he suspected it for the work of a sixteenth century hack. "Sing to the Lord with cheerful voice." It was Carde's part in this tune to maintain the melody, every word and every intonation concise, while Tel flitted around singing various harmonies, and the tune with its variable textures kept them amused for a long time; Tel enjoyed the joy in Carde's face when they raised their voices to it. Anything to kill an hour.

Private Conklin came into the guard shack during the last several verses of the hymn, and on entering he considered ducking out again when he saw what was going on, but then he reconsidered the rain and thought better of it. He removed his sopping cover to reveal wet, bile colored hair, and he slouched back against the door in unmilitary fashion, his mouth a gash over a prominent yet delicate chin. Wet and expecting to be wet for several hours to come, he glared at them.

"To God whom heaven and earth adore," Tel sang.

He sang, "From men and from the angel host be praise and glory evermore," and then, in the same breath he said, "Goddamnit, Conklin." The private's eyes flew around looking for purchase. "Why," Tel asked him, "do you show up without your web gear or your helmet? You know they're all over me about making you guys carry two canteens. I've mentioned this before, Conklin. Dehydration, remember?"

"I'm not here to walk guard. Not yet." Conklin was ever patient with the less intelligent, the poorly informed. "Came to give you some information."

"Well?"

"Hahn can't make it."

"Can't make it?" Tel said as ominously as he could.

"He's sick," said Conklin, well satisfied.

"Yeah? And he's been to sick bay? Got a no-duty chit and everything?"

"Can't go to sick bay," said Conklin.

"Hahn," Tel said. "That miserable little. . ."

"He thought he'd do a little bump before he walked post. Got carried away."

"Well, he's not gonna die or anything. Is he?"

"Grandy's keeping him up," Conklin said. "Got him up and walking around. He's good. He just does this sometimes. It's no biggy, but you wouldn't want him out on post."

"You better hustle back to the barracks," Tel said, "and find somebody to take his place. Quick."

"Nobody around," said Conklin. "Today? Nobody sticks around. I mean, Grandy's there, but he's kind of busy right now. I can walk it myself. Fact I'd rather walk it myself."

"Yeah," said Tel. "And then Sergeant of the Guard comes by, or the Officer of the Day, and we're all in trouble.

I've gotta have two warm bodies out there."

"I'll walk it." Braxton Carde seized on every chance to do the noble thing; just this once it was not annoying.

Private Conklin, who'd rarely had a say in anything, said again, "I'll walk it alone."

"Chop, chop," Tel told them. "We're supposed to relieve those guys in fifteen minutes, and you know they'll raise holy hell if we don't. Get on up to the barracks and get your gear. Don't forget your canteens, and don't forget to fill 'em. Go."

Private Alvin Conklin was new to the Marine Corps, to the rock, and, at eighteen, to life, but it happened Tel knew more about him than almost any other man in the company. According to Conklin's file he had enlisted on the strength of a high school equivalency diploma and then revealed not a single aptitude to the usual battery of tests given new recruits. Had Conklin been merely useless he might have flourished as did so many others, taking orders, but Conklin was a regular at office hours for company punishment, and he was all but permanently confined to barracks, a curious penalty for a confessed barracks thief. Tel had been there to take notes at these hearings, and to see Conklin standing tall before the hearings officer and visibly veering between bravado and craven terror, fantastic and tireless in his dishonesty.

"Boots?" The hearings officer had asked him. "You steal a man's *boots*, and they're two, three sizes too big for you. What were you gonna do? You think you were gonna *sell* those, Private?"

"I found 'em, sir."

"Found? You didn't see Martin's name on the inside, stenciled right where it's supposed to be?"

"Yes, sir. That's why I knew I better get 'em back to him."

"You *found?* Where?"

"In Martin's cube, sir. I got turned around. In my head. I was drunk."

"Just that," the hearings officer told him, "just that much is illegal for you, Conklin. And didn't you also *find* that picture? Picture of somebody's girlfriend. I'm not real sure why you haven't had a blanket party yet, Private. There's vigilantes in every barracks, Conklin. You'll piss blood, and not a bruise to show for it. I'll be the least of your problems if these guys get fed up with you. You know that. You better know it."

Private Conklin had offered precisely the same promise at each of these hearings. "I'll do way better now, sir. I'm squared away for sure." He was very near to being processed out as unfit, and Private Conklin had generated a constant flow of paperwork that brought Tel regularly to his file; Conklin was a documented mess, that file a trajectory guided by neither intelligence nor useful instinct, and reading it had been for Tel a guilty pleasure. But now Braxton Carde had volunteered to spend four hours in company with this oily kid, and Tel had failed to thank him for it, and worse, Tel had not thanked him for it because Conklin's presence somehow made a decent courtesy seem inappropriate. Tel considered he'd spent too much time second guessing himself since he'd been in the Marine Corps, that it was just too damned hard to keep your boots clean in this outfit. He dropped his new sentries on post, and in time that velvet dark that comes under rain had descended on them, and Tel could only imagine poor Braxton Carde going round and round, utterly useless, and with only Private Conklin to ease the misery and monotony, and Private Conklin himself an agent of misery and monotony. All in the sweltering dark.

Tel resolved that when he next relieved post he was

going to say 'thanks' to his friend, and in front of God and everyone. The grand resolution. And how things got turned around here, and how happy he'd be to be off this odd island and its odd situations. Thanks? He'd better find Braxton Carde a decent steak. Carde was a Wayne Newton fan, but this and other oddities were easy to overlook in such a straight shooter, the guy who could never be restrained from doing the right thing and who had likely saved them all some trouble tonight. Tel owed him, though, from long before that, and just for being good old Braxton Carde.

Ordinarily the guard met its relief at the end of the shop building, and ordinarily the men walking guard would not be late to this meeting, but Carde and Conklin weren't there for the rendezvous that night. Tel called for them, and ordinarily they should be within hearing, and he waited for the ritual challenge, 'Halt. Who is there?' But nothing. Maybe the rain. To wait? To look for them? Where? Tel's flashlight made sense of a very small cone of the night immediately in front of him. One of the boys he'd brought with him to walk post was saying, "Fuck this." The other had gone between two tanks to relieve himself, and he yelled, "Whoa!" and backed out still prepared to make water, and it might have been funny if he hadn't been so scared.

Tel came with his light. There between the tanks was Private Conklin with his weapon leveled at them. Helmet gone, poncho gone, rain sluicing down his face, and in Tel's revealing light his eyes showed crystalline blue. The lump behind him, when lit, was Braxton Carde face down in the mud, a dark red cavity in his back, a brighter red brook flowing out under him.

"Nigger," Conklin explained, "thought he was better than me."

"You shoot anybody now," Tel said, "you'll have to get all three of us." He didn't intend this as advice, but as he kept his beam on those icy eyes, he could see it might be taken that way. "You don't have that many rounds."

"Nigger," Conklin said again.

"You're from Maine," Tel said. "*Maine.*"

"Not anymore," Conklin said. The short barrel of his shotgun was just right for bringing the muzzle under his chin and still providing easy access to the trigger. Then, just a twitch.

ULYSSES PUREFOY

Purefoy had come in on a bucking commuter plane through the turbulence between Billings and Great Falls where he'd landed queasy. Taxying in, the propellers whirring immensely beside him now that they were on the ground—on the ground, he should never ask for more—he saw that there would be none of the usual airport preliminaries, no tunnel, no long hallway to be got through. Here the lucky traveler stepped right off his little ride and onto the apron of the tarmac, about sixty steps hence from whatever awaited them in the terminal. The propellers stopped. This was unfolding too fast. Woozy and otherwise in a bad way, Purefoy was grateful for the small delay afforded by men retrieving their tall Resistols from overhead bins. The only black man on the plane, he'd need no sign to identify himself. Process of elimination. On the ground. No turning back.

He'd started by calling his son 'Mr. Harrow.' "Mr. Harrow," he'd said, "we haven't met, but maybe your mother. I don't know if she ever talks about the old days. The Ozark Club? This is a while back. I don't know if she would've mentioned a Purefoy. A Ulysses, maybe? A guy they used to call Up? A friend from. It has been a while. So. I."

"I always knew it," Tel had said. "Have to admit, I was about to give up on you, but I always knew you'd call. Some day."

"You did?" Purefoy had formed the intention to make this call only within the last several hours. He already had two sons, the ones he'd raised in his own house, who were strangers, who'd become whoever they became while he was at work paying for it. He'd been making this very point in an argument with his wife Audrey when he finally acknowledged, "I've got two boys who know my name and don't use it, got another one probably doesn't know me from Adam. Can you see how a man begins to wonder just a little bit about his purpose?"

Audrey, of course, had demanded through her tears such details as her husband could provide and wondered how he could live with his shame. Very amicably, but he didn't mention this, having already lost the argument. She just couldn't imagine how he could ignore the existence of his own child. Pretty easily after all these years. It had been quite some time since he'd given his third son—first son—any thought at all.

Once the subject finally came up, though, and now that he was done concealing it, Purefoy suddenly seized on the idea that maybe his long running secret was somehow responsible for his soured existence. Lately a deepening funk had him casting around for reasons, for answers, and so almost before he knew what he was doing, he was on the phone, tongue tied. One call to information and suddenly he was addressing his son as 'Mr. Harrow', if only to remind himself that he wasn't speaking to the six-year-old boy he'd kept locked in a poorly lit corner of his imagination. Too quick. So easy after all. Easy and quick after all these years; he was speaking to someone who seemed to know who he was.

"So your mother has? She's told. . .?"

"Sure," Tel said.

"Oh," Purefoy said, "I, uh. Well. We should meet. If I'm not getting ahead of myself."

"Sure," Tel had said.

"I mean," Purefoy said, "I bought a ticket. Tickets already, all the way to Great Falls. Maybe ahead of myself. But, of course, it's up to you. It would be up to you. If."

"Sure," Tel said. "Be a shame not to."

"Thursday afternoon. They've got me routed through Denver."

"All right," his son had said.

"I hope I'm not getting ahead of myself."

◊ ◊ ◊

Purefoy knew him at once for his son. Bigger and far more Caucasian than his brothers, his half-brothers, he was a work thickened man extending a work thickened hand, and in bib overalls he was obviously his mother's son—why dress up to come to town?

"Tel, I take it?"

"Mr. Purefoy."

"No," said Purefoy, "I mean, well. . . yes, but. Uhm, well, how do you do. Nice to meet you."

"Sorry I had to make such a flying trip into town," the young man said. "We probably won't have a chance to grab a bite to eat or anything. And I was meaning to bring the girls in to meet you. . ."

"Excuse me," Purefoy pleaded. "Have to excuse myself. Got the whirlies coming in. Sorry, but uh— excuse me."

In the bathroom he ladled up cold water in his hands to bathe his face in it until it was no longer ashen gray. He'd brought no clear idea of what this meeting might be, and now if it was to be as it seemed nothing more than a 'Hi-how-are-you?' then that should be enough; if Purefoy had come only to learn that this young man was a pleasant young man, then that should justify the trouble of his trip. When he got his legs under him, he came out of the restroom and declared, "I'm sure glad I didn't embarrass anyone. That was quite the flight coming in. Light aircraft. I'm all right now."

"I didn't see your baggage on the cart."

"Oh, it's. . . It's just this." Purefoy indicated the gym bag he had in hand.

"All right. Shall we? I've got some drilling I've got to do."

"Drilling?" said Purefoy.

"Seeding. A few hours one way or the other can make a difference in your yield. Need to get it in the ground."

Purefoy hadn't really thought beyond his need to lay eyes on the boy. The boy. The man. And his plan, such as it was, had already fully unfolded, and he'd never even imagined the possibility of going back to the farm. The thought of it now filled him with various forms of dread, and it was with an old man's hollow bravado he said, "Lead the way."

All at once they were out upon the reeling emptiness of that country, in that vertigo he remembered here, and there was nothing for it but for Purefoy to ask a few of the questions a man might rightly ask. "So—" he asked. "Your mother. Is she? We haven't stayed in touch."

"Out in Portland now," Tel said. "She went there after I got back from the service. Been out there ever since."

"She never? She's. . .?"

"Never married," said Tel. "Said she was too mean to marry."

"Mean?" said Purefoy. "I don't remember that at all."

"It's not exactly accurate," said Tel, "but she can be contrary. She went out there, got right after it, and now she's a teacher. She's a rehearsal pianist for a dance school, too. She seems to like it."

"She was wise to pursue that," Purefoy said sincerely, more sincerely relieved that he wouldn't be encountering the woman. If this conversation was difficult, what would he possibly say to Verity Harrow at this point? Maybe it would please her to know she'd conducted a much better life than he had. Maybe she'd like to know she'd provided the purest moments he'd ever known those many years ago. "She was a monster talent, your mother. You have any idea how good she was?"

"Still is, far as I know," said Tel. "Yeah, she was the sound track of my life for quite a while. We heard her just about constantly sometimes." He indicated a road sign requiring passersby to: REELECT G.C. HARROW— County Attorney. "That's Jeet," he said. "Do you remember him? You knew him, didn't you?"

Purefoy did then remember that strange, stiff, speckled child in sunglasses. "Looks like he made quite a success of himself. But it seems impossible, you know. He was just a little guy—and now. Time just goes. Just goes by." Purefoy scanned the several horizons available to his view and found no comfort in any of them. "I never understood how you folks could live in this. This. Makes a man feel so damn small out here."

"You hear that," said Tel. "Not enough people. Not enough trees. People seem to think it's kind of spooky. I'm lucky, I guess. Suits me fine."

"Your mother raised you boys right," said Purefoy.

Tel Harrow was too well raised to affirm that he'd been well raised or be easy with any kind of compliment. Instead, he said, "So, I understand you're also a musician."

"No," said Purefoy, bitterly. "To be a musician you have to *be* a musician, and I didn't do that. You can lose it."

"I know," said Tel. "I used to be a singer myself."

G.C.

As a boy, to fit in as a boy, Jeet Harrow would sometimes resort to the rough and ready. One Labor Day outside Hawarden Hall, full of a Labor Day dinner and with the air beginning to crisp as it can in early fall, he fell into a pickup football game and, always the useful teammate, he'd been assigned to play center. Through the lens and echo chamber of time he lives this day, sees and hears it sometimes more clearly than when it was happening. He sees his own too vivid head bent over a football bloated nearly round and with a bubble of rubber bladder coming through a seam, he sees his hands splayed on the laces, ready to hike, freckled of course, and he sees Larry Lucerne as he could not see him then, standing there behind him, eternally the handsome, quick quarterback, and Jeet hears him calling his signals high and clear to issue over the wind, over the crowd roar in an imagined stadium, the simple signals of that era, "Readeee, set. . ." Jeet has the long perspective now, and he sees Larry Lucerne rushing up behind him, full of fun to kick his unsuspecting center's outspread crotch, kick-off style. How fortunate that merciful memory is not specific in the pain, his newly furred testicles flying through sixty yards of pain, the agony that returned at intervals for about a month afterward, during which he never said a word about it, explaining those grimaces he couldn't resist or conceal as his response to "cramps." When and how had he become such an irresistible joke? The cruelty Jeet somehow inspired required him to be an exceptionally good sport, so his childhood would fester in him forever and burden him with an abiding interest in justice. In one of his lives, he would be given to argue that there is always a price to pay, in another he would demonstrate the principle.

When he graduated law school Jeet got not only his Juris Doctorate but also an automatic license to practice, as was the practice in those days in Montana, and he was good to go that May if he wanted. But after putting himself through all that trouble he didn't seem to want it at all, and so he went back to the farm to sort himself out and try not to be too much in the way, and it happened while he was there that Donovan Grimm died as he had lived, on a bar stool in Fort Benton, and that every other attorney in Chouteau County, citing conflicting obligations, declined the county commissioners' invitations to complete the man's term. So, by default, G.C. Harrow, as Jeet had decided he'd call himself for the hell of it and for professional reasons, was to be the new County Attorney. He'd come somewhat late in life to his first real job, a situation with insurance and distantly scheduled vacations. During school many of his classmates had found internships and other work in the law, entry points into the profession, but Jeet had instead played and dealt poker around Missoula and Frenchtown, an employment more lucrative and easier to schedule, so as he arrived for his first day on the job, he was a lawyer who had never visited a court room, or a commissioner's chambers, or any other official location; he was expert in not one area of juris prudence and completely unfamiliar with procedure.

A card player tricked out in a suit smelling of moth balls, he'd been informed of his appointment on a Monday and was in attendance that Tuesday afternoon for a meeting of the County Commissioners who held a brief, dreamy swearing in for the new County Attorney, an imposter so green he wasn't even sure if he was to stay for the meeting that followed. Jeet reasoned that if he wasn't supposed to leave, then leaving would be the worst possible mistake he could make right now. He stayed on and the commissioners were soon into an exhaustive, exhausting discussion of gravel in its many varieties. Was this to be his working life? This uncertainty and tedium? He was employed, all right, but could see where he'd set himself up to run a long bluff. On taking office, Jeet's mood vacillated between mild terror and mere second thoughts.

Then, it being July and a musty chamber on the top floor of a brick courthouse, and with the commissioners talking of gravel, and of fill dirt, and of the sheriff's fuel problems, the new County Attorney felt a nap coming on. Only moments earlier he'd been scared of his ignorance, alert to a looming failure, and where was that good juice now when he needed it? He dared not yield to his weighted eyelids; he'd been informed through the years that he was a quick snorer, that he might snort like a power saw the moment he nodded off, so Jeet remained awake but only with the aid of occasional little spasms that jolted him back to wakefulness, and these could also signal an early end to his career. Twitching? Was this how G.C. Harrow could be expected to discharge his duties?

How timely and superb of Jolene, then, to choose that very afternoon to be a concerned citizen. She rescued him simply by coming into the room. Compliments of the season—a girl in a sleeveless sun dress. Where the air had seemed medieval only a moment before, now Jeet was effortlessly awake again, and now the great effort lay in keeping his eyes from constantly straying back to her. Her hair-do was a few years out of date, and he surmised from this, correctly as it came to pass, that she was an old-fashioned girl; it flowed in brown abundance fountain like from the crown of her head and smoothly down to flip up just before it reached those bare shoulders, and this whole arrangement bounced with her every movement. She was a collection of soft contours, soft gray eyes, a button nose. Not since earliest adolescence had Jeet known desire so unendurable. None of the official business conducted at this meeting had made a sufficient impression on him even to allow him to forget it, and just as he had always suspected, adulthood was no place for him. He was so easily distracted.

Much the oldest of the commissioners was a man named Homer, a vicious parliamentarian who ran the meeting according to obscure rules and who'd developed two strands of flesh down the front of his throat portending his fairly imminent death. When at last the drone of minutes, and reports, and old business, and new business subsided, Homer turned to the young woman who was on that fair summer day the only visitor to their hellish chambers. He told her that they couldn't usually act on public comment unless the commenter and subject of the intended commentary were properly identified on the agenda beforehand. "But in your case, dear," said the ancient commissioner, "I think we can make an exception." One foot in the grave, and still the man managed to leer at her. Hope, or something like it, springing eternal.

She said that she was Jolene Middlemarch, that she worked the counter at her parents' drug store. But what she'd come to talk about was dogs.

"Dogs?" said Homer, pretending an interest.

"Stray dogs," she said. "I've heard they're being shot. Something should be done."

The commissioners turned as one toward their new legal adviser, three faces the color of beef steak. Jeet could only imagine what his own face must be doing in this heat, under this pressure. They wanted his opinion. Stray dogs. The majesty of the law. Here it was.

G.C. Harrow, so far only conceived, was at that moment delivered smoking from the womb of Jeet's long awaited and now unexpected talent. G. C., an organism Jeet had been brewing up, apparently, in the law library and card rooms, was a somber figure who seemed to know quite a lot about ordinances and the like, the legal imprudence of discharging firearms in city limits, and Jeet was not at all sure how much of this he was remembering and how much he was making up, but it seemed not to matter so long as he said something. He mentioned cruelty to animals, too, but clarified, "It would actually have to be cruel, though, to be a crime."

"How could it not be?" Jolene, lovely in her sympathy, was horrified. "Shooting the poor thing?"

G.C. pressed on, explaining, "Strays. Sometimes they'll get to running game and the warden has to put 'em down. Sometimes they'll run people's livestock, and. . ." G.C. did not say, as Jeet might have observed here, that it was a dog's life, but he offered her something he'd probably cribbed from the television, "Get someone to come forward, someone who's actually seen or at least heard something. Or if you could even show the Sheriff a dog's body, that might be a start." The commissioners seemed pleased with this answer. Jolene was not.

Dog's body. Something from Shakespeare? Jeet was so easily distracted.

"How can that not be cruel?" Jolene asked him again.

◊ ◊ ◊

G.C. was literally born to be a backwater county attorney, and as soon as he'd committed a few useful statutes to his cocksure memory he became a terror around the courthouse, ruffling the long calm his predecessor had established by doing very nearly nothing. G. C. was just abrasive enough to do the job as he saw fit and to keep Jeet constantly amused with himself. He received a regular pay check for this. He must be, he thought, insufferable, and Jeet who was after all still reasonably young then, thought in this flush of self-discovery, or success, this role or the funny assignment he'd tumbled into, that maybe the universe owed him after all. County Attorney. What fun, a series of games he played like a chess hustler in the park, and mostly won. He was on a roll.

One day, dimly in pursuit of his destiny, he went to Middlemarch Drugs, and before he could make his retreat Jolene had caught him mooning at her through the glass door. She was right there at the counter, had seen him and seemed to know him, and now there was no choice but to go on in, and the choice he did make, and instantly regretted, and never subsequently understood, was to develop an unconvincing limp. He limped right up to the counter.

Heart shaped face, lips pursed with concern, "What happened?" Hers were the nasal, flat intonations of the middle of the middle class, and she wore a smock, and still Jeet was beside himself with wanting her.

"I think I might have twisted my ankle," he said. "Running." And he might have, had he ever been running. "Probably need an ace bandage," he said. "Some aspirin. Epsom salts."

"A cane?" she said.

"Oh," he said, "Well, sure. If you have one."

"Will you be needing any injections?" she asked him.

"In. . . injections?" he said. "No. I. No."

"Are you sure it wasn't a dog bite?" she said.

"A. . ."

"Because," she said, "I thought maybe a dog bit you."

His face would be cycling through its most kaleidoscopic display, and Jeet was afraid she'd be alarmed by it. He said, "I hope you didn't think I. I mean, I've." He was here with no particular plan or intention but with that very particular yearning, and he'd dealt himself a bad hand with the limp. "Anyway," he said, "I really am on their side. Man's best friend, and everything, and I know they've got it pretty rough." It was by no means the last time he'd find himself apologizing for laws and circumstances he hadn't authored, but it was nearly the last time he'd do so sincerely.

Later, and not much later, Jolene would confide that it was his sincerity and seriousness she found so attractive, a nice little irony in that these were the very traits that in the past he'd used mostly to fashion his sloughs of despond. She liked him, and she was plain about it. She was saving herself for marriage, and was plain about that, too, but he'd been allowed almost unlimited access to heavy petting on the backroads, and offered an irresistible glimpse of things to come, and eight months later they were married in the church Jolene had attended all her life. Jeet had long ago while out wandering a dire desert promised himself that should he ever escape that desert he would contrive to walk the moderate path and the moral high ground, and now it seemed he'd stumbled right into it, for he was the guy who took the little lady to Sunday services and came home to change his oil in an immaculate garage, smell that tuna casserole, and in the summer he would don a fez and drive a tiny car in parades for the benefit of crippled children, and in the fall he'd go duck hunting, and with his lovely wife forever involving him in good works he was on the library board and gave the Red Cross his blood as often as was medically advisable, and Jeet thought during this era that he must be very near to assembling reasons enough to finally like himself. They lived in a prairie style house Jolene called the Werther House, up on the bluff with a low roof and wide eaves to shed the wind, and every window in that house gave onto some view of the river, and all around it was an aromatic hedge that Jeet kept trimmed up perfectly square, and within that house there had been his mint condition Jolene.

She had saved herself for him, then given herself to him, and in the early going they were agreed that it was well worth the wait. Together they explored Jolene the wonderland, a tawny fleshscape upon which the sun seemed always to shine, so responsive to his long awaited touch. Jeet would never quite escape the suspicion that both his wife and fate were too kind, that happiness as the Buddhists would have it is a hothouse flower. Was there nothing he couldn't complicate? She'd wanted him, and he was freshly astonished at this every night for many consecutive nights. A gift he never tired of opening, she wanted him, and the sheer flattery of it, the length and power of her legs when she wrapped them around him to draw him in—marriage as Jeet encountered it was far better than advertised. What tenderness in those gray eyes. Jolene. The cheerier love songs, as it turned out, had been correct: There is really nothing at all like the love of a good woman.

His wife when he met her was that lucky person whose expectations and understanding of things align almost perfectly; she was an adored daughter entirely at ease in the affections of a world she expected to pass on with the aid of a solid husband; Jeet saw it as an honor to be chosen for such work. His wife wanted to extend the lore of potato salad and lodge politics to another generation, she naturally wished to dote on little offspring as she had been doted upon, and by this means, to her understanding, everything should remain just fine. Her mission lay before her well defined—a family. Whenever Jeet and Jolene as a couple encountered children—her screechy nieces with some frequency—Jolene would melt, and the children would in turn melt, and Jeet would loiter at the edge of these episodes with a big, indigestible glob of molasses in his mouth. Had Jolene considered the possibility that this fortunate generation she intended them to make could come out pink and squinting and stay that way through their beleaguered lives? He might be any kind of genetic mess.

So as not to betray his misgivings about children he avoided speaking of them at all. Jolene also generally gave the subject a pass except for the declaration she'd made on their second date while strolling back from a movie, when in a moment of dawning inevitability—Jeet had already met her mother by then—and mid stroll, she pulled at his arm to stop him, to face him, and though they had not yet shared so much as a kiss she thought the time had come to specify, "I want kids."

"Oh?" Jeet had said.

"Not a lot," she said. "Of kids."

"Oh," he said.

"Two," she said. "Two should do it. Maybe three, depending."

Then, all through their courtship, and the wedding, and well into their marriage they didn't more than glancingly speak of it again. He knew how she felt. He thought she might know how he felt, though he certainly never told her. His feelings on the matter did not flatter him; children were noise, foul odors, bad behavior, and even if he and Jolene should be lucky enough to make their angels in the unmottled, uninflamed complexion of their mother, still Jeet had no desire to share this woman any more than he was already sharing her with her family. She was, his wife, a pool of repose at that time, and he had no interest in shrinking the shoreline. But she must have what she must have after all, and Jeet was willingly along for the ride, making his contribution, taking the risk whatever that might be. She worked in a drug store under her father the pharmacist, so Jeet considered her fate to be in her hands. The young couple were not widely admitted to each other's confidence, and birth control was one of many topics they tended to avoid. He now recalls too accurately that there was not much talking between them even then. Their fucking had been such a complete conversation that talking had for quite some time been superfluous.

So, let the chips fall where they may, baby-wise, she must have what she wanted after all, and he would have what he would have, and unless he was mistaken then, or misremembers it now, he was happy in the arrangement. Happy. In hindsight, though, he can put a date on it; Jeet can name the date and even the hour when he first smelled the thing going sour.

On their fifth anniversary he stopped at the market on the way home from work to buy a brisket, some grocery store flowers, and a bottle of the sticky pink wine Jolene associated with celebrations. Such celebrations might also include a cheese plate, a fruit plate, or both, and salty snacks, and a dark beer, and all these delicacies would be consumed on the sectional sofa in their large, clean living room from which they might simultaneously see the fireplace, the river, and, as the occasion warranted, the moon sliding over the prairie across the river. Here Jeet the case-hardened prosecutor was transformed in a trice to helpless romantic. Such nights, in Jeet's estimation, were more than consolation enough for the daily slings and arrows. That particular anniversary fell on a Friday, and he went home expecting a weekend of making love, taking long, sudsy baths, and slinking around in the mischievous light of the candles she'd set out everywhere; he found Jolene, however, weeping on the very couch where he'd hoped the festivities might begin, clutching a bouquet of soggy tissues.

"Honey?" he said. "Honey."

A look as if he'd summoned her from far away. She was wearing the flannel nightgown he found peculiarly seductive—she'd been planning the same night he had. But now that look, and, jaggedly, "Hi." A cold jolt ran through him. Had someone died?

"What is it?"

"Nuh uh thing," she said, her tears so uncharacteristic that on Jolene they looked like hysteria.

"Nothing?" he said. "Honey . . ." He should comfort her, he knew, but that could be easily misfire since anguish made her even more desirable and since Jeet could not recall successfully comforting anyone, including himself. "Honey," he said. Little by little he dragged it out of her and was made to understand that she wasn't nearly so content as he'd let himself suppose. "Did you know," she eventually said, "we've been trying since the honeymoon? To get pregnant?" She'd been sitting there, waiting for him, and she'd got to thinking about it, and it just struck her—five years—and now she'd made a formula of it, a proof—after five years you just knew something must be wrong. She'd never even missed her period in all that time.

"Well," said Jeet, less than useless, "we'll just have to keep trying."

Continued trying had been their approach to the problem for a time after that, but the results were the same, and there was anxiety, and there were rounds of examination and testing, and eventually a conversation with a specialist in Billings who informed Jeet in what he probably thought were manly terms, "You're firing blanks, bud."

"Oh? Oh. Can that be—fixed?"

"No," said the doctor. "You should be glad, though. You could be emasculated. Got all the testosterone you'll ever need. You're just firing duds."

"Could this be an injury?" Jeet asked him. "An old injury?"

"Possibly," said the doctor, blue jawed, compassionate.

"We'd have to run more tests to really nail that down."

"That's all right," Jeet said. "I guess it doesn't matter."

Bearing the news home, he dreaded throughout the long drive to tell her, but Jolene's first response on hearing it was to console supposedly disappointed dad. Jeet could easily imagine himself being disappointed, too, now that fatherhood had been taken out of his reach. Jolene with strange, quiet insistence said over and over again, "It's not your fault," using the phrase as a sort of caress, but then too much, until she'd scared him with it. Deeply composed, Jolene made him a sandwich on white bread and brought him a glass of milk. She turned on the television. That television or one of its larger, louder successors was to remain on through the rest of their time together. About six months later she was briefly elated at the thought of adoption. It was, she thought, the purest form of love, and wouldn't it be neat if they could maybe adopt a boy and a girl from out of the same orphanage where he'd been adopted?

No. It was never Jeet's place nor his desire to deny her anything, but he must deny her this. He could not be enlisted in the plan. He was pleased that she hadn't noticed the great hole in him, but it was there and had been forever, and he had always assumed it was an artifact of the orphanage. He knew what orphans were. He knew of the big need they would bring with them and that he entirely lacked the means to fill it. In this one thing he must be firm. No.

The television played on; sucked into it, Jolene began slowly killing herself with cheese puffs and Sunshine Hydrox cookies, but because she was a hearty, healthy woman, she only succeeded in adding fifteen pounds of wobbling flesh to her misery every year for some years to come. Her complaining knees and ankles ended her career at the drug store but did not interfere with her civic duties, and Jolene at one time or another chaired nearly every committee formed in Fort Benton; she was the heart and soul of any church rummage sale. At home she kept houseplants alive by the dozen under their many windows; she prepared them delicious, nutritious, and colorful meals. She was with grim determination all the wife a decent man could ever want, dutiful and yielding to whatever desire her husband might be able to summon, and now, having said no to her orphans, Jeet could hardly say no to a dog, so Jolene acquired and maintained a pack of them in their home. She liked small, shrill beasts, Pekingese, and Chihuahuas, and other pocket-sized mutts—goggle-eyed dogs, their little toe nails tapping frantic on the kitchen linoleum, their little bladders demanding release, and in Jolene's pack there was always at least one sonofabitch whose bark would shiver Jeet's whole nervous system no matter how often he heard it. But by far the worst piece in this domestic mess was Jolene's galling way of never in word or deed doing anything unkind to him—this rendered him helpless in his own house.

G. C. Harrow was Choteau County's most devoted civil servant during all his terms of office. It seemed straightforward enough, he would be good by doing good; always at work, he was eventually the oil that fueled and lubricated that courthouse where he considered himself essential and where he was not alone in that opinion, and where if he wished he might glory in his own importance. Ever the player, G. C. had gamed it out, and he knew all the law he'd ever need to know, knew the rules of evidence, the local rules of court; he carried a map of the county in his head, a genealogy chart, and he knew or could easily find out how property lines and water rights ran. He knew the deputies, he knew the clerks, often knew their children's names; G. C. knew where and how things got done in the county, so G.

C. was a big cheese, but Jeet, the worrisome little shit, never ceased nibbling away from within. What if?

In a single election cycle that he would come to describe as "the boob-onic plague," the County Attorney had been shackled with a new sheriff and several new commissioners, and they were all of them the self-actualized kind of assholes who have no use for any pesky legalities their County Attorney might care to trouble them about, and so the people G. C. advised and the people he put in jail had exactly the same regard for the law, and he held them in exactly the same contempt, and he liked to call himself the superintendent of the sewage lagoon. G. C.'s disgrace would seem a sudden thing when it came, but Jeet had been in there worming around in him for a long time by then, troubling him with that old, troublesome mind until simply doing the right thing was no longer simple.

◊ ◊ ◊

"Hey, G.C.," the sheriff was breathless on the phone, more than usually jazzed. "Looks like the bootlegger's trail is open for business again. Caught us a big one. Got an idiot broke down right under the railroad trestle with five pounds of cocaine in his trunk. Five pounds. You'll want to be there for his bond hearing, I expect."

"You seized it, Newt?"

"Well, sure. What else, leave it in his trunk?"

"Can you lift prints off it? Off the package?"

"Uhm," said the sheriff. "Why would we? It was in his trunk."

"Because—" said the county attorney, 'you collect *all* the evidence. Because—there's a thing called 'dominion and control.' Because I might need it. How about chain of evidence? Got it tagged? Logged? Everything okay that way?"

"Oh, sure," said the sheriff, less than certain. "Crossed

the t's and dotted the i's, we've got him in a pickle. You might know the guy. He's from up around your way." For all the years Jeet had now lived in Fort Benton, he was still considered to be from somewhere in the wastes out beyond the city limits "Or maybe up around Big Sandy," said the sheriff. "Or he's from somewhere over there. Says his folks farm. Lucerne? Larry Lucerne? Heard of him?"

"Yeah," said Jeet. "I know him, or I used to."

Upon any reflection at all Jeet understood he didn't know anyone. Know him? They'd been boys at the same time in the same echoing corner of Montana, but separated by a few years in age and virtually opposite personalities—Larry Lucerne had been a well favored one, trailing friends—Jeet had never known him except as the living embodiment of all the shitty inequities of human existence. It would be interesting to see how he'd aged.

The defendant as Jeet found him stood between two deputies and before the Justice of the Peace; he wore a belly chain, a floral print shirt, another chain round his neck of chunky gold links, his hair still in its boyish mop. His wandering grin sought very hard and very much in vain to convince everyone a mistake had been made. He was saying something to that effect when Jeet appeared, and Larry Lucerne seemed relieved to see him, and he addressed him as Jeet, and he said, "Oh, man. Oh, wow, am I glad to see *you*. Maybe you can tell 'em. . ." He'd now acquired his own odd complexion, every appearance of fun-in-the-sun, but if dissipated he was mostly intact, really very well preserved.

County Attorney G.C. Harrow leveled his finger at the defendant's gaudy chest and told him, "You've been accused of a crime. As the judge here will tell you, that gives you the right to remain silent, and you want to use it." Art Blessing had already been summoned to provide Mr. Lucerne with benefit of counsel even for this, his initial appearance, and

Mr. Blessing huffed several blocks with an empty briefcase under his arm; his arrival in Justice Court visibly deflated his new client's already shattered confidence. Never-shined shoes, pleasant, scattered, Blessing introduced himself to and then stood with Larry Lucerne to hear that the poor man was charged with Possession With Intent to Distribute, to hear of the twenty years he might serve for that offense, which snatched the color right off the accused's face, and to learn that he was bound over to District Court to be arraigned at Judge Hand's next law and motion day. They were given a moment to confer in a corner, Blessing and client, concerning matters pertaining to bail, and they enjoyed such attorney-client privilege as might be available with deputies hovering so close; here Mr. Blessing had to convince his client that protesting his innocence was at the moment a complete waste of time, and together they came back to report to the court that Mr. Lucerne was at present unemployed, but his mother and father and brother and sister and a number of nephews were all in the area, and he had land interests in the county, so his ties to the community were strong, and he represented no threat to anyone. A moderate bond was requested along with such conditions of release as the court might consider appropriate.

To this Jeet responded, "State requests the Defendant be required to post a two hundred-thousand-dollar appearance bond. He was arrested with five pounds of a substance that sells for at least a hundred dollars a gram. I haven't done the math yet, but you get the idea. He's not without means. He's got plenty of reasons to run. And no danger? That stuff is illegal because it is dangerous. He's not just dabbling in it with a load like that." A load. The phrase brought to mind Jeet's own history as a smuggler, and he knew hypocrisy when he smelled it, but this would just have to be different enough. This was now. This was cocaine. He was

G.C. Harrow and professionally obligated in such cases to be fiercely self-righteous. As Larry Lucerne was being led away, he shot a sorrowing, wondering glance back at his old school mate. Why so mean? Would he remember the kick? No. There had been no pain in it for Larry Lucerne, so it would have been gone from his thoughts a week after it happened so many years ago. Vengeance served cold on a silver platter, and it could only be too good to be true, but wasn't it G.C. Harrow's job, after all, to do justice, or at least to prosecute a crime?

◊ ◊ ◊

Dan and Laverne Lucerne owned land enough that they might have stood surety even for their son's outrageous bond, but they reasoned that Larry could profit from a little stay in the county lockup, and they left him there where he might finally get his priorities in order. No need even to mention that they'd long ceased to trust their boy. The Lucernes did, however, pony up much hard cash to retain Gamer Schenevar's outfit out of Billings, and the matter was assigned to the firm's youngest and most eager associate. Brian Schenevar was then newly admitted to the bar, and though he hadn't been a lawyer long he had always adored his warring father and had begun taking in legal craft with his mother's milk; now, radiating ambition and a citric cologne he rode north to Larry Lucerne's rescue and a long wrangling commenced.

The FBI came, and Larry Lucerne, acting on advice of counsel and out of deep concern for his business partners' privacy, would say nothing to them, not where he'd got the package, nor from whom, nor to whom it was to be delivered; he would not so much as acknowledge its existence. The stuff had tested very pure. Obviously, Lucerne had made some impressive connections, and after several pointless trips to Fort Benton it soon became equally clear to the Feds that he was not about to reveal those connections to them. One of the agents, a man with a line of tiny moles under one eye, had been conferring with the County Attorney about the deal that might be on offer for Lucerne's cooperation, and after the agent's final fruitless conversation at the Chouteau County Jail he swung by G.C. Harrow's office on the way out of town to say, "Little Larry hasn't done himself a damn bit of good, so go ahead and slam him."

"What about the girl? Could you get anything out of her?"

"She's a coke whore," said the agent. "Last thing she knew for sure probably happened a while back. They make the worst kind of informant."

"I didn't know we had those here," Jeet said.

"You kidding? Got them, probably got some cartel running around—the whole shitaree. It's everywhere. So, like I say, you'll want to kick his ass."

"You bet," said G.C., but startled at the agent's turn of phrase. "If I can beat this suppression motion."

The defense had been busy, young Schenevar filing motions, and the kid from Billings was very good, fogging the air with every mechanism he could bring to bear. The war was to be won or lost, though, around Schenevar's suppression motion. The issue, as is usually the case in drug cases, was not especially to do with the defendant's guilt or innocence, but whether the state had legally obtained the evidence. Briefs flew back and forth. Meanwhile Larry Lucerne sat in jail, and about once a month young Schenevar drove north, charging hours of windshield time either way to appear once more before the Court with another imaginative argument for a reduction in his client's bond that met with Judge Hand's special hatred of hard drugs and those who profited from them. After several months inside, Larry Lucerne's skin and hair were turning gray, his hair had also grown noticeably brittle, and his deteriorating appearance was yet another angle Schenevar used to try and get him out. Larry Lucerne himself was in manner humbler and humbler before the court, but none of it did any good; Judge Hand thought jail ought not to be mistaken for a health club, and he never did deign to lower that bond.

Schenevar had an admirably simple argument to make for his client; he had only to recite the constitutions of the United States and of the great state of Montana for his legal theory, and for facts he had the incontrovertible fact that first Mr. Lucerne's car and then the contents of that car had been seized without a warrant or any other scrap of paper, and certainly without Mr. Lucerne's permission. Schenevar asserted with reams of authority that there was just one remedy in the law for such a goof: The evidence must go. He made a poetic anthology of the many decisions from the state's high court in which the right to privacy had been enshrined and defined as especially broad and sacrosanct in Montana, 'Get off my property' being the state's true motto. Schenevar declared the evidence must go, "… if only to keep the people's immense preference for privacy perfectly safe from unwarranted trespass by the state."

One leg of the aimless journey Larry Lucerne was making on the day of his arrest had him slipping down into the cut the Missouri makes at Fort Benton, down to the cottonwoods and the river, a fuming companion at his side, thinking whatever she was thinking. They'd been going a hundred and twenty all night, or much of it, and Lucerne knew the Corvette was a preening car, an attention grabber at any speed, and that there was no need at all to maintain this pace, a number of reasons not to, but Larry Lucerne and April Newberry were extremely high, and had been up to Cut Bank that night, and back down to Augusta, and all over the place, making excellent time going nowhere. Later he would understand that he should have brought a serious car, a serious attitude, to a serious job of work, but that night he'd been in a mood to run, and nothing he asked of the Corvette had caused her to break a sweat until that following morning she did at some point blow a head gasket, and they'd dribbled oil over a long length of highway, and his oil pressure needle sagged. Only when a red light appeared did he notice anything out of the way. More graphic signs of their trouble followed immediately as his overbored engine began eating itself without lubricant and multicolored smoke seethed out of the engine compartment, and April said, "Stop, you asshole. We're on fire."

"Better get to town," Larry Lucerne said, already grimly aware of a bad bend in everything.

"Slow down," said April.

Just then with a shriek and a heavy clank his whole drive train seized with such force that it slung them around sideways as they came to the trestle, just there where a stone arch supports the railroad tracks over the road, the only paved road coming into Fort Benton from that side, at just that place where as the road signs warn in advance the road becomes a single lane, and right there, across that single lane and under that arch was where they came to rest; Larry Lucerne was appalled at the extent of his bad luck, to be on the wrong side of a one-in-a-million sequence of events. They'd come to rest with stone work a few feet from both bumpers, fore and aft, but Larry Lucerne could take no consolation in the disaster, the collision he'd avoided, because his Corvette would not run, wouldn't even roll, and that was grievous enough, but he foresaw encounters now that might be hard to manage while he was so extravagantly high on cocaine and uncut adrenaline. What happened then would many months later be the subject of the hearing that would essentially decide whether Larry Lucerne was to be reacquainted with freedom any time soon.

◊ ◊ ◊

He had got puffy in jail and his right hand seemed to be perpetually writing something, but there was no instrument in it. Sitting near his attorney he'd acquired the lawyer's luxurious scent but still wore his jail jump suit, a bright ensemble in broad orange and white stripes, accessorized by gray socks and plastic shower shoes. Transfixed by disbelief, he let his face move neither left nor right, neither up nor down, and his eyes remained equally immobile, and this eerie pose persisted even when he was responding to the judge.

"Mr. Lucerne," said Judge Hand, "before we go forward with this hearing, there are a few things I'd like to say to you. You've probably heard them before, but I want them said on the record. First, I should tell you that I have the briefs in hand, and I can rule on your motion with just the briefs. You understand that?"

"Your Honor," said Brian Schenevar, "we've. . ."

"I want to hear from your client on this, counsel. That's why I asked your client the question."

Larry Lucerne moved just enough to speak, and spoke just loudly enough to be heard, "I understand, Your Honor." He seemed to want to seem pitiful.

"And you understand," said the judge, "that this is an evidentiary hearing, and the rules aren't as strict as they would be at your trial."

"Yes," said Larry Lucerne.

"And you understand that if I hear something today that doesn't put you in a good light, then I can't unhear that later?"

"Yes."

"And with all that in mind, and knowing you run a certain amount of risk, do you still want to go forward with the hearing?"

"Let's go," said Larry Lucerne, summoning the remnants of his force. "Your Honor." Everything in his bearing suggested he could use a change of scene.

Weary to his dewlaps, Judge Hand sighed and said, "All right. It's your motion, counsel: Call your witness."

Schenevar called Bob Roberts of Bob's Towing to the stand where Roberts took the oath and assumed an exaggerated air of innocence, a tourist's wonder at being there. Under questioning he established where he'd been on the day in question—at his shop—who'd called him—the dispatcher, and he further affirmed that so far as he knew, yes the dispatcher works at the Sheriff's office, and, yes, the dispatcher works for the Sheriff. Roberts confirmed that the original call for his services must have come from the Sheriff's deputy who was out there directing traffic, but he didn't know for sure.

"And once you were on scene, Mr. Roberts, who told you to remove my client's car?"

"Told me?" Bob Roberts went even wider-eyed. "Nobody had to *tell* me to get it out of there."

"But who, if anyone, *did* tell you, Mr. Roberts?"

"Well," said Roberts, already out of patience for this fancy kid, "*nobody*. Wasn't that what I just said?"

"Is it your usual practice to tow vehicles without any authorization from the owner?"

"Abandoned ones," said Roberts, determined now to be as clever and as uncooperative as possible with this shyster.

"Is it," wondered Schenevar, "your practice to tow vehicles without the owner's permission when the owner is present?"

"My practice?" said Roberts. "I mean—practice? The car was stuck in there."

"Do you recognize my client here, Mr. Roberts?"

"Sort of," said Roberts. "I guess that's the guy."

"And was my client there when you towed his car?"

Dragging that Corvette out from the trestle required all the finesse and know-how Bob Roberts had, the technical difficulties and the oddness of the situation had made the whole thing a kind of career highlight for him until now. Sure, the car's owner had been there, and frantic—'Don't tweak the frame, man, just don't tweak the frame.' A pain-in-the-ass rich guy. "Yeah," said Roberts. "He was there."

"Did he ask you to tow his car?" Mr. Roberts.

Bob Roberts was beginning to harden. "No," he said.

"Did he authorize you to tow his car?"

"No," said Roberts.

"Who did authorize that?"

"Authorize? They call, I come. That's all."

"And by *they*, you mean that dispatch called you?"

"Yeah," said Roberts. "Dispatch. Dispatch. How many times do I gotta say these things?"

"And who, if anyone, told you to tow that car to your impound lot?"

"Told me?" said Roberts.

"Who authorized it?" Schenevar leaned an inch toward the witness.

"Authorized? There you go again. *I* authorized it. It's *Bob's* towing. That's my name on the door panel of that truck. Nobody authorizes me to do a. . . I'm my own boss."

Schenevar, having asked perhaps one question too many, passed the witness to the County Attorney, who asked, "Bob—Mr. Roberts—How long you been doing this? Towing?"

"Since fifty-nine," said Roberts. "Started in high school

on old Dave Quinlevan's truck."

"So," G.C. asked, "do you think you know your way around the profession by now?"

"I better," said Roberts, "by now."

"And what happens," wondered G.C., "if you pull a car out of the ditch, and it's not running? You just leave it there by the roadside until you hear otherwise from somebody?"

"Can't," said Roberts. "If it got smacked into, then that'd probably cost me my business. At least. No, when I grab 'em, I always haul 'em in. Have to, the way I see it."

"And," said G.C., "when you went out there to get the Defendant's car—what is that thing, a coupe?—did he ever tell you *not* to tow it?"

"*Nope*," said Bob Roberts, triumphant at last.

Lawyer Schenevar's main thesis and best shot was that the State had seized his client's car without a warrant and everything that happened after that was necessarily wrong. The County Attorney took the position that the car had not been seized at all, but only removed to safety. So far, the County Attorney was having much the better hearing. Young Schenevar had a weak case, and a strong opponent, and it was hard to watch Larry Lucerne's chance to walk on this thing sliding so quickly out of sight. This was no way to build a reputation. Lucerne, now nearly comatose at the council table beside him, had been so profoundly stupid that it was probably a good thing all in all if he was retired from the drug business by any means not involving his death. Still, a lawyer hates to lose.

The fluorescent fixture in that windowless holding cell had been failing during every meeting Brian Schenevar had with his client there, and in each such meeting either the light or Larry Lucerne had given him a headache. "Well," he said, "that's that. I really didn't expect him to rule from the bench. At least now we know."

"Know what?" said Lucerne, a creature alive in the rocks.

"The evidence would come in," said Schenevar. "The drugs. If we went to trial."

"You said," Lucerne reminded him, "they didn't have a warrant."

"They didn't," said the young lawyer.

"Then why?"

"Because," said Schenevar, "the judge says so." And the judge had said so forcibly, and in some detail only minutes earlier in his client's presence, but it was Larry Lucerne's abiding belief that if he could only keep questioning any reality he didn't like, then eventually he could make it go away.

"If?" said Lucerne, the thin varnish of his charm long gone. "*If* we went to trial?"

"I wouldn't advise it."

"What?" Said Lucerne. "Throw myself on the mercy of the court? We've been trying that. That's a very bad idea. I'm not guilty yet, am I? I mean, what have I got to lose?"

All but, thought Schenevar, all but guilty now. It was a pending formality. "For one thing," said Schenevar, "we're still two and a half months out on your trial date. You'd sit here in county the whole time, waiting. If you lost, they could assess the cost of the trial to you, which isn't cheap. And you've already run through the retainer your folks paid us."

"You can't get me out?"

"No. We've been over that. You've heard the judge on that, too. Many times."

"You can't get the trial moved up?"

"No," said Schenevar. "It's set. They slid it in just under

six months."

"I'll pay you," said Lucerne. "I can pay you."

"That's not my first concern," said Schenevar. "But, frankly, I don't see how you would pay. If you do have any assets left, you'd have a hard time getting at 'em now."

"Well, I want my day in court," said Lucerne. "Talk to my mother. They've got equipment parked all over the place. They'll pay."

His day in court, when it came, would be exactly and only that, a one-day trial offering a breathtaking series of plunges into the many chasms in the defendant's thought processes. By ten, Judge Hand had seated a jury, by ten thirty he'd read them their preliminary instructions and given them a bathroom break, and before they broke for lunch that day, they'd heard testimony from two of the State's three witnesses.

The first of these was April Newberry who wore her hair in the helmet cut of a silent film star and a black, cable knit sweater. G. C. asked her where she was from, and she said Highwood, originally. He asked her what she did. She cleaned motel rooms. In Highwood? "In Missoula," she said. "I was in graduate school."

"Was?" said G. C. "And what became of that, Ms. Newberry?"

"I took my degree," she said.

"Now, Ms. Newberry, we have spoken by phone before, is that correct?"

Ms. Newberry was appropriately embarrassed and wished to be concise. "Correct," she said.

"And when we talked, you told me some things about yourself that I told you could be crimes, is that correct?"

"Correct," she said, relishing these one-word answers.

"And I told you I wouldn't seek to prosecute those possible crimes if you gave us your full cooperation?"

"Correct," she said, set a little free by this truth.

"Did I tell you what to say here today?"

"Tell me?" she said. "No," she said. "Oh, you mean the truth. Sorry. You said to say the truth."

"Let the record reflect, Ms. Newberry, that I am gesturing toward the Defendant where he is seated at counsel table. Ms. Newberry, do you know the Defendant?"

Already she was very near to fabricating the answer she knew the prosecutor wanted. She'd known the man under discussion only a matter of hours, and most of those in the dark of night some months ago, and her dim, distorted memory of him did not much comport with this poor guy they were calling the Defendant today. "Slightly," she said.

"How do you know him?" G. C. asked her.

This, thought April Newberry, was the really embarrassing part, a story she would have preferred not to tell even privately. "We met at a party."

"When?"

"Well, it would be the night before his car broke down."

"Where?" said G. C.

"The party?" she said. "Up at Lost Lake." She had been home visiting the folks and thought she'd revive her spirits by partying as she had in the old days with some authentic non academics, back-home people, friends from high school, and then, just as she'd been discovering round the campfire that these friends were no more authentic than anyone else, and worse, that she now had nothing in common with them but a history they remembered very differently, along came a new element to the party in a low slung, plastic car that had no business on the kind of roads that lead to Lost Lake. It was the creep Larry Lucerne, an older man looking for his younger self, and by instinct he immediately attached himself to April Newberry as she moved round the fire, trying to stay upwind of its smoke.

"What happened," G. C. asked her, "when you met the Defendant at the party?"

"He introduced himself. He mentioned several people, and asked me if I knew them. I didn't. Then pretty soon he asked me if I liked bliss."

"Bliss?" G. C. said.

"That's what I said," April Newberry recalled. "Then he said Peruvian flake."

"What did you understand that to mean, Ms. Newberry?"

"Cocaine," she said, succinct again.

"How did you respond to that question, Ms. Newberry?"

"Told him I didn't know if I liked it or not. The people I associate with are lucky when they can afford their Schlitz."

"Was that the end of that conversation?"

"No," said April Newberry, abashed to say it. "Then we left. I left with him."

About a mile into their trip he had stopped, which seemed a little ominous in such company, that he should stop in the middle of nowhere, before they'd even got back to a county road, but his purpose had been to show her a black plastic brick in the little trunk of his car, and with his Swiss Army knife to work a hole in it, and then to extract a healthy spoonful of the white powder within and ladle it onto an issue of *Car and Driver* where it sparkled a bit even in the wan glow of his flashlight. They took some, he using yet another blade of his knife as a coke spoon, she by rubbing it on her gums. There was a lot of it, and they didn't need to be efficient. They'd continued taking it all night. This was as much of the story as G. C. extracted from her on the stand. Fortunately, she wasn't required to say how exhilarating it was at first, blasting around under that other crystalline substance spread across the sky, how instantly profound it had been to be high that way, and she had never felt it necessary to mention that Larry had at some point boasted he could fuck like a stallion on a drug so pure, and she'd had to break it to him that he wouldn't be fucking her, and after that he'd pouted, and started driving too fast, too carelessly, and they'd managed to drive all night without getting anywhere, and she'd smoked a whole pack of cigarettes and felt sick for days afterward; April Newberry, essentially a goody two shoes, a bookworm, was aware as she left the witness stand that this wasn't the impression she'd left with her neighbors in the jury box. She'd be looking like garbage to them. She'd pledged to tell the whole truth here, and thank goodness she hadn't told it.

G. C. then called Sheriff's Deputy Boler who took the oath with his belly bulging and his boots polished, anxious to recount his biggest bust to date. Later, and for many years to come, Boler would use more private, more complete versions of the story to illustrate the serendipity of law enforcement, the bizarre workings of the criminal mind.

While on routine patrol one morning he'd come upon a traffic jam near the junction of highways 87 and 386 where a car had stalled under the trestle. "Upon exiting my patrol vehicle," according to his initial report, "this officer heard screaming and hollering emitting from several different locations." A Mrs. Gompers and her daughters were screaming in their car, stalled on their way to go shopping in Great Falls. Deputy Boler advised them to stop and that help would soon be on the way. A man stood on one side of the vehicle that was wedged under the trestle, a young woman on the other side; they were also yelling at each other. The car still frothed steam and smoke, and because it seemed the thing could explode Deputy Boler told them to move away from it. The young woman with her scorched eyes left the scene altogether then, walked right off the road, climbed through a barbwire fence, and walked out into the countryside, not headed toward town. "What's wrong with her?" Boler had asked the man he was about to identify as Larry Lucerne.

"Who knows?" Lucerne had said.

According to Boler's report: "This officer did see that the subject was very perturbed."

After the smoking car had finally been extracted from under the trestle, and after Deputy Boler disentangled the traffic backed up on either side of it, he gave Lucerne a ride to the impound lot where he might make his arrangements with Bob Roberts. Looking to be helpful, Deputy Boler had asked the man if he might be interested in parting out his Corvette, and Lucerne only groaned and mentioned the unfairness of everything.

"This officer transported the subject to the office at the impound lot. Mr. Roberts gave the subject the keys to his vehicle, but when Mr. Roberts tried to talk to the subject about impound fees, the subject said he couldn't talk about that at the moment and went out to his car."

Meanwhile Deputy Boler had got trapped in the impound office with Bob Roberts talking about paddlefish. He liked to go downriver to snag paddlefish. Would the deputy care for some pickled paddle fish? The deputy then, trying to disengage, saw Lucerne was opening the trunk of his Corvette, trying to be furtive about it, and just then Bob Roberts had another thought and said, "Why don't you tell that guy he can use my phone if he wants. If it's not long distance."

Deputy Boler stepped from the door of the office. "Hey," he called, and that was all, because this one word caused Larry Lucerne to swerve toward the deputy, his mouth a near perfect O, and then to swerve away and scale the chain link fence though there was an open gate not far away, and run already gasping round the first corner.

"The subject had left the trunk of his vehicle open when he fled. This officer did examine the vehicle and found in plain view in the trunk of the vehicle a package wrapped in plastic."

What a thrill it had been to find that package there, a hole worked in it as if a mouse had got to it, white powder leaking out. What fun when his NIK test confirmed the powder was cocaine. A lot of cocaine.

"At thirteen hundred hours of the same day, this officer was once again on regular uniformed patrol when I encountered the subject again, hitchhiking on Highway 80, just past the bridge. When this officer stopped, the subject entered the patrol vehicle where this officer did place the subject under arrest and transport him to the S.O. for further processing."

Boler's later, more informal account would always conclude with the same observation, "Man, that guy was dumb."

By the lunch break in his trial everyone in attendance had reached roughly the same conclusion concerning the defendant. Brian Schenevar located the County Attorney in the hall outside the courtroom and offered once more to have his client plead to a lesser included offense—straight possession, a much easier beef.

"And why," G. C. asked him, "would I do that?"

Schenevar said it would make things simpler for everyone.

"They're pretty simple for me already," said G. C.

"The guy," said Schenevar, nearly reduced to whining now, "has nothing on his record."

"Yeah," said G. C., "I think you've mentioned that before, but that's about to change, don't you think?"

After lunch G. C. called Clara Dunn from the state crime lab, and he walked her all through her lengthy credentials and experience of science, and together they tracked the progress of the black package on the evidence table, from steaming Corvette to gleaming crime lab and back to its present location. They went meticulously through the processes by which she had concluded that it was cocaine, in fact the purest compound she'd ever seen, so pure in fact as to represent some risk of heart attack to the unwary user, so pure that by the time it reached the street it might well have doubled in volume, abetted by other substances.

"And what would those other substances be?" G. C. asked her.

"We often see baby powder in it," said Mrs. Dunn.

"Baby powder?" said G. C. registering his disgust.

"Ojection," said Brian Schenevar. "Not in the form of a question. Irrelevant. Asked and answered."

"Withdrawn," said G. C. "So—Mrs. Dunn, how many individual doses of this drug would you say are in this package?"

"Too many variables to say with any precision," said Mrs. Dunn, a young woman but with her reading glasses suspended from a beaded glass necklace she was a sufficiently grave one.

"More than a hundred?" said G. C.

"Yes," said Mrs. Dunn.

"More than a thousand?"

"Yes," said Mrs. Dunn.

"State," said G. C. "passes the witness to the defense."

Brian Schenevar's client had been increasingly agitated through the morning's testimony when his attorney asked the state's witnesses only a few harmless questions. Schenevar had tried to prepare him for this in advance, explaining that it was dangerous to ask a question to which he didn't know the answer, and that where April Newberry and Deputy Boler were concerned it would be dangerous to ask questions to which he did know the answers. They were witnesses better left alone. To seem meticulous and thorough then, he required the State's scientist to vouch for the certification of every piece of equipment, every reactive agent she'd mentioned in her testimony, he walked Mrs. Dunn and the black plastic parcel once again through its unbroken chain of custody, and in the end Schenevar failed to find the first hole in the woman's process or her composure, but had only reinforced her testimony and bored the jury to no good purpose.

G.C. Harrow stood and said, "People have nothing further for Mrs. Dunn, Your Honor, and would ask that she be excused. And—the State rests."

A trial is the Defendant's prerogative, and the accused in these matters is supplied with exactly one additional choice, to testify or not at that trial. Driving his legal strategy much as he'd driven his now forfeited Stingray, Larry Lucerne had insisted on both. Now was his long- awaited hour. The only one present who didn't know his fate was already sealed, he just knew he could explain himself. His was a now unfortunate history of talking his way out of things. Alone in the back row of the gallery, in its far corner sat Laverne Lucerne wearing a kerchief on her head, the slim babushka who had at every break gone outside to smoke and pray. She did not wring her hands when the lawyer called her boy up to testify, but had to consciously prevent herself from it. It was nice to see Larry in something other than jail clothes, without the shackles for a change, and his hair was shorter than it had been in years even if someone had done an awful job of cutting it. For all his complaints about jail food, her boy had gained weight in there. Laverne couldn't help it—she was so proud of him—he seemed to be really trying at last. How manly he was there on the witness stand with his hand up, pledging however improbably to tell the truth.

It was a short performance to conclude a short trial. Schenevar had been over and over it with his man. They had to make it very short. The less Lucerne said on the stand, the less meat that the County Attorney would have to tear at on cross examination, so Schenevar agreed to ask him one simple, carefully crafted question, and Schenevar had required him to answer that question in five words or less, and that would be the sum of the performance Larry Lucerne had waited all these months to deliver. He meant to give it his all. His lawyer asked him, "Larry, was it ever your intention to distribute that substance they say they found in your trunk?"

Larry Lucerne, from the depth of his being and almost indignantly said, "No, sir, it was not."

"Nothing further," said Schenevar.

Judge Hand said, "G.C.?"

G.C. Harrow stood incredulous, and he asked the witness, "You didn't intend to distribute the cocaine they found in your trunk?"

"Objection," said Schenevar, "asked and answered."

"I'll put it this way," said G.C., "what did you intend to do with the cocaine they found in the trunk of your car?"

From his slight elevation on the witness stand Larry Lucerne looked down to Jeet Harrow—a pipsqueak of old, and he wasn't about to be pushed around. "Use it," he said.

"You would take a thousand doses?"

"I might share it," Larry Lucerne pointedly said, "with my friends."

And there it was on the flop, Jeet's winning card. The legal definition of illegal distribution in Montana includes even gifts; the jury would hear instructions to that effect, and G. C. had maneuvered him into hanging himself with his own tongue, shredding his last slim hope.

Who wore the boots now?

◊ ◊ ◊

The prisoner had got fatter and further desiccated and his hair was growing out again. Larry Lucerne had spent yet another six weeks in the county jail while the local probation officer compiled a pre-sentence investigation which conceded that, as Lucerne's lawyer had always emphasized, the man had absolutely no prior criminal record. However, except for running a business renting jet skis on Flathead Lake for two seasons, he had no employment history either, no military service, not much at all to explain how he had passed his time or financed his expensive hobbies. He'd listed snow skiing and conversational Spanish as his life's accomplishments. When Brian Schenevar put LaVerne Lucerne on the stand to attest to her son's many good qualities, all she was able to say in that regard was, "He's a good boy." No one else was available to offer even that much in his behalf. With that, Judge Hand told the defendant to rise and face the court, and he spoke of the jury's unanimous verdict, and he weighed mitigating and aggravating factors of the crime, and the judge concluded that the defendant's rehabilitation might best accomplished by remanding him to the Montana State Penitentiary to begin serving a sentence of twenty years. Larry Lucerne felt the rest of his life merge with his watery bowels and his knees buckled. His lawyer grabbed his sinking elbow.

How disappointing for Jeet Harrow, then, that he couldn't seem to enjoy this fine joke, the man's temporary terror. The judge kept reciting and went on to say that of Lucerne's twenty years of imprisonment, fifteen were suspended. Later Schenever would tell him that with time served, and good time, and quarter time, he would likely be less than two years in Deer Lodge before he was shipped off to a halfway house somewhere. But Larry Lucerne would be on papers forever now, under the close scrutiny and control of the pettiest of petty bureaucrats, a fate against which the boy would undoubtedly chafe and chafe, and his fun was officially done. This should be revenge enough for almost anything. He was handcuffed again and led away bewildered. Did he have the slightest notion this fate might be part payment for ancient sins, for some old playground cruelty? No. Was he chastened at all, corrected? No. Larry Lucerne firmly believed, a belief apparent on his moon face, that he was a victim of jealousy, that his only mistake had been letting himself fall into the hands of small, careful, weaselly people who resented a heroic good time.

Jeet had been finding more and more reasons to drive out to the farm. He shared with brother Tel and with niece Carrie a particular sensibility, an understanding, and their regular company was increasingly necessary to him. He had of late been missing very few Sunday dinners with them, and though those dinners could involve fried chicken, and potatoes mashed in sweet cream, maybe a steaming bowl of peas, another of greens, biscuits fresh from the oven, and coffee afterward with cake, or pie, or pudding, and though he gloried in such meals, food was not the main inducement. This kitchen was the source of his inmost self and Jeet felt he'd continue to be tolerated here so long as he didn't bring whisky, waterfowl, or playing cards, and so long as he followed an unspoken protocol; today he was in violation of its cardinal requirement, because he had come without Jolene, because he had left her at home suffering with her sinuses.

"Poor thing," said his sister-in-law. Donna had been raised to despise lawyers but was usually able to make a qualified exception for Jeet.

When Jolene was there, Donna had an ally, an ear, but

today, in Jolene's absence, Donna would be stuck with these three Harrows whose talk she knew would drift along just out of her reach, and she'd be reduced to prompting them through a meal they needed no urging to eat and to waiting for one of them to say something to upset her.

"This guy I've been reading about in the papers," said Tel, "this guy you convicted—is he any relation to Dan Lucerne and that bunch?"

"He's Dan's boy," said Jeet. "You don't remember Larry? No, I guess you wouldn't, he was older. Still is, I guess. A couple years ahead of me in school."

"Was-older," said Carrie, "is-older. You could make a formula for that." New to algebra, she saw it as an all-purpose explanation. "X," she said, would be that guy's age when Dad was born. Dad's age plus x would always equal that guy's age, no matter how much time passed. That guy's age minus x would always equal Dad's age."

"Never thought of it like that," said Tel as if he'd thought of it in any way at all. "If I remember right, the Lucernes got hailed out pretty bad several years in a row here a while back, had a run of real bad luck. They used to have quite an operation over there. Don't know how they're doing these days."

There was a solemn interlude while they considered the possible fates of the Lucernes.

"Man, it's been *cold*," said Tel, remarking the arctic front that had settled on Montana. "I've been quite the iron monger, been making up projects just so I can fire up the forge and bend some metal. It's always kind of relaxing to bang on things with a big hammer. And toasty."

"And your clothes smell like hell after that. Exactly like hell when you've been out there." Donna poured her husband a glass of the lemonade he drank year around.

"So," said Tel. "I guess this conviction is another notch

in your belt, or wherever you guys wear your notches."

"Fish in a barrel," said Jeet. "Wasn't much of a win."

"It's not a game," said Donna. "It's important work. Keeping these people away from us." His work was the one thing she admired in him. He seemed to admire nothing in himself, not for all his efforts that way.

"Well . . ." said Jeet, and to Carrie he said, "How's basketball going? Have you guys had a game yet?"

"It's just junior high basketball," Carrie said, and her mother told her she should answer the question she'd been asked, that she should try and get in that habit, and Carrie said, "I got kicked off the team. Coach Korn kicked me off. Didn't I mention it, Mom?"

"He what?" said Donna. "Why?"

"I said 'crap' in practice," Carrie said.

Tel was beginning to enjoy the story, and Jeet tried not to, and Donna just knew something like this would have to come up, and she said, "For one bad word he kicked you off the team?"

"I think it was the way I said it, maybe. Or because I usually don't say anything. Or. . . Also, I mean, if I could make a shot at all, or dribble, or even catch, I bet I could say about anything I wanted. But I am the worst basketball player of all time. I'm just about dangerous. It's only junior high basketball."

"It is a healthy, wholesome activity for you," said Donna. "Or it was supposed to be."

She fed them more, fed them and fed them, but sullenly. These men found her daughter amusing in a way that Donna did not.

To break another solemn silence, and to get the girl off the hook, Jeet asked her, "How you doing with Raskolnikov?" When he happened to remember reading *Crime and Punishment* in his thirteenth year, Uncle Jeet had given her a copy for her birthday. A peculiar delight.

"I'm reading it again," she said. "Third time already."

"Again?" said Donna. "Not again?" She'd read the back cover of that book, and that was more than enough for her: an old woman murdered, a young man's tortured conscience, whose idea of entertainment was this? Donna worried about her daughter, a girl who, with her unfriendly personality did not need to take on anyone else's problems or go looking through world literature for the gloomy outlook "Why? Why even once?"

"It's about justice," Carrie said. "That's supposed to be important, isn't it?"

"Justice," said Donna. She confronted her brother-in-law, as she seemed to do at least once every time he showed up to the farm. "Jeet, I'd think you'd get enough of that at work."

"No," said G.C., honest among friends. "Almost none. Justice only occurs in the abstract."

"Now, what does that even mean?" Donna was annoyed, just as she knew they would somehow annoy her.

◊ ◊ ◊

It was the coldest morning in several years, a cold that made usually supple things want to break. Getting to work had not been pleasant, and once there G.C. Harrow made himself begin drawing up an Information to charge the pedophile Joseph Brooks with a dozen dreadful felonies. Brooks, at 19, was hardly more than a child himself but already a seasoned predator, and a younger Mr. Brooks had first come to G.C.'s notice as a victim of such crimes. G.C. could not be too enthusiastic about assigning blame to the poor lad at this late date. But that was the job, really, slapping bandages on the current bleeding. An hour into his Monday and the County Attorney was brooding, fidgeting, and it was a something of a relief to be interrupted in his ugly task by a call from a fellow lawyer. It was Brian Schenevar, saying that he was moving to withdraw his appeal in the Lucerne case; Schenevar told him that Larry Lucerne was dead, found on fish row, in the showers, neck broken. There would be an investigation, of course. Foul play, horse play, more bad luck? Hard to know in there.

"Oh, man," said Jeet. "He never even made it out of receiving?"

"Nope," said Schenevar. "My dad's a lawyer, so I sort of knew I should be prepared for things like this. But you get to know the guy and—anyway, I'll withdraw that appeal. It's moot now."

"You did a good job for him," Jeet said. "A person can't cover every single contingency; as long as the thing you're doing at the moment seems like the right thing, then that's the best you can do. And then you hope it works out." Jeet could not at the moment place the slightest faith in his own prescription.

The County Attorney went home to an extremely early lunch, suggesting to his secretary on the way out that gastric distresses may or may not allow his return. Gail was unable to conceal her delight at his departure, urging him to take care of himself and, unctuously, to take all the time he might need. The office, he knew, was more peaceful without him. At home there was a new dog Jolene had named Princess, a relentless yapper, and on the television a large and seemingly varnished woman was holding forth on another large woman's troubles with her lazy teens. Jolene might have been in the studio with them, she had a way of entering into teeveeland so wholeheartedly. Jeet also watched this, but with no comprehension, and he stood at the kitchen counter eating cookies by the handful, washing them down with that morning's cold coffee. He told Jolene about Larry Lucerne, and Jeet wasn't sure she'd heard him at first, but then she said, "So, that means it's over. You won."

"Yeah. It's officially over now."

"Ark, ark." Princess pranced at his feet, glaring up at him.

"I can't see how you'd have any problem getting elected next time," Jolene said. "No one can say you don't get results." His wife had it closely worked out—he had only to win the coming election, and then two more, and then he could retire if he wanted. To pursue other interests. Their steadily throbbing furnace could not keep a house with so many windows more than cool in such weather; Jolene had wrapped herself in quilts.

"Well," he said. "I'd better get back to the office."

Jeet had cultivated no bad habits to distract him from his work and had for that matter very few good ones to claim his attention, so when he was at wit's end and didn't know what to do with himself there was usually nowhere to go and nothing for it but a return to the scene and the source of his irritation; it was back to the office, usually, or to bed. The air just outside his house was charged with a deep, fearsome cold and was hung with prismatic sprays of crystalline ice; it was Jeet's impression that the day meant to make itself memorable.

◊ ◊ ◊

The jailer in charge of the evidence locker that day had been on the job all of three months, and it never occurred to him to question the County Attorney when the man came to sign out all that cocaine. On learning of this the Sheriff was to advise the young jailer that shit rolls downhill and that as a probationary employee he occupied the very bottom of the slope, and, "Don't ever do that again."

"What was I supposed to do? It was the County

Attorney."

"Nothing," said the Sheriff. "Say you lost the key. Say you don't know where it is. Just say you don't know. How you expect to work in public service if you can't even do nothing? Say you don't know. Just learn how to say you don't know."

"He said he didn't need it anymore," the jailer explained. "Said he was going to destroy it."

"Anything," said the Sheriff, "that comes out of that evidence locker, gets logged back into that evidence locker. Or if it does get destroyed, there better be several officers there to witness it. Firearms, anything. Somebody to see it. You know what that package was worth? If we could've got the value out of it? If we could've figured that out, that could've been new cruisers for us, you understand me?"

The jailer did not understand him, but claimed to. "So," he said, "will he be in trouble?"

"Who?" The Sheriff was losing patience with his trainee. "The County Attorney? No. *You* will be in trouble. That's what you need to appreciate."

◊ ◊ ◊

The County Attorney knew the proper procedures, of course. He knew all the rules, a habit he'd formed as a gambler, and how he would have hectored anyone who was doing what he was doing now, absconding with that package. The black package, further wrapped in a clear plastic sack, rode in the back seat of his sedan, radiating like uranium. One day, and probably soon, the County Attorney would be called upon to explain this, and what would he say? He would arm himself as usual with the truth, for he was scrupulous, it was the root of all his security, and he would say, "I wanted a private ceremony. I earned it." This truth, he suspected, would have less traction than most.

Jeet was detecting a trend away from the right decision. He was on his way to Square Butte Bench and the forge in Tel's shop. He intended a purification ritual. Burn it up.

Climbing out from a river clogged with ice, coming up through that coulee that bent toward the farm, Jeet came upon a person whom he'd soon discover was April Newberry, but who was on first sight only a puffy X waving its arms at the roadside, only its nose and upper lip exposed, and these had been scalded by the cold. Her broken car, its tailpipe emitting nothing. He didn't know her as April Newberry as she got in beside him, and even in his fully heated car Jeet had remained bundled, so she didn't recognize him either, and in the pleasant moment while they were still strangers they bonded as the occupants of a small, warm pod with lethal cold all around them.

"Bad time to break down," he commenced with the obvious.

"Every time I come home," she marveled. "Of course, the Comet, that skanky thing kind of breaks down everywhere."

He knew this voice. "Where," he asked, "were you headed?"

"Highwood," she said. "I'm up at my folks' place, supposed to keep the pipes from freezing while they're on a cruise. Went into Benton to visit with Marci, cause I was going stir crazy up there, and. . . Getting to be a long story. I fear it's the bitter end for the Comet."

He knew this voice. "So, where you going now?"

"Well." She said, sifting quickly through her two options.

"Highwood?" he said.

"I know that's not on your way," she said. "Is it? That's not on anybody's way."

"I'm just driving around keeping my heater running,"

he said.

April Newberry sighed. Another creep. There would be creeps on the moon.

"You know who I am?" Jeet asked her.

"No," she said in a terminal way to discourage him from filling her in.

"You remember giving testimony?" he said.

"Oh," she said. "You. Unbelievable"

"Better not let those pipes freeze," he said, and Jeet drove on through the Shonkin toward Highwood, and he told her the news of the late Larry.

"They killed him?" she said.

"I don't know if there was a 'they' involved," Jeet said. "Got this about third hand, so all I know for sure is he's dead. Died down there at the prison."

"That's the first person I've known who. . . He didn't deserve that. Poor guy. I mean he was just a. . . Poor guy."

Jeet could only agree, but didn't think he could decently say so. He didn't require her gratitude, but after a while did not feel it fair that he must suffer this much of her silence. The sky was so blue in such weather, he was taking her home, they were warm—surely, they could find something else to say. "Where they going?" he said at last.

"Going?" she said.

"Your folks," he said. "The cruise," he reminded her.

"Puerto Rico," she said.

"Great," he said. "They won't even have to change currency."

"Exactly why they picked it," she said.

The County Attorney had known her initially as half of several recorded conversations in which several different officers had ached to know what she knew about all that cocaine. She'd been of no use to them. Though her account of her evening with Larry Lucerne didn't incriminate her too terribly, it did incriminate him, so she'd been subpoenaed to testify at his trial where the County Attorney extracted the same tale of aimlessness from her. Now, sunk in a down coat, embarrassment, and a thick knit cap she said nothing at all. Maybe he'd frightened her. Though he'd been one for some time, Jeet had never got accustomed to see himself as a daunting official or a threat of any kind. He sometimes forgot the effect he could have on people.

It was such a brilliant day. It seemed so unfair of her to drag this loneliness into his car. Her tiny grief? His small guilt? She did eventually say, "I was thinking about law school myself. Until all this happened."

"Well," he said, "you weren't charged with anything, so I wouldn't worry about the, you know. You'd be surprised at some of the doozies they let into this profession. You might as well go ahead and apply to the law school if you want."

"And maybe I could be a doozy, too" she said. "Sounds fun."

"Well," he said, "probably is a good idea to know why you want to do it before you do it. Go into the law, that is."

"I know exactly why," she said. "My parents scrimped and saved so I could get a masters, and now I'm cleaning motel rooms in Missoula."

"I saw you had Missoula plates," he said. "Well, people do make a living at it. It's not a bad deal if you've got a high tolerance for mendacity. You do get lied to about a hundred times a day."

"You think I lied to you?" she said.

"I don't care," he said.

"I stuck around," she said, "to watch some of that trial. After I testified. I watched you guys do that lab lady. The science. Kind of liked the formality of it, but, man, you managed to make it so tedious."

"Tactical," Jeet corrected. "You snow 'em with bullshit.

Scientists are great for that. Put 'em on the stand, give 'em their head, and they give you everything down to the nanosecond, and the jury'll believe anything they say, just so they'll quit saying it."

"Yeah," she said. "I doubt I could ever get that strategic about things."

"You might surprise yourself," he said. "when it's your job to win. But I've been wondering," he said, "about that cocaine."

"Yeah? Here it comes."

"No," he said. "About the effect. Obviously, people take it because it's pleasant. But I wonder how. In what way?"

"I hope I'm not authority on that," she said.

"Well, you did look into it."

"It made me feel kind of smart," she said. "Right at first. Like I was taking it all in. Then it made me feel like I wanted more. It's the pure essence of consumerism, cocaine. Can't get enough. Sometimes I'm glad I'm poor. And now, see, that guy is dead, which seems like kind of a waste. You can tell there's an ugliness around it. You keep taking it, though."

"What's your degree?" he said.

"I hold," she said, "a Master of Arts in Comparative Literature. Disqualifies me for about everything."

"What do you read?" he said.

"Read?" This was a question she was never met with in these parts and therefore found confusing. The honest answer would seem pretty snooty, but nothing wrong with that. "The Symbolists," she said. "I've been reading the Symbolists."

"*Fleurs du Mal?*" he said. "If that's how you say that."

"What?" she said. "What have I? Who are you? I feel like I'm being jerked around," she said. "Too many surprises. Tragedies. Coincidences. It's like a nightmare."

"A Season in Hell," he said.

"Quit it," she said. They covered another mile before she said, "So—you have any other surprises for me?"

Jeet inclined his head toward the package in the back seat, which she hadn't noticed before.

◊ ◊ ◊

In Highwood April Newberry said she needed to ask one more favor of him. "You know anything about gas?" she said. The pilot light in her mother's cook stove had gone out, and she was ashamed to say it, but she wasn't sure if she knew how to relight it without blowing herself to smithereens. She was very tired of eating cold cereal. Jeet came in and got the thing burning again, and by way of celebration and thanks April made coffee which they drank in the kitchen like good country folk anywhere might do, visiting. Her face, close at hand and with the muffler removed from it was very broad but with delicate features strangely, closely clustered at its center as if intended for a smaller skull. Her brow, also broad, suggested worried concern or something absorbing. Obsidian eyes, the deuce on a di; was she looking to seduce him? His instincts, such as they were, would not let him hazard a guess; it was flattering enough, whatever her reason, that she wanted to keep him here in talk. Jeet was very rarely mistaken for a sympathetic ear.

"My dad," she said, "teaches history and hygiene and everything you can think of over at the high school. Has forever. Coaches football and track, and on weekends when there are no games or anything he cuts and wraps meat. Mom tends bar. Also forever. So those are my people. God, I hope they have a decent time. This is the first vacation they've ever had—to go anywhere. Can you believe it?"

"Oh, sure," said Jeet. "You get busy and time gets away from you. I've been to Eugene and Denver for trainings, conventions, and I'd just as soon have my teeth cleaned, really. You get in a rut."

With the somewhat obvious exclusion of Larry Lucerne from the conversation, they talked of many things. Jeet became wired on two pots of strong percolator coffee and found himself telling her of seeking the ghost of Garcia Lorca in the Spanish hills, and how fine to tell this long latent story to someone for whom it might have meaning, and April in her turn recounted her turn as a waitress in a truck shop where she called everyone, regardless of a age, sex, race, or national origin, 'honey.' She must have said it too ironically, she thought, because her tips had been terrible.

They had still more coffee. Jeet brought in the cocaine and put it on the kitchen table; he recalled from a law enforcement seminar that the thing to do was roll up a little-circulated bill, something not too creased or greasy, and roll it into a straw, and then, having agreed between them that the French were undoubtedly right and nothing really mattered, and in the spirit of post modernism Jeet made such a straw, and they began inhaling the cocaine through it. Twenty-three hours later April Newberry was to be astonished that her parents had taped 9-1-1 to their phone, the poor dears, did they think they'd ever need to call? From Highwood? Did they think they'd forget? Were they so old? They were so old. She felt terrible. She dialed the number. April gave her name, her location, and quite calmly the reason for her call, "He's killing us," she said. "You'd better come break this up. We can't stop." She was told to stay on the line. She hung up. Then, when the phone rang and rang and it annoyed Jeet, she unplugged it, an old Bakelite thing, and they had entirely forgotten she'd made that call and were arguing about Charles Beaudelair, of all people, when the sirens came swirling into Highwood, and the man on the bull horn must have recognized the car in the driveway, because he said, "Come on out of there, G.C. Let us see your hands."

It was still thirty-five below. Compliant in his way, Jeet Harrow entered into legend then when he threw open the Newberry's front door, stripped to the waist, glistening in sweat, and brandishing one of Mr. Newberry's bowling trophies.

◊ ◊ ◊

Shot in the head, divorced, disbarred, Jeet accepted it all with equanimity as his due, he'd been completely rearranged it seemed before he'd fully regained consciousness; what a dreamy time. There had been a series of awakenings—on the Newberry's stoop with that warm ooze on him, in the ambulance, shackled to a hospital bed. At some point early on he would open his eyes to the gauzy sight of Jolene wrapped in her own embrace at the foot of that bed, weeping triumphantly and asking him, 'Is it true?'

"Probably," he said. He was sure he'd heard something snap, as if she'd been preparing right along for his betrayal and knew just what to do now, knew better than to forgive him. Another vision from those hours was the pitcher on his tray table with water so cold it beaded with condensation. That water, the glass to drink it in, the deepest contentment he was ever likely to know. Both nurses who attended him told him he should be grateful for his luck.

And there had been some luck in it, really, when the ever-eager Deputy Dunn had responded to that call, and when the little zealot, ever forgetful of his weapons training and much too fearful and trigger happy for his work had let slip a nine millimeter zinger in Jeet's direction that carved a deep new part high in his scalp, a scar that he'd come to call the crown jewel in his collection, and a blow sufficient to drop him like a sack of dirty laundry, to bleed him like a pig, and it was a fortunate wound in its way because how else could a man hope to curry any sympathy? A man who'd done the self-same crimes for which he'd only just sent another man to prison and to his death? To be well bled seemed to offer some expiation, but not much. When he was released from the hospital Jeet already lacked a home to which he might return, and he couldn't safely be held in any proximate jail, so he was given over to his brother's custody until the state could decide what should be done with him.

He stayed in the bunk house, using his brother's house, the family home, only as a place to defecate as there was no longer an outhouse on the farm and Donna didn't like him anymore, not at all, not in her house any more than he could help it. His case was being handled by the Attorney General's office, and the Deputy Attorney General assigned to that case was a friend and kindred spirit from law school who was secretly delighted at the facts and who dithered considerably about the full range of charges he should bring. Jeet waited in the bunkhouse with the portion of his library Jolene had been good enough to send him, and in this monkish existence he was peaceful. What a shame he'd had to raise so much Cain just to discover what he'd wanted for himself all along. Jeet could hardly wait to be a ward of the state; he would represent himself like a holy man rather than a lawyer, and he'd be responsible for everything and for nothing, why not? It was an interesting job of work, regaining consciousness. His pot well stirred, Jeet would have confessed to anything if they'd only let him. The incident remained under investigation for some months.

One day during that wait Donna came pounding on the bunkhouse door, and when he let her in, she confronted him about a book he'd given Carrie.

"Which one?" he said.

"That *Ball Jar*," she said.

"*Bell Jar*," he said. "Ball jar's for canning."

"She's going through some things right now," said Donna, "and she certainly doesn't need that kind of thing; all these awful Russians, these unhappy New York people. What do you think you're doing? I'm sending her out to have some time with her grandmother. And you can get your own damn food, Jeet, and bring it out here."

"Verity has a lot of the same books," he warned her. "Same kind of books. That's partly where I got my taste."

"That's not the point," said Donna. "You do terrible things to that girl's way of looking at things. I think she thinks you're some kind of heroic guy. I mean, I don't even know what she's thinking anymore. This whole deal has got me and Tel to arguing, and we never argue, and she doesn't need to see that, so I'm sending her out to Portland for a while, that's all I know."

Even with that, he had not quite finished blowing up his brother's life.

Jeet had come to the farm with a batch of dressings that he could change himself and that gave him the look of a soldier from the Revolutionary War. He wore these until the day Tel drove him into Fort Benton to have his staples removed and the physician's assistant who removed them advised he should now expose the injury to light and air, that he should let it breathe, and it was breathing in the car as Tel drove him back to the farm. Tel had driven him so much lately, to court appearances to confess his guilt, to a psychologist to be found sane, to the clinic to be found fit—Jeet thought himself selfish to make such demands of a man with no holes in his schedule and such a strong distaste for any society, but hadn't it given them a chance to talk, to really talk? Hadn't it given Tel a chance to speak of his divided house, the perennial farm crisis? The brothers had been given to wonder together if it was true as Verity had always claimed that she'd raised them a little too soft.

"This should be it," said Jeet. "They should be able to ship me down to Nevada now. Minimum security. I'll finally be out of your hair."

"Nevada," Tel said.

"It's almost over. You've been, you've been—family. You don't know what that means to me. How much it means."

Tel's great shoulders began to work, convulsions that increased until he was forced to pull to the roadside.

"What?" said Jeet. "Are you? I'm so. . . Are you?"

"It's your head, man. Have you seen it? Jesus, Jeet. Your poor damned head."

CARRIE

In that old farmhouse there could be no secrets except from the deaf, and Carrie overheard the conversation, or her mother's half of it, that would send her off to Portland.

"Just for a while," her mother had said. "Ever since Jeet, oh it's—Tel's started back with the, well he's. . . we worked so hard to get him. . . And Carrie never saw this before. That shaking, you know. . . ah, no, he's been to the Veterans, and they just want to dose him up, or. . . ah, no. He wouldn't do that. But, anyway, when he gets to. . . It really scares her. We're in a rough patch here."

Her mother in the kitchen, on the phone, sounding spent; disembodied grandma in the unknown, a mosquito drone on the line; Carrie Harrow out in the front room, listening.

Donna Harrow wallowed in concern for wounded animals and for her wounded husband, but it seemed to Carrie that her mother had little sympathy to spare for her husband's family, including even her own daughter. It was Donna's rarely spoken but constantly expressed opinion that the Harrows, except for she and her husband, were too strange, too ringy, too often part of the problem. Her problem. "Well, I know he's in prison," she was saying, "but that Jeet, it doesn't take him long to really. . . he already did his damage here. That deal on his head. His head was about half scab where they shot him, and he had that just hanging out there, soo ugly, and things are kind of shaky right now. Tel doesn't do well with that, or with almost any kind of, you know. . . If we could just send Carrie out there for a while, it sure would help. I think it would help everybody. Maybe *you* can understand her, Verity."

Carrie was to remember every word of this, remember its tone. It was that tone, in fact, that she could never quite forgive.

At the bus station, before Carrie could board, her mother had held her at her shoulders, held her at arm's length, her head cocked as if to admire her girl going out in the world, and she told her gamely, "Great big city. Big school. So many. . . Your grandma. You'll have a wonderful time, I bet. You'll get so darn fancy we won't know you when you come back home." Donna's mouth turned down. "You always wonder if, well. . . So, you're going to really. . . So." Her mouth turned down again. Mom. Donna. Sorta sad. Carrie knew as daughters do, despite themselves, approximately what her mother thought of her. Donna had always considered her daughter uncooperative, but lately she had decided her girl was an inhabitant of another world altogether and that there was no reaching her.

Carrie took a seat where she and her mother might wave to each other through the window, their faces arranged haphazardly. There was a rattling, a gust of diesel fumes, and Donna Harrow raised her hand almost as if to call young Carrie back, and that was that. Poor Dad. Poor Mom. Poor me. Carrie was gone before the sense of being gone could reach her. A girl cast off—out on the interstate she suddenly felt sorry for no one.

She had her coloring and her crisp hair from her grandfather, kindly old Mr. Purefoy, a man she'd met just once when she was very young. She was bookish and socially skittish in the manner of her uncle Jeet. From her mother she'd learned to be ashamed of her reticence, to be ashamed of being ashamed—why couldn't she ever put herself out there a little bit? Or try and be nice? Carrie was, primarily, shy, and she had assumed this was her father's contribution to her character, but lately she had come to understand that Dad had earned his shyness, or had it imposed on him by something way back and nasty, some extreme meanness involving their color, or her color, or something, but Carrie had been wary and stuck in herself for as long as she had been, and she didn't think there was any particular reason or cause for it. Carrie did not much like open spaces, and Carrie hated their television from its farm reports in the morning to actresses displaying cleavage in the night and all the news in between, and, thus dissatisfied, Carrie had been living in the muffled cave she made of her room. She had been hoping some grander experience might develop out of this, she'd been dreaming of it, and she had good reason to believe that the grass and everything else was greener out west.

But shy. This was her first trip out of Central Montana. Her folks traveled nowhere if they could help it, and for as much as she had wanted it, Carrie had never been much confronted by the new. The not farm. Coming into Helena she had begun to relax and enjoy the scenery along the way, but there a large one-legged woman got on the bus, made quite a sighing, clattering episode of getting on, and she took the seat directly across the aisle from Carrie's, arranged her aluminum crutches beside her and got an inhaler from out of her dirty pink backpack. Between pulls from the inhaler, the woman struck up a conversation.

"Hello," she said. "Dear." The woman closed her eyes, gathered herself, inhaled again, exhaled gratefully, and said, "So, where are you going?" Her face had a granular texture.

"Portland," said Carrie.

"Wonderful," said the one-legged woman. "Me too. That's where I'm going. Fun."

Carrie's gut clenched.

"Do you live there?" the woman asked. "Is that home to you?"

"I don't know," Carrie said, and when the woman

frowned, she said, "I might. I'm not sure. Live there."

This exhausted the woman's interest in her, so Carrie wasn't pressed to further explain herself. The one-legged woman told tales of medical woe and bureaucratic viciousness to the back of her head as they traveled to and over a set of mountains, and when the woman finally fell silent and took to knitting, Carrie felt they'd begun to glide toward Portland in the belly of a long loping beast; once back on the freeway they rolled irresistibly town to town, an express bus. Carrie enjoyed the peanut butter and jelly sandwiches and the thermos of hot chocolate her mother had sent along—loved, wasn't she?—and Carrie slept, and as the day gave way to night they were moving along a river that flowed opposite any river she had known before. She was on the other side of the divide.

"I was such a kid, so stupid, and I remember wondering if I would miss him. Dad. Or if he'd miss me. Of course, we did. Sure, we did. We always have."

◊ ◊ ◊

Her grandmother, as her grandmother, was somewhat familiar to her, and who else in that terminal could it be standing there under a bolero hat, with red, rectangular glasses on her nose, and wearing a serape and blousy cargo shorts over pouched knees with blue veins running down into Converse All Stars. The old woman was still entirely Square Butte Bench, though, when she opened her mouth, "You made it," she said, and she remembered to offer an embrace, a move that was even more awkward for the seventy-pound sea bag Carrie had slung over her shoulder; the sea bag was the only luggage her family owned and she had no previous experience of carrying it.

"Yeah. It was easy. You just get on, and they take you."

"Hungry?" said the old woman.

"Sure."

"I suppose Tel's warned you about my cooking. Your father was not a fan of that."

"He did say, he said you were using mustard in everything for a while, and he thought that was pretty funny. That's the only thing I heard. But I remember you used to come and help cook for harvest. When I was little."

"We'll grab a bite on the way home," said the old woman. "What do you like?"

"Like?"

"Food," said her grandmother. "Got any preferences?"

"Oh," said Carrie, unaccustomed to choice. "I don't know. I guess I wouldn't know what I like. Mom makes. . . well, I don't know. I like oatmeal. Even if it's not for breakfast. It's, uh. . . It's nice to see you, Grandma."

"Do me a favor," said the old woman. "Don't call me that. I don't know why, babe, but it's just that term. Makes my skin crawl. You can call me anything else. 'Long as you don't call me late to dinner', as the old timers used to say. Well, we better try some pad tai or something, see how you feel about peanut sauce. Give me that damn bag. That strap's about to cut you in half."

The old woman made to hug her again, thought better of it, then took the great bag off Carrie's shoulder to sling it on her own. What did Carrie know of this person, her grandmother? Her scant memories were confirmed already; the woman was lean and strong—hard. For the rest, though, Carrie was better acquainted with her grandmother as the myth her father and her uncle had made of her; they were forever amused by the gal who had raised them, but Carrie wasn't sure why. Grandma, or whatever she was to be called, was a near stranger and suddenly Carrie's entire family of consequence—her keeper. Carrie was forced into a strange gait to keep up with her, neither walk, nor skip, nor jog, but something inefficient, and they rushed down the sidewalk with oncoming pedestrians giving them a wide berth.

"So, what's going on with your dad?"

"Well, he just. . . You know it's always been where he didn't like to be around people?"

"Not always," said the old woman, breathing heavily now. "He wasn't always like that."

Corrected, Carrie said, "Yeah. But since I've, well. . . anyway, I guess he had this real bad memory and it, and that. . . I don't know. He didn't seem that bad to me. Most of the time. They said he had a little breakdown, but he's still doing the same stuff he always did. Which is about everything. Except going places, which he never really did. Since I've been—you know—around."

"Well," said the old woman, "then, how are you?"

"Me?"

"You doing all right?"

"About as good as ever," said Carrie.

"Bastards skin you alive at these parking garages," said Verity Harrow. "I think you pay by the minute."

"Wait," said Carrie. They had been instructed by a blinking icon at a crosswalk not to walk; her grandmother was walking anyway. "Can you see okay, gra. . . Can you see okay?"

"We're fine. Come on." She led the way. "New prescription," she said. "Got some thicker lenses. Come on, before they start honking." A blue minivan nosed toward them as they made their way across, and the driver, a woman in a baseball cap and swinging pony tail appeared to be noiselessly screaming at them. Downtown. Here it was necessary to look up to see anything of the sky. Her grandmother's breathing was labored now, but the old woman had air enough to say with that air of country finality,

"Well—here we are."

"Here?" said Carrie, struggling up the next sidewalk.

"Here *you* are," said Verity Harrow.

"Oh," said Carrie. "Yeah."

They went into a gray and echoing spiral maze, then her grandmother's musty station wagon, then they went out of the parking garage with the sea bag riding in back among flats of pepper starts and a broken old mandolin soon to be used as decoration, then on a soaring green bridge they passed high above the Willamette, then they were among paper lanterns, eating prawns so hot they made Carrie's nose run and sweat stand out on her forehead. Way past dinnertime.

"You're probably pretty bushed."

"No," said Carrie.

"Good."

"I mean," said Carrie. "All this new stuff, I like it."

"Good," said the old woman.

"But I mean," said Carrie, "should I? Like it? Just because it's new? You know—like things? Just because they're new?"

"Might as well: They only stay new for a little while."

"But I feel like I should feel bad," said Carrie.

"About what?"

"Oh—leaving them. When. Or how they don't need, or how they don't want. . . I don't know. I should feel bad, I think."

"You shouldn't ask for it, if you *don't* feel bad. Don't worry, there'll be plenty of things to feel bad about; you never need to go looking for them."

"Nope," Carrie believed the old woman would know. "That's right. That's—That is right." She sniffed and took up a paper napkin. "Pheew. This stuff is great. I really *do* like this."

"*And*," said her grandmother, "they deliver."

"Right to your house? That is so. . . Wow. Uhm, they did say about paying for my food and everything? They said they'd pay for, or keep on paying for. You know. My expenses?"

"You thought I was worried about that, did you, babe?"

"Oh, no. No. But I really do not want to be any trouble."

"That sounds dull," said the old woman.

◊ ◊ ◊

Her first morning in Portland, after a breakfast of espresso, a croissant, and an orange, Carrie found herself holding the legs of a wooden ladder while her grandmother climbed up and down it with a bucket of astringent solution and a brush. "Rain," said the old woman from above, her voice raised to be heard from afar though it was intended only for Carrie.

"Oh. . . Oh!—Don't! No! Please don't lean out like that."

Her grandmother thrust with the brush at blighted spots under the peak of a gable, distracted, acrobatic but not agile. "Steady now. Hold it steady, girl. I probably should've run a few more nails into this ladder, but I don't use it that much. Wants to snake around, doesn't it?" Verity Harrow grasped in one hand the bail of her bucket and her brush, and with the other she held to an uncertain rung; she lay well back from the ladder, inspecting something directly overhead. "Rain," she said again, and Carrie was beginning to see how the old one was all irony nearly all the time, how it sustained her. "That's why I picked this place, said I wanted to go someplace where it rains regular. And that it does—and mold, and moss, and mildew and every other thing seems to think this house is another tree and wants to grow on it. These cedar shakes look cute when you buy the place; natural—then—you kind of expect mushrooms to come busting out. And these god-damned marionberries around here, it's a life's work just keeping those cut back."

"Ooh," said Carrie. "Careful. Careful up there." The old woman was probably brittle.

"Long as we've got the ladder out, maybe we'll take my little chainsaw out to the cherry trees; I've been wanting to lop some of those limbs. I do more actual farming, me, out here in my back yard than I ever did back home. But here you have to *keep* things from growing."

◊ ◊ ◊

They came of the same circumstance, girls born to the farm but never of it, they suffered similar semi fond memories, warm regrets, and wary nostalgia, so they knew each other instinctively. In her room at the farm, on the doorframe of her tiny closet, the progress of her grandmother's vertical growth, or the first five feet of it, was still marked in annual increments. It was the only surface of that room Carrie had never painted or postered over because those marks were her own personal cave paintings, proof of an unimaginable past. She had shared that room with her grandmother, though never at the same time. Now they were housemates, same time and place, and they would be real to each other as only housemates can be. It was her grandmother's farmgirl understanding that everything comes with a price and that such prices should be bravely paid; Carrie might have found this attitude oppressive if her grandmother didn't further understand most everything as a joke.

Verity had lived so long alone that she tended to explain things to the girl, or imply things, just as they occurred to her, with the same kind of random remarks she might have used if she were still alone in the house: Facts, truths, bits and pieces just as they occurred to her and blurted out. Her career? "Just like Mother," she said of that puzzling development. "A damn schoolmarm after all." She had been until her recent retirement a teacher at the high school where Carrie was now enrolled. "They kept having me do the choir," the old woman marveled. "Like I had anything to tell those kids about singing. I think it's mostly how your skull happens to be shaped, how your brain is folded. I often wonder if I ever taught anyone anything at all. But—they pay you, so you show up and act useful, wave your little baton around."

For her music, the old woman gave her housemate just one initial apology. "Comes with the territory; sorry. Got myself locked away in my piano room, like I always do, so it shouldn't be too bad for you." And it was not bad, or never anything near it, but often a haunting, pastel kind of playing that leaked from that room. "I eventually got to where I really do dig Satie. And, you know, Chopin. Things ballerinas like. All these ways, there's all these ways to skin the cat. But, anyway, I keep going back to my little spot, so you'll have to live with that. Just like the boys did. And, I should tell you—I'm strictly live-and-let-live—that's how I was with your father and Jeet, and I don't know if that really worked out. Maybe the boys could've used a little more direction. But I don't care to stick my nose in anyone's business. You'll be sort of on your own that way. Just so you know."

Unmoored, Carrie felt herself being nudged away from the dock, out to sea.

"You all right with that?"

"Mm-hm," said Carrie. "Sounds fine to me. And—you know they're good men, gra. . . They're good men. I think so, anyway."

"I know. Yeah, we'll get along fine here, won't we?"

Carrie's confusion as a teen would consist in discovering that she was the only teen in America, except possibly the religiously addled, who was without a single complaint. Untroubled by the goofiness of riding her bike to school and being a member of its tiny poetry club, untroubled by her abiding disinterest in any romance not somehow committed to print, she had at least been a hacky sacker until the endless talk in those circles of acquiring and rating marijuana wore her out. But Portland, Portland under its clouds was so perfect for her. And her grandmother's house, ringed almost year around by rhododendrons, often by roses, a house that had come here as she would come to learn via a Sears Roebuck catalogue, and full of the small rooms and nooks of that Craftsman era, small rooms like the farmhouse back home but much nicer, and just as she had at the farm, Carrie denned up in her own room where the clouds were never gloomy, and she read, and her reading of other's troubles gave her to understand that she must be unusually happy. Under her comforter, reading, and nothing amiss in this so far as her grandmother was concerned. In a house smelling of coffee and wood polish, Carrie solved their only problem by learning to cook; she cooked and read and ran. Her grandmother played in her room, and went out to play four times a month for her tiny dancers, more often in recital season, and Verity groomed her grounds and fed her cat and read and sometimes entertained a former colleague, a math teacher with a physically disabled wife.

Coming into herself in this cozy existence Carrie discovered that she *was* dull, and eventually that she was glad of it. Just as her grandmother had suggested, she was free to do nearly anything here, and she used this freedom to do nearly nothing, which suited her so well. To keep from melting completely under her comforter and becoming a blob, she ran regularly in Pier Park. She had heard of and attempted meditation but couldn't seem to sit so long without a book in her hands; in running, though, it was impossible not to breath rhythmically, and the footpaths through the park passed through fir and pine so tall that when the occasional sun did slant through them, she dreamed of a long cathedral, her footfalls sounding futile and hopeful in the sublime light. Sometimes a run drained thought away, sometimes she ran into thoughts that didn't otherwise occur to her: Family.

It wasn't long before she had come to think of her mother as 'Donna' because that was what her grandmother called her, and of course no one else was mentioning the woman within her hearing. Donna called at four p.m., Mountain time, every Saturday afternoon; she called on Christmas, on Carrie's birthday, and, in the early years, on Easter Sunday. Donna called and spoke to Carrie, briefly, and then Dad—always and only 'Dad'—got on the line, and they would speak. Also briefly. Because what was there to say? Did they really want her thoughts on Emily Dickinson or mortality generally? Did she ever have plans or events to announce? No. Young love? None in sight. And for Carrie's part, how many times can you pretend an interest in a distant bake sale, their weather of the moment? 'Love you,' was always how she ended these conversations, and this was harder and harder to say, though it continued to be true; it continued, her love, through various hues and through time, and though it continued, Carrie almost never went home, and when she did, such visits were, again, brief. Family.

Donna and Dad.

Donna didn't like her much, or continued to think her disappointing, though Carrie was consistently an honors student and never near any trouble or angst. An acknowledged good girl, Carrie always knew this to be something short of what Donna might have hoped for her, though neither of them knew what more might be wanted. Donna's daughter must always be a little disappointing, that's all. And Dad, oh Dad, who loved her too much and who, it seemed, didn't wish to burden his daughter too much with his love. And these two were 'Home', for that was how Carrie would ever think of it, the farm, and those brief visits only made her wonder how she had ever lived there. High prairie. She couldn't do that anymore.

So, Portland where she slid through high school so contentedly that she had failed to imagine what might be next; she seemed to lack all ambition and lust. One day she happened to answer the phone when her uncle called, and she said, "Hey, you're out." All his calls from prison had to be collect, and this time there were no charges to accept.

"About three months now," he said. "Good behavior. I was a *very* good boy inside. I loved your letters."

One a year, few enough that Carrie felt guilty now. "Great," she said, "I'm really glad. Let me find Verity, and . . ."

"Hang on," said her uncle, "I wanted to talk to you. Where are you going to school?"

"Now?"

"College," he said.

"Oh, I . . ."

"Where did you apply?"

"I haven't," she said. "Yet."

"What? Don't you want to go?"

"Maybe," said Carrie, as accurate as she could be.

"Is it money?"

"Oh, no," said Carrie, "Dad tells me all the time that they want to pay for my education. Higher education—so."

"Sweety," said her uncle, "they can afford it. Tel plowed right through all this farm crisis; he'd keep that thing going through nuclear winter. They're doing fine. But, that's why I called. I've got a little fund, a little windfall I need to invest in, uh, oh something worthwhile. I was thinking a trust fund. For your education. I need to get this off my hands."

"Windfall?" said Carrie. "But you just got out of. I mean—windfall?"

"Yeah," said her uncle. "It's perfectly legitimate, but, uh, complicated. I do have some talents that travel pretty well. And I'd like to invest. You know, immediately. Be nice if. . . Why wouldn't you go to school?" How funny to hear Uncle Jeet sound alarmed about anything.

"I guess I could," said Carrie.

"I'd like to do something worthwhile," said her uncle. "Just to see what it feels like."

"Okay," she said.

On the strength of this agreement Carrie enrolled in a college with public transportation running to and from her grandmother's house so that she might be a day commuter, and she majored in communications, a strange choice, perhaps, for a young woman who spoke to her fellow commuters or her fellow students only out of necessity. College was by her design a small drain on her trust fund, and college was, also by her design, a very small adjustment in her routine.

One day her grandmother, who was as always loathe to intrude, did have to finally wonder, "What is the deal with you, babe? I was already ugly when I was your age, had a lot of other problems, too. And I can see how a person might get sidetracked. But you are *not* ugly. That's one problem you don't have. So, I just. Well. Gorgeous, I'd say. Which is supposed to be an advantage. You and your father—If *I'd* been a knockout like that—you know, you should *use* that."

"I am nothing to worry about." Carrie said.

"I just don't see why everybody needs to be lonely all the time. It shouldn't be necessary. Or—I don't mean everybody. I mean you."

Carrie's successes to date had been to somehow disappoint everyone who cared for her at all, but if there was something wrong with her, it was such a comfortable condition she just could not bring herself to correct it, so she passed through college where she got excellent grades again, even, implausibly, in public speaking, and as her graduation approached, she was anxious as a nun about to be expelled from her order. She read in her room, she read on the bus and in coffee shops here and there, and Carrie made them pasta prima vera, or grilled salmon, or toast, and Carrie felt they were living deliciously, deliberately, but now her grandmother just had to inject this niggling little worry. Carrie had thought her last concern was loneliness. Didn't she have at least three unobtrusive friends? Loneliness? Why did the old woman have to get all spooky and oracular and bring that up? But was she lonely? Could a person possibly overlook something like that?

Or was she only too happy and therefore bound to be misunderstood? These questions seemed linked to the question of what she might do with herself after college.

In her last semester, Carrie bought an old Volvo of indeterminate color with the last of the money remaining in Uncle Jeet's trust fund, this in anticipation of job hunting. She had been told by a counselor to consider looking outside her field, which should, she thought, be easy because she wasn't aware of having a field or any particular expertise. This counselor also suggested she should be fine tuning her resume and seeking interviews.

Her resume would be an absurdity. What could she say of herself, for herself? Apart from a few desultory months of scooping ice cream she'd never held a job, and her life experience could be summarized in a short paragraph. She had always gotten very good grades, so she must seem dutiful; any letters of recommendation would have to be written by some near stranger. Wanting to be wanted was something new to her and deeply unpleasant, and it hurt Carrie to think how so many girls had been suffering similar or even worse pangs from the moment they hit puberty.

Reluctant but responsible, she had soon enough strewn at least a hundred completed job applications around the metropolitan area and the suburbs, and now she winced every time their phone rang, for of those many jobs there were two she might really want to do, and all the rest meant long hours on concrete floors, or dull or degrading activities, or the public. Dealing with the public. Things unthinkable, but when that phone rang Carrie thought of them. And she picked up.

"Hello. Hello? Harrow residence."

"Ms. Harrow?"

"Yes. But which one? Which one would you want?"

"I was calling for Carrie."

"Oh," she said. "Yes. That's me." This might be something professional. "How can I help you?" she said.

"It's Brett," said the caller. "Brett Manfredi."

The name was not the hint the caller seemed to think it should be. "I . . ." she said, stalling.

"I hope you don't mind that I got your name through the registrar, or your number I should say."

To fill elective credits, Carrie had taken several courses in film studies in her final year of college. Manfredi, she now recalled, was the name of the adjunct who had shown the films and graded the essays she had written about them. A graduate now, she said, "Oh. Well, there's nothing wrong with my . . ."

"Oh, no," said the adjunct. "No. Not at all. Nothing. Wrong."

Her memory of him was neither old nor very distinct. Ringleted hair worn long. He had shown her some pretty movies. His way of talking suggested that he was not talking the talk he'd heard growing up, that he was, the adjunct professor, trying on different personalities.

"That's good," she said. "If everything's okay. I know I got my grade and everything."

"You could call me Brett, if you like. If that's comfortable."

"I couldn't call you that before?" She hadn't called him anything before. Or spoken to him.

"Well," said Brett, "of course. But. I'm not. . . But, I mean, would you?"

"What?" said Carrie.

"Call me that."

"Brett?" she said.

"Yes," he said.

"Okay," she said. "Brett. So—is that it?"

"Oh, no, no, no," said Brett. "I called to tell you about my annual film festival. Personally curated. I'm sorry. That was a little weird. I know that was a little weird."

"No," said Carrie. "I mean, usually I am. The weird one. I'm from way out there, you know, so sometimes I'm still kind of, oh—what? Awkward?"

"No," said Brett, shocked. "No, you're. . . So, anyway, I'm not teaching this summer, and now that you've graduated . . ."

"Oh? What are you doing?"

"Projectionist," said Brett. "I'm a projectionist at a brew pub. Which can be hellish. Greasy food and film are just not good together. Marx Brothers, and chicken wings, and ninety-nine styles of microbrews. Well. It's okay."

"Good," she said. Carrie had lately become something of a film buff herself, with stacks of tapes beside her bed and the smallest television that would accept a VHS player balanced on a small stand right at the foot. "Doesn't sound too bad."

"But why I called," said Brett. "About my film festival. I was wondering if you might be interested in, uh. In attending."

"A festival?" said Carrie, sounding impressed because she was.

"Carefully curated," said Brett. "Really, just two films."

"Oh," said Carrie.

"Maybe not a festival. I remembered how much you loved Elizabeth Taylor."

"I read Jane Eyre so many times. I thought she did Helen Burns exactly right, you know just as I. . . Better. To see her do that. And National Velvet. That was great."

"Your paper was very good."

"A-plus," she said. "Yeah. Thanks for that."

"No," he said. "You completely deserved. . . No. But I was wondering if you'd like to come. To the film festival."

"When is it?"

"Oh. Uhm—tonight?"

The street address he gave her had a ½ appended to it which meant he lived in a sort of cottage in someone's back yard. It took Carrie some time to find him way out near Beaverton, and when Brett answered her knock at last, he was too clearly relieved to see her.

"Sorry," she said. "I had quite a time. . . I hope I'm not late." They both understood she could not be late to an occasion that needed her. Carrie was inexperienced, not stupid. "I got a little lost."

"It's that mall," he said, some old grievance.

"Mall?" she said.

"Come in," he said. "Come in. Come in."

As his couch yielded under her she understood it was a single piece of foam and that the only way to be at all comfortable in it was to lie all the way back on it, a deep recline. There was a hookah nearby, and on the wall opposite, just above his television came nosing the great prow of an ocean liner. Cunard. From out of an elegant ocean. A room draped in patterned fabrics, with sandalwood strong in the air. The amount of attention he lavished on his little space; she understood this, Carrie thought she approved this, warmed to it. His television loomed large, stark, blank, and modern. He had set a ceramic leaf out on an improvised coffee table, a platter upon which he'd arranged fruit and cubed cheeses. Some of that fruit had been waiting too long.

"Wine?" Brett said.

"I." said Carrie. "I. If."

"I know you're not a zinfandel kind of person," he said.

"No."

"Merlot? You like a good red?"

Carrie had never tasted, never been tempted, not even when she'd cooked with it. Never tempted. By anything. Anyone. This seemed strange in the moment, and she didn't want Brett to know it. "That might be nice," she said.

The wine was not to her liking—really just grape juice gone bad and a very funny thing for so many people to raise such a fuss about. With cheese, she found, it was better. He had made these little cubes of cheese for her. She could tell he liked saying 'gruyere'.

"Ms. Taylor," he said to summon the star onstage, and thumbing his remote he startled that big television and his VCR into playing, 'Who's Afraid of Virginia Wolf.'

Carrie and Brett reclined at each end of a couch so small that her left knee and his right knee hovered about a half foot apart. Carrie cringed frequently as George and Martha began to deteriorate onscreen and claw so convincingly at each other. Regarding that drunken behavior, Carrie suddenly conceived of her wine as sticky poison and heaved up out of the couch to set her glass on the coffee table. She lay back. One experience experienced. Recumbent, not relaxed. Arms folded across her chest. This Elizabeth Taylor of the constantly twisting mouth, this was not her Elizabeth Taylor, and Carrie could only wonder how much bitterness had been poured into National Velvet's dewy starlet to make her capable of even pretending to be this awful Martha. Carrie winced at the things the woman said—some playwright made her say.

Brett had seen her discomfort. "Intense," he said.

"Mmm," said Carrie.

And no happy ending; they suffered it through to the end of the credits. Embarrassed, Brett rewound the tape and said again as he was removing it from the machine, "Intense," as if the observation had been useful in the first place. "I know that was pretty. . . intense. I just thought you might be interested in her range."

Carrie only wished Elizabeth Taylor had never grown up. The wine was now an aftertaste heavy in combination with the aftertaste of the cheese. "Definitely," she said. "Range. She definitely has that." She could see now why Brett Manfredi had made such a slight impression on her. There was nothing in his face for the eyes to snag on, nothing of interest. Nothing to attract, nothing to offend, nothing. Poor guy. She knew he wanted her.

"We should probably take a little break after that," he said.

Carrie sighed uncertainly.

"You up for another one? It's Burton and Taylor again, but not quite. Not so in... oh—overwhelming. I have more wine. Some different."

"I wouldn't need any."

"Or . . ." he said, his longing was so prominent in such an undistinguished face. He looked at her. "Has anyone ever told you how much you look like Angela Davis?"

"Funny you'd say that," said Carrie. "My girlfriend's mom did. So, I looked her up. Got that gap in my teeth, anyway. Same gap in our front teeth."

"It's intelligence," said Brett. "That's the look."

"Thank you," said Carrie. She thought of him now as a white boy, now an unflattering category, and she wondered if he wanted her for a novelty or something else sad. This was what came of wanting to be wanted. "That hairdo," she said. "That afro she wore. That looked like a lot of work. I doubt I could ever maintain something like that."

"But beautiful," Brett said.

"She was," said Carrie. "Or is, I guess."

"I meant you," said Brett, reddening and a little more interesting for it.

Here was Carrie Harrow with that curious power she'd heard her girlfriends discussing. She didn't like it.

They watched a better battle, 'The Taming of the Shrew' in welcome technicolor and in which Ms. Taylor's marvelous mouth was put to better use. The actors declaimed so that Carrie was content to understand about half their dialogue. Italy looked a little crowded in places. Brett Manfredi's foam couch was becoming an affliction under her and had introduced a crook in her neck. The movie ended. They watched all the credits again.

Something more must happen now.

"What did you think?" This did not appear to be the question actually on his mind.

"If I ever go anywhere," said Carrie. "I think it would be Italy. Out in the country. Looks so sunny." She also thought, could not help thinking, how poorly this Brett Manfredi compared to Richard Burton's Petruchio on a sliding scale of virility.

"Vivid," said Brett.

Carrie said, "Yes. It was."

Brett Manfredi lapsed into a freighted silence and this persisted until Carrie concluded he had made his last move. To own him this way was as heavy to her as the dregs of that wine. Now she had set herself out on a tightrope that wouldn't let her be impolite or at all encouraging, and she said, "Thank you. Thank you. Those were. . . Different. Certainly different. I do see the range."

"She could do anything," Brett Manfredi said. "Be anyone."

"I'm not sure how that would be," said Carrie. "To have that ability. I like being myself."

"Maybe that's what I. . . Yes, I'm sure you do." He touched the knobby protuberance at her left wrist with one index finger and left it there so that they might both consider the significance. For one thing, they were too close now to conveniently look away.

"Oh," said Carrie eventually, an expression of surprise, disgust, invitation; she heard herself as feminine. "Hm." she said, still ambiguous.

"I," he said.

"Hmm," she said.

Brett's upper lip twitched in what seemed a sneer until he burst into tears.

"Oh, gee," she said. "Don't do that. Please don't do that."

"I didn't mean to," he said.

"What?" Carrie said.

"Get it wrong," he said. "This was the last thing I. . . I got overwhelmed. By you."

"Okay," she said. "Okay, that's. . . But don't. . . Hey, you don't have to be this sad. Okay?"

◊ ◊ ◊

"I don't get it," said her grandmother. "I've been making navy bean soup for, well. Back in the old days, that's what you'd have in a restaurant if you didn't have a hamburger. It's almost impossible to screw up. Anyone can make navy bean soup—but this. This is something else."

"I think a ham hock is a ham hock," said Carrie. "I put a new potato in there to thicken it. Bay leaf."

"You got the scald on it, babe."

This wonderful old house. Her grandmother's house. Their place. They sat in the nook near the kitchen, near windows overlooking the kitchen garden.

"Okay," said Carrie with a great inbreath, thinking she might be about to ruin it all.

"What?"

"I. I did something stupid."

"It's about time," her grandmother said.

"Well, this was pretty—I had an encounter. So, yeah—I had this encounter. And I—really, really stupid, you know the way things are out there right now, with the. So I went to the free clinic, which isn't entirely free if you want *all* the tests. But anyway, you know, the *good* news—no diseases. Not even herpes or anything. But I did get pregnant. Which—"

Verity Harrow swallowed the beans in her mouth, then swallowed again. "Encounter? Babe, you weren't?"

"No. It was nothing like that."

"And you're pregnant?"

"I got the test, the home version, and I double checked.

Comes up the wrong color. I'm—yeah."

"We must have quite the hellacious eggs in us," said Verity Harrow with her usual sense of wonder. "Just the one time, and you? Gee."

"Two," said Carrie. "Technically, I think it was two. But they were right together."

"Your beau must be quite a stud," said her grandmother.

"He's not either one," said Carrie. "Not my beau, and he wouldn't be anyone's idea of a stud. He's nice enough, but mmh."

"Now what?" said Verity Harrow. "Do you know what you're going to do?"

"Okay," said Carrie again, preparing to vault, "Okay. This could be my second mistake. But—okay, I'm keeping it. And I don't know how. It? I guess it's an 'it' until. But. I could just never bring myself to. And I know that already. This probably really screws things up. If I'd been a little more experienced maybe—but I wasn't. Not prepared, you know."

"What about the father? What does he think about all this?"

"He's nice enough," said Carrie again. "I think he's probably all right. Maybe a little better than average in some ways. But he's not someone I'd want to be sort of stuck with. We do have this in common. This? I have to find a better way to refer to—sheesh. But—to have to deal with someone and deal with them and deal with them. For—ever. It's not like I picked him for this."

"You haven't told him?"

"No," said Carrie with a finality she liked. "I've spent the last two weeks trying to convince him I'm seeing somebody else. And I even told him it was someone I liked better, and. . . He was pretty hard to shake."

"Do it on your own? You want to do this on your

own?"

"I hadn't thought of it exactly that way," said Carrie. "But—yes. Sorry. I know. I know now I need to really. Well, I don't know everything, how I'll, what all I'll have to do. But, I'll. Sorry."

"Aw, don't be," said Verity. "You're fertile and hard-headed, and that may just run in your—ooh. We'll get it figured out. But in the future, I hope you don't think you have to make every last mistake I ever made. A person might want to learn the basics of biochemistry. If you're a woman."

"Yeah," said Carrie. "So now I suppose I'll have to tell Donna. She might even be happy about it. Who knows?"

ELIZABETH

One of three women who'd had little respite from each other these several months past, she had been pleased for any reason to get out of the house, but now in the Public Defender's office there were signs everywhere requiring everyone to wear a mask at all times and maintain social distancing. Hand sanitizer and paper towels. There was a plant, a single rubbery plant. The receptionist apologized through a pleated mask, taking her name, and explained, "If we don't really enforce all these precautions, we'd have to stop seeing people. Completely." The receptionist seemed to think this would be a shame. "We have those gloves," she said, "we have those gloves available, if you're not allergic to latex." The woman called someone named Maxine to tell her that her one thirty had arrived, and Maxine soon leaned into the hall so that Elizabeth could see her.

"Elizabeth? Is it Hah-row?"

"Hare-row."

"Oh," said Maxine. "Okay," she said, radiating a desire to understand, a tendency to sympathize. "Come on back."

There was a vast macrame hanging on her wall, a framed law degree; there were professionally produced pictures of a well-scrubbed boy-and-girl on her desk. Also framed. Hopeful children. Maxine couldn't lower her mask or offer to shake hands; she remained standing behind her desk, pawing through that day's files. Her eyes weren't very informative. "So, yours was. . . Here it is. Assault. Is that right?"

"I thought it was at the time," said Elizabeth who wore her hair in the style of a Puerto Rican prizefighter, cropped to a kind of skull cap but for a forelock curlicue, blond at the moment, and she didn't need to go much out of her way to seem aggressive.

"No," said Maxine. "Wait. This is, you know, this is pretty serious. Even in City Court, Assault is a serious thing."

"I *was* serious," said Elizabeth. "Sometimes in business you've gotta be extra firm. Especially if you're a woman."

"A step at a time," said Maxine, her eyes opaque but intelligent. How old was that jacket with its moonraker shoulder pads? "Just. . . Don't. There may be a defense here, so. . . So why don't we take it in pieces? Were you defending yourself?"

"Did I think he'd hurt me?"

"Or . . ." prompted Maxine.

"No," said Elizabeth. "Nah. Nothing like that. Kostas? I think he was kind of afraid of me. Even before all this happened."

"But you didn't," said Maxine, "you didn't necessarily. . . I haven't seen an officer's report, if there is one. Just the citation."

"Oh, I hit him. Several times. What else was I supposed to do?"

"I . . ."

"He owed me money," said Elizabeth.

"And?"

"He wouldn't pay. There's a little more to it than that, but those are the basics. He owed me money and he wouldn't pay."

Elizabeth didn't think she should try and explain the incident beyond the basics; she felt a bit guilty now at having poor old Kostas stand in the way of a lot of things that had been pissing her off, most of which weren't his fault; having a tortuous job and then having none; a phone bill that rolled around every month with or without an income to satisfy it; depending so entirely on a mother who didn't have the good grace to resent it; the prevalence of halftruth and lying in this spastic world, the constant insults to her intelligence.

Elizabeth had been in a mood that day, plunging headfirst toward a landing somewhere outside the social safety net, and she had driven her mother's humpbacked, rustbucket Volvo downtown, paid to park it, and stood pounding at the door of Plato's Cave for a long time. Plate glass. She knew he was skulking in back, that he would be avoiding his mother-in-law that day, it was the only thing he strictly scheduled for himself, and she knew that Kostas knew she knew that he was there, and so it was necessary to stand for a long time pounding. She might have to make a scene, no easy thing in such deserted streets. Then Kostas did come, acting so surprised though she'd been calling him, texting him, finally he came out and let her in, and she told him that next time, if there was next time, she would just let herself in, that she still had a key. He had better come to the door. Kostas said he hadn't heard her. Lie number one. She said he owed her money and she named the amount. Kostas said he didn't have it, but maybe he could spot her fifty.

He would just keep lying.

Elizabeth had spitted the meat, and Elizabeth had chopped the lettuce and tomatoes here, and she had run the till, mixed the tzatziki, and ordered all the Cave's stock, and she had even on occasion been dispatched to pay the rent, so Elizabeth well knew the kind of profit Kostas had been realizing. He either had what he owed her, or he should have had it, and at a certain point it didn't matter to her, and she kept naming that amount, sharper and sharper, backing him into a room that for all the azure seas on its many travel posters had the discrete charm of a morgue, coolers forever humming, and how many hours had she spent here, brutalized into not noticing it, unable to turn off the bouzouki music. She must have done something to herself, Elizabeth thought, to tolerate this, and so as she backed Kostas into his hellhole little restaurant his fear was satisfying, hitting him a joy. Doors closed by the health department. Pandemic. A relative with special difficulties in Cyprus. Too bad, too bad, too bad; Elizabeth had backed him up, reciting that number, and hitting him. Fun. Fun at the time.

"So," said Maxine, "we probably won't try and bring that up. It's not a defense at law. Not a reason to hit someone. Legally."

"At law?" said Elizabeth. "Hm. Yeah."

"There are other ways to . . ."

"Take him to court? I was supposed to take him to court for it?"

"Well," said Maxine. "Yeah, I. So, as I say, we may as well set this for trial. The criminal thing, I mean. Probably it falls through the cracks, or this Kostas doesn't show up, doesn't want to be embarrassed, or. Some men might find it hard to admit to being punched out by a, you know. Also, they're not even really having trials right now in City Court. I think a lot of things are going to get lost in the shuffle. I'm advising everyone to plead not guilty; might have to waive speedy trial under the circumstances, but that only goes so far."

Bureaucracy in any form was tiring for Elizabeth. "Couldn't we just get it out of the way? I mean, I *did* hit him. And his nose was still bleeding when the cop showed up. Seems kind of sleazy to try and say I didn't. Why is there always a cop so, uh, *avai*lable? Like, the minute Kostas calls, there's this cop. I thought he was going to arrest me right there, but he just gave me my ticket and this card and told me to leave the Cave. But he did see Kostas bleeding. And, I mean, I *did* hit him."

Maxine was grave. She wore a gray mask. "By serious," she said, "this is the kind of thing that follows you around, that's what I mean. Even in our little file I can see where you've had some trouble before. And it was another Assault. Juvenile Assault."

"Which I thought," said Elizabeth, "was supposed to be sealed. Your juvenile record. After you're no longer a juvenile."

"Just what I mean," said Maxine. "As you can see, these things follow you around. Even when they're not supposed to. That's why it's worth some effort to avoid getting tagged if you can help it. Especially as an adult. Student loans, and various kinds of jobs—military service, you can really compromise your future with something like this. If there's a way around it for you, you should definitely. But, didn't you say there was something else? Was there a relationship or something? Something going on?"

"Nnn," said Carrie, smiling, shuddering, thinking of Kostas and of the matted hair growing almost without interruption from his chest to his chin and even out his ears. A mound of a head on a mound of a torso. "No," she said. "It was strictly a labor negotiation. Which is exactly what it was last time. Back in high school. Guys who wouldn't pay me. I seem to kind of lose it when they won't pay. They were both way bigger than me, too."

"I think I understand," said Maxine, who didn't exactly. "But I think this will probably just slip through the cracks. We'll go down and do the cattle call, plead into the little camera, set it for trial, and that's whenever the world is right again, so. I think a lot of things are going to be misplaced. There's already a huge backlog. Just, you know, show up for your appearance. Failure to appear, a lot of times that's worse than the actual crime in terms of what can happen to you. So, show up. This might not be too big a disaster."

"What's the worst that could happen? If I got convicted?"

"As I say," said Maxine, "having it on your record. That would be the worst. No jail, obviously. You have to be quite dangerous to go to jail these days. They couldn't use that juvenile thing as a prior. So, really, in practical terms, you'd probably have to take the anger management course. And pay for it. They're doing those online now."

"Anger management. I could probably really use that. But I'm sure it's just more bullshit a person has to buy."

Anger was her offense and anger her sentence, an immutable and indeterminate one.

How would this nice lady lawyer really feel about her client, Elizabeth wondered, if she knew that even her sympathy was enough to piss that client off? The lawyer's picturesque children. The fuzzy fucking macrame on the wall—did she think that thing was sterile? Good luck with eliminating everything that was making Elizabeth Harrow mad.

◊ ◊ ◊

"I am not going to Montana in that Volvo," said Verity Harrow. "And I was saying that ten years ago."

"And we haven't been for at least ten years," said Carrie.

"You've got every penny you ever made, babe, so just rent us a car. That's a long haul out there, as you may remember. Lotta places you really wouldn't want to break down. How'd you like to be broke down and stuck out there? You remember that country."

"Sooh optimistic," said Carrie. "I just had it serviced; Klaus thinks I'll make a quarter million miles with her."

"Yeah," said Verity in the voice of a small, dark bird. "Great. It still stinks."

"That's my fault," Carrie confessed. "I let the seats get wet, but. You get used to it."

"No," said Verity. "No. I've got no padding left on my ass."

"Ladies," said Elizabeth. "Isn't this bad enough? Without. Really, those seats are kind of rough, Mom. I mean to sit on? Remember when we went down to Salem that time? I mean, that was just to Salem. How did they get so hard? You would think they'd get softer."

The car that Carrie did eventually rent them was a Cadillac, the most fuel-efficient thing left in the agency's stable, or so she was told. There had been some trouble keeping the maintenance department staffed. It was the Cadillac or nothing, or worse case, try Hertz out at the airport.

"They might have been putting me on," she said. "I never know. But there is some kind of system in here. Apparently, we're hooked up to a satellite. We could call if we got in trouble."

"Call outer space?" said Verity.

"No," said Carrie. "It's via space. Your message bounces off their thing out there."

"Where does it bounce to? Ulm?"

"Ladies," said Elizabeth.

"People buy leather chairs," said Verity. The old woman pressed back in her seat. "I always thought that was kind of dumb, but. I don't know—Pretty nice. Feels like flesh, huh? This isn't my first Cadillac, come to think of it."

From the back seat that Carrie had chosen for her territory, she said, "Elizabeth, do you know how to operate that system? In case? The thing they showed me, with the icon and everything, that's right there, next to the . . ."

"I think you have to pay extra, Mom, to make that work. We've got our phones, anyway. You know, if we need to call outer space or anything."

The luxury of their ride seemed at odds with their mission, the purpose of the trip. Donna Harrow had died unexpectedly. They were traveling out toward a circumstance none of them, somehow, had ever considered. A reckoning maybe. It had been so long, so long in part because none of them had imagined this happening. Road trip. They were not well traveled in the best of times and hadn't traveled all together like this since the last trip to the farm so long ago.

How to feel about it? A person is supposed to know. Wouldn't grief be blunt? Or harsh? And what about that gratitude that your own number hasn't been called? They drove through the Columbia Gorge with the river bucking and the sun shining, and they were alive. Elizabeth's grief so far was slight and lay in pondering how someone supposedly beloved would now be so little lamented. Maybe the shock. Elizabeth had an aproned figure in mind, but one so foggy she might have been from an old ad campaign; a pure whiff of vanilla might also recall her grandmother who'd been permanently assigned in Elizabeth's mind to the baking of a batch of oatmeal cookies. Elizabeth had at times amused her mother and her great grandmother by imitating the cooing Grandma Donna did on the phone when she called them to say little or nothing. Grandma was, of course, how Donna signed her cards, her personal calligraphy under a commercially appropriate sentiment. With a crisp twenty. Happy birthday. Be my Valentine. So, Grandma. This was what Elizabeth knew of her, and all that Elizabeth could truly miss in her absence, and she felt small about it, but Elizabeth told herself it might be poor mental hygiene if she should fail to enjoy summer from this fabulous car. So. Grandma. It could all be sorted out later. Wasn't that what they were going to do when they got to Montana?

The benefit of belonging to this family as Elizabeth saw it was that they allowed each other all the room they might need to be strange, but it was a strategy that left them estranged, too—some by the many miles, and some by other means, but they all of them lived apart.

◊ ◊ ◊

Verity had not driven since a large patch of lint had settled into the center of her field of vision, but she had never in the intervening years learned to trust anyone else at the wheel. "Hey, Sis? How fast are you going?" She had seen this child through her infancy, which didn't mean she had ever known what to expect of her.

"Fast enough," said Elizabeth.

"Where are we?"

"This is Washington," said Elizabeth.

"Oh, I thought I saw combines cutting."

"You did. Up there on the hill. The sign said this is the fabulous Palouse."

"Thought we were already home."

"Not yet," said Elizabeth. "We would've needed afterburners to be in Montana already."

"You get so turned around."

"I've been telling you," Elizabeth said. "We need to get you out more."

"Out where?" said Verity.

"Well. Out."

"You know what I now know?" said Verity. "I was always confused."

"No, you weren't."

"You want to be prepared," said Verity, dangerously thoughtful. "You might want to get yourself a real stupid hobby. In case. Cats are good. Some of the people in this family live and live and live. Keep on living. We use things 'til they're completely used up. You go on and on, and it can get to be a problem. What to do with yourself. You hit ninety, girl, and you only wish you were senile." She nodded to her granddaughter in the backseat, wearing headphones, listening to a calm and calming reading of 'To the Lighthouse', eyes closed in the pleasure of it. "Now, Carrie, she'll be all right. She might not even notice when she gets old. But you, Sis, you might have a little more trouble with it."

"Trouble?" said Elizabeth. "I've got trouble now."

"Not the kind that hurts every morning. One thing— at least your grandmother missed out on that. The worst of it. If Donna was ever sick at all, I never heard about it."

They considered, as they had been considering since they'd first heard of it, a perfectly healthy woman whose husband had found her dead next to him just three mornings previous.

VERITY

"I could never bring myself to like her, and I'm not sure I tried that hard. I always thought she kept Tel too dependent on her, that she kept him so isolated on purpose, so he'd be all hers. But maybe she was just what he needed, and maybe I was just a—you know how people are about the people they love. I can kind of see where she'd get so possessive. Those times when people were depending on me, I thought I resented it, but no, I was always in better shape when I was needed. Gives you a reason, I guess. Now, though, now I'm needing them, and this really galls me. That poor woman. Poor Tel. I'd been thinking I needed to get home one more time, smell it even if I couldn't really see it. Home. Those poor people out there."

CARRIE

"Oh," she said. "So beautiful. The lake." When she finally opened her eyes there happened to be a royal blue stretch of water with wind chopping it and driving someone's sailboat nearly apace with them where the road followed the shoreline. "Idaho?"

"Even I knew that," Verity said.

"We've been in Idaho for a while now, Mom."

"I'd forgotten this lake completely. How pretty it was."

"I'm getting hungry," said Verity.

"I brought some chips. You like those blue corn chips. You've got your teeth in, so."

"We'd better not," said Elizabeth. "In here."

"Why not?"

"She's afraid," said Verity, "that I'll dribble, make a mess, and I probably will, but that's why they have vacuum cleaners, so, hand 'em up. These aren't those ones you get at that Food Barn, are they? You didn't get these on sale, I hope. Because those were—*bad*."

"They should be fine." The pleasure Carrie had in her measured and careful ways, that's what those who teased her never understood. Her pleasure.

She happened to thrive on routine, and though they rarely acknowledged it, this was fortunate for them all. From before Elizabeth's birth, Carrie had been driving over the hill to Hillsboro to work for Trillium Press, a precious publishing house that brought out only gardening books, and only a few of them each year, but these lavishly illustrated beauties weighed upward of fifteen pounds apiece and seemed scented of lavender and fetched ridiculous prices. Heirlooms on acid free paper. Carrie had started as a proofreader and spent several years scanning line after line of Latin in italics and small font—to be sure of the full and official taxonomy for every plant pictured. Without complaint. And she became an editor. Her portfolio and pay grew, and from the beginning she'd had no daycare or housing expense, and because she was cheap and without vices or much vanity, she had kept her daughter far from want and could now keep her grandmother in her own home. Over the hill, day by day, to an office containing none but hushed conversation, and little of that, and lovely books, lovely prints, lovely, quiet people. Carrie was fortunate and knew herself to be fortunate in her occupation, but best, Carrie never had to move. They all lived together, and since Elizabeth had been off work and Carrie had been working from home, they had piled up on each other.

"It's nice to get out of the house, isn't it. You wish it was a different. . . well, I think we all needed to get out."

"It sure is," said Verity, and she mentioned to Elizabeth, as she had mentioned before, "You better not get knocked up, Sis. We are about out of room in that joint, so you better hold off on the babies for a while."

"I think we're all right for right now." Elizabeth grinned at the thought of sex. "It's zombieland right now, so I don't see any sperm getting, you know, exchanged."

"Oh," said Carrie. "See? See why I tune you guys out? These are last year's apples, but they're good." She had sectioned them, put the sections in a baggie with lemon juice and some nutmeg. In this moment, in this car, in this company, and in this thing she had fashioned for herself, she was a funny little essential, and that was fine, to be herself as she had come to know herself.

But the next border they crossed would see them into Montana, and Carrie had made more of this than a line on a map, it seemed a membrane she must pass through on the way back to being previous Carrie. A day, a long day but only a day was needed to drive home, so why so very long since she had done it? They had their digital communications now, their virtual interactions, and these were neither more nor less satisfying or intimate than any actuality she remembered of her childhood. Her childhood, that's where the unreality lay. They had so little to say to each other, then and now, only now Carrie was unwilling to face it, to drive and drive to be weird again with each other, always a little weirder, a little stranger than the time before. The folks, of course, had never peeled away to come out to Oregon for a minute, so—So they hadn't been to Square Butte Bench since Elizabeth was a child. Why? Those voids out there. And Carrie had been busy, but never half so busy as she claimed. And they hadn't been back. Home. Montana. That's where Carrie had been driven off by love—her love, his love, her mother's baffled love, that awful recurrent sadness. Sorry. Regrets all around.

If there had ever been anything to say to her mother, suddenly it was too late to say it.

ELIZABETH

"Okay, Ladies. Lookout Pass, and—there you go, the Treasure State, okay? You're like little kids, 'Are we there yet?' Man. Here we are, but we're only about halfway there. To the farm."

"Well, everything is mystery to me anymore," said Verity. "I'm lost soon as I leave the house. You must drive like a Harrow, Sis."

"Is that good or bad?"

"Bat out of hell. Good if you want to get somewhere."

"I hardly ever exceed the speed limit."

"We do need to be there for him," said Carrie, "so, I wouldn't say there's no hurry. But. I'm sure you're being safe."

"On the interstate?" Elizabeth reveled. "This car? Might as well be flying."

"But down here," her mother advised, "there are more things to run into."

"What? Didn't you get the insurance, Mom?"

"Of course, I. . . Oh."

"She's a Harrow," said Verity. "She'll get you there."

"I don't know why you keep saying that."

"You don't think she'll get us there?"

"Nooh," said Carrie. "About the."

"Well, she is. We all are."

"Obviously. But I'm not sure what that means. 'She's a Harrow.' We're all Harrows and look how . . ." Carrie was about to point out how little the three of them had in common other than their name, but she herself refuted that argument before she could make it. They had much in common, still she did wonder, "She's a Harrow. What does that even mean?"

"Means," said Verity, "we need to get out to the farm.

Not that we can do much, but who knows what shape he's in. Who knows? I don't know him anymore."

"He seemed so calm." Carrie had worried at his eerie voice. "When he called. And he must have called right after."

"I should've talked to him," said Verity. "I guess I still could. Yeah. Why don't I?"

"No bars out here, no signal," said Elizabeth. "It's darkest America right here. But, the poor guy just. That's about the worst thing I ever heard. To find her that way." Elizabeth imagined the aproned lady as a corpse with a face the color of flour.

"I went over this pass once," said Verity, "about two miles an hour all the way, white-knuckle. This pass can be a bear in winter. They all can."

"It's summer now," Elizabeth said. "So, we should enjoy it. I mean, not enjoy it, but, yeah. Enjoy it."

"Til death do us part," said Verity. "She did have a man, anyway. A good one. More than any of us can say."

"Ew," said Elizabeth.

"You think?" said Carrie. "Well, sure. That is one way of looking at it."

"Ew," said Elizabeth. "That sounds to me like you're somebody's *dog*. They must've liked it, but. . . Could we just. I mean, it's *sum*mer, ladies, let's look at *this*."

"You'll have to look at it for me, Sis."

"Very nice," said Carrie.

Tributaries. They followed rivers through the mountains, the St. Regis, to the Clark Fork, to the Blackfoot. Though Elizabeth was doing nothing more than driving it in extreme comfort, the countryside was making her feel heroic, as if she were absorbing it, as if its big, brooding energy had been latent in her, and all the ill tended trailer houses and misguided signage along the way were easy to overlook in such country, and then, after Lincoln there was hardly any clutter, but huge meadows stitched by split rail fence. They paralleled the Blackfoot all the way to its source, another pass, another place claiming to be the crown of the continent, claiming also the coldest temperature ever recorded in the lower forty-eight. Up and over once more, and another descent, a bursting out onto high prairie.

"Did we come this way before? When I was little?"

"You'd have your nose in a book," Verity said, "or your game thingus when we came before. How you could read in the car without getting car sick—neat trick."

"How did I ever miss this?" said Elizabeth. "It's great. It's fucking golden."

"What is?" said Carrie.

"Well, this. Out here."

"You'll notice," said Verity. "There's not many people living in it."

"Yeah," said her great granddaughter. "That's probably the best part. You know, I've been thinking—truck driver. Long haul truck driver. They'll still need those for a while. Try and jump in the industry before it's automated."

"That could be interesting," said Carrie. "You mean you? But, yeah. Why not?"

"They say it's hard on the kidneys," said Verity. "You wouldn't want to screw those up."

CARRIE

"Here I am thinking about myself just when I should be thinking about them. My father. Sure, I've been lonely, it was lonely back on the farm, but I've never been really alone. Which would be different. So. They've been everything to each other, so maybe it's shattering. I hope not. But Dad. But me. I keep thinking about me again, the who-am-I game, which I thought I'd sort of won, but this happens, and as soon as I see Square Butte it all turns up again; she knew I didn't belong out here. Give her credit for that. You see a lot of others didn't belong, couldn't take it. So many abandoned farms. I knew some of those families. But, me. Little old me, and who am I? That comes up again out here. So much of it. Too much of it. Remember how the wind would snatch your breath away? Too much for me. Was that the problem? Was that what made me odd? Or was it being a black woman in a white family? Tan Dad and his little black baby; and you do wonder if you were one surprise package too many. Everyone was so nice, though. Too nice to me in Montana. Everyone was so nice, and so surprised when I wasn't stupid. But I don't think that was it. These people, I mean *my* people, they must have come out here *looking* for this. I know I'm odd, but I also think I'm right. To live my way. That would be how I'm a Harrow, I think. Right down to leaving the smallest possible carbon footprint—I am responsible. What could possibly be wrong with that? As long as I meet my responsibilities? But, Dad. Oh, Dad. Will this be something else?"

JEET

He had driven all night, and his engine ticked cooling when he finally turned it off; he thought he could also hear his heart beat. Mornings here, mornings before the wind or machinery commenced, where in the near absence of manmade noise everything else was so amplified, where the remote sound of your own heart might exalt or terrify, depending on. . . Depending on what? Jeet Harrow had driven all night and right back into an old, unanswered question. But now he was here, and having driven all night he would need to pull himself limb by cranky limb from his car. He was of an age when he seldom had to wait to know the cost of his decisions.

Another man than he'd been since he'd last been on this farmstead, he was revised if not reformed, and the farm was also different, as he might have expected given his brother's energy and focus. Shiny new grain bins, the new house. New things among old things never discarded, but all of it well ordered and ready for use, his brother's farm. His brother who aroused some pity because he could so rarely make himself leave this place, but as he stood on that place Jeet understood and even envied his brother's exile.

A rental car. The others were here.

He stepped up onto a deck of treated lumber, an optimistic or silly feature in a location where people so rarely lounged in pleasant weather. Given the hour Jeet knocked lightly and was startled when the door opened at once; he'd been heard arriving.

She was a street urchin in attitude, a maker of quick appraisals with a well-shaped head and an Afghan round her shoulders. "Uncle Jeet," she said. "I'm Verity's IT person, so I see all your posts. You look more like a biker in person, an old biker, oh, hey, yeah, come in, I'm . . ."

"I know," he said. "I get Verity's posts, too. Yep. How is she? How's your mom doing?"

"Pretty good. Or they were, but right now, well, we got in real late last night, and they got a bottle of whiskey out, Verity's idea, and it had *dust* on it. So, they drank some whiskey. And, you know, none of them drink, and you can tell; I *know* Mom doesn't; so, I think they might be sleeping in, and I'm trying to be quiet. I did make some expresso, though. You feel like some caffeine?"

"I'm already jingling from that drive; your eyes start seeing little extra things after a while. I came up from Jackpot, which is too far in one shot, much too far these days." He flexed his hands, his fingers particularly. "So, you broke out the expresso machine. This'll make Tel proud."

"Proud?"

"You know how long he's had that thing? Just in case."

"In case? Of? Well, I know their coffee beans were all the way in the back of the freezer. It's unreal. Here you are. You are kind of a big thing in my house. I hear about you a lot."

There was a suddenness about the girl that recalled Verity at a certain age, an age that only Jeet was old enough to remember. He did not remark the similarity, not knowing how she might feel about it. "I've had your baby picture," he said. "Had your baby picture in every place I've lived since—since you were a baby. So, yeah, I'd have to agree—unreal. The real unreal, but there you go." Through all the generations and permutations, these two were Harrows, and it never occurred to them to embrace. Jeet's heart, however, was mildly racing, his heart a very active organ here. "Have you ever had the grand tour?"

"Of the farm? Good idea. I'd like to see it. And, you don't like to say it or even think it, but it *is* a little creepy in this house, and even this blanket, it's like she's *in* there, *whooh*. I've got a jacket in the car."

He didn't wish to risk boring this Elizabeth by telling her what she already knew because Elizabeth seemed so very like Verity who had never suffered fools or redundant chatter, but Jeet started by saying something she'd almost certainly heard before. "There's been one Harrow or another here for over a hundred years."

"Verity," said Elizabeth, "kept naming these farms as we were coming in, and I don't know how she even sees them, but she knew where they all were, the old so-and-so place. Lot of 'em were way off, and I could barely see 'em, or there wasn't anything left to see. But she saw. Out of the corner of her eye? They were mostly empty from what I could tell."

"That's why it's something. That they've stuck."

"Our family, you mean? Stuck, huh? Stuck. So, I understand you were an outlaw."

"An idiot."

"Now you're not?"

"Oh, probably. An idiot. But harmless now."

"You look like an outlaw, though. Bandana, moustache and everything. Outlaw or pirate."

"Concealment," said Jeet. "I am about concealment."

Switching subjects, Jeet told his niece the story of the new house and the old house. Her grandmother had troubled her grandfather for some years to have one of those nice new houses trucked in, because they could afford it and the old house had got too hard to maintain, because it was after all a homesteader's shack all cobbled onto and far past its useful life, and so Tel had agreed to their manufactured home, but here stood the old place, and Donna had continued to maintain that old house though they no longer lived in it. Jeet as he told this tale began to realize he was telling it to the wrong audience, that he was telling this story to himself to maybe explain his very mixed feelings about the dear departed, about the only possible end to her odd willfulness. He knew or sensed he wasn't the only one who had considered Donna a necessary evil, but he had no idea what young Elizabeth might think of her, what she might think of her grandmother or of anything.

"They take care of their stuff, don't they?" she said. "You can tell right away that they really take care of their stuff out here. It's like a museum."

"It is," said Jeet. "It would be. Your great grandfather built that house by himself. Before power tools. How would you tear something like that down? Hell-for-stout—I think everything he built here is still standing—might be held up by paint at this point. You have to keep wood painted against all this weather."

Charlie's many structures, the house and bunkhouse white with green trim, a barn-red barn and machine shed, also red the door to the root cellar he had dug, a root cellar still in service when they opened it, its shelves lined with peach and apricot preserves. Charlie had raised the tower here once topped by a windmill, then by a radio antenna, then by a satellite dish, and standing now with no burden at all, but still standing straight and without guy wires. Charlie had planted the shelter belts now fully leaved.

"You knew him?"

"Oh, I wouldn't go that far, but the poor guy wound up being my babysitter. I always thought he knew me, though. You got the impression the old boy could see through steel."

"What about his wife?"

"Dove?"

"Right. See, so pretty. But I've hardly ever heard her name, so I forget it. She must have made something."

"She was before my time. But—Verity. She made Verity, and that's, well. . . She made my, the guy I was . . ."

"Is that what we get to make? Women? We get to make other women?"

"And men," said Jeet.

"And now I've hardly ever heard her name. You know, maybe we should throw a few coats of paint on Verity. She keeps bringing up this Harrow thing. I'm never too sure what that's about or if it's even a thing. Like, more than a name."

"Oh," said Jeet, "it is a thing. I spent a long time wondering about it. If I was part of it."

"It? So, what is that?"

A voice, his voice, deepened by a sleepless night, narrated the sum of his wisdom, "Well, we're related," he said. "We *are* related, and the details don't matter. Distance and time and hurt feelings, funny bloodlines, and at the end of the day or however they're framing it these days, we are re*lat*ed."

ELIZABETH

Food kept arriving throughout the day, a tamale pie, a Tupperware vat of ambrosia, a roast with potatoes and gravy. These were delivered by properly masked neighbor women who didn't offer to come into a house of unmasked Harrows but who called from the door to faces they recognized within. Elizabeth appointed herself to receive these dishes, and the ladies, each of them startled by her naked face, would say something like, "Oh," or, "Then you must be. . ." She would tell them her name, and they would repeat it, exclaim it and tell her how sorry they were, and then their eyes would dart right past her, and the ladies would call in to her grandfather and to her mother whom they called Carrie. One of these visitors, the oldest of them, a woman wearing a white vest cluttered with cloth badges, happened to look in and see and be freshly startled by Verity and Uncle Jeet who must be apparitions from her past.

The ladies came with good food and fond remembrances of Donna, supportive words for Tel, regretful words, if any, for the others, and Elizabeth was displeased during these encounters when she caught herself trying to look crestfallen, but at least the neighbor ladies didn't stay long where she stood breathing on them at the door. Elizabeth had lived all her life in the same North Portland house but knew only two people in that neighborhood, apart from her household, that she might hail by name, and there were many residents of her block she wouldn't even know on sight because she never saw them; they never saw her. Here where everyone lived so far apart it seemed some old intimacy was revived at once with people who hadn't for quite some time lived here at all; the ladies called her mother Carrie as if to sooth a child;

they called her grandfather 'Tel' and kept their sorrowing distance.

It had by then been officially determined that Donna Harrow had not died of Covid but a brain aneurism, which explained the suddenness of her passing and was just the way a tidy woman might choose to go. The body had been released by the medical examiner and the plan was to bury her the next day in the family plot with only the family at graveside. Services would be held after the pandemic when the community might properly gather to pay its respects. In the meantime, here was Elizabeth among hungover and exhausted elders in a house where they were all obviously uneasy, though it was a comfortable, modern house with a granite island in its kitchen, its open floor plan and in the great room a tall picture window looking out on the butte. Too much furniture, perhaps, for the two people who lived here, but it was all in use now, with old people fitfully napping and snoring on it, and speaking from time to time of other elders either dead or about to be. It was a fussy kind of house where a person might in an incautious moment sweep ceramic unicorns off their shelf.

On the cupboard above the refrigerator there was a fanwise display of her school pictures, pictures Elizabeth hadn't seen since she'd brought them home but that her mother, it seemed, had been sending along to her grandmother year by year, and Elizabeth considered her progress in these pictures through her sporting girlhood toward her present inscrutability; there was something a little cute about her and she hadn't quite got rid of it yet. Why did she resent these being here? She was kitsch in those pictures and consistent with the décor, and Elizabeth thought she had been darling much too long, too cute.

They would by unspoken agreement go unmasked in this company, and the same agreement or a lack of service in the region had silenced all electronic devices, and Elizabeth, who was neither exhausted nor hungover was in a bad way for lack of stimulation. It alarmed her that the silences here were so alarming, and she happened to think of the just-in-case expresso maker; she considered this house with its several extra bedrooms, and Afghan blankets draped over nearly virgin furniture, and her school pictures, and with this Elizabeth remembered how often her grandmother had asked them to come visit here. So, Elizabeth felt sorry, and though she'd been expecting and even hoping some sorrow might bite, she didn't care for this guilty pinch at all.

"Man," she said, "I am a barista from way back. Let's get this party started."

Or at least, she thought, something like a conversation. Elizabeth saw that her family, assembled under one roof for the first and possibly the last time, were not inclined to satisfy her curiosity at all, or ease her boredom or distract her from this novel guilt about grandma.

Her grandfather handed his phone to Uncle Jeet who said into it, "A problem? I sure hope you're not trying to breach your agreement. Legalities? Well, obviously, people *are* doing it these days. We're doing it, aren't we? You're being asked to deliver a body in a closed casket, does a mortuary ever get a simpler contract? The medical examiner is fine. . . Well, here's the legal situation—better ask forgiveness than permission. See, we've already got a gentleman coming with his backhoe. If there is a problem, we can sort it out later. I'm fairly confident no one will be digging her up. Aren't you? Good. And it was one, right? Between one and two. And you've got the location? Google? You don't have an actual map? All right. Thank you." Uncle Jeet, freckled bandito, handed the phone back, pleased to have been of use, to haul out the old persuasiveness.

"Why," said Verity, "would anybody want to complicate anything right now? They thought they wanted some kind of paperwork? I don't remember any of that back when. We put Mother in the ground, and then Father, and that was that." Elizabeth had fortified her great grandmother with an Americano and a serving of red meat. The old woman was wearing her teeth.

"It's their business," said Carrie. "They need to be cautious."

"But, I mean it," said Verity, continuing a harangue that had been interrupted by the complications with the funeral parlor. "You boys should retire."

They weren't only old but were in various ways hard used, and the only trace of boyhood left in her boys was an old understanding they shared with a smile.

"Savings," said Uncle Jeet. "I *had* savings. Several times."

"Those casinos," said Verity. "That's an awful atmosphere. The worst." Her pleated lip curled up.

"They've been closed," Jeet said. "It's all private games right now, which is great for me. I can sit in on a private game, felon or not. Been doing great. People are just dying to lose money. Still leaves a lot of time to kill. No, the last thing I need is *more* time to kill."

"Your eyes go," Verity posed, "your memory slips. What then? Then they take *your* money, those people."

"Grand*maah*," said Carrie. "Gee."

"Forgetting," said Jeet. "That might not be so bad."

"And you," Verity charged her son, "you keep sitting

on that equipment. You know anybody out here, anybody your age still farming who hasn't screwed up their back?"

"The tractor I'm using now rides nicer than our car," said her grandfather "Got climate control. That abuse—you don't get beat up in the field anymore. That isn't a farmer's problem anymore."

There were other problems, though, and they could all recite them—endless problems apparently. The market, always the grain market. The Nevada Gambling Commission. Custom combine crews held captive in Canada. Manuscript and ink marooned in Korea. Crap music everywhere. The pandemic generally. Elizabeth recalled a nonsense formula some counselor or speaker had uttered somewhere about the closure of one door always opening another, but here in this company the solution to one problem was typically the source of the next; their stories tended to illustrate the principle and the need for a certain lightheartedness along that troubled track. Often their stories celebrated persistence.

"Elliot Goode," Verity suddenly recalled. "Remember him? Remember the Goodes? He was a banjo player. For quite a while he was the *only* other musician around here; lost three fingers in a power takeoff and they were too chewed up to sew back on; after that he did what he called frailing—with the fingers he had left. I kind of liked that. Frailing. He knew exactly four chords, but he really raked that thing. Never lost any enthusiasm."

Elliot Goode was dead of course; the old folks plotted it out and determined he'd been gone before Elizabeth, or Carrie for that matter, had been born, part of that large local population of the long-gone. It wasn't only space that was expansive in this place, but time, and Elizabeth was not accustomed to think of herself as a newcomer, or as quite this inconsequential. Her family when they reminisced did not tell stories on or of themselves. They weren't talking about her grandmother, either, apart from arranging for her disposal.

Coming out from Portland, Elizabeth had heard quite a lot of concern from her fellow travelers about how they might find Tel Harrow; her mother and great grandmother had always implied an unholy fusion of a marriage out here, so they had come dreading the possibility of a man devastated. As they found him though, her grandfather was to all appearances whole, and Elizabeth didn't know him well enough to know if her grandfather was cold or contained; he had so little to say about his wife. He did finally mention a Debbie. A Dinnie. He said they would be, "Just as happy for an excuse not to come out."

"Debbie?" said Elizabeth, bored, inquisitive.

"And Dinnie," said Carrie flatly.

"Yeah," said Elizabeth. "But who are they?"

"They live out around Glendive," said her grandfather. "Or Dinnie up around Plentywood."

"Oh," said Elizabeth. "But they're?"

"Mom's sisters," Carrie said. "Your—great aunts, they'd be."

"They were quite a bit older than Donna," said Verity. "Weren't they?"

"They were never close," said the widower.

They spoke of these sisters in a particularly level way. Older? Elizabeth tried to imagine these women, much too old for such girly names and living off in locations even her grandfather seemed to consider remote. "I don't remember hearing anything about these . . ." she said. "But they're, they'd be—family—right? Part of our family?"

Mild assent, murmured assent in that room. Then

nothing more, and Elizabeth gave up on trying to get any rise or revelation from them. Not even whiskey the night before had accomplished that with them. Elizabeth foresaw a long day with her family in a house half tomb.

◊ ◊ ◊

Now that they were all here, someone was going to have to sleep in the old house; Elizabeth volunteered, and her grandfather told her, "The plumbing is still hooked up, but not the power." He gave her bedding and a bulky flashlight, though it was still dusk, and she went out with Verity wondering behind her as she left, "What about rats?"

Another question left hanging.

Elizabeth went out to the old house, left her blankets in its screened porch and went around to the other side where there was a clothesline built of steel pipe tees set in concrete pads. She smoked a joint, and Elizabeth pulled deeply, nice, piney hits enhanced for being inhaled with such pure air, and the long day did continue, but pleasantly now, sun melting into the prairie.

"There's something they won't say, or don't say. Or can't say. It's been there all along. Maybe every family is this way. Something they think or something that happened. Something that's supposed to be said. Who knows?"

Elizabeth lounged by the clotheslines until full dark. She had no service here, but there were satellites overhead; she could see them. Satellites, airplanes, stars fixed and falling. She stood in the dark, between the clothesline and the shelterbelt, under an instructive sky.

◊ ◊ ◊

Her mother had wanted to walk to the plot, it was only a half mile from the house, she said, but Verity corrected her and said it was closer to a mile, and, "You know damn well, I'm not walking anywhere near that far." There was also the matter of the two Dans, one of them the pastor at a church Donna had sometimes attended, and the other manning the backhoe. Tel wanted to be sure not to keep them waiting, so the Harrows rode to the plot, Carrie with her father and a thoughtful box of trinkets she had collected, Elizabeth with Verity and Uncle Jeet loaded in the Cadillac. Elizabeth felt silly and superior, driving this vehicle. She was surprised that her passengers, especially her great grandmother, had not one thing to say along the way. Maybe Verity was looking out again, trying to see it again.

At a corner formed by two county roads was a piece of arable ground enclosed by a five strand fence and planted only with lilacs and Harrows. "Just Mother and Father so far," said Verity. "For farm people, I guess we weren't all that productive. Most families were bigger."

The machine that had dug the new grave was parked a respectful distance away from it, the operator wearing a sports coat over his overalls. This Dan was identified to Verity and she asked after his family; the backhoe man mentioned several generations of his people, and the old woman nodded approvingly. There was a rock cairn here, about hip high and not too noteworthy from the road, a brass plaque set in it bearing the few raised letters deemed necessary.

HARROW
Dove   Charles

No dates. Elizabeth might turn completely around in her mind, rotate three hundred and sixty degrees here, and it was all unimpeded horizon. Big view, maybe, for those with eyes to see, but not the prettiest graveyard.

Dove. Charles. According to her sources they had been the source of everything. Now a sunken spot in some unremarkable ground. Her grandfather remarked the empty vase wedged into the cairn. "She'd bring flowers out," he said. "Memorial Day. Pull weeds. Took flowers in for her folks, too, in Big Sandy. Kept their graves nice."

The new hole stood open, and they waited some distance from it but not in their cars, not wishing to be impolite. Pastor Dan arrived in a bad brown suit that he must have worn when he was a bigger man, and he came to them putting on his mask, then quit when he saw it wasn't necessary, and he walked in from the road saying something he thought was clever about social distancing, and her grandfather introduced him, a name Elizabeth forgot at once, just as she instantly forgot the pastor's praise for her grandmother, because it sounded like he really didn't know her that well. A man with no edges, a mild one, but he did say Donna had been kind, which must be true. Those nice cards. That empty vase wedged in the rock. And Elizabeth, who had made fun of her, stood with the others a little apart from the new hole, the empty one, and the view from here made eternity all too easy to picture.

"No wind," said Jeet to appreciate the one thing at least for which they all might be grateful.

They waited, and while they waited it seemed wrong to say much in the presence of others who weren't saying much. Even Verity remained circumspect, and they waited for the hearse, and finally Pastor Dan, who was also booked to perform an outdoor wedding that day, had to excuse himself, so he offered a quick prayer in parting to which only Carrie and backhoe Dan said, 'amen.'

In time Carrie suggested that Verity wait in the car, she had been a long time standing.

"I'm fine," said Verity. "Said I wanted to smell it again. This is a good spot for that."

"I could run back to the house," said Tel, "Get a camp chair."

"I'm fine standing," said Verity. "Cripes, if a person can't even stand up you might as well, well. . . How long can they take?"

How long? An August day progressed, its lack of wind becoming oppressive. The hearse might be lost, or maybe the driver had decided or been directed not to come at all, and no way of knowing. The graveside party waited, each of them reasoning privately that the crew of the hearse would have no good reason or desire to retain a body, so they must be coming, and when at last the poor, flustered, dark suited men did arrive and back their hearse up to the open gate, one of them explained through his black mask that they had relied to their regret on GPS.

The ground was uneven in this cemetery. Elizabeth was recruited as a pall bearer to help carry a casket with a coppery sheen from the hearse to the hole, and the thing was heavy though the bearer right in front of her was Dan the stout backhoe man. The bearers were entirely unrehearsed in this, so there was some awkwardness about setting it down beside the grave. The funeral men had helped carry the casket as well, and they seemed glad for this duty, full of apology because they had come without the usual equipment. "What a mess it's been. Things have been so messed up." They had come without the device they used to lower caskets into graves. Elizabeth wondered if the funeral people had been overwhelmed, if this was one of those communities hit hard by the disease, their dead being stacked in cold storage.

Dan told them he thought it would be okay. He went

to the trailer on which he hauled his backhoe, and he opened a chest at the front of it and withdrew from that a coil of nylon strap, blue and new. "I can rig a sling," he said, "sway it right down in there. No problem."

The senior funeral man apologized again for everything, offered condolences almost as an afterthought for their loss, and left with his assistant who had remained silent and flushed the whole time.

Carrie said, "So—with your machine, you'd? Would you need our help with that?"

Dan said he didn't. He had lowered many a septic tank with this technique.

"Then," Carrie said, "I don't think I want to see that. Could we? Would it be all right with everyone if we said our goodbyes now. Before he? I mean, I don't want to see that."

Elizabeth watched her mother as the poor lady considered the open hole, clutching the cardboard box she'd brought to contain some angels. She wanted to send something along, but as Carrie approached the hole, she thought better of throwing fragile, glassy pieces into it, figurines still catching the light. She wasn't about to open the casket to try and slip them in, so there she stood, hapless.

"If Donna arranged this," said Tel. "It would have gone a lot smoother."

None of them knew what to do next and only Carrie had thought of anything to say, and she said it, "She knew what everyone needed. That's what I know. She knew what we needed, and she made sure we had it. That's what I know. You only hope. I. You just hope. . ."

Heat of the day. Elizabeth watched her family's eyes wander away from the hole, the casket, the backhoe, each other. Heat of the day, and a family pathologically disinclined to say anything insincere; here a prayer would have been useful. For once in her life Elizabeth wished she weren't such a hard ass. There must be so much more to say, but not a word of it occurred to her.

Her grandfather said at last, "She loved it out here. I don't know why, but she loved it. We got that much right."

TEL

His mother had been preparing her flight to the city for some time, so within a month of his return from Okinawa Tel had the farm to himself, high, dry, and lonesome, and this might have been the only situation he could have tolerated just then. He liked to be alone with his shame; he'd known men and a lot of them who had seen far more than he had, marines who'd lived with carnage for months on end, and they hadn't fallen apart, but here was Tel Harrow with his inward quivering, a weakling possibly ruined. A man doesn't like to think of himself as a delicate flower, but there comes a point—one night he went out to a high school football game that he enjoyed until the second quarter—go-fight-win— when he became convinced that someone on the rise behind him, some invisible sniper had a bead on his brain pan. He moved out of that crowd, breathing as if he hadn't quite learned how, his pulse pushing an unsustainable pace and pounding through to his temples, a bright sweat between him and the cold night air, and from that night on Tel feared he might be on track to become another bachelor farmer. He now understood how that might happen, how a person might turn strange. Bachelor farmer. The kind of man everyone makes fun of, and Tel felt himself sinking in that direction.

One day, however, he was in a cavernous store in Great Falls, wheeling a bale of toilet paper down an aisle when he heard his name from behind. "Tel?"

His name?

"Tel Harrow."

It was a clerk as he turned to her, a pretty one with a device for marking merchandise in her hand. "Oh," he said. "Oh. Dinny." A pretty girl, from Big Sandy if his memory put her in the right gymnasium, and out of place here. Proud or brave in her new circumstance.

"*Dinny?*" she said. "It's *Donna*."

"Oh," said Tel. He was on the back foot with this woman, and would be from then on, but she did soon relieve him of his bachelorhood. Donna had attached to him, decided he should not be alone, married him, then spent her life protecting him while never thinking him a coward, a lifelong favor he had rewarded by driving everyone else away. Tel Harrow and his too tender self.

He had to believe Donna had shared his feeling for this place; almost from the beginning he'd had to believe his gratitude would be enough for her, and now Tel must remind himself as often as necessary that she had chosen this.

◊ ◊ ◊

It seemed a betrayal, but he was hungry. Boom—boom, the driver's side door, the passenger's side door—closed— and his daughter sat beside him, so forlorn with that box of gimcracks in her lap, and his wife's burial was only just underway, and Tel was thinking of lunch, which meant he couldn't think too highly of himself at the moment.

"We have to do better," Carrie said. "When they have that service, I'm coming out again, because we need to. *I* need to honor her. Somehow. That was. That wasn't very good."

"She either knows exactly how you feel about her now," said Tel, "or she doesn't know anything at all. Either way."

"Yeah, Dad, but that's what I'm still working out. How I feel, how I felt about her. I mean, in some ways I did know. I thought I might understand better when I became a mother myself, but I'm still, on that front I'm still. Well."

"It's confusing," Tel said. He remembered now how almost nothing undid him like his daughter's distress, and how it had always been her habit when she'd been a girl to avoid distress, but for his sake. While they had been at the plot, he'd seen several cars going by that he knew were probably taking fresh offerings of food, country consolation, to the house. "And, I hate to say it," he said, "but it stays confusing, too."

During the short ride back to the farm Verity had stiffened up, sitting down, and she needed help getting out of the back of the Cadillac. Tel admired the swagger his granddaughter brought to that project. Elizabeth rendered her hand with a polished, "Upsy—daisy," and the old woman was extracted.

Then, indistinct at first, they heard the backhoe working, a distant bang and rattle, and Elizabeth, whose ears were the best among them, was the first to understand the sound, and Elizabeth, to everyone's dismay, burst into tears. Carrie rushed to her side to wrap an arm round her shoulders, not a practiced move. "Honey," she said, "she'll be. It is part of life, and we. Oh, honey. She'll be."

"Mom," said Elizabeth. "Please."

They went into the house to leave her with her leaking eyes. Just as Tel had expected, a fresh smorgasbord awaited them there, but now some uncertainty about his granddaughter had interrupted his appetite, and though he would be the last person who knew how such things worked, he went back out to her. Maybe she didn't really want to be alone. He had nearly always preferred it, but maybe she didn't. So, despite her stated wishes, he went back out to her. Her face was still wet, but she was feline again, stylishly leaning against the fender of the Cadillac, arms crossed, chin cocked, impatient now, and as Tel came out to her Elizabeth inclined her head toward that heavy metal clanking from so far away, huge bumps, out of rhythm. "That," she said, "is driving me crazy."

"Come inside. You can't hear it from inside."

"No," she said. "That would be worse. I do *not* want to be comforted."

"All right," he said. "Well—let's take a drive. Let's take a look at some wheat, why don't we?"

"Sure," she said, "If I can drive. All this driving has been great. I really should get a car, but I don't want to get that hooked into the system."

"Which system?"

"The one I'm already hooked into," said Elizabeth. "I do just *love* to drive, though. So, out here, where you have to anyway—might as well, huh? Drive."

"We better take the truck."

"Even better," said Elizabeth. "Pretty sure I can drive a truck. I can drive Mom's Volvo, and if you can drive that thing, you can drive anything. That car was built before the invention of the automobile."

She apologized once underway for making a fuss, particularly because she had been crying for herself, not for her grandmother or for anyone else, but crying for herself because she had seen the big picture out here, seen her place in it. She said that all those with any memory of the old ones were about to be gone themselves, then they in their turn would be forgotten, then everybody. Then what?

"When no one's remembered?" he said. "I. Well, I try to take it one problem at a time. That—I don't know— would that be much of a problem? Who'd notice?"

"I don't know," said Elizabeth. "But it was mainly me. Nobody will remember *me* some day, which, you know, so what? But it really got to me there. Am I sad for poor grandma, or you, or anybody else? No. It was just me feeling sorry for myself. Scared, sort of. But—I'm over it." With her hands on the wheel, he saw how on each of her fingers was tattooed a tiny, stylized sun.

Tel Harrow had been quite the modern man since internet service had reached Square Butte Bench. His family, except for Donna, was a virtual family, and as a family were well suited to the digital age, speaking to each other electronically far more often and more forthrightly than they ever had during the old face-to-face days. The Harrows recognized the world wide web as a bonanza for shy people; the Harrows liked e-mail. Seeing them in the flesh again, Tel was seeing the wear and tear, scars new and old and more or less subtle and a little too illustrative of souls still unsettled. But how good it had been to see them. "Here's something funny," he said, "you and I were raised by the same woman. I know you had your mom, too, but. You and me. And Jeet. When we were babies. Imagine that."

"I don't think I can," Elizabeth said. "Maybe we lucked out. I don't remember exactly, but I'm sure she let us get away with everything."

Tel kept turning to time out of mind. "The ice shelf stopped right here," he told his granddaughter. "The geologists say this was the foot of the last ice shelf before it retreated, that ran along through here, and that's why we've got the dirt we do. So, that was another stroke of luck, we lucked into some exceptional dirt."

"Her fairy tales," Elizabeth said, "were a little gruesome. I do kind of remember that."

He described their destination then. He was farming a piece of low ground he'd bought just to introduce a new strain, or an ancient but newly rediscovered strain of wheat that he raised and harvested organically with equipment never tainted by contact with herbicide or pesticide. "I sell it straight to a pasta maker down in San Francisco," he said. "No middle man. This is the old-style wheat. Never been tweaked for yield. Supposed to be a lot easier to digest."

He told her he had been meaning to scale back, to raise just this boutique wheat and cut out the custom combiners who now harvested most of his crop, cut out those asses in the commodity markets, sell straight to his consumer. He told her he'd been meaning to scale back and get clean, that the wheat he was about to show her had been the source of ancient civilizations, a crop with a five-thousand-year-old pedigree.

"Yeah," she said. "But what about you? You must be—I don't know."

"Me?" He wasn't an authority on the subject if he could help it.

Tel Harrow knew his granddaughter as the person who kept Verity's passwords straight and who had built a foot-driven potter's wheel in their basement, a kiln in their backyard, and who was according to her mother, 'Deciding what to do with herself.' He told her, "My legs feel like they're not there. The rest comes later, I'm sure. How else I'll feel, but, hey, look at you double-clutching. When I do that, I have to cuss. Cuss my mechanic, which is me. Been fighting that thing ever since I put it in."

"Did something happen? With Mom out here? I've always wondered."

"Happen?"

"Well, you know. How she is. And she's black. From what I've seen, that's a little unusual around here. And we're black-ish. Is that a thing? Was that a problem?"

"No," he said. "Oh, no, no, no. Don't ever think. . . It was me, sweety. I was the problem. I was quite a mess."

"You seem all right to me."

"You really don't bump into evil much out here," he said. "So, when I did run into it and all the. . . It really threw me for a loop. If it wasn't for this. If I didn't have something to do and a lot of room to do it in. Hate to think. I wasn't much good to anyone, especially your poor mother. No. What happened was me. Me, and the mess I brought home with me."

"Mom has been afraid for you."

"No," he said.

They went along a long straight, another big prospect before them. They went along for a while.

"When I said I got scared?" said Elizabeth. "I've been a little bit that way ever since we came out here. It's so—It does kind of scare me, all this. But I like it."

◊ ◊ ◊

The wind came up at last while they were out in the field, a field in full ripeness, stirring, sighing, rolling with every little freshet. He trailed behind his granddaughter who walked stooped before him, leaning forward to stroke the top of the stirring crop. As if it were fur. He pinched off a bristling head, pinched it again and smelled it. "I've got a special gizmo to get the exact number on my moisture content, but I can tell you standing here, I need to cut this right about now." He looked off and away. "Now the problems start. When we cut this specialty stuff, Donna was the driver. She did all the business end of things and was a fair hand in the field, too. It's a two-person operation. At least."

"She was your partner."

"Yes," he said. Pleased the girl understood it that way. Pleased for Elizabeth, and himself. And Donna.

"I can drive the truck for you."

"I was sort of hoping you'd say that." Tel Harrow's crop caught an epic light at this hour, and he too ran his palms over those bearded heads, a move he'd never made before. "You mentioned memory," he said. "These guys don't remember anything the way we do. Probably. But they do know, from seed, to root, to top what to do. They know what they are. And they've known it continuously since the pharaohs. We've got that kind of memory, too. DNA, I believe they're calling it these days."

"What about now? After we do this field?"

"I haven't been thinking about it very long," he said, "but it sure has come up. It's kind of hard to avoid. . . I don't see myself hiring help. I'd probably have to hire three people. Your mother could probably do with some cash. So. For some reason, you can always sell these things. You can always sell ground."

"Yeah, but what about you?"

"I'm not quite so screwed up as I used to be. I'll go somewhere."

"Somewhere?" said Elizabeth.

"Yeah, well, I hadn't given that any thought either."

"Because," she said, "you didn't really want to go anywhere else. I get that."

"Since I've been talking about it out loud, I think I'm seeing where I won't have much choice. Which is all right. A person should get a look at more than one or two places in their life, anyway."

"Where?" she challenged.

"Well," he said, and he ceased thinking of it, and he said, "You always thought the object of the operation was to feed people, but, first things first, you've got to make equipment dealers and bankers and commodities traders rich. Pay your fuel bill. Keep the State of Montana afloat with your property taxes. The idea was to feed people, and we did, but more and more gets in the way."

"Better in the old days?"

"Yeah," he said. "Okay. It wasn't. It was never easy."

The wind worked sworls in his wheat and caused it to speak to them. This field lay in a sheltered bottom that channeled the wind in funny ways. "So," said Elizabeth. "I can code, and it looks like I can drive trucks, and I've done some bookkeeping. I can solder. Prune rose bushes. Point is, I'm pretty good at figuring out how to do things. But the real point is, you can't sell this farm. Not after today."

"Today?" he said.

"Or—after all this time. People are still eating. It's still a good thing to do."

"What do you think? Think you want to go farming? Has your mother ever told you how cold it gets out here? This gorgeous weather, you know, this is real unusual."

"I don't even know what I don't know," said Elizabeth, looking off and away. "And that's scary, too. But, hell yes, let's feed people."

"You know it's more complicated than that."

His granddaughter fixed him with a look, an expression Tel Harrow knew from previous faces, and she said, "I'm sure it is. But it's real, and all we have to do is survive."

∞ ∞ ∞

ACKNOWLEDGMENTS

This book required many questions to be posed to many people over a period of some years. What follows is necessarily a partial list of those to whom the author is grateful for information and insight. Anyone not properly noted here is, none the less, appreciated:

Elizabeth Fee, Ken Robison, Lon Withrow, Henry Armstrong, Peter Rutledge Koch, John Boyle, Jim Todd, Scott McMillion, and Gish Jen.

www.ingramcontent.com/pod-product-compliance
Lightning Source LLC
Chambersburg PA
CBHW051133300726
48978CB00011B/262